www.MinotaurBooks.com

**The premier website
for the best in crime fiction.**

Log on and learn more about:

The Labyrinth: Sign up for this monthly newsletter and get your crime fiction fix. Commentary author Q&A, hot new titles, and giveaways.

MomentsInCrime: It's no mystery what our authors are thinking. Each week, a new author blogs about their upcoming projects, special events, and more. Log on today to talk to your favorite authors.
www.MomentsInCrime.com

GetCozy: The ultimate cozy connection. Find your favorite cozy mystery, grab a reading group guide, sign up for monthly giveaways, and more.

www.GetCozyOnline.com

MINOTAUR
BOOKS

PRAISE FOR JAMES D. DOSS'S
CHARLIE MOON MYSTERIES

"Although less well known than other Native American-based mystery series, the Charlie Moon novels are quickly rising to the top of the pack. Doss has a fine comic touch—playing off Moon's laconic wit against Daisy's flamboyant personality—and he just may be the best of the bunch at seamlessly integrating anthropological and spiritual material into his stories."

—*Booklist* on *White Shell Woman*

"A dash of humor and a sprinkling of romance season Doss's eighth Charlie Moon mystery."

—*Publishers Weekly*

"Doss keeps ringing intriguing changes off the chords of his unusual premise: former Southern Ute police officer Charlie Moon, now a Colorado rancher, solves crimes as a special tribal investigator while sparring with his cantankerous Aunt Daisy, a Ute shaman, who scoffs at Charlie's obstinate refusal to acknowledge the supernatural nature of the universe. . . . Hillerman gets the most press, but Doss mixes an equally potent brew of crime and Native American spirituality."

—*Booklist*

"This latest story, one of pure-handed suspense . . . makes us deeply eager for the next."

—newmysteryreader.com

"Lyrical and he gets the sardonic, macho patter between men down cold. The finale is heartfelt and unexpected, and a final confrontation stuns with its violent and confessional precision."

—*Providence Journal Bulletin*

DEAD SOUL

JAMES D. DOSS

St. Martin's Paperbacks

This book is dedicated to the memory of
Thomas J. Boyd Jr.,
soldier, scholar, and gentleman.

And to his wife and sons,
Nikki, T.J., and Ron.

ACKNOWLEDGMENTS

The author is very grateful to James A. Baran for his helpful suggestions.

PROLOGUE

The heavens over middle world are obscured by a mottle of clouds that grumble and rumble and spit white-hot fire. Midnight's black sea roars over mountain passes, rushes down deep canyons, washes over bone-dry prairies. Stinging winds shriek and moan, limbs of half-dead trees shudder and snap—nocturnal creatures scurry about in search of sanctuary.

The Lawman

In the parlor of the Columbine Ranch headquarters, Charlie Moon's lean, seven-foot frame is folded into a maple rocking chair. His boot heels rest on a redbrick hearth fronting a massive granite fireplace. Amber tongues lick at resinous pine logs, taste the turpentine flavor. Firelight sparkles in the Ute's dark eyes.

The full-time rancher, part-time tribal investigator is a hard-working man who should be in bed at this late hour. But his soul knows that the Long Sleep will come soon enough. This being so, he delays his slumbers to enjoy the intermittent drumming of heavy thunder, a peppering of cold rain on the porch roof. His happy thoughts are of lush, green pastures where fat cattle graze.

Aside from not having a woman under his roof, Charlie Moon is content with his life. Though he has seen many troubles—and knows that more will come—he does not worry about what the morrow might bring.

The Dead Soul

Not so far away, under another peaked roof, inside another lonely dwelling, the thunder and lightning is hardly noticed, certainly not appreciated. Something infinitely more sinister than nature's raucous storm is brewing here.

A peculiar pair occupies this gray twilight-misted space.

In a cedar cupboard, sitting on a cracked saucer, a buffy-brown piñon mouse. The nervous little creature nibbles at a salted sunflower seed.

Seated on a three-legged stool, a human biped. Hardened by intense bitterness, haunted by garish nightmares, the deeply troubled spirit is aware of only three realities. Like tectonic layers grinding and buckling beneath a broken world, one sensation slips past another.

Sickly flicker of kerosene lamp.

Cold muzzle of revolver against temple.

Sinuous curve of trigger under thumb.

Deep breath. *Time to get it done.* Jaw clenches hard enough that enamel cracks on molars.

The wounded soul tries. Tries so *very* hard.

Cannot.

Bone-weary of burdens too heavy to bear, the failed suicide rests head and arms on a sturdy table. Sighs. Slips away into gray oblivion. For a few heartbeats, experiences something almost like rest. But all too soon, the horrific vision comes. It is always the same.

Lumpy projectile enters brain.

Hollow needle penetrates vein.

Then . . . the pointed blade, the painful pricking.

A sharpened spoon cups under the left eye, severs the optic nerve.

The right orb follows, popped out like a ripe plum.

And always, always—filling the black void . . . the silent screams.

The pitiful shrieks go on and on and on. . . .

A desperate groan escapes from the mouth of the dreamer.

The wee mouse twitches oversized ears at the startling noise, abandons its meager supper, scurries away with a clicking of tiny feet.

In the rodent's wake another soul-searing moan. The sleeper awakens, shakes off the remnants of the recurring nightmare. Stares at the revolver. *There must be another way.*

There are indeed alternate paths. Some are bright and lovely. Others, dark and paved with crumbled bones.

There is an eternal instant of indecision before . . .

A choice is made.

Immediately, a hideous notion bubbles up from the depths of that fetid pit where burdensome thoughts settle, take root, blossom into hideous fruit.

The concept is simply awesome. Awesomely simple.

CHAPTER 1

The Earth

Pressed snugly against Colorado's border with New Mexico is the bittersweet land of the Southern Utes. Like the entire universe and every creature in it, this is a work in progress. And a very fine work it is. Splashing, snow-melt rivers follow serpentine paths through broad valleys where willows weep not and lime-green cottonwoods are crowned with shimmering rainbows. Hardy piñon and juniper dot the crests of wind-sculpted mesas. Between these long sandstone benches are dark, silent canyons where spirits who tarry in this world keep company with other shadows.

Presiding above all are the cloud-shrouded peaks, blue-green with spruce and fir. During the frigid Moon of Dead Leaves Falling, the mountain's round shoulders are sprinkled with flakes of aspen gold. But this is a fleeting time; soon their heads will be capped in purest white that does not vanish until June is well past middle age. The early Spaniards named these heights after that beloved disciple who inquired of *Jesu Cristo:* "Lord, who is it among us that shall betray you?" The answer *San Juan* heard still whispers in the winds. From age to age, the mountains remain . . . and the betrayal is repeated.

The Elder

The red-tailed hawk circles high over the creation. Far below, at the yawning mouth of *Cañon del Espiritu*, the bird's clear eye spies a tiny silver speck. It is the body of an antique house trailer. The dwelling has stout steel ribs, aluminum skin that can be sliced with a pocket knife, small windows where an old woman's wrinkled face can sometimes be glimpsed. This is where the Ute elder spends the twilight of her life. By the path of the hawk, her home is an almost equal distance from Arboles, Bayfield, and Ignacio—which is to say about ninety-five furlongs. This is a very considerable distance for one who must depend upon others for transportation.

Though she is far from civilization, Daisy Perika dwells close to the heart of God. Considering her many sins, this might seem unlikely—and indeed is beyond all human understanding.

If she is neither sweet nor full of compassion, there are reasons why. The woman's years have pressed hard, molding her into a leathery bag of brittle bones and bitter memories. Loss and pain have made her greedy and fearful. The elder's tongue is sharp, sometimes vulgar. Despite her many well-meant promises to the kindly pastor of St. Ignatius Catholic Church, the shaman has not given up her clandestine conversations with the dwarf-spirit who dwells in the badger hole. Daisy might well commit theft or even murder if there was no fear of being caught and punished. The poor old soul is fond of only six of her fellow human beings, and barely able to tolerate the rest. Under these circumstances it cannot be expected that Daisy would keep the First Commandment. One who finds her neighbors hateful cannot truly love God.

But that Lover of Souls adores the crabby old woman. And grants her grace upon grace, not the least of which she deserves.

Therein lies the heart of the deepest, sweetest mystery.

The Morning

Daisy Perika pushed herself up from the straight-backed chair, hobbled slowly across the linoleum to peer out the miniature window. Hands resting on the sill, she looked toward the U-shaped formation called Cougar's Tail. Not that she could see the entire curl of the rocky ridge—Daisy could barely make out the mouth of the Canyon of the Spirits. The atmosphere was a stinging swirl of sand and grit that peppered against the trailer like brown sleet.

All night, she had slept fretfully. All morning long, the wind had sputtered and coughed, pausing now and then to gather its raspy breath. With the greater of the gusts, the walls of the trailer rattled and buckled as though the sixty-year-old rivets might pop. Moreover, the entire structure rocked back and forth. And squeaked. And groaned.

It was maddening.

There was this singular blessing—the usually solitary woman was not alone. Charlie Moon, who had arrived with the sunrise, was seated at her kitchen table. The tribal investigator had not said a word since finishing his scrambled eggs and chili-spiked posole. His whole attention was focused on a tattered copy of the *Southern Ute Drum*.

The tribal elder turned to scowl at her nephew. As if he was responsible for the weather. "This wind is going to blow us over into Conejos County."

He grunted, turned a page.

She made a rude, spitting sound. "I can feel the sand between my teeth."

Charlie Moon muttered something unintelligible.

The old woman pulled a woolen shawl more tightly around stooped shoulders. "It's cold enough out there to freeze your shadow to the ground." *And not much better inside.* "I think the furnace is about to give up the ghost—or maybe I'm low on propane."

"And the cow's gone dry and the hens won't lay." He

winked at her over the newspaper. "Other than that, it's a fine day."

Daisy tried hard not to smile; the effort made her face ache. "Anybody who thinks this is a fine day has maggot stew for brains."

He folded the tribal newspaper. "There's not so much dust up at the Columbine. You should go home with me."

The tribal elder shook her head. "No-thank-you. Every time I go to your ranch, something bad happens. And if I'm not here, thieves might break into my house."

Moon glanced around her sparsely furnished home, wondered what anyone would want to steal. Miles from the nearest neighbor, this was no place for an elderly person to live. He repeated the offer he made on almost every visit. "I could fix you up a bedroom at the ranch headquarters." As an enticement, he added, "It'd be nice and warm."

"All your bedrooms are on the second floor," she snapped. "I'm too old and brittle-boned to be climbing up stairs." She followed his gaze around her kitchen. "Besides, home is where your stuff is."

"I could fix you up a room downstairs."

"Where, in a closet?"

Moon, who had been thinking of his rarely used office, grinned. "No, I need my closets. But there's a little pantry just off the dining room. It's got a forty-watt lightbulb. We could clear out some of the canned goods so you could have a shelf for your stuff. It'd be nice and cozy."

She brushed this joke away with the wave of a hand. "Don't you have to be getting home?" The sharp-tongued woman immediately regretted these words.

The rancher consulted his wristwatch. "Now that you mention it." Moon's eye followed his aged aunt as she made her way across the kitchen. "Anything I can do for you before I go?"

"I can take care of myself." The shaman placed a palm on the door of the chugging refrigerator, as if she could feel what was inside. "But when you come back, bring me a dozen eggs. Two pounds of bacon. Pound of pork sausage. Can of lard. Sliced bread. Coffee. Milk. Sugar. Butter. And some red chili powder."

Charlie Moon, who knew her grocery list by heart, got up from the table. He was not able to stretch to his full seven-foot height inside the trailer, and the black Stetson would go on after he stepped outside onto the rickety pine porch. "I may not be back for a week or two. I'll have some groceries brought over from Ignacio. And I'll get somebody from La Plata Propane to have a look at your furnace." He gave her a hug.

The old woman watched her nephew drive away. Cold coils of loneliness tightened around her heart. *Maybe this time I should have gone with him.*

CHAPTER 2

The Shaman Sleeps

Evening has come to the high country. The overworked winds heave a last sigh before settling into the canyons for a night's rest. Dust and sand drift slowly down to earth. Twilight grows old, dusky gray . . . withers into inky blackness. One by one, sharp prickles of starlight burn holes through the outer darkness. A yellow-eyed owl calls once, twice, thrice. She leaves her lookout on a piñon's gnarly shoulder, wings hopefully toward a perch on the pale crescent moon. Night after night she does this.

Now a taut stillness occupies the land. The unseen audience is hushed, expectant. Waiting for the velvet curtain to be drawn, the darkling players to appear onstage and prance before the backdrop of mesa, mist, and cloud.

Weary as she was, the old woman was also restless. Daisy Perika turned onto one side, found no comfort there, rolled onto the other. She tried lying on her back, staring at an invisible ceiling. The tired old soul listened to the clock's metallic tickety-tick. She heard the recurring call of a distant owl, the sound of something small scurrying across the roof of the trailer. A squirrel, she thought. The elder closed her eyes, tried hard to find sleep. She could not, and finally gave up the search.

Moments later, Sleep found her.

A luminous balloon inflated with soul-stuff, the dreamer felt herself floating upward, passing through the roof of her trailer home. Over there, jutting up between Snake Canyon and *Cañon del Espiritu,* were the familiar stone formations on Three Sisters Mesa. She was drifting higher now, above the snowy peaks of the San Juans, moving rapidly toward that distant place where the sun would appear to bring a new day. As if covered by a multitude of unblinking eyes, the shaman saw everything—above and below, toward all four points of the compass. A thin sliver of moon hung over the earth, as if suspended on an invisible cord. There was a lake to the south; it was shaped like a leg bent at the knee. Starlight reflected off the glassy waters. There were headlights of automobiles, inching ever so slowly along unseen highways. And then, in a twinkling, the mountains were far behind her. A flash of blue-green light, and the sun was well above the horizon—but not as she had seen it appear on thirty thousand mornings. The incandescent sphere was just *there.* Not moving. As if time itself had frozen.

The dreamer felt herself falling, falling.

Daisy Perika was on her back. The shaman felt a thick carpet of grass under her bare legs. She pushed herself up on elbows, inspected the backs of her hands. As she had expected, there were no wrinkles in the skin. No pain in her joints. The elder was young. Her eyes searched for the sun but could not find that bright orb. The sky was thick with gauzy clouds, the air moist and heavy with the perfume of wild roses. She was in the center of a great meadow, dotted here and there by an isolated oak, maple, or elm. But mostly there was thick grass and fragrant wildflowers. Daisy got to her feet, brushed off her nightgown. The great field was bordered on one side by low, wooded hills, on another by a wide river. This place was not real like Middle World, where her aged body slept. It was real in a completely different way.

And it was very still. *Something is wrong here.* But what? Like a hound on a scent, she sniffed.

The atmosphere fairly crackled with the expectation of some awful calamity. Having had a thousand visions, Daisy Perika was not unduly alarmed. Morning would find her safely back in her bed near the mouth of *Cañon del Espiritu.* Knowing that these visions always had a purpose and that something would certainly happen, she waited.

It was not necessary to wait long.

Daisy felt a slight tug at her skirt. She looked down at the elfin creature whose head barely reached above her knee. It was the Little Man. The *pitukupf* was dressed in a green cotton shirt, buckskin breeches, beaded moccasins. He also wore a floppy black hat and a dark expression.

The shaman stared at her power spirit, waiting for him to speak.

He uttered not a word. But the dwarf did raise his arm. Point.

Daisy looked up, saw something approaching through the mists. The intense silence was penetrated by the rhythmic beating of hooves on turf. Appearing over a low ridge, there it was—a magnificent white horse. Upon the great beast, a rider. She felt a surge of joy to behold this marvelous sight. To own such a fine mount, this one must surely be an important chief. But as horse and rider came near, she realized that this was not a man of the People. This was a white—a *matukach.* More from prudence than alarm, the Ute woman took a step backward. She watched him rein in the horse, dismount. The tall man wore tightly fitted white breeches, a pale yellow silk shirt with lace at the collar, a long blue cloak. His knee-high black boots glistened like polished midnight.

She stared. *Should I know this man?*

The stranger took note of the Ute woman and the dwarf; a wry half-smile passed across his face. He made a slight, formal bow to the visitors from the West.

The shaman returned the bow, smiled. This was a good-looking fellow. And quite the gentleman. Daisy brushed a wisp of hair from her face, hoped she didn't look too frowzy in the patched nightgown.

The muscular horse snorted, stamped a hoof against the earth. Three times.

The tall man comforted the animal with words that Daisy could not hear. The shaman looked down to consult with her power spirit. The dwarf had vanished.

This was, as visions went, a rather pleasant one. She waited for the white man to speak to her, but the handsome stranger remained silent. Indeed, he now took no notice of the Indian woman's presence. He gazed off into the distance, toward the great river. His eyes turned glassy. He was as one whose vision penetrates things present—to see another, more distant world.

There was a slight puff of wind that dried her eyes. Daisy blinked.

The white man was standing by a tripod-mounted surveyor's transit. He waited until the suspended plumb bob had damped its pendulumous motions, then checked the compass and the leveling bubble. Apparently satisfied with the instrument, he squinted through the eyepiece. Marveled at what he saw so many years hence. The sighting done, vertical and horizontal verniers were consulted, angles and bearings duly noted. He consulted a map, inked numbers and symbols onto the lined pages of a small ledger.

Again, the shaman blinked.

The man was on his knees with a triangular trowel. He had already laid a sure foundation that rested on bedrock. Now he was setting the massive cornerstone.

Daisy blinked a third time.

Now the man was old and frail, his thinning hair white like lambs' wool. He rested in a rocking chair, under the pleasant shade of a hawthorn tree. The *matukach* elder watched a great number of workers—far more than the Ute woman could count. They were raising many fine buildings. A great city of milky marble, black-peppered granite, fine red brick. Though weary from all his labors, the elderly man seemed pleased with the work on the foundation he had so carefully laid.

This was, the shaman thought, a most pleasant thing to see.

But in an instant, the air around her lost its fragrance. Wildflowers wilted, drooped their heads. There was a rumble of distant thunder, a flash of electric fire.

The old woman felt a thrilling chill pass through her.

The clouds turn coal-black. A cold mist of rain begins to fall. Not so far away, a crooked finger of lightning reaches out to touch an oak perched on a grassy knoll. Woody limbs explode with a flash of blue-white fire. Thunder shakes the earth. A white dove flutters in flight . . . falls from the sky.

Daisy Perika heard herself whisper, "What does this mean?"

Something is drawing near. Something wicked. A great horse appears, iron-shod hooves striking sparks on flinty stones, eyes demon-wild, insane with fury. The animal is the hot color of flames. It is mounted by a presence composed of sulfurous smoke. The sinister rider carries a heavy sword—the weapon is two-edged, and longer than a man is tall.

The shaman watched in horror as horse and rider approached the old gentleman in the rocking chair. "Look out," she croaked. "Look out. . . ." She lost her voice.

The fiery red horse—now within yards of the matukach *elder—comes on at a hard gallop. The dark rider raises the edged weapon like a scythe.*

Daisy tried to rush forward to prevent the attack, but like the lightning-struck oak, her feet were rooted to the earth. And so she stood on the grass, mute and paralyzed. The seer tried to close her eyes, but could not. Neither could she turn her face away. The elderly white man remained in his chair, seemingly unaware of the approaching peril.

The shaman tried to cry out. Again, the scream was smothered in her breast.

The dark figure swings the blade in a long, flashing arc, severing human flesh and bone as if the tissues are warm butter. There is a guttural shout of victory from the shadowy assassin. With a final flash of lightning, blazing horse and murderous rider are gone.

The decapitated head rolled across the wet grass, leaving a smearing trail of blood. The horrendous object stopped at the shaman's feet; the pale face looked up at the woman. Tears flowed from the eyes. The lips moved. She could not hear his words. Neither did she know how to help him. Still unable to speak, she thought, *Who are you?* For a fleeting moment, something flickered in that dark closet where her memories were kept. She tried hard to remember, but it was like trying to recall a dream upon awakening. A hint of recognition was swept away like old cobwebs before a broom.

But the shaman did know something about the rider on the fiery-red horse. The sword-wielding phantom who had decapitated the distinguished elder was a hollow, empty spirit. A dead soul.

CHAPTER 3

Two-Toes

The sun would not show its warm face for another hour, but Charlie Moon was already in the spacious kitchen, appreciating the rich aroma of freshly brewed coffee. He cracked three brown-shelled eggs into a cast-iron skillet where plump patties of pork sausage sizzled in hot grease. The radio was blaring a tearfully sad Hank Williams ballad. *That fella could yodel a man to a pleasant death.* He removed a pan of biscuits from the oven. *Yes, sir—this will be a fine breakfast. And a fine day.*

The cattle rancher heard a booming knock on the parlor door. It had to be Pete Bushman. An ordinary cowhand who wanted an audience with the boss would not show up before first light, or bang so hard on the door. Moon frowned at the skillet. From the sound of it, Pete had something urgent on his mind. The Ute, still in his sock feet, padded out of the kitchen, across the dining room, through the parlor.

Another heavy knock.

"Hold on—I'm coming." He opened the door to see his bewhiskered, bleary-eyed foreman. "Good morning, Pete."

Stomping past his employer, Pete Bushman grumbled that he was barely able to stomach these "Mr. Sunshines, who is filled to the gills with goodwill before they's had a bite a breakfast" and made a beeline for the kitchen.

Pete poured himself a half-pint of coffee, threw his head back, swallowed half the scalding brew in one gulp. He set the cup aside, wiped his whiskers on the sleeve of a denim jacket. Belched.

Moon tended the eggs in the skillet, which were burning brown and brittle around the edges.

The foreman helped himself to a biscuit, which he buttered. After consuming this delicacy, Pete began to drum his fingers on the kitchen table. This was a signal that he was ready to have his say.

The boss pretended not to notice.

The foreman drummed harder.

Moon salted his eggs. Peppered them. "You want something to eat, there's eggs and sausage."

"I suppose those who don't have to bother themselves about the bad troubles all around us can feed their faces. Me, I got to do the worryin'. So I'm not in the mood for grub." He had another biscuit. With a large dab of butter, a generous helping of blackberry jam.

Moon scooped eggs and sausage onto a platter, seated himself across the table from his employee.

Pete Bushman realized that the boss was not going to ask what was wrong. "I hardly got me a wink a sleep last night."

"Sorry to hear it." Moon didn't look up from his breakfast. "A working man needs a good night's rest."

Pete clicked his teeth. Like a hard case cocking his pistol.

Uh-oh. Here it comes. Moon selected a biscuit.

"Boss, we got troubles."

"All of God's children have troubles."

"Not the kind that comes with a mouth fulla sharp teeth." Like one about to announce the first installment of six kinds of apocalypse, the foreman affected a dramatic pause. "It's ol' Two-Toes."

The Ute speared a sausage with his fork.

Pete sniffed. "I reckon you don't know about him."

The rancher did know. According to cowboy gossip, the fabled mountain lion had chewed his paw free from a bear trap. Taking the foreman's gravity lightly, Moon frowned, as if puzzled. "This Two-Toes, he that new cowhand—the gimpy one from Carson City who can't see good out of his left eye?"

Pete went wide-eyed with astonishment. "Cowhand—Lord no!" *How ignernt can a grown man get?* "The new hire you're thinkin' of is Ben Schaumberg from down in New Mexico. He's an ironsmith. Good man."

"Oh, yeah. Schaumberg." Moon eyed his foreman. "I understand you've got him shoeing some quarter horses."

"He's been welding a new drive rod on the Farmall tractor." Bushman scowled at the absentminded Indian. "Two-Toes, he's a full-size daddy mountain lion."

Moon took a sip of heavily sugared coffee. Enjoyed it.

The gloomy foreman propped his elbows on the table, leaned forward. "When that cougar was young and fulla piss and vinegar, he used to do his killin' next door on the BoxCar range. That was when the BoxCar was a workin' ranch and had some stock for the big cat to pull down." Bushman snorted. Senator Davidson had ruined a perfectly good cow operation. Turned it into a sissy tinhorn spread. "But nowadays I guess Two-Toes figgers the pickin's is better on the Columbine."

The Ute looked across the table. "He killed any of our stock?"

Pete reached for another biscuit. "Not that I know of. But he's been a-slinkin' around."

Moon's eyes twinkled merrily. "A-slinking around where?"

"Over by the Misery range. Mostly at the bottom end of Dead Mule Notch."

"As long as this cougar don't bother the stock, we'll leave him alone."

Bushman buttered the biscuit, eyed several jars of sweet

stuff, selected a spoonful of apricot preserves. "That might be a mistake."

"How so?"

"Some of our cowhands say Two-Toes has been stalkin' 'em. And there's those two horses we lost last year."

Moon thought about it. The carcasses had never been found. It was most likely sickness. Or some trespassing city hunter had mistaken the horses for elk. But it could have been the mountain lion. "You figure that big cat has developed a taste for our riding stock?"

"I expect Two-Toes is pickin' his teeth on whinny-bones and belchin' up horseshoes." The foreman shot a grim look across the table at his boss. "And maybe for dessert, he'll swaller a couple of our cowboys whole."

A decision was necessary. "Till we can sort out this cougar business, issue these orders. Nobody works by himself."

Pete's head bobbed in agreement. "Right."

"The best marksman in every work crew will carry a rifle—and I don't mean a twenty-two."

The foreman wiped at his mouth with the edge of the cotton tablecloth, got up from the chair. "I'll see to it."

"And one more thing. I don't want anybody taking potshots at mountain lions for sport. First cowboy who does can find himself a job with another outfit."

Pete Bushman made a halfhearted salute. "I'll tell 'em."

CHAPTER 4

The Cyclist

Twilight's diaphanous mists had been inhaled by night; the sky was streaked with puffy wisps of feathery clouds. The moon had not yet made its silvery appearance, but there was sufficient starlight to keep the nocturnal wanderer from bumping into signposts, brick walls, or trunks of trees—if the night traveler knew his way around the campus.

Wilma Brewster knew her way around. Without using the ten-speed bicycle's small headlight, the young woman slipped confidently along the back lanes and unlighted byways of the virtually deserted grounds of Rocky Mountain Polytechnic University.

The part-time campus police officer, full-time undergraduate student was in high spirits. The last of her final exams had been completed. Two As, if you please, a respectable pair of Bs, and a single C. Not bad. And rookie officer Wilma Brewster was determined to enjoy a glorious Christmas vacation.

Being delightfully young, recklessly fearless, she had no thought whatever of personal safety. The well-oiled bicycle seemed an extension of her lithe limbs. Darting across empty parking lots, flitting silently along bricked sidewalks, careening around blind curves—it was all absolutely intoxicating. The hum of thin rubber tires was the only sound in her small universe. The rider leaned, made a careening left past the domed football stadium, zipped along Moab Avenue.

A hundred yards ahead, under the branches of a maple, Wilma thought she saw something move. Jarred by this intrusion into her private world, she brought the sleek ten-speed almost to a halt, held her breath. *Is this my imagination?* Another flutter of movement. *No. There's really something there.* Probably an animal. Stray dog, maybe. Or a coyote. It moved again. No, definitely not a canine creature. This *something* walked upright. And so in her mind, the shadowy thing became a man. *Probably just an insomniac taking a late-night stroll.* But there had been several cases of vandalism in this area. Only last week, some bone-head had broken a half-dozen windows in the new preschool. *Better call it in.* Wilma reached for the small holster on her belt. The radio transceiver wasn't there. *Oh, dammit!* She had checked it in just before signing off duty. *So what do I do now?* The answer was obvious. *I'll keep an eye on this guy. Find out what he's up to.*

She shifted to low gear, followed the dark figure that was now moving along the sidewalk toward the preschool. This might be the vandal, getting ready to heave a few rocks through the undamaged windows. Wilma was confident that she had not been seen, but fear rippled along her limbs. There was something oddly familiar about the way this person moved. *Could he be someone I know?*

Presently, the figure paused at the campus preschool, leaned against a chain-link fence enclosing a small playground. For a spine-chilling moment, she was certain that the phantom looked back. At her.

Wilma guided the bicycle behind a bushy shrub, gripped the handlebars, waited. Not a sound. *He didn't see me—it was just my imagination. I hope.* Stretching her neck to look over a branch, the campus police officer thought she spotted her quarry. *So what are you going to do now?* There was no movement for almost a minute. Doubt began to gnaw at her. *Maybe I'm looking at something else. Maybe he's gone. Or maybe he's doubled back and he's behind me now and*—There was a creaking sound as the dark figure opened a gate in the fence. She watched the shadow-person move onto the playground, pass by a set of miniature teeter-totters, a slide, a sheet-metal assembly resembling an enormous beetle. The amorphous form stopped under an elm. Sat down.

What on earth is he doing? From somewhere deep in her brain stem, an urgent message surfaced. This voice of her most basic instincts was simple, imperative: *Danger. Stay away.* For a full five seconds, she heeded the stern warning. But curiosity overcame the young woman's underdeveloped sense of self-preservation. *I need to get a closer look.* She got off the bicycle, pushed it closer to the boundary of the preschool play lot. Wilma stood behind a mulberry tree, squinted toward the spot where she had last seen movement.

The moon showed its brow over the snowy crest of a round-shouldered mountain.

Whoever it was, was still there. She could see this person more clearly now, sitting in a place where, during the daylight hours, small children played. Wilma squinted. The shadowy figure was doing something quite peculiar. Technically, it appeared to be a matter of theft. Petty theft, to be sure. *But why on earth would anyone want to steal*— This thought was interrupted when the shadowy form paused in its work. Looked up. No doubt, this time—invisible eyes stared directly at her. Wilma's heart hammered against her ribs. The campus police officer found a voice that squeaked with fear. "Hey—what're you doing on the playground?" She could see precisely what this strange person had been doing. The question was *why*.

The figure was now erect. Moving toward the young woman. Again, there was something hauntingly familiar about the way the dark form moved.

"I'm Officer Brewster, Campus Police. This is a lawful order—stop right where you are. And identify yourself."

The shadowy trespasser did not stop.

Even as the young woman's joints rattled with fear, she reminded herself about duty—and standing one's ground. As she entertained these virtuous thoughts, the urgent message from her brain stem fairly screamed, *Run! Run!*

Duty was forgotten, ground surrendered. In a wild panic, Wilma mounted her bicycle, kicked off the ten-speed, pumped the pedals until her legs ached.

By the time she was half a mile away, her face burned with shame. *I'm behaving like a silly, frightened child.* The righteous thing to do was turn the bike around, return to the preschool playground, confront the trespasser. Or at least go back to the campus police headquarters and report the incident. But there would be no one at the playground by now. Best to forget the matter. *Everything will be fine when I get home.*

Not so. Once inside her small apartment, she could not dismiss the peculiar incident from her troubled mind. Like a deranged serpent, the poisonous thought coiled in a tight circle, fastened teeth on tail. A hoop with no beginning, no end. Over and over and over.

It's too late to do anything now.

I can't report what happened—how could I explain running away?

I'll just have to forget about it.

It's too late to do anything now. . . .

The young woman looked at trembling hands. *This is crazy—what is wrong with me?* And then it hit her. *Did I take my meds today?* She tried hard to remember. *I'm sure I did.* But she was not sure. She hurried to the tiny bathroom, opened the medicine cabinet, removed the brown bottle. Perphenazine. *I'm supposed to take two pills every day, whether I need them or not.* She stared at the bottle shaking in her hand. *No, I'm sure I took them this morning. I don't want to overdose.* She put the pill bottle back in the cabinet. For the short term, something else was called for. Distraction. *I need to get out of this apartment for a while.*

Have some fun. Her holiday vacation had just begun. *Maybe I should take a trip somewhere.*

She brushed her teeth, enjoyed a quick shower in the rusting stall, slipped on the white dress (it went *so* well with her bright red hair), applied crimson lipstick, glanced occasionally at the television. As a final ritual, Wilma hurried around her small off-campus efficiency apartment, doing a bit of fine-tuning. Dusting off the coffee table she'd picked up at Goodwill, picking up tiny bits of fluff and stuff from the worn carpet, forcing some stray underwear into an already overstuffed drawer, checking to verify that all four burners on the gas range were turned off, and the oven.

It seemed that the brisk, mindless activity had been the right prescription. If not entirely gone, the jitters were at least suppressed.

Time for the final ritual. She slipped on the red high heels.

Glorying in this victory over what her mother called "nerves," Wilma paused to stand before the full-length mirror on the closet door. She inspected what she considered a not unattractive freckled face, then stuck out her tongue at the image—which responded in saucy fashion. One hand on a slender hip, the willowy young woman posed seductively, frankly admiring the reflection of her trim figure. Which was several notches above "not unattractive." This dose of narcissism was highly therapeutic. She turned to see a commercial on the television screen. A seriously cute little boy, sitting in a sandbox. The tot was shoveling sand into a blue bucket. A spaniel came, licked his ear. The child giggled.

The jitters returned.

Dammit!

She switched off the TV, fed a disk into the gaping mouth of the cheap CD player. The first of nine delicious Strauss waltzes dripped like warm honey from the cone. *There. That's better.* She closed her eyes. *Okay. I am in control.* Deep breath. *I will put the whole thing out of my mind.* Exhale. *Out goes the bad.* Inhale. *In comes the good.* Exhale. *Replace bad thoughts with good ones.* With an admirable effort of will, she concentrated on lovely things. Deep in a dark forest, a small pond. Ripples in the sunlight, spreading. Emerald lily pads, tilting with each sigh of the waters. Creamy white cup-shaped blossoms springing up magically from an acre of velvety lily pads. And there . . . something moving underneath the waters. An astonishingly beautiful golden-scaled fish about to break the crystalline surface? No. It was a *person* coming up from the depths. Out of the darkness. Dripping wet, the phantom surfaced. Head. Shoulders. Torso. Legs.

The legs walked toward her. She could see the face quite clearly.

Wilma Brewster opened her eyes, absolutely certain that what she had witnessed at the preschool was not just petty theft. *Something terrible is going to happen.* She had no idea what.

High heels clicking, delicate hands clenched into fists, she began to pace around the small apartment. *What should I do?* Abruptly, she came to a decision. *I need to talk to someone I can trust.* Wilma's hand went to her neck, grasped the jasper crucifix dangling on a gold-plated chain. *I could talk to a priest.* She smiled. *Or maybe I should find me a real kick-ass cop.*

CHAPTER 5

A Chance Encounter

Charlie Moon was helping his groaning aunt out of the F-150 pickup when he heard a familiar voice. He turned to see Father Delfino Raes, pastor of St. Ignatius Catholic Church. The short, slightly built Jesuit had a gaily wrapped parcel under one arm. The Ute nodded a polite greeting to the priest, who served both the reservation and the non-Indians who lived in and around Ignacio.

Daisy squinted suspiciously at the cleric. "Who's that funny-looking little man?"

Her nephew rolled his eyes. *Here it comes.*

The sly old woman clasped a large purse protectively against her chest. "The television news says there's lots of riffraff hanging around these big parking lots—especially pickpockets and purse-snatchers."

Father Raes forced a smile that hurt his face. "Hello, Daisy."

"Oh, it's *you.*" She lowered the walking stick, managed to look down her nose at the kindly man. "I guess my money's safe—till next Sunday morning."

"Sorry," Moon said. "My aunt's having one of her off days."

"Really?" *She seems perfectly normal to me.* Father Raes

tipped his black fedora at the elderly woman. "I shall look forward to seeing you at Mass." *Forgive me, Father, for I have lied.* After exchanging a few pleasantries with Moon, he excused himself and hurried away.

Daisy watched the receding form and called out, "Next time the Pope phones to ask how you're getting along, tell him hello for me!" Her day made, the mischievous woman cackled with delight.

Knowing that his expression of disapproval would only encourage the incorrigible old woman to new heights of wickedness, Moon held his silence.

But Daisy Perika had a darkly sweet secret that she shared with no mortal soul. In fact, the truth of it was hidden so deeply inside her heart that the woman herself did not fully fathom it. God alone knew how much the shaman loved the priest.

The Walking Corpse

Grunting as she thumped her oaken staff across the parking lot, Charlie Moon's aunt hobbled along by his side. The long-legged Ute found himself taking very short steps. It was much like going for a walk with a two-year-old. *Poor old woman. Wonder if this is how I'll be getting around when I'm her age.* He comforted himself with the thought that it was highly unlikely he would live so long.

Daisy Perika muttered without looking up at her nephew. "I still got some Christmas stuff to buy. I'm glad you brought me here."

Despite her rudeness to the priest, he had noticed that she was mellowing with age. Now, not less than once or twice every year, the cranky old woman would say something that sounded almost like *thank you.* "I hope you have a good time. Buy everything in sight." He smiled at the scarfed head bobbing along at his left elbow. "We'll fill up the pickup, haul it all home. As long as you brought plenty of cash."

Daisy patted her flowered purse. "I got my Social

Security check right here." She slowed, squinting at the storefront. "I can't recall what it is, but there's something about this place I don't like."

It was too good to last. Moon prepared himself for the inevitable complaint.

The Ute elder stopped in her tracks.

"What's the matter?"

"I remember now." She pointed her walking stick at the entrance. "This is where *he* hangs out."

"Who?"

"You've seen 'im." The tribal elder made an ugly grimace. "That nine-hundred-year-old white man."

Her nephew frowned. "What're you talking about?"

"Clyde," she sneered.

"You know his name?"

"Sure—it's sewed onto his vest. That's so when he can't remember who he is, all he has to do is check his label."

"You talking about the elderly gentleman who greets the customers?"

"When that old buzzard got so feeble he couldn't tie his shoes and started to slobber in his oatmeal, I guess his family was too lazy to dig a hole and put him in it. So they propped up Gran'pa Broomstick to frighten the children when they come in the store."

Children come in all ages. "That's no way to talk about one of the greeters. Besides, you've got a good ten years on him."

"In case you hadn't noticed, there's a big difference between being old and being *dead.*" She snorted. "That man is a walking corpse."

She gets worse every year.

Daisy clenched his arm in a grip surprising for one of her years. "They put those zombie white men right inside the door just to keep 'em off the street." She shuddered. "What's the matter—ain't there enough *matukach* graveyards to hold 'em all?"

"Now listen—"

"It's a wonder they didn't put him in the carnival. Lotsa

folks would pay two bits to see the old freak—Clyde the Tooth-Clicking Dead Man."

"Are we going inside or not?"

"We'll go, but if that old bag of bones pops his teeth at me just one time, I'll lay his skull wide open with my stick."

The amiable Ute looked to the heavens. *Why me, Lord?*

They passed through the portal into the bright land of plastic-wrapped merchandise.

"Look out." Daisy clenched Moon's arm all the harder. "There he is." She withdrew behind her nephew.

"If you keep acting like this," he murmured, "I'm not going to take you anyplace."

"Hush—Clyde looks like he's about to pounce. You keep him away from me."

The skinny man in the blue vest had indeed spotted the potential customers. He took a halting pace forward to meet and greet. His wrinkled face creased into a merry caricature of a smile, exposing a pearly set of dentures that did not quite fit his gums. The false teeth clicked as he spoke. "Hello—anything I can do for you?"

Moon smiled at the greeter. "Not right now, thank you." *Just a few more steps and I'm home free.*

Clyde Sprigg recognized the tall Ute and leaned sideways to see behind him. *Yes, there she is—that peculiar old Indian woman.* She was always good for a laugh. He tipped an imaginary hat. Clicked the porcelain teeth.

Daisy peeked around her nephew's elbow. "Back off, Walking Dead—or you'll find out what it feels like to get this laid across your ugly head." She raised the oak walking stick in a menacing gesture.

The old man snickered.

"Sorry," Moon said. "Once a month they let me take her out of the Home. I'm afraid she's forgot how to behave in public."

His flippancy was rewarded by a dark oath from his aunt, punctuated by a sharp rap on his ankle.

"Ouch."

The official greeter nodded with a sad expression. "I know how it is, sonny. My poor old mother is just the same. Momma don't get her little yellow calm-me-down pills, why she's pure hell on wheels." He pointed down a broad aisle, past a cluster of checkout stands. "You want to drug the old lady into a stupor, our excellent pharmacy is down that way."

"Now there's a notion," the Ute said. "Or maybe I'll go over to Pet Supplies—buy me a leash."

"Well, she *is* cute as a spotted puppy under a little red wagon." Clyde winked a bleary eye at the Ute elder.

Daisy ground her teeth. *These men stick together like a gob of cockleburs.*

Moon managed to separate the pair without further insult or physical threat.

Inevitably, time passed. Delightful items were purchased. Wounds were healed.

By eleven-thirty, they had strolled through Women's Clothing, Kitchenware, Paints, Electronics, Sporting Goods, and finally the Lawn and Garden Center where Daisy selected a small bag of fertilizer, several packets of seeds.

Moon had been confident that she would be worn out by now.

But the crusty old woman was getting her second wind.

Her nephew was getting his second appetite. Since breakfast, he had not had a bite. He cast a hopeful gaze at a small cafeteria. Sniffed heavy aromas floating in the air. Read the sign over the plastic counter. There were choice delicacies at bargain prices. Meat loaf special. Polish sausage and sauerkraut. Grilled ham and cheese sandwiches. Milk shakes. *Some of that would hold me till lunch.* He leaned close to the old woman. "You ready for a snack?"

She shook her head. "I got more important things to do right now. Besides, I don't want to spoil my appetite—you're taking me to Bennie's Kitchen." In Daisy's opinion, this was the best restaurant in Durango. Really fine peach pie.

"Right." His stomach growled. "Guess I can hold off for another hour."

"Oh, go ahead and stuff your big face. While you're busy making gas, I'll do some browsing."

"You sure—"

She waved him off. "Go on—leave me be. I won't get lost."

The plastic stool was small and hard—like sitting on a cedar fence post. Charlie Moon smiled at the plump woman behind the counter. He ordered the Frito pie. Large fries. And a chocolate milk shake, if you please.

Daisy Perika was watching a highly entertaining display of rainbow-hued tropical fish dart about in glass tanks when she first noticed the redheaded woman. There were hordes of shoppers wandering among the mountains of merchandise, but this one was staring at Charlie Moon. Like she wanted to go up and say something to Daisy's nephew, but couldn't quite get up the nerve.

The Ute elder was about to pass by the gawker when she noticed the frustrated look on the white woman's face. In an attempt to get her attention, the Ute elder sidled up beside the young lady, faked a wracking cough.

The pale creature took not the least notice.

Daisy put on her best manners. "What're you staring at?"

Still no response.

Louder: "Hey, you—Carrot-Top!"

At this, the woman turned—looked Daisy straight in the eye. Her expression suggested mild surprise.

"That young man you been gawking at—that's my nephew. Charlie Moon."

There was the merest hint of a smile.

Maybe she's a lunatic. "You got some business with him?"

A nod.

"What about?"

• • •

Feeling a tug on his sleeve, Charlie Moon turned away from the Frito pie to see his aged aunt. "Didn't think you'd be back so soon." He shoved a red plastic basket toward her. "Want a french fry?"

Daisy Perika shook her head. "My legs hurt."

"You've been working 'em too hard." He helped the weary woman onto a stool.

She grunted at the effort.

He concentrated on the greasy snack. "I'll be done here in a minute. Then we'll head for Bennie's."

His aunt's face wore a worried look. "I need to tell you something."

"No. Don't tell me. Let me guess." He assumed an expression of intent concentration. "Oh, yeah—I got it. You've spent your whole Social Security check. And you expect to tap me for a loan."

"I just ran into somebody who wants to talk to you."

He squeezed a plastic bottle, squirted a stream of tomato catsup over the fries. "Who?"

"A young woman. She's been watching you."

Young woman. Well, now. The tribal investigator straightened his string tie, turned on the rock-hard stool. "Where is she?"

"I thought that'd get your interest." Daisy pointed. "She's right over . . ." The woman was not there.

"Which one?" The store was packed with female persons of every description.

"I don't see her now." The old woman's eyes searched the crowd in vain. "After I went up and asked what she was doing looking at you, I think she must've got spooked."

"Imagine that." He turned back to his food.

"Don't you get sassy with me, Charlie Moon. You can eat later—right now, you got to go find that girl."

He grinned sideways at the tribal elder. "Why do I got to?"

"Because she's in trouble."

"What kind of trouble?"

"She didn't say. But that girl's afraid of somebody." And it was always a man that ruined a woman's life. "And don't ask me how I know—I just *know*."

Damn. He lost his appetite. "She have any cuts or bruises?"

"Not that I could see. But sure as woodpeckers peck wood, somebody's knocked her around one time too many. That's why she wants to talk to a policeman."

"I haven't been in uniform for almost four years. Why would she—"

"Well, that's plain as the nose on your face," Daisy snapped. "She's somebody who remembers you from way back when."

He stared at his aunt. Most of the time, the old woman seemed to live in a dreamworld. Then she would surprise him with a display of common sense. "Yeah. I guess she could know me from my time with SUPD."

"Which means she's probably from Ignacio." Daisy eyed the french fries. "And she probably knows you're still doing police work for the tribe."

"Give me a description."

"Pale-skinned *matukach*. Skinny. Stringy red hair. Freckles. Blue eyes. Not more'n twenty-four years old."

Moon was impressed with his aged aunt's powers of observation. He could think of at least two women in Ignacio who matched the description. "What's she wearing?"

"White dress. Red shoes."

This one wouldn't be hard to spot. "Stay here."

Daisy watched her nephew disappear into the throng of shoppers. She reached for a french fry. Bit off the end. The starchy stalk was soaked with grease, crusted with salt. She dipped the remnant in a gob of catsup. *Pretty good.*

It was well past noon when the tribal investigator returned to the lunch counter. In response to the question on his aunt's face, Moon shrugged. "Couldn't find her. She must've had second thoughts about talking to me." It was standard behavior for battered women. First, they couldn't wait to tell a cop about how the husband or boyfriend had beaten them up. "Drop the bastard in the darkest dungeon," they'd say. "Throw away the key!" But love makes a strong bond. Even the warped kind of affection that keeps a woman with a ham-fisted bully. So when she looked the cop in the eye, finally had the opportunity to jug the animal, the abused woman typically thought of a dozen reasons not to make a complaint. Like: What will I do without him. What will he do to me if I file charges. What will the children do without a father. What will my parents say. And worst of all—maybe it's really *my* fault.

Moon took a last look around the six-acre store. *Ten to one, this redhead has gone home for another beating.* He mounted the stool, stared at the cold remnants of the Frito pie. Thanked God that he no longer had to deal with such dismal matters on a daily basis. There were uniforms for that. Poor underpaid, underappreciated bastards.

Daisy glared at her nephew. "You going to give up just like that?"

"I'll give her description to the Durango and Ignacio PDs."

Daisy nodded. "Well I hope *somebody* will do something useful." *You sure didn't.*

"This redhead—she say anything at all that might help the local cops find her?"

"Like what?"

"Like who she is, where she lives. Why she didn't approach a uniformed law enforcement officer. Why she wanted to talk to me in particular."

"No."

Figures. He drained the last of the chocolate milk shake.

"And just so you won't think I'm a silly old fool, I did ask her what her name was."

There was no point in asking. "But she didn't tell you."

Daisy tapped her walking stick on the floor. "She didn't tell me who she was. Or exactly where she lived. But she said, 'Tell him he can find me in Arroyo Hondo.' "

Well, that's better than nothing. There were at least three

Deep Arroyos within a couple of hundred miles. The nearest one was an abandoned mining settlement halfway between Granite Creek and the Columbine's eastern border. It was listed as a ghost town on the Forest Service map, but there might be a few down-and-out squatters hanging about. Also, that particular Arroyo Hondo was in Scott Parris's jurisdiction. Moon paid his bill, tipped the congenial waitress more than he could afford.

Ignacio, Southern Ute Reservation

It was quite late, almost the eleventh hour. Having said his prayers, Father Raes Delfino crossed himself, got into bed. He stretched out on the lumpy mattress, found the familiar hollows that cupped his hips and shoulders. Having come as near to comfort as was possible, he rested his head on the pillow, closed his eyes. *I am so very tired. . . .* He began to drift away into that diffuse shadowland that divides ordinary consciousness from the near death of sleep. The Jesuit priest was about to dream his dream when—

There came a knock-knock-knocking on the rectory door.

He groaned, raised himself on an elbow. *Oh please, God—not a caller. Not at this hour.* Muscles tensed, he waited for a second knocking.

It did not come.

Pleased to have his prayer answered so promptly, the priest yawned. And fell into the most peaceful of sleeps.

CHAPTER 6

Blood Ceremony

The razor-edged ten-inch blade was tinted with crimson. There was not a hint of pity in the white man's hard eyes. The object of his attention was a *thing*. A piece of meat. He got a better grip on the elk-horn handle, set his square jaw, savagely plunged the blade into the flesh until tempered steel was deflected off the surface of moist bone. *That's better.* In an age-old gesture of triumph, he lifted a sliver of pink tissue on the tip of the deadly instrument, stuffed it into his mouth. Closed his eyes. Chewed. *That's mighty good.*

The sole witness to this brutish exhibition suppressed a surge of nausea. The aged Ute turned his face away from the grisly scene. "Patch, you're the only man I know who brings his own knife to a restaurant."

Patch Davidson pointed the sliver of tempered steel at his dining companion. "Oscar, a man needs a heavy blade when he's cutting meat. None of these flimsy little steak knives—" He was interrupted by a buzzing sensation that tickled his ribs. "What's that?" Colorado's senior United States senator scowled as he reached into his jacket pocket. "It's my cell phone." He unfolded the charcoal-tinted instrument, held it against his ear. "Start talking." He listened, tapping the knife blade on a china plate. "Sure, Billy. Take your time. We'll be here for about another hour." He snapped the instrument shut, slipped it back in his pocket. "That was Billy."

The chairman of the Southern Ute tribe nodded. "I thought so."

"He's hanging out at that sleazy bar on the west end of town."

"The Mountain Man?"

The senator nodded. "I asked him to have dinner with us, but I guess this place is not to his taste."

Oscar Sweetwater was not eager to walk down this path. But Billy Smoke was an enrolled member of the tribe. "He doing a good job for you?"

Senator Davidson wiped at his mouth with a linen napkin, sawed off another chunk of very rare beef steak. "Billy's one of the best drivers I've ever had."

Sweetwater gathered bushy eyebrows into a fuzzy frown. "I hear some worrisome talk. Rumors he's acquired some unsavory friends."

The senator forked a buttery chunk of baked potato. "I suppose Billy does hang out with some roughnecks."

The elderly Ute, who had a highly sensitive digestive system, helped himself to a spoonful of cream of mushroom soup. After thinking about it, he said, "You want me to have a talk with him?"

"Wouldn't help. Billy's a grown man—he'll choose his own drinking buddies."

"I could ask Charlie Moon to do some poking around. Find out who these buddies are."

Patch Davidson expertly speared a floret of steamed broccoli with his fork, looked across his plate at the tribal chairman. "I thought Charlie had given up law enforcement." The former Ute policeman now owned one of the largest ranches in Colorado. And Moon's Columbine bordered the senator's BoxCar Ranch.

"He's a special investigator for the tribe," the chairman said, and added: "On a part-time basis."

"Interesting," the senator said. "Charlie have a private-cop license?"

Oscar Sweetwater nodded, crumbled a pair of saltines into his soup.

As their pleasant supper continued, the pair of politicians discussed several issues of mutual interest. Charlie Moon's prior success as a tribal policeman. Charlie Moon's huge ranch. Charlie Moon's aunt Daisy, who reputedly communed with sundry ghosts and spirits. Why the senator had carried only fifty-two percent of the tribal vote in the previous election. A legal battle between the tribe and the state over water rights in the Piedra Basin. What to do about the ever worsening mess in the Bureau of Indian Affairs.

A smartly uniformed waiter pushed aside a red velvet curtain to enter the small dining room. The space was reserved for special parties and infrequent VIP guests. The senator—who cherished these intimate meals with influential constituents and old friends—loved the occasional luxury of privacy. He always entered and left by a rear door that exited into the employee parking lot.

The Sleeping Man

Billy Smoke had three cans of Coors beer under his belt, along with a greasy order of fish and chips. The Ute belched as he eased the black Lincoln into the employee parking lot behind the Blue Light Cafe. He shifted to park, cut the ignition. The senator's chauffeur glanced at his wristwatch, checked it against the clock on the dash panel. "The old man shouldn't be stuffin' his face much longer," he mumbled. "Probably having his dessert right about now." He thought about going inside to let his employer know he was here with the car. Then, there was the lazy man's solution—he could call the senator on the cell phone again. *If I go inside I could order some strawberry short-cake to go. With ice cream.* But feeling sleepy, the chauffeur decided to sit awhile in the Lincoln, let his supper settle. He switched the radio on, pressed the Seek button until the receiver locked in on the FM signal from the Rocky Mountain Polytechnic radio station. KRMP was broadcasting a *Prairie Home Companion* rerun. The lovely voice of a woman singing slipped across the airwaves. Swing Low Sweet Chariot.

A cold rain began to fall from the heavens. Droplets peppered hard on the windshield, threatening to become sleet.

The chauffeur leaned back in the luxurious seat, closed his eyes. There wasn't much more a reasonable man would ask for. Full belly. Fine music filling his ear. The sweetly soporific drumming of cold rain on the steel roof. This triple blessing was too much. The chauffeur slipped off to sleep. He snored. Dreamed of the well-endowed barmaid who'd poured his beer at the Mountain Man Bar & Grille. Charlene was bouncing on a blue trampoline, higher and higher. And she was singing in a sonorous, bluesy voice, " 'Swing low . . . coming for to carry me home.' "

There was a rhythmic crunch of footsteps on the wet gravel. The figure treading the fragmented stone seemed immaterial—a misty shadow that had somehow raised itself up from the earth. It approached the Lincoln. Slowed. Stopped. Stared through the rain-splattered window at the sleeping man.

The bouncy barmaid was inviting him onto the trampoline. Billy tried to get aboard the contraption, but it was too high, his legs too heavy. She reached out with a wand. Rapped him on the head. Tappity-tap. *Why did you do that?* The Indian's absurd dream was interrupted by a second tap-tapping sound. He grunted, opened his eyes. It took Billy Smoke a long moment to remember where he was. *In the senator's car.* A second later, he remembered that he was the senator's driver.

Still another tap-tap on the window.

He blinked at the dark form on the opposite side of the rain-streaked glass.

Oh, hell's bells. The senator's standing out there in the rain. And me asleep and with beer on my breath. The mean old sonofabitch'll chew my ass for this. He opened the door, the apology already spilling out of his mouth. "Sorry about that, sir—I just closed my eyes for a minute and—"

Something hard smashed into his face, flattening his nose, driving a sliver of bone into the base of his brain. Another crushing blow to the temple. Billy slumped to his side, rolled onto his back. One hand was slightly raised, as if in supplication. His eyes were closed. Forever.

Oscar Sweetwater watched the white man finish a slab of Mud Pie. Far more separated the mismatched politicians than the linen-covered table. But the Southern Ute tribal chairman reflected that he genuinely liked the powerful *matukach*. One thought lead to another. He mused that a desire for power was what led to most of the trouble in the world. And power was what politics was all about.

A silent waiter appeared with the check. When Oscar Sweetwater insisted on paying the bill with a tribal credit card, the wealthy senator made a show of protesting. But the Southern Ute chairman was a lobbyist of sorts, so it was understood that he would pay for the eats. The waiter departed.

The senator smoked an expensive cigar. Told a few off-color jokes.

The tribal chairman smiled at the appropriate moments. And thought his thoughts.

The waiter returned with a credit card receipt. Oscar signed it. The evening was over.

Because the elderly Ute felt the need to pay a call on the urinal, they said their good-byes inside the private dining room.

The rain, true to its threat, had been transformed into pea-sized pellets of sleet. Wind whistled in the eaves, scattered dead leaves. It was the sort of night that reminds even a powerful, successful man that he is much like ordinary mortals, who toil and fail and laugh and cry. And die. That he is made from the same stuff as the earth.

And to dust you shall return.

Senator Patch Davidson did not tolerate such humbling thoughts for more time than it took to dismiss them. Having pulled on his overcoat, he stood just outside the employee exit, musing about whether the meeting with the Southern Ute tribal chairman had accomplished anything useful. Next election, Oscar Sweetwater's good- will could add two or three percentage points on the reservation. He allowed his eyes time to adjust to the night. The employee parking lot was darker than usual. *Something seems different.* He realized what it was. The single lightbulb that normally illuminated the graveled space was black as an eight ball. Senator Davidson leaned forward, as if this would help his vision penetrate the damp blackness. *Where's the car? Billy knows he's supposed to turn the lights on when I come out. Maybe he's still hanging out in that sleazy bar. Maybe drunk. Maybe I should call him on the cell phone.*

As he collected this handful of maybes, the senator's pupils dilated just enough. He spotted an outline that resembled the big Lincoln. The barge-like automobile was parked less than ten yards away. "Well, turn on the lights, Billy-Boy." It occurred to him that the chauffeur might not be able to see him in the darkness. He pulled the coat collar close around his neck, started across the parking space toward the black sedan, heard his footsteps in the soaked gravel. Crunch. Crunch. Crunch. As he approached the automobile, he noticed that the door was open just a crack. Davidson leaned to peer through the window. "Billy?" He pulled at the door. The dome light switched on, bathed the luxury car's interior in soft amber light. The front seat was empty. "Now where the hell is he?" *Maybe he went inside looking for me. Probably stopped at the john to take a leak. That's why I missed him. Sure.*

Senator Davidson heard footsteps, turned, expecting to see the approaching form of his good-natured Indian chauffeur.

His bladder relieved, Oscar Sweetwater was at his Buick, fumbling in his pocket for the keys, when he heard the sound. The tribal chairman turned toward the rear of the restaurant, where Billy Smoke always picked up the senator after their late dinners. There it was again. Something between a whimper and a groan.

Sweetwater unlocked the Buick, removed a flashlight and a very old Colt .32-caliber revolver from the glove compartment. As he walked slowly toward the sounds, he opened the cold steel cylinder and ran his finger around it, feeling the rims of brass cartridge cases, counting six. *Ready for business.* Rounding the corner of the cinder block building, he heard an indistinct thumping sound—a car door closing? He waited, then called out, "Who's there?" The silence was prickly-cold. The elderly Ute switched on the flashlight. He swept the beam across a half dozen parked sedans, a rusty Chevy pickup. And the senator's Lincoln. But no sign of a living creature, human or otherwise. The pitiful whimpering had ceased. A sea of silence washed over the graveled parking lot.

The tribal chairman took a half dozen steps toward the Lincoln. "Hey—Patch. You there?"

The answer was illuminated in the beam of his flashlight. The senator, easily identifiable by a shock of silvery-white hair, was stretched out on his side. The Southern Ute tribal chairman knelt by the still figure. "Patch—are you . . . dead?"

There was a faint, answering whimper. Sweetwater played the flashlight beam around the lot. Barely a dozen paces away, immediately behind the Lincoln, he saw another body. *Must be Billy Smoke.* Right size. Right shape. Right hair color. But it was impossible to be certain if it was Billy. Much of the man's face was caved in. Sweetwater was certain of one thing. Only one of these men would need medical attention.

The tribal chairman grasped his friend by the shoulder. "Hold on, Patch." The aged man managed a stiff, bowlegged gallop toward the restaurant. Oscar Sweetwater heard someone screaming for help. It was his own voice. The Ute didn't realize he was speaking in his native tongue.

The cashier looked up in openmouthed alarm as the wild-eyed maniac burst through the restaurant door. It was an old dark-skinned man waving a flashlight in one hand, a pistol in the other. He was shouting in a choppy language she did not understand. The woman, who had been robbed three times in five years, automatically raised her hands over her head. She nodded at the cash register. "Hey, take it all, Pops—just don't shoot me!"

Oscar Sweetwater pointed the revolver at a telephone, sucked in a deep, rattling breath. "Call an ambulance."

"Yes sir." She snatched the phone off the hook.

"And the police—call them too."

CHAPTER 7

Four Months Later

Late morning sunshine bathed the columbine in a spray of purest gold. On the wintertime side of the ranch headquarters, the river—swollen with snow melt—roared over black basalt boulders. At the edge of the south valley, the mirror-surfaced glacial lake nestled like an emerald on the throat of the mountain. Charlie Moon, who owned this rugged corner of paradise, was leaning on a steel-pipe fence beside a fat, bearded trucker who smelled of beer and tobacco. Both men were watching Moon's ill-tempered foreman and a half dozen dusty cowboys unload twenty head of Herefords into the holding corral. The purebred animals were a fine sight to behold. Fine enough to make a stockman's eyes go moist. When the last of the costly beasts were unloaded, the trucker said a hearty good-bye to Moon and thanked the rancher for a first-rate breakfast. The heavyset man went to button up his rig in preparation for a long, empty run to Fort Worth.

With the throaty rumble of the diesel engine, the cowboys shouting and cursing, the clanging of gates, the snorting and stomping of half-ton animals, the corral was incredibly noisy. Moon, who had his back to the ranch headquarters, had not heard the arrival of the sedan. Neither was he aware of the small man making his cautious way down the slope from the big house. He was startled when a thumb poked him in the ribs.

He turned to see the wrinkled, smiling face of the Southern Ute tribal chairman. The rancher shook the elder's outstretched hand. "Hey, Oscar—you sneaked up on me."

Oscar Sweetwater took a place at the fence. Admired the fat cattle. "Looks like you're doing all right for yourself."

"I haven't gone bankrupt yet. And," the former tribal policeman added, "it beats hauling drunks to the jailhouse."

"But you still carry a badge." Sweetwater was not a man for making small talk. He had a reason for reminding Charlie Moon that he was a special investigator, reporting to the tribal council. Which, for practical purposes, meant that he did an occasional piece of work for the tribal chairman. If Moon had the time. And the inclination.

The rancher was on his guard. "You here for pleasure—or business?"

Sweetwater looked up at the seven-foot Ute. "I am a fortunate man. For me, business is always a pleasure." He jutted his chin to indicate the animals in the corral. "I think you like your business too."

The younger man clapped his big hand on the chairman's thin shoulder. "Let's go up to the house."

Oscar Sweetwater's small form was almost swallowed up by a huge, overstuffed chair. The old man's eyes were closed. He would occasionally open them, take a sip from a mug of coffee laced with milk.

Charlie Moon stood in front of the massive granite fireplace that dominated the north side of the parlor. Flames crackled in the stack of split pine. The rancher warmed his hands.

Sweetwater cleared his throat. "Seems like a long time since we buried Billy Smoke."

Moon, half mesmerized by the flames, nodded. "How's the senator getting along?"

The chairman moved the mug in a counterclockwise motion. A dark whirlpool formed in the black liquid. "Patch bought himself a fancy motorized wheelchair."

"Will he ever walk again?"

"Don't look like it. Some people think he'll resign from the senate. But Patch knows this attack will get him lots of sympathy—and plenty of extra votes come next election. And the next election is all he cares about. You mark my words, Charlie—he'll be back in Washington before the first snow. Tootin' around on his electric scooter. Making big things happen." Sweetwater smiled at the picture in his mind.

The rancher seated himself on a leather couch, pointed his knees at the fireplace. "You been keeping yourself out of trouble?"

"What do you mean by that?"

Moon allowed himself a smile. "Just wondered if you'd managed to stay out of the pokey."

The tribal chairman snorted. "I don't know what's wrong with those cops in Granite Creek. Throwing me in the jailhouse when I was an innocent bystander reporting a crime."

Moon nodded. "It is a mystery. All you did was run into a restaurant at midnight, wave a loaded pistol at the cashier." He grinned at the chairman. "And with two bodies lying outside in the parking lot."

"All I wanted was for that dopey cashier to call the police, but I was all outta wind. And I forgot to talk American. Them dumb coppers locked me up like I was some kinda criminal. And," he added in an accusative tone, "one of 'em is your buddy."

"If the chief of police wasn't my buddy, they might've kept you in that cell for a week. Scott Parris called me to find out if you had a history of criminal behavior." *Or lunacy.*

"Speaking of your lawman friend, has he got anything new on who killed Billy Smoke?"

Moon intertwined his fingers over a silver belt buckle. "Not the last I heard. He figures it was some lowlife transient looking for a quick buck."

Firelight twinkled in the elder's dark eyes. "Is that what you think?"

The tribal investigator nodded.

"Think they'll ever catch him?"

"Habitual criminals like that eventually end up in prison. Or dead from an overdose of heroin or lead. But it's a hundred-to-one shot against us ever knowing his name."

The chairman snorted again. "That makes it easy for your chief of police buddy—he's got nobody to look for." He was silent for a moment. "But maybe the killer was somebody who knew Billy. Somebody who wanted him dead."

The randomness of senseless evil was always hard to accept. "The evidence is pretty clear—it was a robbery gone wrong." Moon stretched his long legs toward the fireplace. "Wallets were stolen from both of the victims."

The chairman shook his head stubbornly. "Billy Smoke's mother don't believe that. She thinks whoever killed her boy had a grudge against him."

"Who'd have a grudge against Billy Smoke?"

Sweetwater ignored this question. "And most of the tribe agrees with her." He gave his host a sly, sideways glance. "That's why I want you to look into the matter."

Well, I saw that one coming. "Granite Creek PD has already looked into it. And because a U.S. senator was assaulted, the FBI has investigated the incident."

Oscar Sweetwater dismissed this with a wave of his hand.

Moon sat for a long time, staring at the flames. "It's been months since Billy was killed. If the right suspect isn't arrested within twenty-four hours of the crime, he usually gets away clean. If he's not picked up within a week, the chances of ever catching him are so close to zero that—"

"Don't quote me no statistics," the chairman snapped. "I know it won't be easy. But look into the matter, Charlie. If you can't find nothing, then you can't. But we got to at least make a show of trying to find out who killed one of the People."

Make a show. Of course. It's always about tribal politics. "Oscar, after all this time, I wouldn't know where to start."

"You could talk to the senator. He's your next-door neighbor."

Next door thirty-some miles away. "The FBI must've talked him to death already."

Sweetwater grinned. "Patch Davidson don't much like the federal cops. All he gave them was a written statement through his lawyer."

Moon turned to the old man. "He refused to be questioned by the FBI?"

The chairman nodded. "Damn right. Ol' Patch, he don't mess with folks he don't like."

"What's he got against the Bureau?"

A shrug under the old man's plaid shirt. "Patch just don't like who he don't like. That's all."

"So what makes you think he'd talk to me?"

"You, he likes."

"How do you know that?"

"I just know." He winked at the former tribal policeman. "Might have something to do with that time years ago."

"What time was that?"

As if you don't remember. "You can ask him."

"Oscar, it'd be different if I could see how me messing around in this business could help find Billy's killer. But it won't. Besides, I got lots of cow-related work to do."

"From what I hear, you're more or less a nuisance around here."

"That's an advantage of being the owner." Moon grinned at the cantankerous old man. "I can be a nuisance whenever I want to."

"If you'd get away more, this ranch might start showing a profit."

"Sounds like you've been talking to Pete Bushman again."

"He's a capable foreman. You ought to leave the running of the Columbine to him."

"Tell you what, Oscar." Moon pointed. "I'm going to pick up that telephone. Call the BoxCar Ranch. Tell whoever answers that I'd like to drop by for a chat with the senator. If I get an invite, I'll go and ask him about the assault. If I don't, that's the end of it. Agreed?"

The tribal chairman put on an offended expression. "Looks to me like you're trying to weasel out of doing some useful work for the tribe. And it's not like we don't pay you enough."

"Hey, you claim the senator likes me. So is it a deal or not?"

The old man sighed. "Well, if that's all you'll do—what can I say?"

Moon thumbed through the telephone directory.

Sweetwater gave him the number for the BoxCar spread. *Old man has a good memory.* Moon dialed.

A female voice answered. "BoxCar Ranch. Miss James speaking."

"Uh—hello, this is Charlie Moon. I own the ranch next door, and I just wanted to—"

She interrupted. "Why, hello, Mr. Moon. Thank you for calling. The senator is anxious to speak with you."

"He is?"

"Of course. Your tribal chairman advised us to expect your call. Please hold for just a moment." There was a click in his ear.

Moon put his hand over the mouthpiece. "Oscar, you have flimflammed me again."

The old man's eyes widened in feigned innocence. "What do you mean by that?"

"You know exactly what I mean."

"Sure I do. But I like to hear you say it."

"You are a devious old man. Full of deceit and treachery."

The Ute politician nodded his agreement with this assessment and smiled. "Thank you kindly."

The rancher heard the senator's gruff voice in his ear. "Charlie Moon—that really you?"

"Yes, sir. Oscar Sweetwater is here. He asked me to talk to you about—"

"Right. Can you drop by the BoxCar on Thursday morning?"

"Well, I suppose I—"

"That's great. Make it around ten."

Moon accepted the invitation. When the telephone conversation was terminated by the powerful politician, Charlie hung up the phone and turned to the tribal chairman.

Sweetwater avoided the tall man's stare.

"Oscar."

The chairman concentrated on the fireplace. Reflected flames danced in his merry eyes. "Did I hear somebody call my name?"

"Anything else you might want to tell me about the senator?"

The old man frowned, deepening furrows in an already wrinkled brow. "I don't think so. Except . . . maybe one thing."

Moon waited for the boot to drop.

"Patch—he might have something else for you to look into."

"What might that be?"

Oscar Sweetwater shrugged bony shoulders. "He didn't spell it out. But I think it has to do with security on his ranch." He turned, smiled playfully at Moon. "I expect somebody's been stealing old Patch's beef cows."

"Last thing I heard," Moon said, "the BoxCar don't have any cattle."

The chairman nodded thoughtfully. "Them damn rustlers must've got away with all of 'em. No wonder the senator is so upset."

Minutes after the tribal chairman had departed, Pete Bush-man showed up at the front door. The Columbine foreman was shaking his head, growling.

Moon invited his employee into the parlor. "What's on your mind, Pete?"

"It's that damn cougar." Bushman shook his shaggy head. "This mornin', he made a run at Alf Marquez."

The Ute felt a sour coldness in the pit of his stomach. "Is Alf hurt?"

"Not this time. But that big scat spooked the Mexican's mount, and Alf got throwed." Pete pulled at his beard. "Two of the men was with him, one took a shot at the cat an' scared it off. If he'd been workin' by hisself, Alf'd a been cat food for sure."

"Where did this happen?"

"Right where you'd expect it—over at the foot of the Notch."

Moon went to a window, looked westward toward the half-mile-wide, saddle-shaped crevasse in the Miserys. Dead Mule Notch was the big cat's range. If he wasn't able to bring down the occasional whitetail, Two-Toes must be getting slow. That could make him a potential man-killer. "Pete, maybe we should pull all of our cattle over to the lowlands—out of that cougar's range."

The foreman glared at the boss. "Well if you ask me, and even if you won't, I don't think we oughta let this overgrown house cat run us offa two prime sections of the Columbine grazing. I say we get us some trained dogs that can track the sneaky rascal down. We get him treed, we shoot 'im, we skin 'im. Nail his sorry hide to the barn wall."

Moon shook his head. "Forget the dogs."

"What do you want to do then?"

"I'll think on it."

Sure. And while you're thinkin' on it, we'll lose half the herd. Bushman stomped away.

CHAPTER 8

Terminal Building

Charlie Moon noted the sign erected by a Grand Gunction construction company, nosed the F-150 onto the lane linking the main highway with the site of the yet-unfinished Patch Davidson Airport. A crisply uniformed employee of a private security firm waved him down, stared through reflecting sunglasses at the tribal investigator's ID. After a comically ludicrous attempt to intimidate the Ute, the officious Robocop waved him on without a word.

The old county airport, six miles to the north, had a runway intended primarily for private pilots who buckled small, single-engine propeller aircraft to their butts. The new facility, named after Granite Creek's favorite U.S. senator, boasted runways that would accommodate a Boeing 737 with five hundred yards to spare. He crossed the freshly blacktopped parking lot, slowed to a stop between a county fire truck and a matched pair of black-and-white GCPD squad cars. The red and blue lights were not flashing, presumably because there was no problem with traffic or gawking onlookers.

Moon got out of his pickup, stared at what was left of the new terminal building.

Inside a rectangle of yellow tape were two acres of blackened ruins. It was apparent that there had been a terrific explosion and a scorching fire. But not in that order. Aside from four walls of reinforced cinder block, little remained of the structure. Sections of Propanel roofing were strewn well past the taped border and into the edge of a forest of pines and cedars. A long row of seven-foot-square plate glass panes had been reduced to crystalline shards that were scattered over the parking lot. Where the glazing had been mounted, metal frames bulged outward from the force of the blast. Jagged remnants of the glass around the rim of the frames gave the eerie appearance of shark teeth lining enormous, open jaws. The inside of the terminal building shell was crusted with black soot. Metal-frame furniture and wooden partitions had been reduced to twisted skeletons and heaps of gray ash. A dozen helmeted firemen were picking their way about the ruins, spraying flame retardant on stubborn pockets of embers.

The tribal investigator headed toward a cluster of men stationed just outside the perimeter of yellow tape.

Scott Parris, who had been listening to a report from one of his officers, turned to see his friend approaching. "Mornin', Charlie."

"Good morning yourself." The tribal investigator exchanged perfunctory greetings with Officers Eddie "Rocks" Knox and E. C. "Piggy" Slocum. Both men were somewhat wary of the Ute.

Knox scratched at the artificial leg under his trousers. "Damn thing itches worse'n the real one."

In the superior tone of one who is well informed on such matters, Piggy Slocum offered this advice: "That's because you're always scratching at it."

The pair of policemen walked away, arguing about wooden legs, phantom limbs, and what made them itch.

The chief of police shook his head at the departing duo. "Charlie, you ever want to be a real cop again, you let me know. I'll put you to work right on the spot."

"That'll be the day." Moon nodded at the smoking ruins. "What've we got here?"

"Big explosion late last night. Or to be more accurate— this morning, at about two-thirty. Rattled windows up to four miles away. And according to reliable reports, several cows went dry and a black cat gave birth to six adorable little kittens and a Dalmatian puppy." Parris was watching the helmeted firemen. "Fire department is trying to make sure there's no chance of a new flame-up."

"Accidental?"

"Fire chief's best guess is that some dumb-ass kids started a small fire in the terminal building. There was lots of construction material stored here, most of it flammable. Plywood, paint thinner, gasoline for the contractor's electrical generators, acetylene for welding, and a tank of propane for a portable heater. The fire must've gotten out of control—at which time the kids scram. Eventually, the flames ignited what was left of the gas in the acetylene and propane tanks. This makes a serious boom."

"Anybody see kids out here?"

"Nobody saw nothin'." The chief of police screwed his face into a painful frown. "It could have been a professional arsonist."

Moon found a peppermint in his pocket, peeled off the plastic cover. "Prime contractor must have plenty of insurance."

Parris nodded at the inference. "I'll be checking into that today." A builder in financial trouble might well drop a match in some tinder. "I'll know a lot more after the state arson investigators wrap up their investigation." He glanced at his watch without noting the time. "But they're not even here yet."

"Were there guards on site last night?"

Parris rubbed his eyes. "One old geezer with a hearing aid. Used to be a cop over in Pueblo before he retired on a disability. That's his office." The Granite Creek chief of police pointed toward a camping trailer almost two hundred yard away. It was set up near a huge, roofless hangar.

"Guard swears he was wide awake." Parris mimicked the old man's quavery voice. " 'An' I didn't see nothin' unusual, didn't hear nothin'—not till all hell tore loose and the 'splosion knocked me on my ass.' " The good-natured man chuckled. "One of my officers was within four miles when the big boom blew the terminal building apart. When he got here about five minutes later, the guard was still trying to pull his boots on."

Moon took a look at the battered trailer. "So he was sleeping on the job."

"You know how it is. Damn hard to find good help."

The rancher thought about his motley collection of cowboys. "Tell me about it."

The friends walked back toward Moon's truck.

"So, Charlie—what's on your mind?"

"I'm doing a favor for the tribal chairman."

"No, don't even give me a hint. Let me see if the old ESP is working." Scott Parris pressed fingers against his temples. His mouth wrinkled into a wry imitation of a grin. "The Billy Smoke killing."

"You're always one step ahead of me, pardner."

"I got wind that Oscar Sweetwater wasn't satisfied with our findings." The chief of police sighed. "When we don't make an arrest, nobody likes it. Including me. But the FBI and the state police agree with my department on this one. It's a no-brainer, Charlie. You know the basic facts. Billy's wallet was missing. He was murdered during the process of an opportunistic robbery. And the senator had the bad luck to show up before the guy scrams. So he gets mugged and robbed. Lucky for Colorado we didn't lose Patch Davidson."

"You a big fan of the senator?"

"Not particularly. But he's got tons of seniority, and that helps the state." Parris looked back toward the charred terminal building. "It was Patch Davidson that got us the federal money for this new airport. Which makes just about everybody happy, and that will get him another two or three thousand votes come next election."

"Anybody not happy about the new airport?"

Parris shrugged. "Any new construction on this scale is bound to piss somebody off. There's been some complaints from a couple of environmental groups. But they haven't been able to make any headway in court."

A possible arson at the new airport was interesting, but Moon reminded himself that nosing around in Scott Parris's business was not going to help him get his job done. He directed the conversation back to the tribal chairman's concern. "Billy Smoke's stolen wallet—was it holding any plastic?"

"We determined that Mr. Smoke had been issued a Visa and Conoco. Both had been used by the victim within a few hours prior to his murder. So the cards must've been in his wallet when the perp bashed his skull in."

"And so far, nobody's used either card for a purchase."

"You got it. But that ain't so surprising. Few hours after he does the dirty deed, the bad guy finds out he's assaulted a United States senator. That makes the killing of Billy Smoke more than just your average run-of-the-mill homicide. The criminal knows that half the cops in the country will be on the lookout, waiting for him to make a dumb move. So you know what he does with Mr. Smoke's credit cards."

Moon nodded. "Drops 'em into the nearest sewer."

"You bet."

"If I remember right, you've got the murder weapon."

"Your memory's working just fine." Parris jammed his hands into his pockets. "Fourteen-inch piece of rebar. Found blood on it—Billy Smoke's and Patch Davidson's."

"But no prints."

"Life is full of bitter disappointments." Parris looked sideways at his friend. "So where do you go from here?"

"I'll go do some rooting around." Enough to satisfy Oscar Sweetwater. "I'll see a few people. Ask some questions. Then I'll call the chairman."

Parris was recalling former cases they had worked together. This canny Ute had a way of stumbling over things. "Charlie?"

"Yeah?" Moon kicked at something among the glass shards. It looked like a flattened piece of metal. Soft metal.

"If you should pick up anything important—you'll let me know."

"Sure I will, pardner. But don't hold your breath." Moon squatted to have a closer look at the object. It was a flattened piece of lead. He looked up at the chief of police. "What do you make of this?"

Scott Parris picked up the chunk of metal with plastic-tipped forceps. He gave it a professional once-over. "I sure hope this wasn't a bullet, because it'd have to be at least half an inch in diameter. Hell, that's all I need—some gun nut shooting a fifty-caliber machine gun in my jurisdiction." He found a plastic evidence bag in his jacket pocket.

"Could be a slug from one of those old black-powder buffalo guns. Maybe some Daniel Boone–type shot a hole through the terminal window, punctured the propane tank."

"Well thank you. Some guy in a coonskin hat shooting out windows. That makes me feel lots better." Parris bagged and tagged the lumpy artifact, dropped it into his pocket.

Moon leaned on his pickup. "I'd like to get this Billy Smoke business behind me. I've got a lot of work to do at the ranch."

Parris grinned. "Like what?"

The stockman's expression was solemn. "For one thing, we got a big cougar threatening the stock. He might even be a danger to my cowboys."

"A cougar. Boy, I'd change places with you in one second flat." The white man grinned at his best friend. "So when're we gonna go fishing?"

"Soon as I get this work for the tribal chairman finished."

"You do seem to be awfully focused on that."

"Well, now that you mention it—"

"You'd sure appreciate any help."

"Glad you took the hint."

"Whatever you want—all you got to do is ask." Parris looked up at the taller man. "For starters, would you like to read the official report on the investigation into Mr. Smoke's death?"

"Cover to cover, pardner."

"It'll be dull as daytime TV."

"That's good—if I've suffered some, it'll help my conscience when I cash the tribe's check." He had an afterthought. "The postmortem, it turn up anything unusual on Billy's remains?"

"Unusual—like what?"

"Tiny transmitters hidden under his skin by aliens. A twenty-dollar gold piece in his stomach." Moon hesitated. "Or drugs."

Parris shook his head. "Not unless you count the legal kind. Mr. Smoke was just a smidgen under the blood-alcohol limit."

"Tell me the rest."

"Word has it, the man was drunk fifty percent of the time and not quite sober the other half."

"Sounds like Billy had no business driving a motor vehicle."

The chief of police almost shuddered. "Gives me the cold chills to think about a drunk chauffeuring our senior senator around in that big Lincoln."

Moon frowned. "I just remembered something I was supposed to tell you about."

"So tell me."

"Aunt Daisy met this young woman at a discount store in Durango. She was just a kid—probably needed to talk to a social worker."

"So what was her problem?"

"My aunt thought she was scared of somebody."

"Who was she?"

"Didn't mention her name."

"When did this happen?"

"A few months ago." Moon grinned. "Like I said, it sorta slipped my mind."

The chief of police stared at the Ute. "Last night on a TV talk show, there was this Harvard psychologist. She said as we get old, the memory's the second thing to go." He feigned an expression of intense concentration. "But damned if I can remember what the *first* thing is . . ."

"The *reason* I forgot might be important. Just a few hours after my aunt had her chat with this gal, something happened that distracted my attention."

"And what was that?"

"Billy Smoke was murdered. Senator Davidson got his legs busted up."

Parris raised an eyebrow. "You think there might be a connection?"

The tribal investigator shrugged.

"Any notion where this Jane Doe hangs her hat?"

"Aunt Daisy said the gal mentioned Arroyo Hondo." The old mining settlement was in GCPD jurisdiction. Which made it Scott Parris's official business.

The busy chief of police shook his head. "Nobody stays at Hondo on a permanent basis. And it's been quite some time since your aunt talked to this young lady."

"I know it's a long shot." Moon looked toward the western highlands. "But what if she's out there in the wilderness, hiding from some bad-ass." His eyes twinkled. "Poor thing could be living in a cave. Wearing filthy, flea-infested rags. Eating roots and grubs."

Parris grimaced at the image. "I guess I could send a couple of officers up to have a look."

"Now you're talking."

"What does she look like?"

"Aunt Daisy said she was white. Early twenties. Slender. Freckle-faced."

Parris snorted. "Well that sure narrows it down."

"And she's a redhead."

The chief of police, who had been jotting notes in his pad, paused to stare at his best friend.

"What?"

"You've just described a young woman we got a call about last winter. Brewster—but what's her first name." Parris closed his eyes, scratched at thinning hair. "Oh yeah. *Wilma* Brewster."

The tribal investigator searched his own memory. "Name doesn't ring a bell."

"She's an engineering student over at RMP who went AWOL. Her mother reported her missing about . . . let's see . . . I think it was just before Christmas. One of my officers took the complainant to her daughter's apartment, got entry from the supervisor. No sign of foul play. The mother wasn't sure whether any clothes were missing. The daughter's university-issue bicycle was in the apartment."

"What was she doing with university wheels?"

"Miss Brewster worked part-time for the campus police force."

"And she just upped and left without a word to anybody?"

"That's about the size of it. And the girl has had some medical problems."

"Such as?"

"Schizophrenia. This isn't the first time she's wandered off. But according to her mom, the symptoms have been pretty much controlled for the past three years—as long as she takes her medications." Parris grimaced. "Bad news is that when Miss Brewster left her apartment, she also left her prescription pills in the medicine cabinet."

"How'd a schizophrenic get a job with the campus police?"

"I doubt they had access to her complete medical history. Even if they did, they might've given her a chance. There are a lot of sick people who manage to function well enough to get by." The chief of police shook his head. "Are you not familiar with the two or three borderline psychotics working in my own department?"

"Say no more."

"Thank you. It is not a subject I wish to dwell on."

"This missing gal own a car?"

"She did. The Toyota was parked right outside her apartment. Dead battery."

"So the bike's in her room, her car won't start. How does she leave town? Hitchhike?"

"Quite possibly. But I should point out that Miss Brewster's apartment is on the north side of Eikleberry Avenue, between Gish Lane and Arnett Street."

Moon closed his eyes, visualized a mental map of the small town. "Right across from the bus station."

"You got it. Grumpy old duffer working behind the counter wasn't much help—said, 'Maybe I seed her, maybe I didn't—damn scruffy college kids are comin' and goin' all the time.'" Parris grinned. "He sells lots of tickets. Denver. Rock Springs. Albuquerque. Salt Lake. Wilma Brewster could've gone anywhere. But from what you're telling me, sounds like she ended up in Durango."

"There been any activity on her credit cards?"

"The kid didn't hold any plastic. She had a spotty credit record—her Visa was pulled last year."

"Wherever she's living, maybe she got some kind of job. Any employment reports on her Social Security number?"

"We haven't tried that hard to run her to ground. I figured she was hanging out with some friends—or maybe bumming her way across the country." Scott Parris squinted sad blue eyes at his Ute friend. "Sometimes college gets to be too much. A fair number of these kids get burned out. Some drop out and go home. Others join the Peace Corps— or the Marines. A few, like Miss Brewster, just walk away." The chief of police scratched at the stubble on his chin. "Maybe Durango PD could turn up something. If she's still hanging around down there."

Aunt Daisy was certain the redheaded woman was scared of something. Or somebody. Moon wondered who the young woman might be running from. "This Wilma Brewster, she have a boyfriend?"

Scott Parris shook his head. "I don't know."

"You have a picture on file?"

"We got a high school yearbook photo from Wilma's mother. It'll be in the folder—I'll get you a copy made."

"Tell me about her mother."

"Jane Brewster. Widow. Early to mid-sixties."

"Where would I find her?"

Parris gave his friend a complicated set of directions.

The tribal investigator scribbled notes on a small pad. "The mother have a job?"

"Mrs. Brewster mostly lives off her Social Security check. But she picks up some work here and there. Whenever she can."

"What kind of work?"

"Cleaning homes. Laundry. Ironing. But primarily, the woman is a first-rate cook." Parris held his tongue for a moment. As if he didn't want to say it. "Before her daughter left town, the old lady spent three or four days a week fixing meals for Senator Davidson."

The Ute gave his friend a look. "Seems like all roads lead to the BoxCar Ranch."

The chief of police bristled his eyebrows into a frown. "Charlie—I sure hope this is a coincidence." He looked up at a cloudy sky. "You hear any more from this Wilma Brewster look-alike, you be sure to let me know."

"I'll do better than that—if this redhead contacts me, I'll give her your unlisted telephone number. Tell her it's okay to call you any hour of the day. Or night."

"Thanks, pardner." Scott Parris felt like he was getting a fever. "And if I should pick up a serious case of the flu, I'll be sure to cough in your face."

CHAPTER 9

The Widow

Concerned that he might have taken a wrong turn, Charlie Moon continued down the weed-choked dirt road. Around a hard left turn, he passed under the brittle arms of a diseased elm and slammed on the brakes. The little-used lane was blocked by a rusted Dodge pickup; the hulk was perched precariously on wooden blocks.

The tribal investigator checked his scribbled notes. This layout was more or less what Scott Parris had described. Between an orchard of sickly peach trees and a tumbledown barn, there was a small cottage. The dwelling had a pitched roof covered by tar shingles, deathly gray clapboard walls, a red brick chimney that leaned ever so slightly southward. In stark contrast, the sparkling clean windows were flanked by freshly painted green shutters. The dusty yard had been broom-swept. The overall effect was a melancholy mixture of grinding poverty and stubborn pride.

This has to be the place.

The Ute got out of the truck, approached a sagging porch.

A small mixed-breed dog appeared from under the house. After scratching at an invisible colony of fleas and shaking off some excess dust, she yapped dutifully at the intruder. Turned to look expectantly at the front door.

Moon paused to offer a kind word to the half-starved animal.

The mutt responded with a wag of a drooping tail.

A woman, looking a decade older than her sixty-some years, appeared at the door. Jane Brewster wiped reddened hands on a cotton apron. Dark red hair bobbed on plastic curlers. The work-hardened face was flat, without expression except for a hint of don't-mess-with-me-buster. Only the eyes were alive. Her frank blue orbs engaged the Ute's dark face. Her voice was tired. "You the Indian policeman?"

"Yes, ma'am." The visitor removed the black Stetson. "Charlie Moon."

"The chief of police—Mr. Parris—he told me you'd be stopping by."

"Hope this isn't a bad time. I would have called first, but . . ." Jane Brewster's telephone had been disconnected.

"I didn't pay the bills, so they pulled the plug." She laughed mechanically. "Anyway, don't worry about schedules. Out here, one time is about the same as another." She clicked her tongue at the dog. "I expect there's something you want to talk about." There was not the least sign of curiosity on her face. "It's too chilly to stand out here on the porch." She turned toward the door. "C'mon in."

The inside of Jane Brewster's home was like the outside. Well worn, but clean.

At her direction, Moon seated himself at the kitchen table. He accepted her offer of coffee. He eyed the small sugar bowl, decided to do without the usual six teaspoons of sweetener.

After lowering the flame under an aluminum saucepan filled with Great Northern beans, Jane Brewster turned her back on the sooty kerosene stove. She removed the apron, hung it on a nail by the back door. The woman smoothed a wispy tuft of gray hair, sat down across the table from her visitor. "This about Wilma?"

He looked at the cup, nodded.

"Ain't seen her since last December." Jane Brewster's eyes glazed over. "First time she wasn't home for Christmas."

"Heard anything from her since then?"

"Not a word." A half smile. "O'course I haven't had a phone for a couple of months now."

He took a shot in the dark. "Anybody else seen her?"

"Oh, sure. Every time I get out, I see somebody claims they've spotted my daughter." She waved a bony arm in a gesture of hopeless frustration. "Hey, Jane—I saw Wilma up in Grand Junction at the Kentucky Fried. Over in Pueblo at a flea market. Down yonder in Salida at the post office." She rubbed the back of her hand over a moist eye. "I don't know why she don't write me a letter." Her tone and expression had turned bitter. "Maybe because I don't have no reg'lar work—or any cash money to help pay her tuition."

"Was she having any problems at the university?"

Jane Brewster shrugged under the oversized print dress. "How would I know—my daughter never told me nothing." She stared at the Ute. "There's something else you've been wanting to ask me about. It's all right. Go ahead."

Thanks for making this easy. "I understand she was using prescription medication."

"Wilma was a sick girl. But as long as she took her pills . . ."

An unpleasant picture was forming in his mind. "Mrs. Brewster, what might happen if your daughter didn't take her medicine?"

"Most of the time, nothing too serious. Other times, she could get a little crazy. Hear voices—see things that wasn't there. Sometimes, she'd get pretty excited. One time, when she was still in high school, my ninety-pound daughter punched out her gym coach." The woman smiled. "He was a pretty big guy, but she broke his nose." Jane Brewster looked across the table at the Ute. "Where's this going?"

Good question. "A young woman matching your daughter's description has spoken to my aunt. It was in Durango."

A faint spark of hope glimmered in the pale blue eyes. "What'd she say?"

Another good question. "Not a lot. But it sounded like she wanted to talk to me about something." Moon gauged his words with care. "Far as you know, could she have left town because she was afraid?"

The woman's eyes flashed blue fire. "Afraid of what?"

"I don't know. A boyfriend?"

"Wilma didn't tell me about any boyfriends." She cast a wary glance at the tribal investigator. "Aside from the fact that she spoke to your aunt, why's an Indian cop interested in my daughter?"

"I'm working on something for the tribe. When Senator Davidson was assaulted, one of our people was killed."

Jane Brewster rubbed a callused finger over a stubborn crease in the blue and white oilcloth. Her rough-edged voice took on a defensive tone. "What does that have to do with my Wilma?"

"Probably nothing. But I know you did some cooking for the senator."

"That's why you're here?"

"That, and the possibility that the young lady my aunt spoke to might be your daughter." *Mostly, I'm just shooting in the dark.* "There must be a reason this young woman wants to talk to me." The tribal investigator slowed to a trot before jumping the next fence. "When you worked at the BoxCar, did your daughter ever drop by to visit you— maybe help with the cooking?"

She coughed up a bitter laugh. "Wilma couldn't boil a thimble of water if she had a blowtorch."

"So she was never on the ranch with you?"

The hardworking woman rubbed rough palms together. "Sometimes when I couldn't get a ride out there, Wilma would drive me over to the BoxCar. Other times she'd come pick me up when my work was done. But she never stayed long."

"When was the last time she was at the ranch?"

Jane Brewster studied her hands for a long time. As if

she had never really seen them. When the examination was complete, she looked up at the Ute. "It was the last time I saw her. She drove out to pick me up that afternoon. It was the Thursday before Christmas." She closed her eyes to concentrate. "That must've been on the twenty-first."

"Anything else happen that day? I mean—anything unusual."

Mrs. Brewster smiled without mirth. "Yeah. I didn't know it at the time, but it was my last day at the BoxCar. And it was just three days later—on a Sunday—the senator got crippled and his driver got himself killed." She looked through a cracked windowpane at nothing in particular. "Patch Davidson was in the hospital off and on for almost two months. I never got called back to work. Guess that rich man found out he could get along fine without me."

"Tell me about that day when your daughter came to pick you up."

A listless shrug. "Nothing special. She showed up. I finished cleaning up the kitchen. We left. Next day, she went to work at her university job. Wilma was a part-time campus police officer. Wore a spiffy uniform. Rode around on a shiny bicycle."

Outside, the bored dog barked at nothing. The shack was surrounded by acres and acres of nothing.

Moon accepted a refill on his coffee.

She watched him drink. "You have any idea where my daughter's holed up?"

There was no point in mentioning Rio Hondo. "She's probably staying with some friends."

She anticipated his question. "If she has any friends, I don't know who they are."

The tribal investigator stared at the surface of the black liquid.

Her elbows on the table, the woman leaned forward. "You find my Wilma, you tell that girl to come see her mother."

It's time to go. Moon thanked her for the coffee and conversation. At the front door, the Ute fished a thin wallet out of his hip pocket. Hesitated. The F-150 was running on fumes, and there would be six dollars left for gasoline. He gave the woman his last twenty.

She looked at the greenback, then at the tall man. "What's this for?"

"Expenses." Moon avoided the intelligent blue eyes. "If you hear anything about your daughter—or think of something I need to know—I expect you to go into town. Find a pay phone, call me."

The woman opened her mouth to speak, said nothing. The reddened eyes teared up.

Embarrassed, Moon turned away. "Well, I better be getting on down the road."

Jane Brewster found a hoarse voice. "I don't know. I never took nothing from nobody that I didn't earn. I just don't think it's right to—"

"Sure it's right—think of it as a bribe." He flashed her a smile that lit up forty acres of twilight. "And you'll earn it. From time to time I'll drop by and make a nuisance of myself."

She showed him a careworn face that had once been pretty enough to inspire foolish young men to hang around her father's front porch. "You're quite a sly fellow, Mr. Moon."

He tipped the John B. Stetson. "Call me Charlie."

She crumpled the bill in a fist. Watched the slender man make long strides toward his pickup.

CHAPTER 10

Ghost Town

Long wisps of fog hung like spiderwebs under the spruce. Unseen things rustled among the dark ferns, a demented owl who didn't know noon from midnight hooted at the intruders. It was enough to make even a sensible man muse about ghosts and goblins and other unmentionable horrors. Neither of the police officers measured above zero on the sensible scale.

Leaning forward, his back muscles painfully tense, Officer "Piggy" Slocum steered the GCPD black-and-white along a forest service road slippery from recent rain. He stated his candid opinion to his fellow, Eddie "Rocks" Knox, who was yawning. "This is stupid, Eddie—no young woman in her right mind would be camping out at Arroyo Hondo."

"So maybe she's a nutso." Knox allowed the interrupted yawn to play out. "Quit your bellyaching—we get paid by the hour, don't we? If we wasn't looking for this redheaded gal, we might be doin' lots worse duty back in town."

Slocum gripped the steering wheel with white knuckles. "This ain't no four-wheel-drive Jeep. We could get stuck out here."

"So what if we do?"

Visions of cold and hunger loomed in the damp mists hanging over the dirt road. "I don't like gettin' stuck way back in the boonies."

"Relax, Piggy. We got a radio, don't we? If we have a problem, we call dispatch for a tow. Then we sit here as long as it takes. Eat our sandwiches, drink our coffee, swap lies. And if the wrecker truck takes a long, long time getting here, we draw some time-and-a-half. All for sittin' on our butts."

The driver brightened. "Yeah. I guess that wouldn't be so bad."

"O'course it wouldn't." Knox, who enjoyed tormenting his timid partner, frowned at the dark forest. "Not if we got help before the bears showed up. Started sniffin' around the unit, trying to find a way inside—so they could eat all that fat under your shirt."

Piggy Slocum pretended to be unconcerned. "Bears eat berries, not people."

Officer Knox reached down to scratch the wooden leg. It kept right on itching. "Piggy, you are ignernt as a post. Why this time of year, when they're startin' to think about puttin' on weight for the long winter's sleep, a hungry bear'll eat *anything*. Road-kill skunks. Moose turds. Even fat, greasy cops."

Slocum tried a comeback. "Well, after Mr. Bear et me, he'd sure as hell have you for dessert."

Knox shook his head. "No, he wouldn't."

The driver glanced at the confident man. "Why not?"

"First of all, 'cause he'd be all full up after swallerin' somethin' big as you. And second, if he did bare his teeth at me, I'd just give him this here artificial leg to chew on. He'd realize right off that a bite of Officer Knox didn't have no nutrition."

The driver attempted to find some chink in this logic, but was unable. So he changed the subject. "I'll bet you ten dollars to five that this Brewster gal ain't out here."

Knox yawned again. "You can keep that bet."

They topped the last ridge. Officer Piggy Slocum slowed

to a stop, looked around the barren remains of a mining settlement that had died out before Teddy Roosevelt was elected president of the United States. There were remnants of tar paper shacks, heaps of fist-size pebbles where make-shift chimneys had once stood, scattered sheets of rusted roofing material. But aside from a raven perched on a lightning-seared snag, not the least sign of life. Including bears. Which the chubby policeman was thankful for.

Knox opened the passenger-side door, got out stiffly. He hobbled his sideways gait a few paces down the forest service road, alert for evidence of recent visitors. There were a few tire tracks, but the officer estimated them to be at least a week old. Probably left by the single overworked forest ranger who patrolled over a thousand square miles of federal land. The policeman leaned on the wooden prosthesis, cupped hand to mouth. "Helllloooo . . . anybody here?" He was answered by an echo off the sandstone cliff above the arroyo. The police officer needed about fifteen seconds to come to the inevitable conclusion. *There's no use wasting time here.* Knox, who had several times skirted very close to death, had gained a deep intuition about such matters. *Aside from me and Piggy, there ain't a living human soul within ten miles. But even so . . . this ain't a healthy place to hang around.*

Piggy Slocum felt beads of cold sweat popping out on his forehead, a sourness settling in the pit of his ample belly. At the corner of his eye, a shadowy something darted under the spruce. He stuck his head out the window. "Hey Eddie, let's get goin'." *Something ain't right here.*

CHAPTER 11

The Visitor

Two long rows of floodlights illuminated the boxcar airstrip. In a vain attempt to find some comfort, the elder statesman scooted around in the plush rear seat of the Lincoln. Senator Patch Davidson consulted the platinum Rolex on his wrist, hunched forward to complain to Henry Buford. "He should have been here by now."

The man behind the steering wheel shrugged.

Davidson scratched under a steel brace at one of his wasted legs.

"There." Buford raised his right hand to point.

The wealthy politician pushed his nose against the window, squinted at a spray of pinprick lights over the eastern peaks. One of the stars seemed to move . . . and wink, as if it knew a delectable secret. The senator allowed himself a smile. That would be the blinking white strobe light on the fuselage. Soon, he could make out the alternating red and blue lights on the wing tips. The aircraft was losing altitude. "That must be him."

Henry Buford got out of the luxury automobile, went to meet the visitor.

The boxcar manager held onto the brim of his hat until the pilot cut the engine and the propeller came to a jerky halt.

The hatch opened, a single passenger climbed out of the small airplane. The short, stocky figure was wrapped in a London Fog raincoat that was the sooty gray color of night. The ranch manager grinned. "Art Westerfield—it's good to see you."

The Defense Intelligence Agency attorney raised a finger to his lips, glanced over his shoulder at the pilot. "Dammit, Henry—don't say my name."

Buford laughed. "What's the matter, you give up your job as legal counsel to become one of Uncle Sam's secret agents?"

"Please—nobody's supposed to know I'm here." Disoriented by the dark of night and the rows of runway lights, he looked around. "Where's Davidson?"

"The senator came to the airstrip to meet you. He's waiting in the car."

"What car?"

"It's parked behind the hangar."

The visitor had no idea where the hanger was. "Can Patch see us?"

"Not unless he can see through steel walls, like Superman. Does it matter?"

The DIA employee fidgeted, leaning first on one leg, then the other.

"Let's get going, Art. The boss hates to be kept waiting, especially by two-bit government lawyers."

Arthur Westerfield decided to confide in a man he had always trusted. "Henry, the senator has a problem. A very serious problem."

"Then you'd better go tell him about it."

"That's what I'm here for. But first, I think I should tell you."

"Look, Art—I manage the BoxCar for the old man. I drive him around in his big, shiny Lincoln. I fix things that are broke. Now and again, I even shovel horse manure—and other things that smell bad. But I never, never stick my nose into politics."

"This is about considerably more than politics." The

attorney lowered his voice. "I'm talking national security. And you used to work for the Agency."

"That was way back then. This is here and now."

"Dammit, Henry, I only got a New York minute to tell you about this. So shut your big yap and listen!"

Henry Buford shut up. And listened.

The DIA attorney said his few words, waited for a response from the ranch manager. "Well?"

"If this is on the level, the senator should contact the FBI. They'll know what to do."

"My sentiments exactly. But you know how Patch Davidson hates the Bureau. If you have any influence at all over him—"

"I doubt he'll confide in me about something like this. But if he brings it up, I'll advise him to call in the feds."

"Thanks. That's what I wanted to hear."

"Well, you've heard it. Now let's go say hello to the senator."

Arthur Westerfield walked stiffly as he followed Henry Buford toward the Lincoln. He exchanged brief greetings with Patch Davidson, then settled into the rear seat beside the senator. On the short drive to the powerful man's home, they talked about the weather. And the president's push to reform the Social Security and Medicare programs.

After Buford had delivered his passengers to the sandstone mansion, the ranch manager wandered off to the kitchen to find a snack, leaving Patch Davidson alone with the quirky DIA attorney.

The senator, secure in the warmth of his parlor, settled into the Moroccan leather comfort of his Electric GroundHog. In command of his mobility, Davidson felt more the man for it. He pushed the joystick forward, felt the surge of power as the battery-powered scooter hummed obediently across a thick, chocolate-colored carpet. He braked expertly at a walnut liquor cabinet, turned a craggy face toward his guest. "What would you like?"

"Straight whiskey." The employee of the Defense

Intelligence Agency, still cold from the flight from Denver, was rubbing his hands together.

His host poured two thumbs of amber liquid from a crystal decanter. "How was your trip?"

A listless shrug. "Okay."

Davidson passed the shot glass to his guest. "The hour is rather late for meeting guests. Not that I'm complaining."

"Couldn't be helped." Westerfield took a sip of whisky. "Grabbed a late flight from Dulles to Denver, found me a freelance flyboy. Paid him cash, and a fifty-dollar tip not to file a flight plan. Gave him a John Doe—so he wouldn't know who he brought here."

The senator chuckled. "You're not usually so paranoid. I fear that the nature of the work must be getting to you."

Judging from his grim expression, the visitor was not amused.

What is eating him? "Perhaps we should retire to the conference room and discuss this urgent business that brings you to the BoxCar."

The Agency attorney cast a nervous look down the long hallway, shook his head.

"Very well." Davidson blocked a yawn with the back of his hand. "Then I suggest we both get some sleep. Whatever's on your mind can surely keep till after breakfast."

Westerfield shook his head. "I got a pilot and plane waiting—at two hundred and ninety bucks an hour, whether the tin bucket's on the ground or in the air. Thirty minutes, I'm outta here. I got some official business in Denver tomorrow. That was my excuse for the trip."

"Arthur, you're beginning to worry me—"

"Don't say my name out loud in here," the guest hissed. He pointed toward the door. "Let's go outside."

"Outside—is that really necessary?"

The DIA employee was already on his feet, heading for the door to the south porch.

Davidson had paused long enough to yank a wool blanket off the couch. He spread this over his legs, and was grateful for the warmth. "You rent a charter under an assumed name. You tip your pilot to avoid filing a flight plan. You don't want to discuss your business inside my home. Now what is all this cloak-and-dagger nonsense, Arthur?" He smiled in the darkness. "But excuse me—I suppose I should refer to you as Mr. X."

Westerfield buttoned the raincoat against the night chill, exhaled frost-white breath with his words. "I guess we can say whatever we want out here." He looked down at the crippled man. The senator's soft, shadowy form had melted into the blackness of the electric conveyance. "I appreciate all the favors you did for me over the years. Especially the one back in 'ninety-nine—when I damn near lost my clearance over that alleged leak and my marginal polygraph result. If you hadn't intervened—well, I don't know what I'd be doing now." *Maybe chasing ambulances.* "But I sure wouldn't be working for Uncle Sam."

"I was happy to help." *Get on with it, Art.*

"I'm eternally grateful to you, sir. That's why I'm here now—to return the favor." *And then we're square.* Arthur stared at the empty shot glass in his hand. Wished it was full.

The senator waited. Wondered whether he really wanted to hear what this man might have to say.

A meteor fragment slipped across the sky, burning white-hot for a hundred empty miles. Its glory expressed for an instant, the galactic ember was reduced to a dark cinder, to fall to earth where no human eye would ever see it. The DIA operative watched this ominous symbol. *That could be my career. Might as well get it over with.* "Last January, I got a promotion."

"Well-deserved, I'm sure."

"I'm DIA's senior rep on the IAC."

"For pity's sake, Arthur—we're not inside the Beltway. This is my home. So do not confuse me with acronyms."

Absently, the attorney sipped air from the dry shot glass. "Interagency Analysis Committee. Last Thursday, we had a meeting at Langley." He lowered his voice. "Something came up. About you."

Senator Davidson listened to the silence drift along in the deep river of night.

"I really shouldn't be talking about this."

Still, the politician did not respond.

Damn. Maybe he already knows about it. "Okay—here it is. We got some hot intel. HUMINT, I think—but I'm not certain. I can't mention the particular foreign power involved, but it's a major player." He rolled the cold glass in his hand. "All I can say, Senator, is that there's been some serious leaks from . . . well, it must be somebody on your staff."

There was a long silence before Arthur realized that while Patch Davidson would listen to his illegal monologue, he would take no part in it. That would transform it into an illegal *conversation*. Participation could make the canny politician culpable. *Why didn't I keep my big mouth shut? I could've done him some other favor. One that wouldn't be likely to land me in a federal penitentiary. What if he turns me in? Well, Art—you're already up to your ass in Mud Creek. Might as well wade all the way across—and then get the hell outta here.* "From what I heard at the IAC meeting, either your office in D.C. or your Western headquarters are targets of espionage. That's the reason I didn't want to say anything inside. Your house—especially your secure meeting room—may be bugged."

A cold breeze whipped across the open porch.

The DIA attorney continued. "I don't know if the FBI counterespionage office has been notified. But if they haven't, they will be. It's just a matter of time. And the more people get involved, the more likely somebody will talk. First, it'll just be the usual rumors. Then some smart-ass columnist will write a piece for the *Times* or the *Post*. That's why I wanted to give you a heads-up." He hesitated. "If you want my advice, I think you ought to go to the FBI

before they come to you. You don't have to let 'em know
that you've heard any rumors. Make up some other reason.
Maybe you got somebody on your staff that you don't feel
altogether comfortable with. Tell 'em you want every place
you hang your hat swept for bugs. Your office on the Hill.
Your home in Georgetown. And for good measure, this
place." The visitor buttoned his coat. "Well, Patch—I gotta
get going now."

Senator Davidson stared into the dense night. Wondered
what it would look like when the sun came up. If it ever
did.

"Tell Henry I'm waiting in the car." The DIA visitor
walked away across the neatly trimmed lawn.

In his heart, the politician yearned to say "Thank you,
Arthur." Or at least good-bye. But his mind was in firm
control of his lips . . . they would not part to offer a word
of acknowledgment to the man who had risked his career
to save another's.

Henry Buford stood beside the DIA attorney. They watched
the pilot remove nylon ropes from steel eyebolts set in asphalt.

Despite the heavy raincoat, Arthur Westerfield was shiv-
ering in the cold. "Well, I told him."

"Good."

"I have no idea what he'll do with the information. But
I hope he calls the FBI director."

"Patch didn't get where he is today by being stupid,"
Buford said. "He'll do what needs to be done."

The DIA employee stuck his hand out. "Good-bye,
Henry." He glanced toward the aircraft, where the openly
curious pilot watched the two men. Arthur Westerfield lowered his voice. "And for heaven's sake, don't say my name
out loud in front of this civilian flyboy."

"Gotcha." The ranch manager grinned. "See you later,
Mr. McSpook."

Westerfield sighed. "One last thing, smart-ass—you take good care of Patch."

Henry Buford's face lost the grin. "That is Job One." *Some yahoo sets out to harm the senator—he'll have to get by me first.*

CHAPTER 12

The Misery Range

Moon emerged at dawn to plan his day. He loitered on the west porch with a cup of sugary coffee, took a long, thoughtful look at his faithful F-150 pickup. The much-used Ford was dented in a dozen places, the fenders were rusting out, the windshield was cracked and sandblasted. The V8 engine smoked like a coal-burning locomotive. It was, in its waning years, a pitiful-looking vehicle. Not suitable for a visit to a rich man's fancy ranch. *I'll drive the Expedition.* The fine-looking four-wheel-drive automobile had recently been washed and waxed. Moreover, the ranch's namesake flower was painted on the driver's door. And then he remembered. The Wyoming Kyd had taken the Columbine's flagship into town for a brake job. So the battered F-150 would have to do. *Well, at least the truck has character.*

After a breakfast of pork chops and scrambled eggs, the tribal investigator inspected both of his suits, selected the gray one. He slipped on a crisply new white shirt, looped a black string tie under the collar. He pulled on knee-high cotton socks, a pair of soft bullhide boots. Like the gray suit, the boots were reserved for special occasions. Marriages. Baptisms. Funerals. The expensive footwear had not gotten much use.

Following a telephone conversation with his gruff fore-man, who lived a half mile down the lane, Moon donned his dove-gray Stetson and went outside to inhale a full mea-sure of crisp, high-country air. His destination was to the west, on the far side of a blue granite ridge that peaked out at over thirteen thousand feet. The Misery Range had been named by an early prospector who had presumably suffered many hard trials in that barren, lofty wilderness. Moon's Columbine and the senator's BoxCar Ranch shared an ill-defined border that meandered over and around and across these jagged mountains. Though Moon's drive would be about thirty miles to the entrance of the BoxCar, the ranch properties abutted in the Miserys at the highest elevation of Dead Mule Notch, which was a few yards over nine thousand feet. If a man was of a mind to ride a sure-footed horse through that broad, boulder-strewn gash in the moun-tains, the Columbine headquarters was barely twelve miles from the BoxCar's home base. Aside from an urgent desire to suffer, there was no reason for such a daylong punish-ment of man and horse. Especially in the backyard of an aging cougar who was getting too slow to bring down deer or elk—and who might have developed a taste for horseflesh. Or something more exotic.

The Gatekeeper

After forty-five minutes on the road, Charlie Moon slowed for a better look at the personification of the BoxCar Ranch. The logo, situated a few yards off the highway, was a rusty red boxcar. Faded, yard-high white letters were evidence that this hardware had once rolled for the Atchison, Topeka, and Santa Fe. It rolled no more. Separated from its fellows, the former carrier of freight now sat alone on a concrete pad. Like the rest of the senator's property, it was behind a fence topped with three strands of barbed wire.

Three hundred yards down the road, the seemingly end-less fence was interrupted by a steel gate under a massive pine log arch. In case a passerby had missed the meaning of the full-scale boxcar resting on rusting iron wheels, a yard-long ornamental version was suspended on brass chains from the arch. It swayed gently in a southerly breeze. Squatting darkly beside the gate was a sturdy log building. A pair of narrow horizontal windows suggested slitted eyes. On the peak of a pitched, red shingle roof, a vertical antenna was strapped to a sandstone chimney that needed chinking. The Ute pulled the pickup to a halt by the gate, waited.

A full minute passed.

Finally, the gatehouse door opened. An aged cowboy emerged. He was a short man with skinny legs, skinny arms, a neck about the size of his wrist—and a pendulous belly that hung over his belt. The sallow face wore a dazed, grumpy expression, like a bear whose winter sleep had been disturbed.

Moon watched the man's swaggering approach.

With the easy manner of one who is familiar with deadly instruments, the gatekeeper had a carbine slung in the crook of his arm. Beady eyes squinted under a new straw hat. "Who're you?"

"Charlie Moon."

The armed guard pulled a pad from his pocket, licked his thumb, flipped a few pages. Frowned as he attempted to decipher his own crude printing. "Oh, yeah. You're expected." He removed a cell phone from a clip on his belt, pressed the buttons, waited until the woman's voice tickled his ear drum. "Hidey, ma'am—this is Ned. Mr. Moon's at the gate." He listened. "Yes, ma'am. I'll send him right in." He turned his back on the visitor, vanished inside the log building.

The steel gate's lock clicked like a well-oiled rifle bolt. Moon heard the painful, grinding sound of an electric motor driving a gear shaft. After a couple of hesitant jerks, the gate began to swing open. The tribal investigator eased the truck through as the aged cowboy emerged again from the log building. As if the visitor had a choice, Ned pointed the carbine to indicate the direction. The graveled road disappeared into a gathering of gray, piñon-studded knobs. "Ranch house is six-point-one miles thataway."

The hollow-eyed man looked painfully lonesome. Like he wanted to talk. *Maybe he'd know something about Billy Smoke.* "I've never been on the BoxCar Ranch spread before." Moon gazed at the far hills. "Guess the pasture must be pretty good this year."

The wrinkled-apple face under the straw hat pursed thin lips, spat. The gatekeeper wiped his mouth against a soiled sleeve. "BoxCar's not a actual ranch anymore. Don't have a cow on it. Has some horses, but they're not workin' broncs. They's for soft-butted city dudes to ride on." He spat again.

"This must be a good place to work."

"Work?" The aged stockman grinned, exposing the half dozen remaining teeth in his jaws. "That's a good one. Hell, sonny—if I'd a wanted to work I'd a got me a real job. There's nothin' to do here anymore. No hay to bale, no stock to take care of. Oh, it's a fine place to look at. All the windmills is runnin'—fer to water little fish ponds and raise acres and acres of purty grass that'll never get inside a cow's mouth. But I'm not complainin'." He pointed the carbine at the gatehouse. "This so-called job is a soft spot for an old man." He wondered whether this well-dressed fellow in the beat-up pickup had come to see the senator about a job. "You from around here?"

"Ranch to the east." Moon pointed with his chin. "Other side of the Miserys."

The pot-bellied cowboy leaned closer, exhaling a mixed scent of raw whiskey and garlic. "That new owner at the Columbine—he a good man to work for?"

"The very best."

Ned scratched at his whiskers. "I hear he's an Injun—a Paiute or 'Pache or somethin'."

"Southern Ute," Moon said.

"You and him pals?"

"I'm about as close to him as a man can get."

"Now is that a fact?"

"He don't make a move without my say-so."

Rogers, who knew the Columbine foreman, cast a doubt-ful look on the visitor. "Who're you?"

"I am that Injun fella."

This statement took a moment to register, then produced a dry cackle. "Well, don't that just about cap the bottle." The almost toothless man managed a low whistle. "You must be rich as a Rockyfeller to own a big spread like that." He fumbled in his shirt pocket for a pack of cigarettes.

Moon's mouth made a sad smile. "I'm what they call land-poor."

The gatekeeper touched a lighted match to the tip of his Lucky Strike. "Me an' your foreman—we's old buddies from way back when ol' dogs was jus' puppies."

"I didn't know Pete Bushman had a friend in the world."

"Pete is a sour old cracker, ain't he?" The gatekeeper stuck out a hairy paw. "I'm Ned Rogers. Some folks call me Shorty."

Moon shook the liver-spotted hand. "Glad to meet you."

"If this soft spot I got here ever plays out, maybe you could hire me on. I ain't young anymore, but I still got plenty a vinegar in my veins. And I knows cows."

"I'll keep it in mind." Moon looked up the road. "I un-derstand the senator lives here practically by himself."

"Well, the old man does like his privacy—but he's not all by hisself." Rogers began to count on his fingers. "First, there's Patch's nephew, Allan Pearson. The senator took him in some years ago after the kid's folks died. I guess it turned out to be a good thing for Patch to have some extra family in the house to keep him company, 'cause it wasn't long after that when Miz Davidson took that bad fall down the stairs an' broke her neck."

Moon shut off the pickup ignition.

The gatekeeper turned down a second stubby finger. "Then there's Henry Buford—he's the straw boss around here. Henry, he kinda looks after the place, 'specially when the senator's away in Washington. Which hasn't been all that much since some mean sumbitch busted up Patch's

legs." He counted a third finger. "And then there's the senator's assistant, Miz James. Nice lady." Ned Rogers
winked. "And a purty little thing." He paused to call up the
pleasant image.

"Must take a sizable staff to take care of the senator's
business."

"Oh, there's them *staffers* that's in an out from Washington all the time. Sometimes they stay for a few days,
but then they're gone again. And there's a few local folks
who work on the BoxCar. But they don't stay on the property—they show up in the mornin' and leave before the sun
sets. Like there used to be this woman who did the cookin'.
What in the world was her name . . ." Ned Rogers closed
his eyes to concentrate.

Moon waited.

"Oh, yeah. Now I remember—Miz Brewster." He made
a gummy grin at the visitor. "The ol' gal ain't Mexican—
I think she's shanty Irish. But she can whip up a stacked
green enchilada that makes my mouth water just to think
about it." Rogers bowed his head in an expression of despair. "But she don't work at the BoxCar no more. Now
mosta the eats is brought in."

This sounded odd. "Brought in—how?"

"Little panel truck. Had a sign on it."

Moon knew of only one caterer in Granite Creek. Patch
Davidson and his friends must be eating high on the hog.
"How's the senator managing—with his injury?"

"He's doin' pretty fair for a bunged-up ol' cripple. Patch
is in his 'lectric scooter 'bout all the time now. 'Cept when
he's in bed."

"He hired a new driver yet?"

"No need to. Since Billy Smoke got kilt over in G-
Creek, Henry Buford's been doin' all the drivin'. Henry,
he's a strong bugger—he heists the old man up from his
scooter and into the car like Patch wasn't nothin' but a peck
a beans."

Moon managed to squeeze a few more drops out of the
old sponge before it went dry. The gatekeeper hinted at the

occasional presence of Very Important Visitors. They came
to the BoxCar from everywhere. Denver. Dallas. San Fran-
cisco. New York City. Washington, D.C. "Even from some
o' them foreign countries." The old cowboy lowered his
voice to a hoarse whisper, as if someone might eavesdrop
on this conversation in the middle of an empty prairie.
"Some real big shots drops in at the BoxCar." He glanced
over his shoulder. "You'd be surprised who takes over my
job sometimes."

The tribal investigator pretended ignorance. "Well, I
guess if the governor was to come to visit Senator Davidson, the state police would—"

"I'm not talkin' about none a your common John Laws,
young man. Besides, here at the BoxCar, guv'ners and such
is common as red dirt." Ned Rogers leaned backward so
he could look down his nose at the Ute. "Sometimes that
little log shack is chock full of them people from the Secret
Service." He pointed the carbine at a flattened spot on the
sparse grass. "Right over there is where they land them big
whirlybirds."

Moon assumed a doubtful look. "You're not telling me
that the president of the United States visits—"

The gatekeeper raised a shushing finger to his lips. "I
never told you nothin' about no *president*. You didn't hear
that from me. No, sir."

Moon observed that it must be interesting work, watching all those important folks come through this very gate.

"Oh, very few comes through here." Ned Rogers
squinted at the sky. "Most of 'em flies in." He explained
that there was an asphalt runway north of the ranch headquarters, more than long enough for the senator's jet airplane. The aged cowboy informed the visitor that the
BoxCar was mostly a gathering place for big shots and no-
goods. Not that there was necessarily "a helluva lot of difference."

The gatekeeper's telephone buzzed on his belt. It was
Miss James. She was concerned that Mr. Moon had not
shown up. Might he possibly have had car trouble along

the ranch road? The old cowboy assured her that he had not. Mr. Moon would be there d'rectly. Adopting a cool, professional demeanor, he waved the guest on with the carbine.

Moon eased the truck away. In the rearview mirror, he watched Ned Rogers enter the log shelter, saw the massive steel gate swing shut behind him. Heard it close with a heavy *thunk*. It was an unpleasant sound that spoke of finality. Of fateful decisions made that could not hereafter be revoked. The Ute had a bad feeling in his gut. *Coming here was a mistake.*

CHAPTER 13

The Boxcar

Charlie Moon's pickup slipped along the undulating ebb and flow of the earth's rippling crust. Underneath the F-150 tires, the road ribboned over a high, shortgrass prairie that soaked up ten inches of rain in a good year. For as far as the eye could see, the arid land was dominated by native buffalo grass, with only occasional growths of western wheatgrass and side-oats grama. To the east, fingerlike ridges reached out to pull at the skirts of the blue mountains. The Misery Range stood protectively between the senator's remote estate and the Columbine, a broad-shouldered picket line separating the rich man's limbo from the Ute's paradise. This was the way Moon saw it.

His thoughts were interrupted by a roaring sound. He had just noticed a puff of dust in the rearview mirror when a cherry-red motorcycle roared by the F-150, the right handlebar almost nicking the pickup fender. "Damn!" The former SUPD officer barely had time to notice that the rider with the straw-colored hair was not wearing a helmet.

A light breeze wafted the dust away; it was as if the motorcyclist had never been.

As the road dipped through a shallow valley, Moon saw a rambling log house in a cluster of cottonwoods. There were tire tracks in the driveway, but no vehicle. He pulled to a stop, checked the odometer. He had driven almost four miles from the gatehouse, so this clearly was not the senator's home. More likely, it was a house used by one of his employees. A floppy-eared bluetick hound appeared from under the porch, shook off some dust, croaked a single bark.

The Ute smiled at the dog, pulled away.

The ranch lane curled around isolated clumps of juniper, took him up a long, steep grade.

Can't be far now.

Finally, the F-150 topped the ridge. And there it was, in all its glory.

Barely aware of what he was doing, Moon pulled the pickup to a halt. He got out, completely absorbed by the panorama of a darkly lush emerald valley. It was like a magic lantern's projection cast on a sandy screen of barren land. Island groves of aspen and spruce floated in an undulating sea of wind-rippled grass. In the foreground, an anachronistic windmill turned, topping off a five-acre pond that would surely be stocked with flashing rainbow trout. Emerging from a dark cleft in the mountains, a long necklace of snow melt made a plunging loop into the bosom of the estate, liquid facets reflecting golden sunlight. Set as a gaudy jewel on this glistening chain was the wealthy man's home. Like the verdant valley, the sprawling structure seemed to have been transplanted from someplace far away. Someplace where farmers got sixty inches of rain in a drought year.

But Moon reminded himself that there was no magic here. The senator's oasis was fertilized with wagonloads of greenbacks—and precious water, sucked from far beneath the dry hills.

As Charlie Moon approached the BoxCar headquarters, details of the magnificent structure gradually came into focus. The politician's two-story palace was constructed of blood-red Wyoming sandstone, crowned with a pitched roof of burnt orange Spanish tile. Counting the windows, he estimated that the place must have at least thirty rooms. A long, open porch swept around the west end of mansion and across the south, ending at the entrance to a massive garage that interrupted the first floor.

The candy-apple red motorcycle was leaning against a whitewashed hitching post.

The Straw Boss

A pair of expectant eyes watched from between parted curtains. *He's here!*

Moon mounted the porch, stood before a massive door. Hewn of a single slab of pine, it was varnished a pale yellow tint. Centered on the door was a polished iron horseshoe mounted on a brass rod. He reached for the knocker.

"Hey—you."

Moon turned.

The broad-shouldered man standing in the yard was tall, a good six-four. The chin was square, the jaw set, booted feet firmly planted on the watered grass. The eyes were shaded under the brim of a felt hat, but Moon could feel the hard stare.

The Ute descended the porch steps.

"Who're you?"

"Name's Moon."

In a movement almost too casual to be noticed, the man's right hand brushed against his unbuttoned denim jacket, parting it just enough to expose a black canvas holster on his hip. It was home to an ebony-handled automatic.

The tribal investigator pegged it as a 9mm Glock. Not your typical cowboy's choice for a sidearm.

The mouth under the hat brim spoke again. "What's your business on the BoxCar?"

"I'm here to see the senator."

"You expected?"

"I expect so."

There was a look of disbelief, then a mutter. "Nobody told me about you." The unseen eyes glowered. "You got some ID?"

The Ute reached under his jacket to a shirt pocket. He flipped open a small wallet, displayed his Southern Ute picture identity card. The gold-plated shield flashed sunlight in the man's eyes.

Broad Shoulders leaned to scowl at the color photograph on the plastic card, glanced at the Ute's face for a comparison. "Indian cop, huh." He looked suspiciously at Moon's suit coat. "You packin'?"

The Ute pulled his jacket back.

The shaded eyes did a quick search. "I'll have to make a call." He pulled a cell phone from his jacket pocket, punched callused fingers at the small buttons. He watched the suspect visitor until someone answered. "This is Henry. I got a Mr. Moon here at the big house. He on today's visitor list?" A pause. "Uh-huh. Well, somebody shoulda told me." He pointed the instrument at the guest. "Looks like you're okay."

Hard-bitten cowboys tended to be direct to the point of rudeness and Moon was not easily offended. But this was a little less than one expected of western hospitality. He returned the ID wallet to his shirt pocket, then leaned sideways to peer behind the man.

"What're you lookin' for?"

"Thought maybe you was pulling the Welcome Wagon."

The hard mouth relaxed into a grin. "Didn't mean to seem unfriendly. But it's my job to look after things around here. Since the boss got assaulted—well, I guess I'm more'n a little touchy about strangers." He pushed the hat back on his head.

Now Moon could see all of the man's leathery face. The hard eyes were narrowed by years of squinting into the sun. The Ute stared at the slits.

Realization dawned on the man's face. "Wait a damn minute—you that Indian fella who owns the Columbine?"

"Same one."

"Well I'm extra sorry for the cool reception. Before the boss got all busted up, I didn't behave like this. Now, every stranger looks like an outlaw." He stuck out his hand.

The Ute accepted it. Like the rest of the man, it was hard and knobby.

"No harm done, Mr. Buford."

"Sounds like you already know who I am." He gave the Ute's hand another hearty shake. "But call me Henry."

"Okay, Henry."

"Tell you what—on your way out, you stop off at my place. If you're hungry, I'll heat up some stew. If you're thirsty, we'll toss down a drink."

"Your place must be the one under the cottonwoods. With the bluetick hound."

Buford grinned. "That's where I rest my bones."

"Thanks for the invite." Moon nodded toward the senator's massive, blood-red house. "Anybody at home here?"

"Only way to find out is bang on the door." Henry Buford turned on his heel and marched away in the rhythmic, purposeful stride of a man who knew where he was going, and why—and how to get the job done when he got there.

The Ute watched him go. *Former Marine, maybe. Or Infantry.*

The Nephew

Before Charlie Moon could rap the horseshoe against the varnished pine slab, the door opened. A face appeared.

It belonged to the straw-haired motorcyclist, who was lean and lanky. Dressed in dirty khaki shorts, a dirtier white linen shirt, and oxblood leather sandals, the young man smelled like he hadn't bathed in a month. The sandals and short pants were right for the mild weather. But the motorcycle daredevil wore long sleeves. And, though he had been inside the house for several minutes—dark glasses. The tribal investigator imagined enlarged pupils under the opaque lenses. Needle tracks hidden under the linen sleeves.

The man spoke in a thin voice that managed to be condescending without sounding unfriendly. "You must be Mr. Charles Moon."

"That's me."

"I am Allan Pearson."

"The senator's nephew. And the guy on the red Suzuki who passed me a couple of miles back." *Like a bat outta hell.*

"You are both well informed and observant." A mocking smile. "But then I suppose that is to be expected—considering your profession."

"I'm a stockman."

"I am quite aware that you raise Hereford cattle. I also know that you are a Native American—"

"Southern Ute."

"—who, in a former life, was a tribal police officer. You are currently licensed as a private investigator."

"You are also pretty well informed."

"I know everything that goes on for miles around." This did not have the tone of an idle boast. Alan Pearson stepped aside and made a slightly exaggerated gesture with the sweep of a pale hand. "Do come in."

The Ute followed the senator's nephew across a sunlit parlor covered with ankle-deep carpet, then down a red-tiled hallway.

The guide spoke over his shoulder. "My celebrated uncle is with Miss James, his personal assistant. They are in the secure meeting room, on the telephone with villains of such exalted rank that one fairly shudders—who can even imagine what evil deeds are being planned?" Allan Pearson's sandals flopped comically as he padded along the ceramic tiles. "I dare say my uncle does not give a diddledy-damn whether you live or die, but Miss James asked me to express his deepest regrets that he is unable to greet you personally. And so there you have it."

Moon smiled at the back of the young man's head.

Pearson turned a corner, passed by an acrylic painting of a massive Hereford bull. The work of art was illuminated by a fluorescent lamp.

The Ute rancher stopped to admire the image of the magnificent beast. *Man alive. What I could do for my herd with an animal like this.*

Pearson paused, beamed an amused smile at the Indian. "You are, I take it, an ardent admirer of highly inbred bovines?"

Having barely heard the remark, Moon nodded dumbly at the Hereford facsimile. *Wonder what something like that would set me back.*

"Personally, I detest the very thought of putting the slaughtered flesh of innocent animals inside my body."

The rancher, mesmerized by the bull's image, nodded amiably.

His agitated host was rocking heel to toe. "When you have had your fill of this sad little piece of poster art, please come with me."

Moon tore himself away from the painting, followed Allan Pearson into a large room. After the dimly lighted hallway, it was like walking into a greenhouse under the noonday sun.

"This is the senator's library."

Charlie Moon looked around. Did not see any books.

Allan smiled at the guest, exposing a pearly set of teeth. "Would you like a cup of tea? I'd be glad to brew up some of my special blend."

I bet you would. "Thanks, but no."

"Coffee, then?"

Moon thought about it. "Wouldn't want to trouble you."

Pearson's fingers played with a copper bracelet on his left wrist. "I assume you would not mind informing me as to the purpose of your visit." The young man offered a mocking smile. "Unless you are here on highly confidential business."

So. Your uncle didn't tell you. "Tribal chairman has asked me to look into the Billy Smoke homicide."

"Really?" The eyes went flat. Allan Pearson turned to look out the east-facing window. "The Southern Ute tribe's interest in the murder of one of its members is quite understandable. But unless I am mistaken, the federal authorities have exclusive charge of the investigation."

"It's a shared jurisdiction. FBI is collaborating with Granite Creek PD."

Pearson sniffed. "Which leaves you . . . precisely where?"

"I have no official capacity, except as a representative of the tribal chairman."

The senator's nephew affected a slight curl of the lip. "And what do you expect to accomplish that the FBI, with all its considerable resources, cannot?"

"Hard to say." The tribal investigator wondered what was bothering this young fellow. "Guess I'll just poke around some. See if I can get under somebody's skin."

Pearson clenched his delicate hands into tight little fists. "That sounds like a good working definition of an irritant."

"Does, doesn't it?" The tall Ute fixed his inquisitor with a flinty stare. "It'll be interesting to see who gets itchy."

Quite unconsciously, the senator's nephew scratched at his neck.

Moon grinned. *I am having too much fun.*

"Please excuse me," Pearson snapped.

Moon watched him leave, heard the sandals flip-flopping down the tiled hallway.

The Woman

Having been deprived of his smelly, irritable host, Moon felt lonely. As an exercise, the tribal investigator made a visual inspection of the "library." There were a dozen overstuffed chairs. Two matching couches long enough to nap on. A scattering of small tables, all topped with pink marble. An antique bar—apparently salvaged from an old saloon—ran almost the full length of the north wall. On oak paneling above the bar, there was a framed painting of a pale, plump woman reclining on a gilded couch. Her cheeks were blushed with embarrassment—apparently because her ample form was draped in translucent yellow silk. The opposite wall was a jarring contrast, fairly bristling with state-of-the-art electronic equipment. The centerpiece was a large-screen television. Flanking this were an array of speakers, concealed behind acoustic mesh in five-foot-high enclosures. There was a scattering of expensive-looking VCRs and DVD players. An audio spectrum analyzer. Two computers. Several telephones. Something that looked like a shortwave transmitter. In a corner by itself, an anachronism—an antique radio. A black horn speaker curved gracefully over the varnished maple enclosure, which boasted eight tuning knobs. On a massive shelf just above the television screen, a hundred-gallon aquarium fluoresced in a faint purple glow from cunningly concealed illumination. A dune of lavender-tinted sand was heaped on the bottom of the glazed tank, and this was speckled with glistening stones of various sizes and colors. But there was not a drop of water. Behind the thick glass lurked a black and yellow Gila monster, its scaled belly plumped out on a flat rock. Moon wondered whether the thing was alive. More likely this was the product of a skilled taxidermist's hand. To get a better look; he leaned close. The venomous lizard twitched a fat sausage tail.

The descendant of stone-age sages watched with fascination. If it could talk, what would the scaly creature say to him?

The Gila monster shot the Ute a poisonous look. Opened its mouth . . .

"Mr. Moon?"

The startled man stared at the reptile for a long moment. *No. Couldn't be.* He turned.

The woman in the doorway was a vision from the 1890s. She wore a ruffled yellow blouse, an ankle-length blue skirt, an enigmatic smile. An antique cameo was nestled against her throat. Glistening black hair spilled in rippling waves to a slender waist. For a disjointed moment, Moon completely lost his reason—he fancied that he had encountered a spirit who haunted the halls of the palatial sandstone home.

The faery queen floated across the space between them, offered her hand. "I am the senator's personal assistant, Miss James."

He heard himself saying something about being very glad to be here. Which was a sizable understatement.

"We are happy that you could find the time to pay us a visit." She squeezed his hand.

I think she likes me. Charlie Moon grinned so hard his jaws ached.

"The senator is pleased that you have arrived." The oval face was looking up at him.

I bet you have to beat the men off with a stick. But he sensed something hidden somewhere behind the astonishingly pretty face. A deep sadness.

"At the moment you arrived, the senator was occupied with some unexpected business, and it was necessary for me to assist him. We regret that there was not someone here to greet you properly, but the senator prefers to keep the staff at his western home to an absolute minimum."

"His nephew let me in."

She hesitated. "I do hope Allan has taken good care of you."

Allan? "Oh—yeah."

"Would you like to see the senator now?"

"No."

She echoed. "No?"

"No, ma'am. I'd much rather talk with you."

Miss James arched a pretty eyebrow. "About what?"

Anything at all.

She waited.

Moon felt his face burning. *What do I say now?* "Uh—it's my job. Talking to people, I mean. Asking questions." He looked over her head. Tried to think of a question. "You like living out here?" *I am an idiot. And that's a compliment.*

"I adore it." She closed her eyes for a moment. "All the open space. The quiet."

The drowning man grasped at this fragment of flotsam. "I own the ranch next door. The Columbine."

"I know. I have heard that it is an absolutely lovely place." The silver dollar-sized eyes sparkled with mischief. "But it may be that these are mere rumors. Perhaps the Columbine's reputation is inflated."

"There's only one way to find out for sure."

"Why, Mr. Moon—is that an invitation?"

"No, but this is—Miss James, would you like to drop by for a visit?"

There was a flicker of uncertainty; she looked away. "I don't know. My responsibilities here keep me rather busy."

"Not a problem. I'll tell the boss man to give you a day off."

"Oh, no—that will not be necessary." She studied his face. It was a nice face. "When?"

"Tomorrow."

"So soon?"

"Life is short."

Miss James gazed out the window, toward the jagged range of granite peaks. "Perhaps on one of my days off—"

"Okay, then. It's a deal."

A telephone warbled.

She withdrew her hand from his, slipped the instrument under a long strand of raven hair, taking care not to press it against a tiny pearl mounted on an earlobe. "Yes." She listened. "Certainly. I will be there directly." Miss James pressed a button to silence the telephone, smiled at the tall man. "I must be off to assist the senator for a moment. I do hope you don't mind waiting for him a little while longer."

"I mind a lot," he said. "But I'll hang around."

She flashed a man-killing smile, vanished.

It was as if the sun had gone down. Forever.

CHAPTER 14

The Senator

All alone in the wealthy man's library-without-books, Charlie Moon was at peace with himself. As he gazed out the window at sun-streaked clouds slipping over granite peaks, his happy thoughts drifted along with them. *Maybe she'll like the Columbine. And want to come back again. Then, maybe . . .*

The rancher's blissful daydream was interrupted by the sound of a raspy cough. He turned to see a bushy-haired man under the entry arch. The lower half of Patch Davidson's spare form was concealed in a high-tech vehicle mounted on four plump pneumatic tires. There were control panels on both armrests, a telescoping antenna erupting behind the Moroccan leather seat. The chrome logo on the sloping hood asserted that this was a 4WD Electric GroundHog.

"Glad to see you." The politician beamed the patented charismatic smile at his guest.

"Same here." Moon reached for the extended hand; it grabbed him like an iron pincer.

Patch Davidson maintained the smile. "Sorry I wasn't here to greet you personally."

"No problem."

"I understand you've met my nephew. I hope Allan took good care of you."

"I'm a low-maintenance kind of guest."

The senator laughed. "And you've met my personal assistant."

Moon grinned. "Yes, I have."

"Miss James is a highly valued member of my staff." Davidson tapped at a steel brace on his right leg. "Since my injuries, she has become absolutely indispensable." He gave the Ute a searching look. "Charlie, it's been a long time. Do you remember when we last met?"

The tribal investigator shook his head.

"Later on, we'll talk about old times." Davidson pointed at a couch. "Try that one." The head of the house reached into an inside coat pocket, produced a slender Cuban cigar. He clamped the stogie between his teeth, fixed the Ute with a look of melancholy. "I can't light the damn thing, because I have given up smoking. I also refrain from drinking strong spirits. And I avoid profane language as much as is humanly possible. I have said good-bye to my bad habits—I am a new man since my injury."

"And you're a busy man," Moon said, "so I appreciate you giving me some time. I expect you know why I'm here."

"Sure I do. Politics."

"I don't involve myself in politics, Senator. My tribal chairman asked me to look into the killing of your driver. Billy Smoke hasn't lived on the reservation for twenty years, but he was an enrolled member of the Southern Ute Tribe, and the chairman isn't entirely satisfied with the results of the official investigation."

Senator Davidson removed the unlighted cigar from his mouth, tapped it against the knuckles of his left hand. "Oscar Sweetwater is a fine fellow, and a good friend of mine for these many years. But your tribal chairman is also a politician. And a damned effective one. He wants you to look into the death of my Ute driver—not because there is any doubt about what happened, but because this course of action will please the voters on the reservation. You know what they'll say: 'When one of our people gets bludgeoned to death, Chairman Sweetwater doesn't sit still. He sends Charlie Moon to check on the work done by the local PD, the BIA cops—even the FBI.' So in the larger sense, your visit is about politics." He aimed the Havana at Moon's chest. "Even if you don't know it."

Moon stared at the dormant cigar. "I've already had a talk with the Granite Creek chief of police, and I'll be contacting a special agent in the Durango FBI office. After I've come to a conclusion, I'll report my findings to Oscar Sweetwater."

Patch Davidson seemed amused by this speech. "Very well. I'm a professional politician—you're a professional lawman. We see things from our own perspectives. So let's discuss what's on your mind. You want to know whether I recall anything that isn't in the written statement I submitted to the authorities. The answer is *no*."

"Fair enough—but just so I can tell Oscar I didn't waste my time coming here, why don't you tell me what happened."

"Oh, very well. Oscar Sweetwater and me, we're at the Blue Light enjoying a late dinner. We finish our dessert, I smoke a cigar." He stared with great longing at the unlighted cylinder in his hand. "We say our good-byes. Oscar leaves by the front exit, I go out the back way into the employee's parking space, where I expect Billy Smoke to be waiting with the Lincoln. It is raining and sleeting to beat the band; I am getting wet and cold as a trout. When I finally spot the car, I find out that Billy is not in it. Figuring he has probably downed a beer or two or three, I suppose he's gone off to take a pee."

"You didn't notice his body behind the Lincoln."

"I did not. I'm about to get in the car when I think I hear Billy coming. That's when it happens."

Moon was trying to wrap his mind around this. "Somebody smacks you on the legs?"

"Not immediately. First, I am struck on the head. Next

thing I know, I am flat on my ass, sleet falling in my face. But my head hurts like sixteen kinds of hell, and I can't move a muscle. That's when the bastard starts to bash me some more. I think he kicks me in the ribs a couple of times, but the worst blows are to my legs. I never experienced such terrible pain. Soon as I can get my breath, I start screaming—or trying to. That's when your tribal chairman hears me. As Oscar Sweetwater approaches—pistol in hand—the mugger takes off. Oscar tells me not to worry, he'll get help. Then he trots off to summon the police, the paramedics—hell, maybe he calls out the National Guard. A few minutes later about a hundred cops show up." Senator Davidson twirled the joystick; the Electric GroundHog responded with a snappy one-hundred-eighty-degree about-face. "That's the whole story. I did not get more than a glimpse of the miserable so-and-so who killed Billy, and busted up my legs."

Moon stared at the blunt rear end of the four-wheel-drive conveyance. It resembled a small automobile. A black plastic bumper sported a pair of square taillights. Above the bumper was a compartment marked BATTERIES. "There was only one assailant?"

"Hell's bells, I don't know. But one was all I saw." Another twist of the joystick. Another one-hundred-eighty-degree turn. He was facing Moon again. "The official investigation concluded that I interrupted a robbery that had escalated to homicide." Patch Davidson wrinkled his brow. "Do you hold a different opinion?"

The tribal investigator stared out the window at the Misery Range. "I don't know enough to have a right to an opinion."

"Well, enough talk of morbid things. Let's go outside. I would like to show you the grounds."

The four-wheel-drive GroundHog was in its element on a sandstone-paved path that meandered aimlessly across damp grass, under the delicate branches of watered aspens, over a picturesque stone bridge that might have been imported from a Civil War battlefield in Virginia. They passed through a slit in a circular hedge that enclosed a rose garden. The plants were puny, the blossoms small. Patch Davidson explained that even with all the irrigation, the combination of low humidity and short summers was a tough challenge for the delicate plants. The paraplegic halted his machine beside a bush with fairly presentable pink blossoms. He cupped a flower in his hands. "Pitiful, isn't it?"

The Ute was wondering how much water the BoxCar pumped from the earth every day. All for lush green lawns and lowland flowers, where Bermuda grass and roses were not meant to be.

The politician's voice was soft, like the rose petals. "Yes. A sad little blossom." He looked up at the towering man. "But no matter. I did not bring you out here to appreciate the flowers." He released the prickly branch.

Moon waited for the monologue to continue.

The older man cleared his throat. Fidgeted with the joystick on the GroundHog control panel. "I am obliged to you, Charlie."

"For what?"

"You damn well know."

The Ute shook his head. "I don't."

"Allow me to refresh your memory. It was some years ago—middle of Reagan's second term. I was in a red-hot primary campaign. Running against that silly used car salesman from Fort Collins." He paused, pulled hard on his memory. "I cannot even remember the simpleton's name. But it does not matter. We were running neck and neck, as the horsy crowd would say. Six days before the polls opened, I was driving a bit too fast down by Ignacio. I had also belted down a couple of drinks. Ran my Caddy over a speed-limit sign, then into a ditch. Well this is bad news. I have a busted radiator. Not to mention a pretty woman in the car with me, who is young enough to be my daughter. I do not know her name, but I am reasonably certain that she is not my wife. And what do I see behind me? Blinking red and blue lights. John Law, coming to mete out justice to the besotted sinner. Well, I know that my political goose is cooked. Probably even my marriage." He smiled at the Ute. "But Patch Davidson is in luck. The officer in the black-and-white is Charlie Moon."

The Ute nodded. "Oh, yeah. Now I do remember."

"You let me off with a stern verbal warning. I was extremely grateful, Charlie. And I remain so."

"If you had been legally drunk, I'd have hauled you in. The woman wasn't driving and I thought she must've been over twenty-one."

"Not by much." The senator smiled at the memory. "You took us to your home on the riverbank. A round house, constructed of Paul Bunyan-sized logs. The ceiling reminded me of a spoked wheel."

"I still have that place. It's rented to a librarian."

"You boiled us a gallon of coffee. I still remember it, Charlie—that was the strongest brew I ever got past my lips. After we were cold sober, you dropped the pretty young thing off at her apartment in Durango. Then you drove me all the way to my office in Granite Creek. You could have ruined me with a casual remark. But in all these years since, you have never breathed a word about it."

"Senator—"

"Don't interrupt I am not finished."

"Go ahead, then. Get it out of your system."

"And after saving my political hide, did you ever once ask the rich and powerful Senator Patch Davidson for the least little favor?" He shook his head. "You did not."

"Now that you bring it up, I've been thinking—maybe you could put in a word with the president. I think a cabinet position would be just the thing. My aunt Daisy would be awfully proud to tell her friends that I was Secretary of Agriculture."

"Don't make light of what I'm trying to tell you." The politician's eyes went moist. "You helped me because you are a good and decent man. And you never asked for anything in return. That is why I hold you in the highest esteem,

Charlie Moon. And that is why I would trust you with my life."

Embarrassed, the Ute looked away.

"So I just wanted to say—thank you."

"Well, for what it's worth, you're entirely welcome." Moon patted the crippled man on the shoulder. "You ever find yourself in another ditch, you give me a call. Now that I'm a serious rancher, I own a fine Farmall tractor. With a long enough chain, I could pull you out of Grand Canyon."

"I will keep it in mind."

The dark profile of a lone hawk soared overhead. The hungry creature circled once, then winged its way westward, chasing after something unseen by the eyes of men.

The politician inhaled, then slowly allowed the warm breath to leave his body. "Charlie—I have a problem."

"Not a bad one, I hope."

"Sufficient unto the day." He smiled, as if at some sweet memory. "Inside the Beltway, you know what the high mucky-mucks call the BoxCar?"

Moon shook his head.

"Camp Davidson."

The Ute returned a blank look.

"It is a reference to Camp David. A place of perfect solitude and security, where the president meets with other big shots. Holds important conferences. Makes earthshaking decisions that fix the fates of nations."

"Sounds like fun."

The powerful politician smiled. "It is no exaggeration. Over the years, five presidents have visited the BoxCar. I do not remember how many heads of state. A potful of cabinet members, ambassadors, chiefs of staff, supreme court justices. I host some very important meetings here, Charlie. Most of them deal with extremely sensitive topics. And you—my next-door neighbor—you didn't know that, did you?"

"Never heard a word about it before today." From the old cowboy at the front gate.

The senator's tone was triumphant. "There is rarely ever

a hint in the media of what goes on here. The VIPs land
at the BoxCar airstrip. We conduct our business. When the
work is completed, my guests depart. I have always prided
myself on the excellent physical security here at the ranch,
which is primarily due to our splendid isolation. And needless to say, I have absolute faith in the reliability and discretion of my staff. But nevertheless, I have a problem."
His mouth clamped shut, as if some part of the politician's
brain was loathe to release another word. After an internal
struggle, he continued. "It is possible that sensitive information may have been leaked from high-level meetings
here at the BoxCar." He twirled the black joystick; the
Electric GroundHog twirled obediently. The politician
glared at his guest. "What do you think of that?"

Moon thought about it for a moment. "Sounds like a
problem." *But not my problem.*

The senator's face twisted into a painful grimace. "I am
not talking about leaks to the press about the latest scandal
in the Oval Office—or which member of the president's
cabinet did not get invited to the British ambassador's annual tea-and-crumpets bash in the limey lilac garden because last year at the same party he got sick and vomited
on a precious stone lion." As if someone might be hiding
in the rose bushes, he lowered his voice. "Charlie—it is
being asserted that this sensitive information has been revealed to representatives of a foreign power."

Moon realized that his initial forebodings had been right
on the mark. *I should've stayed at home.*

"This is an extremely serious issue." Senator Davidson
wagged the dead cigar like a baton. "Potentially, everyone
on my staff is suspect. Which, quite naturally, is a reflection
on my unblemished personal integrity."

The Ute put on his best poker face.

Patch Davidson chewed on the cold cigar. "It is simply
too bizarre, but I cannot rule out the possibility that dis-
cussions inside my home are being monitored." He made a
sweeping gesture to indicate the rose garden. "That is why

we are having this conversation in my rose garden. And why I need your help."

Uh-oh. "I'll give you some free advice that's worth twice the price. Contact the FBI. Tell them about your concerns."

"I have already done that."

The tribal investigator was both pleased and surprised. "Good move. You can leave the rest to them."

"My office in Washington is a fairly straightforward matter. I will provide written permission for entry, and a key. After working hours, the FBI technicians will show up with their equipment, do whatever it is they do, then depart well before dawn. No one on my staff—not even my D.C. chief of security—will be the wiser. But there is no straightforward way to have a half dozen federal cops checking out the BoxCar headquarters without raising an eyebrow here and there. My primary concern is that someone in my employ will realize that the FBI is checking the house for espionage gadgetry—and draw the obvious conclusion."

Moon nodded. "And next week, the story's in the *Washington Post*."

"Charlie, my staff is as competent and professional as that of any senator on the Hill. Which is to say that they simply cannot resist the temptation to gossip. And if word gets out that I have a security problem at my western headquarters—well, its hard to exaggerate the potential impact. The immediate effect would be that I would have to cancel several extremely urgent meetings. And beyond the inconvenience and embarrassment, there would certainly be political ramifications. The very hint of a security scandal—right here under my nose—could cost me five or six percentage points in the next election. And that could easily get me bounced out of the Senate."

Moon thought it time to raise the obvious question. "Why are you telling me about this?"

Davidson moved the GroundHog forward slowly,

bumping it gently against Moon's leg. "Because you can help me."

"I don't see how." *And don't want to know.*

"For this damned bug check to work—both on a technical and a political level—nobody outside the FBI can know the counterespionage technicians are in my house. Aside from myself, of course, and the president. And the thing must be done quite soon—within the next few days. I must be in Washington for the next couple of weeks. And I damn well am not going to allow the FBI to snoop all over my house unsupervised. Gad, for all I know, those lawyers-tuned-gunslingers may plant bugs of their own!"

Moon smiled. "I wouldn't worry about that."

"Of course you wouldn't—you don't have to worry because these federal gumshoes will not be snooping around inside *your* home. Peering under the rugs with big magnifying glasses. Vacuuming dust out of your closet. Copying your computer disks."

"Senator, I've worked with agents at the Bureau for years. Ninety-nine percent of 'em are straight-arrow cops. They go by the rules."

Davidson put on a pleading look. "Charlie, I absolutely must have someone here to keep an eye on them—someone whose discretion is beyond question. And," he added slyly, "you are my closest neighbor. All I am requesting is some neighborly assistance. Metaphorically speaking, I find myself stuck in another ditch. I need you to crank up that big tractor you boasted about. Pull me out."

This was a persistent old man who was accustomed to getting what he wanted. "This ain't exactly a ditch we're talking about."

"All I ask at the moment is your consent to act as my official liaison to the FBI. It is just barely possible, of course, that more would be required of you than merely spending a few hours with the feds while they search my home for hidden electronic devices. I would also want you to interact with them on any related matters that may come up."

"You mean like if they actually find a flea-sized microphone in a plastic olive?"

"Exactly." The expert angler smiled, prepared to set his hook. "The less detail I know of such issues, the better for me. It is a matter of plausible deniability—should some media shark question me about foreign bugs in my home, I must be able to shrug the notion off as so much nonsense. Nor would I want anyone on my staff to be privy to such titillating information. Charlie, you are the man I need."

Moon watched bulbous clouds grow thick and dark over the Misery Range—a crop of hideous black mushrooms. Here and there, they sprouted roots of electric fire.

Sensing that his fish was not quite enticed to bite, Senator Davidson dipped the barbed hook into honey. "While I would naturally consider this service on your part as a personal favor, there are certain advantages to you."

"I'd like to hear one or two of them."

The senator counted on his fingers. "Firstly, you get paid. Secondly—"

"Whoa! Secondly can wait its turn. I want to hear more about *firstly*."

The senator sniffed at a wilted rose blossom. "Whatever that skinflint Oscar Sweetwater is paying you, I will gladly double."

Moon tried hard not to look overjoyed. "Tribe also pays my expenses."

"Certainly I would cover your expenses. That goes without saying."

"Say it anyway."

"Miss James will see that you are issued a credit card on the BoxCar account. Platinum, I should think." He attempted a stern look. "All expenditures would have to be justified, of course."

"That goes without saying. Now we can get to secondly."

"Secondly, my instructions to the Bureau will stipulate that in any issue related to physical security at the BoxCar, or to my personal security—which of course includes the assault upon and maiming of myself, and the brutal murder of your fellow tribesman—that Mr. Charles Moon shall be considered my personal representative. Any request said Mr. Moon shall make in regard to these issues will hereafter be treated by the FBI as coming directly from myself."

The tribal investigator shook his head. "They'd never agree to that."

The senator smirked. "Sir, you obviously have not the least idea of the influence of my office."

"Maybe not. But I've got a pretty good idea what Mr. Hoover's feds will say to your proposal."

"You seem very sure of yourself. But perhaps it is all pretense."

The Ute removed a greenback from his wallet, stuck it on a rosebush thorn. "Here's five bucks that says they'll laugh in your face."

Davidson blinked. "You are proposing a wager?"

"What's the matter—rich fella like you can't afford to lose a few bucks?"

"Alas, I have no cash on my person."

"I'll trust you for it. So go ahead, give the FBI your best shot."

The senator closed one eye. Pointed the cold cigar under the looped finger of his left hand—aimed toward an imaginary cue ball. Snapped his head back. "There, did you see that?"

Moon shook his head. "You must've slipped one by me."

"Aha—the hand is indeed quicker than the eye. The nine ball is in the corner pocket. Has been, in fact, since last evening."

"I didn't think that shot was on the table."

"You were mistaken. The most high and mighty director of the Federal Bureau of Investigation has already agreed to my conditions. Mr. Charles Moon is accepted as my liaison to the FBI. For the official record, the purpose of this arrangement is to aid in Mr. Moon's investigation into the reprehensible murder of his esteemed tribal member and the ruthless maiming of one of this nation's most respected and beloved—not to mention modest—members of the United States Senate."

"The director didn't even put up a fuss?"

"Actually, he did do some moaning and groaning. But not about you. Before your name came up, I suggested that my personal attorney—a man highly detested by the Bureau—would act in my stead. My plucky lawyer is practically a charter member of the ACLU. Worse still, he has effectively represented at least three despicable persons who allegedly shot at and wounded FBI special agents. Not a one of these probable felons has yet seen the inside of a federal penitentiary. When I uttered my attorney's name, the director—normally a rather placid fellow—screamed shocking obscenities into the telephone. One pithy reference had to do with myself ice-skating in hell on the Fourth of July. In light of my specific injuries, I considered this reference bordering on insensitive. But truth be told, I did not actually want my attorney to act as my liaison. The point was to make Mr. Hoover's most recent successor happy to hear any other name—like 'Charles Moon.' As might be expected, the director does not know you personally. But it turns out that your contacts in the Durango office—while not entirely enthusiastic about your previous alleged poaching in their exclusive game park—do give you high marks for integrity. And discretion. And so the director has agreed. You are the man." Davidson snatched the fiver off the rose bush, stuffed it into his pocket.

Charlie Moon realized that he had underestimated the politician. *Not a smart thing to do.* "Well, I'll say it straight out—I sure wouldn't a thought you coulda done it."

Senator Patch Davidson gave the unlighted cigar a yearning look, imagined a fragrant corkscrew of gray smoke curling from a red-hot tip. "Faint praise, indeed. And somewhat lacking in verbal harmony. Nevertheless, sweet music to my ears."

"So it's a done deal."

"Except for the paperwork. You will require a limited-

access security clearance. My able staff has already prepared the necessary forms for your signature, and the FBI
director assures me that your application will be put on the
fast track."

The tribal investigator cocked his head. Looked at the
thing from all angles. It was like an old, tired horse. Moderately ugly. Swaybacked as an upside-down rainbow. Ribs
sticking out. Probably blind in one eye. But if a man sat
easy in the saddle—didn't put a spur to it—why, he might
be able to ride the nag all the way to the bank. And so he
gave the senator's scheme his blessing. "This arrangement
could work pretty good for both of us."

"You have spoken rightly, sir. The uphill path of your
investigation into the brutal murder of Mr. Smoke has been
appreciably leveled. And in the instance of my unwanted
collaboration with those hip-shooting lawyers from the Federal Bureau of Investigation, the consequent risk of an embarrassing exposure is minimized." He grinned like a small
boy. "You and me, Charlie Moon—we are the A-team. And
we are playing a win-win game." He looked toward the
massive sandstone house. "I do believe that concludes our
business."

"There is one other thing. You used to have a Mrs.
Brewster working for you. In the kitchen."

Avoiding Moon's penetrating gaze, the politician examined five perfectly manicured nails on his right hand.
"Yes. Jane is an extraordinary cook."

"You miss her?"

"Indeed I do." He rubbed at an inflamed cuticle. "I assume there is a reason for your interest in my former domestic help."

Moon thought about it. "There's a reason." Maybe not
a good one. "Mrs. Brewster has a daughter. Wilma was an
engineering student at Rocky Mountain Polytechnic."

Davidson cocked an aristocratic eyebrow. "Was?"

The Ute watched the wily politician's face. "Miss Brewster has not been in contact with her mother—or in her
own apartment—since last December. Just a few days

before Billy Smoke was murdered in the back lot of the Blue Light Cafe."

"I had not heard about Jane's daughter being missing." Davidson raised a hand to shield his eyes from a sudden spray of sunlight. "Is there any evidence of foul play?"

"Nope. But the young woman left town without telling her mother why."

"Well, I am sorry for Jane. But surely her daughter's absence has nothing to do with Billy's death. It must be a coincidence."

"You're probably right. But I don't much like coincidences." The Ute squatted by the crippled man's battery-powered scooter. "Why isn't Mrs. Brewster still working for you?"

"I do not like being cross-examined about my help."

Moon waited, knowing the white man would not be able to bear the silence.

"Oh, very well. I was in the hospital, then in a rehab center for several weeks. During that time, Jane simply wasn't needed here at the BoxCar. When I got back . . . well, I got into the habit of ordering food from the caterer. Also, I have a need for quiet. Jane was always banging pots and pans about. And singing loudly. Jarringly off-key, I might add."

"That's it?"

"I don't understand why you're quizzing me about my former cook." The politician shot the tribal investigator a curious sideways glance. "You onto something?"

Charlie Moon dodged the question. "If Mrs. Brewster was filling out an application for a job, and it called for a recommendation from her previous employer—should she write your name in the blank spot?"

Patch Davidson hesitated, then nodded. "Of course." He played with the GroundHog joy stick. "All this talk about food has whetted my appetite." He licked his lips. "You will, of course, join me for a meal."

"Thanks for the offer. I have to be going." Moon thought he saw an expression of relief in the rich man's face.

"Another time, then."

"Sure."

"Well, then, I have some things to attend to. I will say my good-bye."

The Ute watched the electric scooter make its way up the slight grade toward the BoxCar headquarters. The crippled man seemingly a captive in its clutches, the sleek machine beetled around among barbed bushes and misshapen shrubs.

CHAPTER 15

Supper With Henry

Moon pulled the F-150 off at the boxcar manager's log house, parked under an aged cottonwood with bark that was afflicted with a plague of bulbous lumps resembling lemon-sized warts.

Henry Buford emerged onto the front porch before the Ute cut the ignition. The hound did not bother to appear whole—only a long snout and a pair of luminous eyes were visible under the rough plank porch. The beast stretched a skinny neck, strained to produce the croaking bark.

Buford grinned at the shy beast. "C'mon out, Grape-Eye."

The hound came forth, received an affectionate pat from his master.

The ranch manager welcomed his visitor with a hearty handshake. "C'mon in." The dog followed the men inside.

The Ute entered a large, old-fashioned parlor. A corroded brass light fixture dangled from the beamed ceiling. Three of the four sixty-watt bulbs pumped out yellowish light that was promptly absorbed in the dark corners. There was a scattering of dusty, mismatched furniture, but the place looked lived in and comfortable. A brick fireplace on the far wall was topped with a granite mantelpiece, flanked by bookshelves that were populated by a few dusty volumes, several yellow stacks of *National Geographic*. "Nice place," Moon said.

Henry Buford looked around curiously, as if seeing this inner space for the first time. "Some years ago, this was the BoxCar's main ranch house. But when the senator bought up the spread, I guess he wanted something a dang sight more grand. So Patch built himself that big house down in the valley. I'm glad he did—this is the better place and I have it all to myself."

Hanging over the fireplace was a grainy, enlarged photographic print of a man who looked exactly like Henry Buford. The likeness was flanked by a pair of pewter candlesticks on the mantelpiece, producing the effect of a shrine. Except that there were no tapers in the candlesticks.

The ranch manager noticed the Ute's gaze hanging on the picture. "That's my brother. As you might've guessed, we're twins." He took a long, wistful look at the framed image, then removed a wedge-shaped piece of stone from the mantel. "Here's something you might find interesting."

The Ute held the grooved stone axe head in his hand. The polished surface was mottled with black-and-white spots the size of dimes. "This is a fine artifact—and an unusual type of porphyry. And I'd lay odds it was found east of the Mississippi."

Buford nodded. "Way back when, my old man was a farm kid in southern Indiana. He used to find arrowheads and stuff. He picked this item up in a cornfield. Funny— this is the only thing of Dad's I have."

Moon passed the precious object back to the owner.

The ranch manager placed the artifact back on the mantel. "I got hot stew in the pot, cold brew in the icebox."

"Stew sounds just fine." And it smelled good. "I'll have coffee if you have some, or water."

Buford grinned, cocked an eyebrow. "What's this, Charlie—you a member of the Temperance League?"

"I'm an alcoholic."

Buford's white face reddened. "I'll brew us up some coffee."

"Go right ahead and enjoy your beer. Won't bother me a smidgen to watch you drink it."

"No way. You fall off the wagon and start prowling seedy taverns, sleeping in alleys—I don't want it on my conscience."

Charlie Moon enjoyed the evening, as did his host. The men ate hearty beef stew, drank strong coffee, listened to an archaic vacuum-tube radio, laughed at dumb jokes. They talked about many things. The cattle business. The weather. Politics. Pickup trucks. Gasoline versus diesel engines. Dogs. And, of course, women and all their mysterious ways.

A thousand words after the sun had gone down, Moon pushed his coffee cup aside. "Henry, I appreciate your hospitality. But I got to be going home."

The ranch manager stretched his long legs, propped the scuffed heels of his boots on a straight-backed chair. "I don't believe it—you gonna leave without asking me any questions?"

The tribal investigator offered his host an innocent look. "Questions—about what?"

Buford grinned. "You're a Ute cop. Billy was a Ute. Regular cops still haven't found out who canceled his ticket, and crippled Patch. So you're at the BoxCar to turn over some rocks, see what crawls out. So go ahead—see what you can pry outta me."

"Okay. If it'll make you feel better." The tribal investigator rested his elbows on the table, laced his fingers into a massive fist. "What kind of people did Billy hang out with?"

Buford shook his head. "So you've heard about that."

Moon waited.

"Rumor was, some of your tribesman's buddies was dabbling in the drug business—and I don't mean they owned a piece of the Rexall Pharmacy down on Main Street."

"Aside from alcohol, the autopsy didn't show anything unusual in Billy's system."

"Maybe that's because he thought liquor was quicker."

"Then he wasn't a user?"

"Not that I know of. But talk was, he did some peddling. Small stuff."

"With talk like that going around, how'd he keep his job with the senator?"

"Ol' Patch, he liked his Indian driver. And nobody tells a rich man what he don't want to hear." Buford's eyes narrowed. "But I'll tell you straight—if it had been up to me, I'd of fired Billy's ass a long time ago."

"I wish you had."

"Me, too. My hindsight is twenty-twenty." An amused expression crinkled over the ranch manager's leathery face. "So what else would you like to know?"

"Can't think of a single thing to ask you."

Buford chuckled. "And me just aching to talk my fool head off."

"Well, I'd hate for word to get out that I didn't at least try to do my job. Why don't you tell me about some of the other folks at the BoxCar."

"There ain't that many of us—we happy few."

"Let's start with the old cowboy who guards the gate."

Buford rubbed at a stiff bristle of two-day-old beard. "Nothing much to tell. Old Ned's another drinker, but he's harmless enough."

"How about the senator's nephew—he harmless enough?"

"Allan?" The BoxCar manager thought about it. "He's pretty much your average young fella. Wants to make something of himself, but can't manage to keep his attention focused on anything long enough to see it through. Allan has attended a half dozen universities, graduated from nary a one. He hangs out with all kinds of weirdos, supports any political cause that's liable to embarrass the senator, travels around the world to exotic places, tinkers with computers and electronic gadgets. His latest ambition is to qualify as a skilled mechanic—and he shows some promise. You seen his fire-engine-red hog?"

Moon nodded. "Passed me on the road."

"Going pretty fast, was he?"

"Carrying the mail."

"Someday he'll wrap that fancy toy around a tree. But Allan can take that machine apart blindfolded, put it back together, and it still runs."

"Impressive."

"Yeah, he's got a talent for stuff like that. Lately, the little twerp's been pestering me for work to do around the BoxCar. Now and then, I let him help me with a job—but only when I'm looking over his shoulder."

"He live in the BoxCar headquarters?"

"Sure, Allan's got an apartment in the big house. But when the kid's on the ranch—which is maybe half the time—he spends most of his hours over at the old line shack."

"Where's that?"

Buford jerked a thumb over his shoulder. "East side of the property, bottom of the Notch. It's a smelly dump, which makes the senator pretty unhappy."

Moon smiled at memories of his own youth. *Which is probably Pearson's main reason for hanging out there.* "What does he do over there all by himself?"

"Don't know for certain; contemplates his belly button, I guess." Henry Buford looked out a darkened window toward the Misery Range. "I should probably go over to the line shack from time to time and check up on the place, but I don't. For one thing, Allan's not an employee—he's what's left of the senator's family. For another, he likes his privacy." Buford looked around his kitchen. "I guess that's the one thing him and me got in common."

"Sounds like you don't like the young man."

"Men, I either like or I don't. Allan's a pissant. He never takes a bath, he don't eat meat, and he hates dogs." The ranch manager glanced at his sleeping hound. "Especially ol' Grape-Eye here."

Moon pushed the probe deeper. "I understand Pearson's an orphan."

"Yeah." Buford tapped a teaspoon on his coffee cup. "His parents died about ten years ago."

The tribal investigator wondered how much this man would tell him. "They die at the same time?"

"Yeah." Buford grimaced. "House fire."

"Somebody smoking in bed?"

He avoided the tribal investigator's intense gaze. "From what I heard, the investigation was inconclusive." He started to speak, rephrased his words. "The senator believes the fire was accidental."

Charlie Moon watched the man's eyes. "Does the senator believe his wife's death was accidental?"

Buford took a sip of bitter coffee. "Why do you ask?"

"I hear she fell down the stairs. Broke her neck." Not long after the nephew showed up at the BoxCar.

There was a prickly silence before the ranch manager responded. "House fires. Women falling down stairs. That kind of subject don't help my digestion. Let's talk about something more pleasant."

"I'm all for that," Moon said. "Tell me about Miss James."

The ranch manager closed his eyes to call up the woman's image. "That little gal—now she's a sweet Georgia peach. Treats everybody nice, minds her own business. And she takes good care of the senator."

Moon looked at the ceiling. Then, with studied casualness: "What's Miss James's first name?"

"Miss." Buford laughed at Moon's expression. "And from what I've been able to find out, she don't much care for us rough-around-the-edges cowboy types."

The Ute tried hard to grin, but couldn't do it. "You had a go at her, then?"

"Sure, I did." Buford snickered like a teenager. "Hell, I may look old and worn-out, but I ain't dead yet."

Charlie Moon waited for more.

The spurned man sighed. "Last year, I asked her if she'd

like to go to the Roundup Rodeo with my honorable self. Her refusal was what cultured folks call *polite*. But Mrs. Buford's little boy knows when he's been told to get lost." He drained the cup. "Anybody else you want the lowdown on?"

"How about the manager of this high-tone outfit?"

"That's a fancy title. Officially, I'm not even on the senator's payroll. In exchange for what few services I provide, I get the use of this old ranch house. And all the groceries and supplies I need."

"But no actual pay?"

Buford shook his head. "Not a greenback dollar. But I got a disability pension from the government."

Moon thought the sturdy man did not look disabled.

The ranch manger read his thoughts. "I got a back injury from when I was in the Marines. And no, I didn't get wounded in action. I slipped on some sawdust and fell off a loading dock in East St. Louis. Got an honorable discharge and a monthly check for the rest of my life. It ain't much, but a man with room and board don't need a lot."

"So you give up life as a grunt to run the ranch for Patch Davidson."

"Not right away. I had another job in between."

"Ranching?"

"Nope. I was at Defense Intelligence Agency for almost ten years."

"DIA, huh? Must've been interesting work."

Buford smiled at the probe. "Oh yeah, it was great fun. Spent most of my time driving tight-assed generals around D.C."

"And you prefer the BoxCar to the nation's capital."

"You said it right."

"You think a lot of the senator, don't you?"

Buford picked his words with care. "Patch Davidson is the most important person in my life. If it wasn't for him . . ." He clamped his jaw shut.

Moon let that dog lie.

A clock on the wall struck ten times.

"Thanks for the meal." The Ute got to his feet. "It's about time for me to hit the road."

"I've enjoyed your company, Charlie." The BoxCar manager picked up a bowie knife from the bread platter, turned the glistening blade on a hard, callused palm. His voice was crisp as a September breeze at the crack of dawn. "Before you go, there's something you need to know. Somebody harms one gray hair on that old man's head, I will rip him from gills to asshole and then some. When I get done, there won't be enough left of the bastard for a peckerwood's breakfast."

Charlie Moon looked deep into the flint-hard eyes, and knew this was no idle boast. Henry Buford would make a fine friend. But God help his enemy.

CHAPTER 16

A Job of Work

The sun was an hour high when Dolly Bushman heard the Ford F-150 pickup rumbling along the graveled ranch lane. The boss usually stopped on his way out, and Charlie was always game for some coffee. The plump, middle-aged woman went to the screened door, wiped her hands on a red cotton apron. She watched Charlie Moon's long legs take the three porch steps in a single stride. He looked to be in good spirits.

"Come inta house and sit yourself down." The ranch foreman's wife gestured to indicate a sturdy chair at the kitchen table.

He hung the everyday black Stetson on a battered coatrack, seated himself. "Where's Pete?"

"My old man is off with some of the hands"—She pointed—"working on one of them irrigation ditches over by the west alfalfa."

"Hay crop's looking pretty good this year."

"That's what I hear." This slender man was looking thinner than usual. She gave him a worried look. "You want me to whip you up some breakfast? I could fix some eggs and ham."

"I should say no. But I'd hate to hurt your feelings."

"I got a half pan of biscuits I made fresh this morning. They're still warm."

"Well, if you'd hold a gun to my head, I'd eat one or two."

She pulled a cookie sheet out of the oven, shoved it in front of him. "Want some butter?"

"If it'll make you feel better."

She unwrapped a stick of Grandma's Pride, put it on a saucer.

Moon opened a biscuit with a spoon.

The expert cook sliced off a half-inch slab of ham, plopped it into one of her well-seasoned Tennessee Forge cast-iron fry pans. She cracked four eggs for the black skillet's twin. There was a delicious sizzling. "I expect Pete will be back in a hour or so."

"Can't stay that long." He took a wistful look out the window. "I need to get into Granite Creek while the sun's still low."

Dolly Bushman snapped a faded dish towel, wiped at a plate from her husband's breakfast. "What's the big hurry?"

"Got an assignment from the tribal chairman." He gestured with a biscuit. "Today, I am going to investigate the killing of Billy Smoke. By this time next week, I expect to come to a thoughtful conclusion."

She flipped the ham slab over. More sizzling and popping. "All in seven days?"

"That's all the time I can spare from things I need to be doing."

"Like what?"

"Like managing this ranch." *Like fishing.*

She hunched her shoulders. "Hmmph."

"Dolly, I heard that *hmmph.*"

"Well, I'm glad your ears are still working."

"What did this particular 'hmmph' mean?"

She told him. "A job worth doing is worth doing well."

"Now that's a pretty proverb. Here's her twin sister. Don't spend seven months doing a job than can be finished in seven days—with time out to rest on Sunday."

Her brow pinched into a suspicious frown. "I never heard that one."

"It's in the book. Look it up."

"Charlie Moon, I never know when you're teasing me." She slapped his back with the dish towel.

He helped himself to another biscuit. "Ma'am, d'you have any jam?"

"I got strawberry preserves. And blackberry. And some orange marmalade."

"That'll do just fine."

The Medical Examiner

Charlie Moon was about to knock on the hundred-year-old oak door when it was jerked open by an elfin, white-haired man who appeared to be the same age as the varnished wood. "Well, what'n hell do *you* want?"

The tribal investigator removed his black hat. "Sir, I am selling magazine subscriptions to work my way through medical school—and you're my last customer today. If you'll purchase just three cut-rate subscriptions to *Popular Quack Medicine*, I'll receive this enormous cash prize, become a rich and famous heart surgeon, and help the living stay that way. If you don't take pity on me, I may have to become a pathologist."

"Don't get fresh with me, Charlie Moon." The medical examiner turned away with a groan. "Come inside and let me show you something dreadful."

"No, thank you." The Ute had seen too many dreadful things in the ME's basement laboratory.

"Oh, don't be such a sissy—it's not a cadaver."

Thus reassured, Moon followed the plump, round-shouldered man down the dark hallway past a parlor on the left, a spacious office on the right. The paneled hall terminated in a high-ceilinged kitchen that had been remodeled in 1898. There was a sizable puddle of water on the tile floor. It was trying to get larger, and succeeding. "So that's why you're in such a nasty mood."

"I am an old man who suffers from rheumatism, gout, and general distemper—so nasty is not a *mood* with me, it is a permanent condition." Dr. Walter Simpson wagged a finger in his guest's face. "And don't tell me to call in a plumber. I telephoned the scoundrel almost two hours ago, and as you can plainly see, he ain't showed up yet."

Moon put his hat on a heavy pine table, poked his head and shoulders under the sink. Water sprayed into his face. He turned off the cold water supply valve; the spray slowed to a drip. "You got a good-sized adjustable wrench?"

"Just a minute." There was the sound of wet slippers pattering away. Presently, the physician returned with a plastic toolbox. He shoved it under the sink. "Have a look in there."

Moon unclipped the lid. All the tools looked new and unused. There was no adjustable wrench, but he found a pair of channel-lock pliers, tightened a brass nut on the fitting. Thankfully, it did not break. He got to his feet with a grunt.

Dr. Simpson was swiping at the floor with a soggy mop. "Did you really fix it?"

"For now. But you better get that plumber to replace some of these antique pipes and fittings."

The ME's cherubic face reflected his inner bliss. "Can I fix you a cup of coffee?"

"At least."

"I have some highly fattening pastries. Apple fritters. Cinnamon rolls."

"Bring 'em on, doc."

Nine minutes later the plumber knocked on the door. After a three-minute stay, the skilled craftsman departed.

Dr. Simpson's smile was also gone. He waved an invoice in Moon's face, as if the Ute was to blame for this outrage. "This is simply scandalous. Sixty-eight dollars and some odd cents for making a call—and he didn't do a damned thing." He glared at his guest. "I shouldn't have let you monkey around with my plumbing. I paid a professional to do the job and got an amateur fix."

Moon took the last bite of a sugar-crusted apple fritter. "Life is tough."

"Spare me the pithy philosophical observations. Why are you here?"

"You remember examining Billy Smoke's body?"

"I am going to take that as a rhetorical question. Otherwise, I would be forced to respond with some such acid remark as: No, I have forgotten all about the most notorious and brutal murder to occur within Granite Creek city limits for almost a decade." About nine years ago, there had been that RMP graduate student. Poor, poor girl. But that didn't bear thinking about.

Moon wiped his mouth with a linen napkin. "Tell me about Billy's corpse."

Simpson shifted to his professional persona. "There was no mystery about the cause of death. Senator Davidson's chauffeur was struck once on the temple, twice on the forehead. Once on the bridge of his nose. Any of which would have led to his demise, but the trauma inflicted on the temple resulted in virtually instantaneous death." Walter Simpson took a sip of mint tea from a delicate porcelain cup. "The instrument of murder was more or less cylindrical. Diameter about an inch and a half. And heavy." He paused, glancing sideways at his visitor. "Like a tire iron. Or an old-fashioned lead pipe."

The tribal investigator wondered whether the old man had forgotten that the murder weapon had been found at the scene. "Or maybe a section of rebar."

The medical examiner frowned over his teacup. "Well of course I know that a piece of iron reinforcement bar was used in the crime. Blood from Mr. Smoke's head and the senator's legs was recovered from the infernal thing." The old man's eyes sparkled with mischief. "But I have pipes on my mind right now."

Moon did not bite.

Simpson leaned forward. "And speaking of pipes, would you like to hear my well-informed view on a matter of considerable economic and social importance?"

"No, I would not. In fact, I'd rather have a red-hot scorpion crawl into my ear and hatch out three dozen youngsters. But I know that won't stop you."

"Very well, since you encourage me. I contend that plumbers should be regulated. More particularly, I am in favor of firm price caps. Say . . . twenty dollars an hour. No minimum price for house calls. If they do not fix the problem, they should not be paid one brass shekel."

"Shekels were generally silver. Or gold."

"Don't show off, it is unbecoming in one of limited erudition."

"You're right. I don't even know the meaning of the word." Moon reached for a cinnamon roll. "How about pill pushers—you in favor of a price cap for them?"

A merry twinkle danced in Dr. Simpson's bright blue eyes. "Physicians, men and women of the cloth, teachers in public schools—and let us not forget librarians—should get a special rate from the local pipe-twisters. Say . . . wholesale price on parts and ten dollars an hour for labor."

"I think you missed the point, doc. Issue I raised was whether there should be a cap on services provided by an erudite sawbones like yourself."

"No, you did not."

"I did not?"

"Let me clarify. You were clearly suggesting that those involved in vital services to humankind—such as myself—should receive reduced rates from otherwise exploitative plumbers. And with due humility, I am obliged to agree with your point."

"Guess I was confused about what I was thinking. Thanks for setting me straight."

"Don't mention it."

"I won't. So what sort of a discount should an ex-policeman turned rancher get on his plumbing bills?"

"The question is moot. As you have already demonstrated whilst toiling under my sink, such rough-and-ready folk can manage their own repairs."

CHAPTER 17

The Surgeon

Moon ducked under a prominent sign posted to warn potential trespassers that the inner chamber was for EMERGENCY ROOM STAFF ONLY. There was a single person in the room, which housed a motley collection of vending machines and extraordinarily ugly furniture.

The young surgeon was hunched forward in a plastic chair, her elbows on a Formica-clad table. The blue eyes were bloodshot, her somewhat plump figure was concealed in bulky cotton greens, most of her wispy brown hair was tucked under a white plastic cap. Having popped a couple of No-Doz tablets, the physician was feeding herself from a bag of Super Size Cheez Kurls.

"Excuse me." Moon removed his hat. "You are Dr. Eden?"

She pointed a yellow-stained finger at the nameplate on her blouse. "That's what it says. What's your handle, *hombre*?"

He told her.

The ER supervisor looked him up and down. *Nice specimen.* "So what's on your mind, Charlie Moon?"

"Business." He removed the leather folder from a shirt pocket, flashed his gold-plated Southern Ute badge.

She raised a hand in front of her eyes. "Please—you're blinding me."

He smiled, put the ID away. "Mind if I ask you a coupla questions?"

"Not if I can ask you a couple first."

"Go right ahead."

"You're a cop. Why aren't you totin' a gun?"

"I only tote when there's a need to tote."

"So from time to time, you have a need to shoot human beings?"

He lost the smile.

Happy to have scored a point, the ER surgeon upped the ante. "Tell me, Mr. Moon—how many people have you killed?"

A dozen gray faces flashed across the Ute's consciousness.

"Oh, come on now, don't be modest. How many unfortunates have you sent to the grave?"

He leaned over the table, locked gazes with the woman. "Let's make a deal."

"Name it, cowboy."

"I'll tell you my number. But first, you tell me yours."

The surgeon's pale face burned crimson. "That's not a fair comparison—I'm in the business of *saving* lives."

"So'm I." The tribal investigator put on his hat, turned on his heel.

She stood up. "Wait."

He stopped, looked over his shoulder.

"Guess I've had to patch up too many shooting victims."

"Know what you mean. I've patched up a couple myself."

"And not that it's an excuse for my rude behavior, but I haven't had any sleep for almost thirty hours. I was way out of line. I apologize."

"Accepted."

"So tell me, how can I help you?"

"When Senator Davidson was brought to the emergency

room last December, I understand you were the physician on duty."

"You understand rightly, sir."

"I'm sorry to ask you to plow the same ground all over again—I know you've already been interviewed by the local police. And the FBI."

"Don't forget the state police. And the BIA coppers." The ER surgeon stuffed a Cheez Kurl into her mouth. "Everything I told 'em is in the official records."

"I've read the medical report on the senator. But maybe you—"

"You want to know if there's anything I could add to what's in his folder."

"How'd you guess?"

"You cops are so predictable." She stuck the plastic bag under his chin. "Want one?"

He considered the offering. *I'd rather eat a live caterpillar with the hair on it. But just to please her . . .* "Sure." He selected a sample. *That was pretty tasty.* "So?"

She chewed on the junk food. "I can only tell you what you already know. Bottom line—both of the senator's knees were smashed to jelly."

"Any other injuries?"

"Minor bruises on his rib cage. Another on the left elbow."

"But his ribs weren't broken. Or his elbow."

"No. And the bruises were consistent with a fall—which apparently occurred during the assault. If the perp hadn't smashed his knees, Senator Davidson would've been perfectly well in a few days." She grinned over the Cheez Kurls bag. "I watch all the cop shows on TV. Tell me— do you guys really use hokey words like *perp?*"

"All the time."

"Why?"

"The whole word has four syllables. Which is big trouble, 'cause some of us can't deal with more than a couple. But 'perp' just pops right out of a cop's mouth—easy as spitting a watermelon seed."

"You don't seem to have any trouble with words."

"Tribe sent me away to college." He pointed at the plastic bag. "How about another one of those ugly things?"

She offered him the remnants. "Anything else I can tell you?"

He helped himself. "Tell me about the senator's head."

The physician frowned. "What about it?"

"Were there were any lumps or bumps on his noggin?"

She squinted up at the fluorescent lights, tried to remember. "Senator Davidson did report that he'd been knocked unconscious, but there was no superficial indication of an injury. We did a whole-body CAT scan. I'm certain it didn't show any trauma to the cranium. But the shock of the attack may have caused him to temporarily lose consciousness—happens all the time."

The tribal investigator turned this information over in his mind. Billy Smoke's life had been terminated by several blows to the head, by a section of iron rebar that had been found not far from the body. The senator had suffered the same type of injuries to his knees. But if Patch Davidson's memory of the event could be trusted, he had also been struck on the head—*before* his knees were smashed. Apparently by some sort of weapon that didn't leave much evidence of a blow. But this emergency room doctor was probably right. Most likely, Patch had fainted. Moon knew from his own head injury that memories of a traumatic event were murky at best. The most likely explanation was that the blow to the head never happened. But. There were always buts. If it *had* happened, maybe there were two muggers. One felon wielding a piece of rebar, another with a bag of lead shot. Not that this helped much. Unless one bad guy decided to snitch on the other.

He had almost forgotten about the surgeon.

She was watching him. Wondering what he was thinking about.

Moon was thinking that maybe this investigation might take a little longer than a week.

He's sorta cute. And he looks familiar. "I'm pretty sure I've seen you here before. In the ER."

"Could be."

"Did you ever get injured in the line of duty?"

"Two or three times."

"Give me a for instance."

"One time I was changing a tire for a lady in a Saab. It was on New Year's Eve. Bad ice storm. Bumper jack popped loose, banged me on the shin." *Boy, that hurt.*

The surgeon shook her head. "When you were admitted here at Snyder Memorial, it wasn't on New Year's Eve. And as I recall, you were unconscious."

"That was about three years ago. I got smacked on the bean."

"Well, you've had plenty of time to recover from a concussion."

"You'd think so." He frowned. "But my aunt Daisy says I've not been right since."

CHAPTER 18

The Second Encounter

The pair of elderly women were seated in a booth by the front window, their wrinkled faces pinkly illuminated by a loopy neon script alerting the passing gourmet that this was Angel's Cafe. In contrast, the hand-painted sign on the roof claimed that the establishment was Angel's *Diner*. To locals in Ignacio, it was simply Angel's—the home of three-quarter-pound Certified Angus beef burgers, mouthwatering banana creme pie, and *chili verde* that even a displaced Texan could learn to love.

Angel Martinez, short two waitresses, had come to take the order. He forced a smile under the brushy mustache. "What will you ladies have?"

Louise Marie LaForte squinted through tiny rimless spectacles at the grease-spotted menu. "Oh my, I don't know." She peeked over the optics at her companion. "Daisy, dear, why don't you go first. That'll give me a moment to decide."

The Ute elder glared over the menu at the owner of Ignacio's most popular restaurant. "I want something that won't give me gas."

The smile on Angel's face was beginning to ache.

"Perhaps some vegetable soup, and a nice grilled cheese sandwich."

"Oh, no you don't." Daisy Perika shot him an accusing look. "That'd block me up for sure. Last time I had one of your cheese sandwiches I couldn't pass anything for almost a week."

The patient man's forced smile was gradually morphing into a snarl. "I could bring you some prunes." *And a tall glass of heavy-duty drain cleaner.*

It would not have occurred to the respected Ute elder that this Mexican hash-slinger would dare to make sport of her intestinal infirmities. "No, I don't much like prunes." She flipped the menu aside. "Bring me a bowl of green chili stew. And a big glass of water. With ice. But not too much ice." The Ute elder reminded Angel that she and "Frenchy" qualified for the senior citizens' ten percent discount advertised over the cash register.

"Of course." *Half a century ago, you qualified.* He turned to the smaller of the two women. "And you?"

Louise Marie requested an iced tea. A small green salad. And—licking her lips—a grilled cheese.

Daisy smirked at her French-Canadian friend. "You'll be sorry."

Angel hurried away, spewing dark oaths from under his mustache.

While they waited, Louise Marie chattered about the usual subjects that occupied her mind. Her many ailments, from the sugar diabetes to a touch of Parkinson's. The prices of everything, how they just kept going up. And those *terrible* stories in the newspaper. Like the one about the black bear sow who broke into an old woman's trailer west of Pagosa, mauled the poor thing to death. And chewed up the body something awful. Predation—that was what the medical examiner had said.

Daisy Perika was only half listening. It was not the gruesome story about the marauding bear that made her skin tingle. The Ute shaman was certain that someone was *watching* her. She allowed her gaze to sweep over the other

patrons in the restaurant. No, they hardly seemed aware of
the two elderly women in the booth by the window. The
single waitress was busy passing out steaming plates of
stacked enchiladas to a family from Arboles. Angel was in
the kitchen, whipping the sweating cook to greater efforts.
The Ute shaman closed her eyes. She could feel it. The
stare was tingling on the left side of her face. Very slowly,
she turned her head. Looked out the window.

And there she was, across the street—the pale, skinny
redhead. The one she'd talked to in the discount store, up
in Durango. Daisy felt a warm surge of satisfaction. *I was
right. That woman is from Ignacio. That's how she knows
Charlie used to be a policeman here, and that he's a tribal
investigator now. She must want to tell me something. Well,
she'll just have to come in here. I sure ain't going to go
outside in the chill of the evening just to ask some* matukach
woman what's on her silly mind.

And so Daisy waited.

Louise Marie LaForte chattered on about a recipe for
candied yams.

The redheaded white woman across the street stood
there. Staring at the Ute elder hard enough to make the side
of Daisy's face itch.

*Like she thinks I should come to her. Not on a hot day
in January.* But the old woman had a nephew. And Charlie
wanted to know who this was, where she lived. Duty called.
Daisy pushed herself up from the comfortable seat in the
warm restaurant.

Louise Marie interrupted a fascinating commentary
about how a pair of skunks had taken up residence under
her house. "You goin' to the powder room?"

The Ute woman chuckled. "I never heard anybody call
it that except in old movies." Louise Marie had probably
been a grown woman when the new "talkies" were all the
rage. "I think the ladies' room is occupied, so I'll just go
outside."

"What for?"

"To take a pee in the alley."

Louise Marie gasped. "Daisy, don't you dare!"

"Don't let Angel leave my chili on the table where it'll get ice-cold. You tell him to keep it hot till I get back." Having passed on this instruction, she was gone, the front door flapping behind her.

As she crossed the street, the Ute elder recalled her previous conversation with this redheaded *matukach* woman. Charlie Moon would have a mouthful of questions, and she didn't intend to look the fool. As Daisy approached, the pale young woman stared at her with a penetrating curiosity.

"Okay, Carrot-Top. I'm out here getting chilled to the bone on your account. So let's get right to it. First of all, what's your name and where do you live?"

From the security of the warm restaurant, Louise Marie LaForte watched her Ute friend through the window. *What on earth is she doing out there?* It was a rhetorical question. Daisy Perika's behavior was beyond explaining.

When the Ute elder returned from her errand, Angel was placing food on the table.

After their small meal was finished, Louise Marie got up the courage to ask. "What were you doing across the street?"

Nosy old hen. Daisy wiped at her mouth with a paper napkin. "Talking to that white woman."

The French-Canadian woman ducked her head. "Oh."

Her Ute companion explained what had happened in the discount store in Durango. How the skinny, redheaded woman had been watching Charlie Moon. "She wouldn't tell me much that first time I saw her. But this time, I wasn't gonna let her leave before I squeezed a few things out of her."

"This woman . . ." Louise Marie hesitated. "Did she tell you anything?"

Daisy revealed the essence of the brief conversation. Waited for a response that was not forthcoming. She leaned forward, peered across the table at the aged white woman. "You got something on your so-called mind?"

Louise Marie had several very specific thoughts. But sometimes it was better to keep your mouth shut. "It's getting late—I think I'd better be getting on home now."

She's acting kinda peculiar. Daisy pressed harder. "Is something wrong?" *Probably that cheese sandwich.*

"It's nothing." Despite the steamy warmth inside Angel's Cafe, Louise Marie felt a sickening chill.

The Ute elder's eyes glittered with green fire. "You know that redhead, don't you?"

The French-Canadian woman clamped her small mouth shut.

Daisy banged a fist on the table. "We ain't leaving this greasy spoon till you tell me what you know about her."

No response.

The tougher of the two women assumed a detestably smug expression. "You know you're going to tell me, so you might as well go ahead and get it done with."

Louise Marie summoned all her courage. She stared eye-to-eye at the stubborn Ute woman. *Daisy can't make me tell her. And I won't.* She jutted out a stubborn chin. *No matter how hard she begs or threatens. Not if she twists my arm into a pretzel. I absolutely will not say one word. Not in a million, jillion years.*

But of course, she did.

Charlie Moon was at his desk, reading the latest copy of the *Stockman's Report*, when the telephone jangled. He pressed the instrument to his ear. "Columbine Ranch."

"Charlie—is that you?"

The tribal investigator smiled at his aunt's voice. "No. This is a recording. Please leave a brief message when you hear the beep." He made a beeping sound.

"Don't mess with me. I'm weak as watered-down coffee and I need to go to bed. But I won't be able to get a wink of sleep unless I tell you something first."

Another beep.

"Shut up and listen to what I got to say."

"Sorry, your time is up."

"I talked to that woman again."

"What woman?"

"That *matukach* with the stringy red hair. Same one I saw in the Wal-Mart—looking at you."

He pushed the trade magazine aside. "What did you find out?"

She hesitated. Louise Marie had been able to see it right off. Or, looking at it another way, she *hadn't* been able to see it. "Charlie, listen to what I'm saying—something about that white woman is *wrong*."

Aunt Daisy thought everyone was odd. On the other hand, the schizophrenic had skipped town and left her medicine behind. "Wrong how?"

"I'd rather not say." *I've already said too much.*

"What makes you—"

"For one thing, she still won't tell me her name."

"Maybe she's afraid of somebody."

"I'm not sure. . . ." *I'm not sure she can remember her name. Sometimes, they can't.*

Moon listened to an empty silence on the line. "You there?"

The tribal elder sniffed. "I don't like it when you ask me all these questions. It makes me nervous."

"Okay, let's do it like this—I won't ask any more questions. Just tell me what you found out."

"Well, she said . . ." Daisy's voice trailed away.

"Said what?"

"That's a question."

"Sorry, Your Honor—I withdraw the question." He waited.

The line was silent while Daisy gathered her scattered thoughts. Finally, a resigned sigh. "She said she saw somebody stealing sand." *There. Now I've said it.*

"Stealing sand." He stared at a calendar tacked above his desk. Above the month was a stunning photograph. Impossibly blue ocean. Silver-white beach. Palm trees. A lovely tanned woman on a pink blanket. *I'd like to be there. Without a telephone.* "Guess I'd better not ask *who* was swiping sand."

"That *matukach* girl didn't say." Daisy twined a lock of coarse gray hair around her finger. "But she mentioned Arroyo Hondo again. Said that's where you should look for her."

Scott Parris had promised to send some officers to check what was left of the old mining settlement. He printed AR-ROYO HONDO in block letters. Underlined it. "I won't ask you if there's anything else."

Daisy gripped the telephone so tightly that her arthritic knuckles ached. There was something else. She told him.

"She saw someone putting the sand in a *what?*"

"You heard me the first time."

Moon wrote it down.

Daisy cleared her throat. "That's all I have to say."

The tribal investigator was relieved to hear this. "Next time you see this young lady, give her my phone number. Tell her she can call collect."

"Charlie . . ."

"Yeah?"

The tribal elder took a deep breath. "You be careful."

"Careful is my middle name."

"I coulda swore it was Jug-Head." She hung up. *Okay. I've passed her message on to Charlie. Now I'll be able to sleep.* Hours later, her dark eyes were still wide open. Staring at a place where the ceiling should be. Above her was a dark, infinite abyss. Daisy Perika hoped—prayed—that Charlie Moon would not fall in.

CHAPTER 19

The Sandman

Charlie Moon was making a batch of flapjacks. While occupied with this pleasant task, he mused about one of life's many conundrums. Almost three years ago, he had taken a hard blow on the head. The neurosurgeon had made it clear that the concussion was a serious injury. The clinician had not exaggerated. To this very day, he had not recovered completely. *But Patch Davidson claims he is knocked unconscious by some hardcase who had already beat his driver's head to a pulp—and the politician doesn't even get a bump on his noggin.*

Life was just one prickly puzzle after another.

He removed a pancake from the cast-iron skillet, put it on the stack, poured in the last of the batter. These dregs were a lumpy mix: a multitude of miniature islands floating on a thick, yellow sea. The great puddle sizzled and popped around the edges. Gradually, disparate elements coalesced into a single disc-shaped continent.

Charlie Moon stared at the flapjack sizzling in the iron skillet, but did not see his breakfast. His mind was focused on something far more interesting. Sand. *A regular thief might steal a truckload. But another man might just take*

just a handful. Because that's all he needed. He watched
the pancake burn to a crisp.

Standing at the rear entrance of the Blue Light Cafe, Charlie Moon made a careful inspection of the employees' parking space. There was not much to see on the graveled lot.
Three sedans, a rusty Japanese pickup, a muddy mountain
bike chained to an iron post. The blacktopped area for customer parking—where Oscar Sweetwater had been when
he heard the senator screaming—was off to his left and
around the corner of the cinder-block building. To Moon's
right was Nelson Street, where Billy Smoke had entered
the smaller parking lot in the black Lincoln. Across Nelson
there was a crumbling brick building. It was shared by an
Ace Hardware, the Loco Lobo Pawn Shop, and Martin's
Twenty-Four-Hour Laundromat. In front of him, along the
opposite side of the small parking lot, a scraggly row of
cottonwoods and elms bordered a drainage ditch. A large
sheet-metal building squatted just beyond the ditch. If the
yard-high letters painted on the side of the structure were
to be believed, this was the P.I.E. CARTAGE WAREHOUSE.
The tribal investigator turned to study the rear exit of the
Blue Light Cafe, where Senator Davidson had emerged on
that dark, wet night, looking for his Ute chauffeur. A metal
sign was nailed above the door.

NO SOLICITING
NO LOITERING
VIOLATORS WILL BE PROSECUTED

Below the threat, as if in symbolic warning of the stern
punishment to be meted out for petty misdemeanors, a naked lightbulb hung on a twisted cord. While Moon watched,
a five-mile-long cloud blotted out the sun. The photoelectric
element embedded in the bulb's socket sensed this false
twilight; a sixty-watt filament was heated to a pale yellow
incandescence.

Having memorized every detail of his immediate

surroundings, the tribal investigator turned to his inner landscape. Charlie Moon seemed to be taking in the modest skyline that defined the small university town, but he was barely aware of the gathering of peaked roofs congregated about the soaring steeple on the First Methodist Church, or even the mountains, where a swirling, ice-speckled shawl wrapped itself about blue-green peaks. While the Ute thought his thoughts, he also waited. And presently, his patience was rewarded.

A sleek GCPD sedan pulled into the employee parking lot. A stocky, square-shouldered man got out of the black-and-white Chevrolet, pulled on a faded denim jacket.

The Ute smiled at the chief of police. "And they say the cops never come when a citizen calls."

Scott Parris zipped the jacket, buttoned the collar snugly about his neck. He muttered something about hating these chilly days that threatened a hard winter to come. In his imagination, the blue-white monster lurked just over the mountains—a roaring blizzard of a storm whose sole purpose was to make a policeman's life utterly miserable.

A sudden gust whipped up whatever it could from the parking lot.

Charlie Moon stood shoulder to shoulder with his best friend, holding onto the brim of his black Stetson. Like a pair of stubborn sentries, the chief of police and the tribal investigator leaned against a brisk wind that whipped across the open space, flinging stinging sand and grit into their faces. Along the ditch bank that bordered the employee parking lot, bare limbs of cottonwood and elm shuddered and shivered in their nakedness. The worst of it was over in seconds.

"Well," Parris grumped, "I guess our two weeks of summer are about done with."

"Rain or shine, hot or cold, it don't matter a whit to me. I am content in all kinds of weather."

The six-footer looked up at the taller man. "Charlie, nothing in this dreary world is more annoying than a man who is always happy as a fuzzy puppy. And won't keep it to himself."

Moon patted his friend on the shoulder. "What's chewing on your leg, pardner? You're a tad more testy than usual."

The white man's face twisted into a painful grimace. "Anne and me . . . we've split up."

Having nothing to say, the Ute said nothing.

"But I'm doing all right." *As long as it's light outside. But after sundown . . .*

"You should take some time off. Come out to the Columbine."

"What would I do at your ranch?" Parris snorted. "Shoot at snuff boxes and kick cow pies?"

"I'd put you to doing some productive work." *That'd get your mind off the woman.*

Parris rubbed at his cold nose. "Hell, Charlie—I'm no kinda cowboy."

"No need to apologize—everybody knows you're a pathetic tinhorn. But I could find something simple enough even you could do it."

"Like what?"

"Let me think."

"Hey, take all day."

"You could clean out the stables."

"Why'n hell would I want to do that?"

"Shoveling manure makes it hard for a man to think about his love life."

"Thank you kindly. But I'd just as soon stay in town and be miserable in a more hygienic fashion." *Maybe I'll take out a second mortgage; buy me a brand-new red Corvette.*

"Suit yourself." Unexpectedly, the sun came out. Moon grinned at this welcome omen. "We could go fishing."

"Fishing." A dreamy look slipped over the white man's face. "Yeah. I could swallow a big dose of that."

"Then we'll do it."

"Great."

"You feel better now?"

He squinted at the Ute. "Charlie, don't expect instant results. My fiancé has left me. I'm passing through middle age at ninety miles an hour, and it's all downhill from here."

"Anne's leaving is already history. And getting old and feeble is way off in the future. Try to think about here and now."

"Okay. Right *now,* I'm standing *here.* Freezing my ass into brass."

This was a hard man to cheer up. "Where did Billy park the Lincoln?"

Parris pointed toward the trees lining the drainage ditch. "Over there. Under that big knotty-looking cottonwood. When the first two officers showed up, they found Patch Davidson about six feet from the driver's door, which was open. The old man was on his back, hurting like hell and cussing a blue streak. Mr. Smoke was behind the car. He was way past complaining." The lawman sighed. The wind sighed with him. "But what am I beating my gums for? You've read the report. Seen the photographs."

"Yeah." *About twenty times.*

"So clue me in—what are we doing here?"

The Ute exhaled smoky breath onto his hands, rubbed palms together. "Where was the chunk of rebar found?"

Scott Parris pointed again. "Right behind where the Lincoln was parked—at the edge of the drainage ditch. And like I already told you, there's no doubt it was the murder weapon. We found smears of blood on it. Most of it was from your tribal member, the rest was from the senator. State police lifted a few fibers off the rebar—they were from common cotton work gloves, made in Argentina. In the previous six months, over six thousand pairs were sold in Colorado." He paused long enough to growl. "We'll never know who did it unless we get a lucky break—like if the guy is picked up and convicted for another capital crime and confesses to this one. Or maybe he gets high and brags to one of his buddies about killing an Indian and busting up a U.S. senator."

"Maybe this wasn't a random robbery attempt, pardner. What if somebody got here before Billy Smoke showed up in the senator's Lincoln, then waited for him?"

"Waited for Billy—why would you think that?"

The Ute nodded to indicate the electrical fixture over the Blue Light's rear door. "The light was out. So the bad guy could wait in the dark."

Parris followed his friend's gaze. "Look, Charlie, I was here that night, not twenty minutes after the killing. Restaurant manager told me he grabbed a shotgun and ran out back right after Oscar Sweetwater reported the assault. The lightbulb was burned out. Manager told the dishwasher to replace it. By the time my uniforms showed up, there was a new bulb in the socket."

"Anybody talk to the dishwasher?"

Parris thought about it. "I don't remember."

"I found him this morning. Nowadays, he's burning beef over at the Burger Barn. Fella told me he went to replace the bulb, just like he was told. But when he started to unscrew the bad one, he noticed it was already pretty loose in the socket. So he tightened it just a tad—and there was light. Somebody had unscrewed it just enough to turn it off."

There was a long silence before the *matukach* policeman responded. "If the bad guy did loosen the bulb, that does cast a dark light on the random-mugging theory. But it don't necessarily prove that the guy with the rebar was waiting for Mr. Smoke in particular."

"If not Billy, then who?"

"I dunno. Some restaurant employee going home."

"All the Blue Light evening crew leaves at the same time—midnight. Think about it. Nine or ten people coming out the back door within a couple of minutes. Not exactly prime time for a mugging."

Parris considered the tribal investigator with a thoughtful gaze. "You've really been working hard on this."

Moon assumed a virtuous tone. "You take the tribe's dollar, you do the tribe's work."

"Okay. I admit it. You've got a point about the loose lightbulb."

"There's something else."

Parris grinned. "Wait. Don't say another word—allow me a moment to speculate." He closed his eyes. "Aha—I got it. You already know who murdered Billy Smoke and maimed Patch Davidson."

"Better'n that." The Ute nodded toward his F-150. "Got that sorry sack of bones in the back of my pickup. Trussed up like a hog for slaughter."

For the flicker of a moment, the white man's eyes widened. Then he remembered who he was talking to. "When you get some spare time, drop him off at my jailhouse."

"Before that, I'll need to get a signed confession."

"How'll you manage that?"

"Bury him up to his neck beside to a boom box. Make him listen to Harlem gang rap for six or seven days. Whichever comes first."

For the first time since Anne had informed him that they were basically incompatible, Scott Parris laughed out loud. It felt extremely good. Right down to the tips of his toes.

The Ute waited for the right moment. "Like I said, pardner—there's something else."

"Whatever it is, I don't want to hear it." *I want to go fishing.*

The tribal investigator shrugged. "Okay. But don't say I didn't tell you." *Twenty seconds should do it. One. Two. Three.*

"It won't do no good—standing there doing your silent-Indian routine. I said I don't want to hear about it and I flat out don't. And that's final. Phoenix can freeze over. Yuma to boot."

Twelve. Thirteen. Fourteen.

"Oh dammit, Charlie—don't stand there sulking. Go ahead, have your say."

"Seventeen," the Ute said.

"Seventeen what?"

"You don't want to know."

"Dammit, Charlie—"

"Senator Davidson says he got bopped on the head, lost consciousness. When he woke up, the guy with the iron bar was bashing him on the legs."

"So?"

"There's no medical evidence the senator was hit on the head—not with something as hard as rebar."

"So maybe the perp slugs Davidson with his fist. When Patch bites the dust, he gets whacked across the legs with the rebar. The bad guy is about to go to work on his noggin when your tribal chairman comes to the rescue and the mugger takes off."

The Ute nodded. "Could've happened like that."

The white man squinted at his dark-skinned friend. "But you don't think so."

"Nope."

"Is there a sensible reason for this emphatic 'nope,' or are you just naturally contrary?"

"If you hit a man hard enough in the head to knock him unconscious—whether you use a honey-cured Virginia ham or a chunk of firewood—it'll generally leave a good-sized bump and a bruise the color of a ripe plum. The doctor who treated Senator Davidson at the emergency room told me there wasn't any evidence of serious trauma to his head."

"Victims of violent assaults often disremember what happened. Hell, the senator probably never even got hit on the head. Or maybe he bumped his noggin when he fell down—*after* he got clipped on the legs."

"Maybe."

"So what's your explanation?"

"I hate to bother you with it."

"Go ahead, bother me." Parris snickered. "And don't worry that I'll be disappointed—it's not like I've got high expectations."

"Well, since you put it like that, here's my notion. If

Patch Davidson did get smacked on the bean, maybe the bad guy used a sap."

The chief of police raised an eyebrow. "You mean, like a blackjack?"

"Could be. But those Chicago antiques are hard to find. More likely, it was something homemade. Like . . . oh, I don't know. Maybe a tobacco bag fulla lead shot."

"Charlie, why would a guy who already has a serviceable piece of iron bonk the senator with a bag of lead BBs, then start beating his legs to a pulp with the rebar?"

The Ute allowed his friend ample time to consider his own question.

"Unless . . ." Parris pulled at an earlobe. "Unless there was *two* guys. Bad Guy Number One has a handful of rebar. Bad Guy Number Two, he has a bag of lead shot. Number One is the team's heavy hitter, Number Two's probably the lookout. When the senator interrupts the murder-robbery already in progress, the lookout saps the new arrival. After Patch Davidson hits the ground, the heavy hitter goes after him with the iron bar. And would've probably killed him if Oscar Sweetwater hadn't heard Patch yelling—and come running to see what was going down."

"Might have happened exactly like that."

"You keep saying that. It is very annoying."

Moon was staring across the small parking lot. At the warehouse.

Parris stamped his boots. "Charlie, it's too cold to play games. Now tell me straight out—do you know something I don't or don't you?"

"Run that past me again."

"You know what I mean."

The Ute pointed toward the P.I.E. warehouse on the other side of the drainage ditch. "What do you reckon they keep in that building?"

"PIEs," Parris said through bluish lips. "Apple PIEs. Blueberry PIEs. Rhubarb PIEs. I'm told they haul 'em up from Pie Town, New Mexico. By the truckload."

"I guess your guys must've looked around over there."

"Around the warehouse? Sure. We searched for footprints. Calling cards. Photo IDs. Anything a thoughtful criminal might've left behind for the benefit of us dumb coppers. No such luck."

"You check out the top of the building?"

The chief of police fixed his gaze on the pitched Propanel roof. "What is wrong with me." He slapped his forehead. "Charlie, I am embarrassed beyond words. Astonishing as it may seem, it did not occur to me that the criminal might have leaped thirty feet onto that slanted, slippery sheet metal while in the process of making his escape. But if it would make you feel better, I could bring in a ladder and check the roof for footprints."

"Wasn't exactly footprints I had in mind."

Parris gave him an odd look.

"About the sap," Moon said, "I got this theory—"

"Yeah. So you said."

"I think the bad guy pitched it onto the roof."

"Is there any reason at all why you think such a thing?"

"When Oscar Sweetwater was running to help the senator, he says he heard a thump—like a car door slamming. So everybody naturally assumes that the bad guy left the employee parking lot in a set of wheels. But one of your fine police officers interviewed a Mrs. Bale, who was across the street in the Laundromat waiting for some sheets and pillowcases to dry. This very observant lady said she saw the big Lincoln pull into the employee lot behind the restaurant. But she did not see another motor vehicle until the cops showed up."

"Okay," Parris said. "So maybe the perp—or let's say perps, just so we'll have a second guy with your sap—let's assume they have IQs of at least forty-six, which makes them way too smart to park the getaway car right at the spot where they intend to commit a major felony."

"But if the bad guys don't have a motor vehicle parked close by, what did Oscar Sweetwater hear that sounded like a car door slamming?"

"You tell me."

"The sap," Moon said.

"You really got a fixation on this sap business."

"The bad guy doesn't want to get caught with it, so he gives it the old heave-ho. My guess is"—Moon pointed across the ditch—"it landed on the roof of the warehouse."

"Okay," Paris said. "Let me get this picture framed in my mind. Bad Guy Number One is beating hell outta Senator Davidson when his victim starts to yell. Oscar Sweetwater—who is over yonder in the big parking lot—hears the call for help. Here comes the fierce Indian, thirty-two-caliber *pistola* in hand. Our bad guys decide that it is high time to depart. Bad Guy Number One drops his chunk of rebar and runs like a gazelle. Bad Guy Number Two gives his sap a heave, and it lands on the warehouse roof with a resounding thud. That's the sound Oscar heard—and thought it was a car door slamming. This is how you see it?"

Moon nodded. "More or less." *Mostly less.*

"There's a big hole in this bucket, Charlie. If Bad Guy Number Two doesn't want to be apprehended with a sap in his pocket, why doesn't he just drop it like B.G. Number One drops his chunk of rebar? Why go to the trouble to throw it onto the roof of the warehouse?"

"Now that is the question, pardner."

"Charlie, please don't take this the wrong way, but I think your line of reasoning is pretty thin."

Moon assumed a hurt look. "You are beginning to undermine my self-esteem."

"And another thing—why're you so sure our perp flung his sap on the warehouse roof?" Parris squinted at the metal building.

"Well, I guess it looks like a long shot to you." The Ute's deep voice took on a decidedly stubborn tone. "But that's my theory. And I'm sticking to it."

"You really think the sap is still up there?"

Moon took a deep breath. Hesitated. "Well . . . yeah."

"You sure of that?"

"Sure I'm sure."

"Sure enough to bet cash money on it?"

The tribal investigator shrugged. "Well, I don't know if—"

"Hah."

"That 'hah' has a nasty ring to it."

"If you really believed this silly sap-is-on-the-roof notion, you'd be willing to lay your money down. Like the true gambling man I thought you was."

"Well, since it's kinda a long shot, you'd have to give me some pretty sweet odds."

Parris jutted his chin. "How's ten-to-one taste?"

"Well, I guess I might have a bite of that."

"Okay, then." Parris removed a crisp twenty-dollar bill from his wallet. "This here Andrew Jackson covers a pair of your cherry-tree choppers."

"You mean if I'm right, all I take home is twenty bucks?"

"Name your poison."

"How about five of your Jacksons against a pair of Great Emancipators?"

He's getting too eager. "Charlie, you are lucky I am your best buddy. Otherwise, I would take your pair of fivers. But I am not by nature a greedy man."

He's getting nervous. "Okay, then. Two Washingtons against your man from Tennessee says you'll find the sap on the roof. Or," the Ute added casually, "in the gutter."

"Gutter?"

"Technically, a gutter is an extension of a roof." Moon shrugged. "The sap could've slid down the roof into the gutter. Or maybe it even got washed into the down spout. Hey, I'm only betting the mugger flung his sap onto the roof. I ain't saying exactly where it might of went from there."

The chief of police leveled an accusing look at his companion. "Charlie, are you trying to snooker your best friend in the whole galaxy?"

Moon was wide-eyed with innocence. "What do you mean?"

"I mean have you already checked out the roof on that warehouse?"

"Well . . . maybe I had a quick look."

"And did you find anything there?"

Moon shook his head.

"How about in the gutter."

Another negative response from the Ute.

Scott Parris knew his man. "So the sap's in the down spout."

"Well, now that you mention it. It might be. Possibly."

"Charlie, you are a sneaky rascal who would pick his best friend's pocket for a measly twenty dollars. Or a hundred, if you could run the bet up."

"I hate to have to remind you, pardner, but the wager was entirely your idea. In fact, it might be said that you deliberately shamed me into it."

"Bull hockey. You mousetrapped me and we both know it. But I can see that you're just busting your britches to brag about how you worked this out. Go ahead. Lay it on me. I'll pretend to be enormously impressed."

"I did have a little help."

"You mean somebody told you—"

"Not exactly, pardner. And not entirely."

"Thank you. That clears things up considerably."

"First, she told my aunt Daisy, not me. She said she saw somebody stealing sand."

"Who the hell is *she?*"

"The skinny redheaded gal."

"Wilma Brewster?"

"So you say, pardner. I've never laid eyes on the young woman."

"You been holding out on your buddy. Why didn't you mention this sand business the first time you told me about the redhead talkin' to your Aunt Daisy?"

"First time you and me discussed the matter, my aunt had only talked to her once, at the discount store in Durango. The part about some person stealing sand—that came up when the redheaded gal had a chat with Aunt

Daisy in Ignacio. Across the street from Angel's Café."

Parris ground his teeth. "*What* person was stealing sand?"

"The redheaded gal didn't say."

The chief of police scowled at the Ute. "And I bet we still don't know where to find this phantom witness."

"Pardner, I hate to say this. But every time I offer you a fine, shiny apple, you do have a hurtful way of finding a worm in it."

"Okay, I may be just a teensy bit overly critical. So to make amends, let me say this—despite the fact that you tried to steal my hard-earned money, and even though you had the benefit of a tip, I am greatly impressed with the way you have worked things out."

"Well, pardner, that makes me feel some better. But being modest right down to the marrow, I am compelled to point out that it was mostly luck on my part."

"How so?"

"When I got here early this morning, it was raining hard. I noticed that water was spilling over the side of the warehouse gutter—but just barely dribbling outta the down spout. Well, you can see how easy that was. Even a chief of police might've figured that something was blocking the flow."

"Charlie, you should've been a detective. But don't let me interrupt your story with overly generous praise. What'd you do next?"

"Borrowed a ladder. Climbed up. Had a look."

"And what exactly was this something that was blocking the down spout?"

"Well, I couldn't be absolutely certain. After all, pardner, if I knew for sure, it wouldn't have been entirely fair to accept that bet you pressed on me."

"I am duly impressed with your integrity. But go ahead—take a wild-ass guess."

"Well—it might've been a sock."

"Sock?"

"Sure. The redheaded gal told Aunt Daisy she saw this

person putting the sand into . . . well, a sock."

The chief of police shook his head wearily. "And what kinda sock did you find in the drain pipe."

"I think it might've been wool. Dark blue. With three red stripes."

"You think?"

"It could be evidence in a capital crime, pardner. And I'm just a humble private cop who wouldn't even think of poking around a pig that's inside my pardner's pen." Charlie. Moon assumed a righteous expression. "No, sir. That wouldn't be right."

CHAPTER 20

Heartburn

Charlie Moon was nearing the Granite Creek city limits when the dull, persistent pain hit him right below the belt buckle. This was a chronic condition, occurring three or four times every day. A remedy was called for. By some quirk of misfortune, he was approaching the Mountain Man Bar & Grille, a monstrous two-story construction of creosote-soaked pine logs. Standing on the porch roof was a chain-saw-hewn image of a scruffy-looking fellow in a coonskin cap. This oversized facsimile of a frontiersman gripped a rugged wooden tomahawk in one hand, a nine-foot-long Pennsylvania flintlock rifle in the other. Moon slowed the pickup. *This is where Billy Smoke was hanging out a few minutes before he was beaten to death.*

During the lunch hour, the Mountain Man catered to those very few locals who were bereft of functioning taste buds or good sense, plus the occasional innocent tourist who would never darken its door again. When the sun went down behind the mountains, the place was a watering hole for sunburned cowboys, long-haul truckers, and beer-swilling bikers. It was midafternoon, the slow time. The graveled parking lot was vacant except for a dusty Subaru Outback.

As Charlie Moon pushed the door open, an electric bell chimed his entrance. He found himself in a barnlike room that served as restaurant and bar. The Ute paused to allow time for his pupils to adjust to the smoky twilight.

A big-hipped, moderately attractive blonde stomped along the rough boards behind the bar. The name tag on her blouse read "CHARLENE." She looked through limpid blue eyes at the potential customer. "You wantin' somthin' to drink?" Her sad countenance expressed the unspoken hope that the man seating himself on the stool was just passing by.

This lady needed some cheering up. "Ma'am, I am ready for some serious good eats."

His cheerful luminosity fell into the black hole of her despair. "Then you came to the wrong place, mister. Our cook died this mornin'—from serious food poisnin'."

"This is sad news. I hope his death was not painful."

Charlene grimaced, exposing a great multitude of teeth set in matching horseshoes of pink gums. "The owner of the joint does the cookin', but right now BoBo's gone to the post office."

His stomach growled. "This is even worse news."

She found a filthy rag, took a halfhearted swipe at the bar. "I s'pose I could whip somethin' up for you."

Reassured by this offer, Moon smiled. "I sure could go for a hot ham sandwich and a bowl of homemade soup."

"Don't have no ham." She pointed at a row of red and white cans on a shelf behind the bar. "And the soup ain't homemade."

The optimistic man's hope was not diminished at this news. "What do you recommend?"

Charlene poised a ballpoint over her order pad. "Could you go for a Chuck Wagon Elkburger and some Mountain Man Chili? Chili's leftover but I could warm it up."

"I expect that would hit the empty spot just right."

She rattled off the list of potato options.

Charlie Moon informed her that he preferred German potato salad over fries or mashed.

Charlene scribbled *CH/EB/PS* on her pad.

There was loud banging on the front door, coarse laughter, a heavy clomping of boots. The waitress scowled; this trio of bikers was well known to her. "Excuse me for just a minute." She went to confront the unwelcome customers. "Whatta you guys want?"

They told her.

She snorted. "In your dreams, you buncha pea-brained jackasses."

Cheered by this sociable exchange, they demanded beers.

Charlene filled the order, returned to take care of her other customer.

Moon watched the new arrivals in the mirror behind the bar. Three rough-looking white men nursing Buds from long-necked bottles. They had the pale, indolent look of boozers who spent much of their waking hours in darkened bars. The largest of the bikers filled one side of the booth. The tribal investigator did not know why he was paying them the least attention. But something made the hair stand up on the nape of the Ute's neck.

"Okay, I'm back." Charlene was watching the bikers over his shoulder. "Whacha want to drink, cowboy?"

Moon informed her that a tall glass of lemonade would be satisfactory.

There was a snicker from the bikers. One of these philosophers offered his considered opinion that lemonade was a pansy drink.

Charlie Moon ignored the unseemly remark. "And bring me an extra napkin, please."

The waitress's lips curled into a smirk. "One napkin ain't enough for you?"

"No, ma'am." He lowered his voice to an embarrassed whisper. "When I'm at the peak of my appetite, I tend to make a big mess. And I'm real hungry." *Hungry enough to eat here.*

"Well, I don't see how nobody could make a mess with a Elkburger."

"You forget the chili."

She rolled the blue eyes, disappeared into the kitchen. Moments later, the woman could be heard swatting flies, screaming shrill curses at those insects who got away.

The lemonade, which appeared shortly, was of the type concocted from a mixture of powdered concentrate and alkali water dipped from a stagnant pool called Poisoned Well. All the sugar he could mix into the greenish liquid did not overwhelm the bitter undertaste. After a few sips, he left it alone.

Charlene plopped his lunch in front of him. "Bowla chili. Elkburger with fries."

He was about to remind her that he'd ordered the potato salad. *No. Best to eat what's already here. Sooner I'm finished, sooner I'm outta here.*

One of the bikers yelled for more beer.

Moon took a bite of the Elkburger. *Tastes like road kill.* Grease floated on the chili. He tried a spoonful. Awful. *I should've waited till I got home to eat.* But the tribal investigator reminded himself that there was another reason to be in this pathetic excuse for a restaurant. The diner looked over the lemonade glass at the blond waitress, who was putting plastic-packaged crackers into a dish. "You worked here very long?"

"Long enough to regret it." She slammed the plastic cracker bowl on the bar. "Why d'you ask?"

"I'm with the Colorado Board of Welfare Investigation."

The waitress elevated a penciled eyebrow. "No kidding."

"I never make jokes about my work."

"So why're you askin' me questions?"

He crumbled a pair of saltines into the chili. "My specialty is child labor law enforcement. And you don't look old enough to work in an establishment that serves liquor."

She cackled a laugh. "That's a good one. Besides spreading bullshit, cowboy, what line a work are you in— really?"

He presented his tribal ID.

She stared at the dark face in the photograph, the gold-plated shield. "Real pretty."

"Thank you. A homely man appreciates a compliment now and then."

Charlene flashed a gummy smile. "I meant the shiny badge."

He looked at the burger. "I sure wish you hadn't told me that."

She picked up a beetle off the bar, watched eight little legs wiggle. "So what brings an Indian cop to the Mountain Man?" The waitress dropped the unfortunate insect onto the floor, stomped on it. "It cain't be our reputation for dishin' out edible food."

He showed her a photograph of Wilma Brewster.

Charlene found a pair of reading glasses in her apron pocket, propped them on the bridge of her nose. She stared at the pale, freckled face under the red hair. "Who's this?"

"You don't recognize her?"

The waitress shook her head. "I won't swear on no Bible that I've never seen this kid, but she sure ain't one of our regulars."

Moon returned the photo to an inside jacket pocket. "Last December, just a few days before Christmas, a fella I know had himself a beer in this fine establishment."

"Is that supposed to mean somethin' to me?"

He knew she knew. It was written all over her parchment-pale face. "Billy Smoke. Senator Davidson's driver."

"Oh, yeah." Charlene took another swipe at the greasy countertop. "Now I remember. I was here that night."

Moon stirred the chili. "Late that evening, after he'd had a few drinks, Billy left the Mountain Man. He drove the senator's Lincoln over to the Blue Light Cafe to pick up his employer. Before Patch Davidson came outside for his ride home, somebody else found Billy in the Blue Light parking lot. They beat him on the head until he was dead."

Her lips went thin. "Everybody knows what happened

after Billy left the place." She averted her face from Moon's penetrating gaze.

Forgetting himself, he took a sip of bitter lemonade. Regretted it. "I'm looking into the matter for the tribe. If there's anything at all you could tell me . . ."

"Look, mister, I already talked to the cops till I was blue in the face." She was looking past him.

He saw a flicker of fear in her eyes. Heard the creak of a board in the floor behind him. Moon glanced at the mirror behind the bar. *Uh-oh. Here comes trouble.*

The heaviest of the three bikers had left the booth. He was a massive, swaggering man with enormous biceps, a belly flopping over a thick leather belt, a mop of straw-colored hair secured by a dirty red bandanna—beady, piggish eyes. A fat black cigar dangled from thick lips. Four-inch-high yellow letters on his black T-shirt spelled out HALF-TON. Two yards short of the Ute, the monstrous man stopped. In something resembling a smile, the lips parted to expose yellowed teeth.

Moon turned on the bar stool. Took a look at Half-Ton's companions. Though watching their comrade with intense interest, they remained in the booth. That, at least, was a hopeful sign.

The massive man removed the cigar from his mouth, spoke in a low growl. "I know who you are."

"So do I," Moon said. "And I know how to spell my name. That's why I don't need to have it printed on my shirt."

This produced a belly laugh that shook the biker. "That's a pretty good one. For a dumb-ass Indian cop."

"Ah—then you know me by reputation."

"Sure I do." He raised a finger the size of a Polish sausage, pointed at the ID in Moon's shirt pocket. "And your redskin badge don't mean nothin' here."

"I'm a working man—don't have time to waste in idle conversation. So why don't you get right to the point."

"Awright." A happy chuckle rippled along the mammoth

belly. "I am going to pull your ugly head off—and stuff it up your ass."

"You want to fight?"

The huge man's eyes twinkled merrily. "In the worst way."

"I'd like to oblige you Mr. Half-Tub—"

"It's Half-*Ton*."

"—but I've had a long, hard day. I'm tired to the bone."

"Sounds to me like you're 'fraid you'll get your ass whupped."

"Well, if you and me was to tangle, I suppose the outcome would be unpredictable." The Ute took measure of the monstrous creature, who had a distinctly alien look about him. "I have never done battle with a life-form that was not carbon-based."

Half-Ton stared through the pig eyes. "Are you bad-mouthin' me?"

"Certainly not—that was a compliment. I recognized you as a life-form."

The huge biker glanced over his shoulder at his buddies, snorted. "I say you're a yella scum-sucking hound."

Moon considered the insult. "A good effort for a third-grade dropout. But it won't quite do."

Half-Ton sucked in a breath of stale air. "Then you're a lily-livered sissy. A stinkin' coward. Afraid to stand up and duke it out, man to man."

The Ute sighed. This three-hundred-pound gorilla was not going to go away.

The biker sneered. "On toppa that, you're a damn pervert."

The Ute tensed. "What was that?"

"You're a candy-ass pervert." He added gleefully, "The kind whut wears women's underwear."

"What kind?"

Half-Ton's tiny swine eyes bulged. "Women's!"

"No, I mean what kind of women's undergarment are we talking about?"

The oversized thug concentrated all the power of a

walnut-sized brain until he had the picture. "Pink panties. With little red hearts. And black lace."

Moon grinned. "So you got yourself a girlfriend. What's her name—Quarter-Ton?"

"I don't like Injuns." Half-Ton's lip curled in utter hatred. "Specially redskins whut drink limmenade."

"Well, that tears it. You've gone and hurt my feelings." Moon smiled. "But I still won't fight you."

The huge man waddled up to the bar. "You know what that there bowla chili puts me ta mind of?"

Moon made a wish. *I wish you wouldn't tell me.*

Half-Ton told him with some relish. Laughed like a lunatic hyena. Then ground the red-hot tip of his cigar into the chili. It made a hissing sound.

"You should know better than to mess with a man's food." Oh so slowly, Ute raised himself from the bar stool.

From the far booth, the remaining bikers—who also wore personalized T-shirts—watched the slender, broad-shouldered man unfold to an alarming height.

Pie Eye muttered to Yazzoo, "Oh my gawd, but he's a big 'un."

Said Yazzoo, who had a red patch over his bunged-up left eye and a slight measure of good sense, nodded. "I'd estimate . . . hmm . . . about two hundred and sixteen. Give or take a pound." He had spent the summer of '99 estimating patrons' weights with the Ullibari Brother's Greatest Carnival and Circus West of the Atlantic. "And he'll measure a good four-foot-forty with the hat."

Pie Eye wiped a smear of beer foam from his mouth. "I say we go back up ol' Half-Ton."

"Nah. The big guy can take that Indian. Besides, you know the boss don't want any help—it's against the rules."

"Hell with the rules." Pie Eye drained the last of his Bud, grasped the neck of the bottle in a hairy hand. "Backwater if you wanta, but I'm goin' to get me a piece of that tommy-hawk flinger before Half-Ton tears his head off."

The more prudent of the trio watched Pie Eye leave the booth. Yazzoo had a plan of his own, which did not include being present when the blue suits showed up to sort things out. There was always the possibility of confusion when the local Gestapo started stirring the pot. On occasion, the boundary between rowdy participants and innocent by-standers could become murky. Yazzoo had no intention of being dropped into the Granite Creek jug along with this pair of ignorant felons.

Half-Ton raised a pair of arms, flexed biceps the size of watermelons. "Say nighty-night, Injun."

Moon recognized the inevitable when it spit in his face. *Just so it's clear he started this fight, I should let him take the first swing. That would be the righteous thing to do.* But it would also be stupid. The Ute launched a hard right.

Half-Ton caught the blow full in the face, staggered two steps backward, blood gushing from his mouth.

The Ute was pleased. *Okay, one down.*

But the buffalo-sized man did not fall. He staggered, spat out a yellowed pair of teeth. Grinned merrily at his opponent. "Now, Geronimo—you *really* pissed me off."

Alas, this was not the end of the bad news.

Pie Eye came high-stepping it across the barroom floor, knocking chairs and tables aside, yowling like a banshee on fire. A six-inch switchblade glistened in his hand.

For about two minutes, Charlie Moon's life was intensely interesting.

Scott Parris braked his aging Volvo to a halt in front of the Mountain Man Bar & Grille. Two squad cars had already responded to the call from the frantic waitress. The chief of police normally would not have been bothered with a common bar fight, but the description of one of the participants had caused the GCPD dispatcher to notify Charlie Moon's best friend. Parris, who had been enjoying his day off, arrived only shortly after the officers already on the street and a good ten minutes before the ambulances. He braced himself with a deep breath of the crisp air, went inside. Had a first look. *Damn.* This was bedlam carried a notch too far. Chairs and tables smashed. Blood splattered about as if by a chain saw massacre. One good-sized fellow was stretched out on the bar, faceup, eyes wide open, staring up at nothing. He appeared to be dead. An absolutely enormous man was crawling around on hands and knees, moaning pitifully, evidently searching for that which was lost. Each time the hippolike figure picked up a tooth from the dirty floor, he cursed. Every time he cursed, he spat more blood onto the floor. Not that one more mouthful of crimson liquid made a noticeable difference.

Charlie Moon, seated on a bar stool, was ignoring a string of questions being put to him by officers Knox and Slocum.

The waitress was fussing over her favorite customer. "Honey, are you sure you're all right—d'you want some coffee?"

The Ute nodded.

The chief of police elbowed himself past his ineffectual officers. "Charlie?"

Moon turned to present a battered face. "Hi, pardner."

Parris grimaced. "Are you okay?"

"I been better." The Ute's lips ached, his left shoulder was dislocated, and from the sharp pain in his side, he supposed that a rib had cracked under the force of Half-Ton's monstrous bear hug.

The chief of police waved his arm to indicate the scene of destruction. "What in hell has happened here?"

"Fight."

"Well, I can see that." He nodded to indicate the biker laid out on the bar. "Did the fat guy kill this one?"

"Oh, no—I did that." Moon leaned to study Half-Ton's prone sidekick. "Only I don't think he's altogether dead."

Parris was fascinated by the huge biker, still on his knees. Half-Ton was laboriously counting a handful of teeth. "You took on *both* of these apes?"

"Coulda been worse." Disabled by a split lip, Moon grinned crookedly. "A third one hightailed it when the rhubarb started. And I appreciate his leaving—I'm not sure I coulda managed all three of 'em."

Parris stared at a deep cut over the Ute's eye, the front of his bloody shirt. "Looks like you may need a transfusion."

"Nah, that's Half-Ton's juice." The Ute made a big fist and frowned at it. "But I think I hurt my hand when I hit Pie Eye in the head." *Should've used a bottle.*

Parris ordered Knox and Slocum to cuff the massive biker. He put a finger under Pie Eye's jutting jawbone, felt a weak, irregular pulse. "What was this brawl about?"

"That big moron started it." Charlene pointed an accusing finger at Half-Ton, who—in an attempt to evade the cuffs—had dropped a handful of broken teeth on the barroom floor. The whalelike man was blubbering like a small child whose double dip of strawberry ice cream had toppled off the cone to go *splatt* into the mud.

Parris eyed his friend. "He hit you first?"

Moon offered the lawman a solemn expression. "Worse'n that." He pointed an accusing finger at Half-Ton. "That man put his cigar out in my chili."

The chief of police deeply regretted taking the call. He turned to the waitress. "So what should I charge these bums with?"

She glared at the pair of bikers, then looked uncertainly at the Ute.

"He doesn't mean me," Moon said.

Parris held his tongue. *Don't count on it.*

"What to charge 'em with'll be up to the boss, and he ain't here right now." Charlene frowned at Pie Eye's outstretched body, then at the behemoth biker sitting on the floor. "But I expect it'll be for disturbing the peace. And destruction of private property." She grimaced at Half-Ton's bloody, four-chinned face. "If it was up to me, I'd add on being more ten times more ugly that the law allows."

Scott Parris aimed an official glower at his best friend. "And how about this one. He had a piece of this, too."

"Oh, don't bother Mr. Moon—he didn't do nothin' wrong." She patted the Ute's hand.

The tribal investigator grinned at her. "You can call me Charlie."

She bared the impressive gums at the charming man. "All right . . . Charlie."

Moon turned to the chief of police. "Anyway, it was self-defense."

"Don't matter none to me," Parris said. "I can't play favorites. I got to charge you with something."

The Ute surveyed the wreckage. "How about . . . littering."

CHAPTER 21

The Dancing Woman

Daisy Perika felt old as Moses' great-grandmother. Getting out of bed was hard work. Moreover, her knees and shoulders ached. By all rights, the weary woman should have spent the chilly morning sitting at her kitchen table with a strong cup of coffee, listening to broadcasts of bad news from the tribal radio station, wondering, *What is this poor old world coming to?* But the Ute elder felt an urgent need for a walk in the canyon. And so she pulled on her dead husband's wool overcoat, wrapped her fingers firmly about the stout oak staff, plodded away toward the mouth of *Cañon del Espiritu*. With the shallow waters of Snow Creek splashing along at her side, she moved slowly up the slight grade. For most of her journey, Daisy followed the rutted dirt lane that cousin Gorman Sweetwater used to truck in hay to the few of his wild-eyed, white-faced cattle that inhabited the many nooks and crannies of the canyon.

The bottom of the deep, narrow gorge was dotted with great sandstone boulders, prickly clusters of yucca spears, fragrant congregations of juniper and piñon, even an occasional ponderosa. Cottonwoods and willows huddled along the rocky stream bank, shuddering in the slightest breeze. Owls and ravens talked to the shaman while she

walked, and she answered them. Daisy ignored those irritable squirrels who scolded her with chattering barks, arrogant flips of bushy tails. As the sun was nearing its zenith,
the shaman passed close by the *pitukupf's* underground
home, but did not give the abandoned badger hole a glance.
This was not a day for communing with the dwarf. Daisy
did not know how she knew such things, but she knew.
The lane eventually faded into a narrow deer trail that crisscrossed the stream a half dozen times before branching into
several barely discernible paths that led to nowhere in particular.

Her strength almost spent, the tribal elder seated herself
on a blackened pine stump. *Ahhh . . . that feels good.* Daisy
Perika laid the walking stick across her lap. The silence
was perfect. She closed her eyes, felt the pleasant warmth
of the sun on her face. *Nice place for a nap . . . except I'd
probably fall off this stump and break my collarbone.* But
it was hard to stay awake. And so the shaman dozed. She
was startled to hear the sound of padding footsteps. The
Ute elder opened her eyes. In the shadows near the west
wall of the canyon, was something very odd.

Daisy's mouth dropped open. *What on earth . . .*

The gaunt form was comprised of knobby limbs, grayish
flesh. The specter's torso was clothed in a diaphanous garment, the face was hidden behind a webbed veil. As it
walked, its knee joints went squeak-squeak-squeak. The
thing looked vaguely like a female. But none such as the
shaman had ever seen—not even in her terrifying journeys
into Lower World.

Apparently unaware of the astonished observer, the enigmatic figure approached without so much as a glance at
Daisy.

This unwarranted intrusion was all quite annoying to the
Ute woman, who had a remarkably low threshold of irri-
tation. "Hey!" she called out. "Who are you?"

If this odd-looking personage was blind to the Shaman's
presence, perhaps it was also deaf. By all appearances, the
visitor did not hear Daisy's words.

The tribal elder was searching her memory for an appropriate insult to shout at the impertinent trespasser when it emerged from the shadows. Yes, this was certainly a woman. Or the residue of what once had been. In a shaft of sunlight, Daisy saw through the webbed veil—and wished that she had not. The face was black as tar; a swollen tongue protruded from the mouth. Something was twisted tightly around the neck. Something that looked like a turn of heavy wire.

Remembering who she was and *whose* she was, the Catholic crossed herself.

Now, the lonely phantom did the most astonishing thing—she stretched out skinny arms as if to embrace an unseen *someone*. Slowly, with a macabre grace, she waltzed to a ghastly symphony the shaman could not hear.

Daisy Perika crossed herself a second time, began to mutter the Lord's Prayer.

When it seemed that the unseen orchestra had ended the piece, the strangled phantom was stilled. She paused for an eternal moment, stared through the veil at the shaman.

Daisy prayed again. Harder. *Please. Make her go away.*

And the gaunt figure did depart. She moved through the pink bark of an aged ponderosa, appeared on the opposite side of the mossy trunk, then passed across a small clearing and into the surface of a massive, potato-shaped boulder. There was, thankfully, no second emergence. It was as if she had never been; there was no sign of her presence. Except for the squeak-squeak of dry knee joints, which continued for a few heartbeats, fading finally into a haunted silence.

The old woman raised her eyes to heaven. *Thank you, God.* Though bathed in the midday sun and perspiring under the heavy overcoat, Daisy shivered as she pondered the meaning of what she had seen. The eerie visitation raised several troubling questions. The Ute elder had a strong conviction that she and this spirit were connected in some peculiar way. She wondered whether the vision was from the past, or the future. Or elsewhen. Whatever the case might be, Daisy Perika was certain about one thing. *Whoever that was, she wasn't from around here.*

And so the world turned.

CHAPTER 22

Blunt Instruments

The Chief of Police sat across a table from the Ute tribal investigator. "You look awful. Like a cross between a corpse and the bogeyman."

"Yeah, I know." Moon rubbed at a half-closed eye. "Every time I look in the mirror, it scares me."

"How're your ribs?"

The Ute rubbed at a torso wrapped in several layers of tape. "Let's talk about something else."

"Okay." On the surface between them was a one-gallon plastic ZipLoc bag. Inside the transparent container was a navy-blue wool sock with three red stripes. Inside the sock—and partially spilled into the bag—was a quantity of light brown sand, a scattering of small pebbles, a few tiny pieces of vegetable matter. Scott Parris opened a white folder, consulted a sheaf of papers. "FBI forensics lab was extremely helpful. They informed me that what you found in the P.I.E. warehouse drain pipe is a sock. With sand in it."

"It's always gratifying to have our suspicions verified by the experts."

"You bet. But that was only for starters." The chief of police read from the official document. "Material—reprocessed wool. Said sock was fastened at one end with a green wire tie." He looked across the table at the tribal investigator. "Said wire tie is provided with the best-selling brand of plastic garbage bags in Colorado and thirty-six other states."

Moon tried to talk without moving his split lip. "That's it?"

"Oh, no—there's more. The woolen garment is tinted with a common blue dye. Object of apparel was manufactured in South Korea about two years ago." He pitched the folder aside. "You don't even want to know how many pairs of these fine socks have been sold in the continental United States of America by Wal-Mart—just to mention one major outlet."

"What about the sand?"

"There the news gets better." From the tilt of his head, Parris gave the impression of being very proud of himself. "I did some police work. As you already know, Miss Brewster—who told your aunt about somebody stealing sand—worked as a part-time employee for the Rocky Mountain Polytechnic Campus Police. I checked out her assigned work pattern on the campus, also the most likely routes she would have used between the RMP police station and her apartment. I took samples of every source of sand along the way. You'd be surprised how much of that stuff is lying around."

Moon faked a yawn. "I hope this isn't gonna be one of your hour-long stories."

"Not a chance—I shall be the very soul of brevity. The sand in the blue sock is from a preschool playground. Which is located on the university campus." The chief of police paused for dramatic effect.

He wants me to ask. "How do you know that?"

"Forensics techs found some bits of vegetable matter in the sand that was in the sock. Turns out to be fragments of elm leaf. Being an observant fellow, I noticed this big elm that leans over a playground sandbox. I got a DNA analysis done. Perfect match."

"Well, pardner, what can I say?"

"You'll think of something."

"Okay. I am very nearly impressed."

"Thank you."

Moon thought about it. "But why does our mugger select this particular spot to fill his sock? Sand, he can find anywhere."

"A good question, Charlie. I gave it some careful thought. The sandman must have some connection with the campus."

The tribal investigator felt a twinge of pain from a cracked rib. "That preschool where you found the sandbox—isn't it pretty new?"

"Yeah. Construction was just finished a few months ago." Scott Parris thought he knew where this was going. He didn't like the neighborhood. "So?"

"Didn't Senator Davidson get a sizable piece of funding for that project?"

"That he did. Our beloved public servant scared up over three million federal bucks for the campus preschool facility." Parris cocked his head at his friend. "Nickel for your thoughts."

"That's five cents more'n they're worth." Moon smiled at his best friend. "Well, pardner, you've done a fine piece of police work. Made some real progress."

"Oh yeah," the chief of police grumped. "I have identified a sandbox. And thanks to you, where I formerly had only one felon to find, now I have two. A sadistic bastard who uses a piece of rebar to do his dirty work—and a more sensitive soul who prefers to tap his victim with a sock full of sand."

Maybe. The Ute looked out the window at a day filled with golden sunshine.

Scott Parris leaned forward. "I need to interview Wilma Brewster. Find out why she skipped town. And more importantly, get her to tell us who she saw at the playground—stuffing sand in a sock."

"Aunt Daisy said the redhead mentioned Arroyo Hondo

again. You ever get around to sending somebody to check the place out?"

"I sent Knox and Slocum. It was a snipe hunt. No sign of anybody camping out up there." Parris drummed his fingers on the table. "Maybe Wilma Brewster's hanging out at the Arroyo Hondo down near Taos. I'll send her photo to the New Mexico State Police. I've already alerted the PDs where your aunt has seen Miss Brewster."

"Any response from Durango or Ignacio?"

Parris shook his head.

"She'll turn up. There can't be that many skinny, red-headed young women at large who enjoy talking to Aunt Daisy."

Parris was scribbling notes on a yellow legal pad. "Oh yeah—on another subject. Those motorcycle thugs you tangled with. The one that was in a coma, what's his name . . ."

"Pie Eye."

"Yeah. Pie Eye was released from the hospital. Fat one's already cut loose." Parris waited for a protest, but Moon seemed oddly unperturbed by this news. "District attorney had a long talk with BoBo Harper, owner of the Mountain Man. BoBo refused to file charges. Said his insurance would cover the damages."

This had a funny smell about it. "That was extremely tolerant of him."

Parris squinted blue eyes at his Ute friend. "I been doing some checking on the motorcycle gang. There's rumors of drug peddling, some probable assaults in other jurisdictions. Bottom line is this—these bozos have a reputation for getting very nasty with folks who cross them. I expect they communicated this fact to BoBo. And he decided to leave well enough alone."

The injured man got to his feet slowly, clapped the black Stetson on his head. "Sounds like a challenging law enforcement problem."

"It is. And I am dealing with it."

"You need any help, pardner, don't give me a call."

CHAPTER 23

More Heartburn

At midafternoon, the Mountain Man Bar & Grille was as expected. Cool, dark, dirty. An environment well suited for the growth of bacteria and fungi. Aside from the waitress and a sour smell of stale beer that clung to the dank atmosphere, the cavernous interior seemed to be empty.

Charlene, busy filling the cash register tray with rolls of shiny dimes and quarters, heard the door chime "ding" to announce a potential customer. She looked up from her duties. "Well, I don't hardly believe it—never thought I'd see you here again." She patted her fluffy, butter-yellow hair. "I mean, not that I mind or nothin'."

Charlie Moon, walking slowly to avoid jarring the cracked rib, seated himself backward on a bar stool, looked at an assortment of new furniture that clashed with the tables and chairs that had remained undamaged from the knock-down-drag-out brawl.

Charlene leaned across the bar. "So how you doin'?"

"Better." He rotated to face the waitress.

She cringed. The big Indian had a puffed-up lip; his left eye was swollen almost shut. "Honey, you look just terrible."

He grunted.

"So what brings ya in, sweetie?"

"Must be your pretty smile."

She leaned on the bar, flashed him the gummy grin. "I like a man who can look me right in the eye and lie like there's no tomorrow."

"Okay. It's only partly your smile. Mainly, it's them big blue eyes."

"Now that's more like it." She fluttered the glued-on lashes. "So tell mama what you want." *Just name it, big boy.*

He frowned at the chalked menu behind the bar. "Something to drink."

She pouted. "Is that all?"

"But no lemonade. I'll have an ice-cold Pepsi-Cola."

Even beat-up, he ain't so bad-looking. "The boss is in the kitchen today. Think you could go for a Elkburger and chili?"

Moon grinned; it hurt his mouth. "If you hold a gun to my head."

She giggled. "You are such a scamp."

Manfully, Charlie Moon finished his meal. And wondered whether it would finish him. He paid his bill, gave the waitress a twenty-dollar tip that would be added to the expense account. The tribal investigator fully expected this to be a worthwhile investment. Judging by Charlene's wide-eyed response, he would not be disappointed.

She stuffed the likeness of Andrew Jackson into her starched blouse. "Well, sweetie-pie, you sure know how to please a hard-working woman."

He hesitated.

"Oh, don't be bashful, honey. I know what you want."

"You do?"

"Sure. You want to know what I know about Billy Smoke and what happened on the night he got hisself killed. Who did he talk to while he was in here. Did he drink a lotta booze. Did he have any argymints with the

other customers. Did I see anything strange—anything I
forgot to tell the reg'lar cops. Am I right?"

He nodded.

"So go on and ask your questions."

"Ahh . . . you've already asked 'em pretty well."

In an effort to concentrate, she fixed her gaze on an
unwashed shot glass. "Billy was quiet when he was sober,
but he was the kinda drinker who gets a loose tongue after
a couple a beers under his belt. You know the kind. Laughs
a lot. Back-slapper. Real friendly-Freddy. I remember he
talked to some a the other customers that night."

"Which customers? Remember any names?"

She shook her head. "Few days later, local cops asked
Sheila and me to make a list of ever'body we could remember who was here that night. But we couldn't be sure.
There's a few regulars, but we get a lot of transient business. You know. Truckers. Salesmen. Cowboys on the
bum."

"Sheila?"

Charlene nodded. "Sheila used to be the extra night waitress—she ain't employed here anymore. Married a dental
hygienist, moved to Montana, I think. Or maybe one a them
Dakotas." She shivered. "I don't remember for sure, but it
was some cold place."

"Those bikers I had trouble with—were they here that
night?"

"Those hooligans? Well, they're kinda regulars." Charlene closed her eyes, tried to call up the faded memory.
"Might've been. But I just honestly cain't say." She cracked
the lids. "But that reminds me—one of them uglies came
in late last night. Had a message for you."

"I can't wait to hear it."

"Said they'd be in touch."

Well, that's just dandy. "Guy who left the message—
was it the big one?"

"Nope. It was Yazzoo. He's the one with the eye patch
who bailed out when the fight started. There is about a dozen
of 'em. They fight and drink a lot. Use vulgar language.

Never get a bath unless they fall in the creek. And all of 'em has probably seen the inside of a jailhouse." She shrugged. "Just run a the mill customers."

"Do they deal drugs?"

There was a long silence before she responded. "Mr. Moon, you already used up that twenty-dollar tip."

"Few minutes ago it was Charlie."

"That was then. This is now."

He reached for his wallet. *I'll charge it as an expense.*

She raised a hand to protest. "No. I don't want any more a your money. I got to work here. And there ain't generally no big cowboys or Indians around to protect me."

"Thanks. I guess that's answer enough."

"Well, you guess wrong . . . Charlie." She made a cross-eyed focus on a passing fly, snatched it in her hand. "Fact is, I don't know how those crazies make their money. And I don't want to know. I just want to stay healthy."

At that moment, the owner emerged from the kitchen. BoBo Harper was an even six feet, heavy shoulders, walked like a man used to throwing his weight around. He glanced at the Ute customer. "So you're the guy who tangled with them bikers."

The Ute admitted to this folly.

"You guys sure trashed my place." BoBo turned to the waitress. "The economy around here is in the toilet. Business is lousy."

Having heard this a thousand times, Charlene nodded absently.

He glared at Moon. "You know what the problem is?"

The customer looked at the chili bowl. "Yeah. I think so."

"Sure you do—it's location." BoBo spat on the floor, rubbed a soiled apron across his mouth. "Hardly anybody passes this place anymore. The tourists and truckers, they're mostly taking the bypass. And another thing." He pointed accusingly at the customer. "The damn chain restaurants. Hamburgers, fried chicken, pizza joints—that's where they're all going."

"What you need," the Ute said, "is a business consultant."

"Consultant—you kidding me? I can't even afford Charlene."

"That is a problem." Moon got up. "I'll give it some thought."

Charlie Moon emerged into the warmth of bright sunshine. This should have made him feel better, but the greasy meal had settled in his gut like five pounds of overripe catfish bait. Acidic digestive fluids rose in his esophagus, singed his throat. He turned, looked back at the coonskin-capped figure atop the porch roof. The Mountain Man's chiseled face was also twisted in pain. *He must've eaten his last meal here when Charlene was just a pup.* But it was not a total loss. Charlie Moon admitted that he was no longer hungry, and probably wouldn't be for a day or two. Eating at this place had a way of putting a man off his feed.

He cranked up the F-150, kicked up some gravel until the tires grabbed the asphalt, headed west toward the Columbine. By the time he had ascended onto the high prairie, Charlie Moon had forgotten about his troubles. The blue mountains appeared on the horizon—*his* mountains—and the Ute's spirits soared with the misty peaks. All in all, it had been a good day. *And I'll be on the Columbine in an hour. Home, by the grace of God! Sitting on my front porch, rocking in my rocking chair, sipping a cup of fresh-brewed coffee. Watching time and the river ripple by.*

He passed a Greyhound-sized RV with Alabama plates. Turned on the dashboard radio. Listened to the energetic twang of a bluegrass banjo, the mournful wail of a steel guitar. He mouthed the words: Get outta the way, Old Dan Tucker. *Yes sir, the small troubles of this day are behind me. Nothing bad can touch me now.*

Something touched his boot.

What was that? Probably something rolling around on the floor. Flashlight, maybe.

He drove another quarter mile.

There it was again. Bumping against his ankle. Harder this time.

He slowed. Looked down at it.

It looked back at him.

The driver of the Alabama RV frowned. "My, my," Marvin Pitkin said from the corner of his mouth, "would you look at that!"

Marge Pitkin, his able helpmeet, looked up from her *Reader's Digest* article, "Alaska—America's Last Frontier." "Lookit what?"

He pointed. "That there guy just ran his pickup right off the road." Marvin lifted his foot off the accelerator. "I better go see if he's all right."

"No," his wife snapped. "It's just some drunk. Let him sleep it off."

Ignoring her protests, he pulled over. Marvin listened to the RV's diesel engine idle, studied the pickup parked in the sage. The old truck looked undamaged, and puffs of exhaust from the tail pipe proved that the engine was still running. He could see the driver's head and shoulders. The fellow wasn't moving, and he was sitting straight up. But he wasn't making any signal that he needed help. Maybe Marge was right. *Just some fool drunk run off into the brush. Leave him alone and eventually he'll sober up. Mess with him and maybe I get a beer bottle busted over my head. But I can't just drive off and do nothing at all. Maybe the poor guy has had a stroke or something.* He squinted at the F-150 through his bifocals. "Marge, honey, get a holda that cell phone."

She reached for an enormous carpetbag of a purse. "What're you gonna do?"

"If that fella is hurt or sick or somthin', I'm gonna call for an ambulance." Phone in hand, he got out of the RV and headed across the brushy ground toward the pickup.

Marge stuck her head out of the window. "Marvin, you better stay away from there. I just got a bad feelin' . . ."

"Calm down, honey. I'll be fine." When he was within

a few yards of the vehicle, Marvin thought he heard the
driver say something. Sounded like, *Don't come any closer.*
The good Samaritan paused. "Hey—you okay?"

No response.

"If you want, I can call for some help."

Stony silence from the pickup.

"Mister, are you hurt or something?"

The reply from the F-150 was slow and precise. "Call
Granite Creek PD. Ask the dispatcher to send the chief of
police out here. But don't come any closer."

The prairie wind whipping past Marvin Pitkin's ears pre-
vented him from hearing all the instructions. What he heard
was this: "Call . . . Granite Creek PD . . . dispatcher to send
. . . don't . . . any closer." The tourist backed away a few
steps and wondered, *What in blue blazes is going on here
anyway?*

The dispatcher interrupted a routine report of a citizen's
lost wallet to take the Nine-One-One. Clara Tavishuts identified herself as affiliated with the Granite Creek Police Department, asked how she might be of assistance. She was
swamped by a flood of words from the concerned citizen.
"Yes, sir. I understand. Please identify yourself. And just
in case we're disconnected, please give me your telephone
number." She made neatly printed notes on her duty pad,
jotting down the phrases arriving over the telephone line:

*Ford pickup . . . veered off road . . . engine running . . .
man in truck told me to keep away.*

"Sir, is there any sign of fire or other hazard?"

There was not.

"Does the occupant appear to be injured?"

Not as far as he could tell.

"Is the occupant armed?"

Not as far as he could tell.

"Can you give me the license plate number on the subject's vehicle?"

He could and did.

She wrote it down, asked for and got a fairly precise

location. "Sir, could you stay on site while I dispatch officers to the scene?"

He could and would. But he did not intend to go near that pickup again. Something weird was going on out there.

After Clara had dispatched a pair of GCPD officers to the scene, she forwarded the license number to the state police computer for an ID.

Life in this world is never sweeter than when it is about to end. This being so, Charlie Moon had one overriding goal—to stay alive. The Ute's tactics were simple. He prayed to God for help. And remained extremely still. Even his breathing was barely perceptible. Moreover, he assured himself that if the enormous rattlesnake scooting around on the floorboard struck at him, it would be at a location well below the knee. And even a big diamondback like this one would not be able to penetrate the tough cowhide boots under his denims. Or could it? Moon tried to recall how thick the walls of the Ropers were. Eighth of an inch? Under the grim circumstances, this dimension seemed paper-thin. He sought other avenues of reassurance. Eventually, Mr. *Togoa-vi* would slither under the seat. Maybe even behind it. *Then I'll be outta the door faster than you can say*—

He heard the distant wail of a siren. The tourist—bless his sweet soul—had called the police. Charlie Moon closed his eyes, imagined the chief of police arriving. Scott Parris was a resourceful man who always knew just what to do. When Scott understood the situation, he would call for a helicopter. Bring in that Forest Service expert who handled all kinds of snakes. He could picture the reptile wizard wielding a long pole, a loop of transparent nylon cord on the end—snagging the snake, yanking it from the cab.

Moon heard the squad car slow to a stop, fat tires crunching on roadside gravel, two car doors opening, then slamming. Scott had brought someone with him. *Thank you, God.* Things were looking up.

The Ute opened his eyes. Looked down. Supported by

a massive, muscular body, the rattler's head floated over the edge of the seat. Beady eyes locked with Moon's, a forked tongue flicked around, scenting his fear. In a moment, the serpent was on the seat beside him, head poised over his crotch. *Oh, God. Things can't get any worse than this.* The optimist heard a pair of familiar voices. Officer Knox. Officer Slocum.

Things can always get worse.

Despite the impediment of an artificial leg, Eddie "Rocks" Knox was two paces ahead of his chubby sidekick. "Hey, Piggy—that looks like Charlie Moon's old bucket a bolts."

"And that looks like Charlie's black hat," Officer Slocum said. "Wonder what's happened to him now? Maybe some of them bikers' tough buddies has caught up with him—shot him dead."

"Nah. It'll be a blowout on a front tire," Knox opined. "Or maybe his steering column busted."

Slocum found a flaw in this line of reasoning. "Then why's he still in the truck?"

"Could be he's broke his back. Or he's impaled on the steering column." The morbid possibilities were endless. This was what made police work so interesting. Knox snickered. "Or maybe he's parked out there with a sportin' woman."

The plump officer thought this doubtful, and said so.

As they came near the pickup, Knox called out. "Hey, Charlie—what'n hell you doin' out here in the sagebrush?"

The officers heard an unintelligible response from the Ute.

"He's not moving," Slocum said. "Can't even turn his head. I expect he's paralyzed or something."

"He sounds drunk to me," Knox said this with an old-maidish air of disapproval. "Imagine. After all these years of sobriety, ol' Charlie's back on the bottle." He leaned to look in the open window at the driver. "What's wrong with—"

"Get back." Moon said this almost without moving his lips.

Now 'Rocks' Knox was not a man to take orders. Not from his own chief of police. Not from the president of these fifty United States. Certainly not from some oversized Ute Indian who wasn't even a real cop anymore. He leaned over to get a better look inside the pickup. "Charlie, we come all the way out here to—" His normally pink face turned the color of dirty chalk. Officer Knox, who had lost his leg in a face-to-face shoot-out with a Mexican *bandito,* had never once backed down. Until now. He was two yards away from the pickup in one eighth of a second.

Officer Slocum stuttered. "Wha-wha-what is it, Rocks?"

The one-legged man was, for a moment, speechless. He sucked in a deep breath, pointed at the pickup. "Charlie— he's got a great big rattlesnake in his lap."

Slocum stared in incomprehension. "Why?"

"Damned if I know, Piggy. Maybe it's some kinda pet."

They heard Moon again, still speaking softly. "Stay away. And don't make any loud noises."

Knox frowned at the side of the Ute's head. "You want us just to stand here?"

"Go back to your car. Call Scott. Tell him to bring that snake handler who works for the Forest Service."

Both officers understood. They were not considered competent to handle the situation.

Knox set his jaw. "We don't need no fancy snake handler. We'll take care of this."

"Eddie," Moon said in monotone, "if you cause this snake to bite me, I won't die right away. And before I give up the ghost, I will get out of this truck, yank your wooden leg off and beat you to death with it." *It will be the last useful thing I do in this world.*

"Because you are not yourself, I am going to overlook that remark." Eddie Knox said this with an expression of saintly patience. "Now you just sit still—and be real quiet. Me and Piggy, we will rectify this situation."

"I give up," Moon muttered. "Just shoot me."

Officer Slocum offered the view that while suicide might seem to be an easy way out for the Ute, shooting him would not be strictly legal.

Knox addressed his partner with a weary shake of his head. "Charlie is just joking, Piggy. He don't actually want us to shoot him."

Moon looked straight ahead. *I'm good as dead.*

Eddie Knox summoned Slocum to his side. "I figgered out a plan."

The victim with the rattlesnake draped across his thighs tried not to listen.

"What we'll do is this. We move up to the window, side by side. I'll have my sidearm ready. You sorta wave your hand a bit, get that ol' snake's attention. When he raises his head to see what's a-goin' on, I'll shoot him right betwixt the eyes."

Piggy Slocum nodded. "Yeah. That ought to work."

Moon looked to the heavens.

The police officers moved closer.

Piggy waved hopefully to the reptile.

Eddie 'Rocks' Knox aimed his .357 Magnum revolver in the general direction of the snake. Which was in the general direction of Charlie Moon's crotch.

It seemed to the team of Knox and Slocum that the plan was going well. The diamondback did raise his triangular head, focus his beady eyes on the visitors. Wanting a scent, the reptile flicked the forked tongue at this odd pair of human bipeds.

Though it was unnecessary with a double-action revolver, Officer Knox cocked the hammer. He did this for dramatic effect.

Piggy Slocum wagged his trembling hand. "Here, Mr. Snakey-Snakey."

Knox closed one eye, sighted down the barrel. "Now hold still. Okay . . . gotcha."

The potential victim knew the score. *The best that can happen is I get my leg shot off and bleed to death. Well to hell with that!* Moon snatched the deadly viper, flung it out the window.

There were shrill squeals and terrified yelps from the startled policemen. Knox's revolver discharged, shattering the F-150 steering wheel into shards. Piggy was running backward at a full four miles per hour, and accomplishing this feat with a grace admirable in one so heavy. Knox stumbled, landed on his back, became disconnected from his artificial leg. The revolver discharged again—puncturing the truck's gas tank. Moon exited the pickup by the passenger-side door, keeping his head low to minimize the chance of stopping the next round from Knox's hand-cannon.

The five-foot rattlesnake departed in a huff, never again to be seen by the eye of mortal man.

"Barroom, brawls. Now a rattlesnake in your lap." The chief of police shook his head. "Charlie, you do like to live on the edge."

The Ute held his silence.

Scott Parris shoved a padded chair toward his friend. "Why don't you have a seat."

Moon continued his pacing. "Can't afford to sit down." He rolled his hands into fists. "Who knows when one of your fine police officers will bust in here, try to shoot a chigger off my ear."

The former Chicago beat officer tried hard not to grin. "Eddie Knox did make a poor judgment call. But he was trying to help you out of a bad situation. And the department will pay for the repairs on your pickup."

"Next time I see Knox, I'm going to break his *good* leg. Put him out of action permanently. It'll be a service to the community."

"I guess this would be a bad time to tell you that Officer Knox intends to file a complaint against you."

Moon paused in his pacing, looked blankly at his friend. "What did you say?"

"He intends to charge you with reckless endangerment."

"Scott, I've had a pretty tense afternoon—do not kid around with me."

"It's no joke. He claims you purposely threw a venomous reptile at him." Parris cleared his throat. "With malicious intent."

Moon continued to stare at the chief of police. "You know, now that you mention it, I do feel some malicious intent. Take me to Knox and I will provide him with some hard evidence."

Parris chuckled. "I've never seen you quite so worked up."

The Ute clenched and unclenched his hands. "I should've tied that rattlesnake around his neck."

"You can do that later. Right now, we got more important issues to be concerned about. Like how did that snake get into your pickup."

Moon closed his eyes. Took a deep breath. Exhaled.

Parris pressed on. "I found a grass sack behind the seat. It'd been tied, but apparently not very tight. Somebody intended for the snake to get free."

Moon nodded. "Somebody who don't send me Christmas presents."

"I had a chat with that waitress at the Mountain Man. Charlene says one of those biker thugs left a threatening message for you."

"Wasn't exactly a threat. Just said his bunch would be in touch with me."

"Right. And I bet they intend to give you some sort of award for knocking the teeth out of the fat guy's head, and almost killing the other one."

"What do you want me to do?"

"Please sit down."

Moon sat.

Parris leaned forward, tapped his finger on the Ute's knee. "Whether we can ever prove it or not, it's a sure thing—while you were in the Mountain Man, one of those crazy bikers put that rattlesnake in your pickup. I figure it was the fat one. Half-Ton."

At the mention of the man who had bear-hugged him almost to death, Moon felt a sharp twinge of pain in his side. "You think he's mad enough at me to do a mean thing like that?"

Scott Parris grinned at his best friend. "You do have a way of getting on a man's nerves."

With considerable attention to his bandaged ribs, the Ute eased himself up from the chair. "I got some business to attend to."

"Charlie, I know you'd like to have another go at them bikers. But take some advice from your best friend and—"

"This isn't about the snake. Or the bikers." The Ute was headed for the door. "I got some work to do for the senator."

CHAPTER 24

Clean Sweep

The long, cold night—having overstayed its allotted time—was withdrawing in a huff, dragging its dark, dusty cloak over the arid highlands. The western horizon was a smear of deep purple, rippled with streaks of greenish yellow. To the east was the promise of a new day—a halo of silver shimmered over the shark-tooth peaks of the Misery Range.

Charlie Moon was parked at the BoxCar airstrip in the Expedition, listening to the early morning *Farm and Ranch Report* on AM radio. He watched a dark speck appear over the mountains, turned the radio off.

Nine minutes later, dawn's perfect silence was shattered by a King Air 200's twin turboprops.

The tribal investigator watched the sleek aircraft descend at a seemingly precipitous angle, glide along barely above the asphalt runway, take a slight bounce, sit down with a brief shriek of rubber. The twin-engine airplane taxied to a roaring halt near the senator's hangar. Almost immediately the engines were cut; a hatch dropped to make a stairway. Two figures emerged down the suspended steps. They wore crisply pressed gray suits, white shirts, blue ties, polished black oxfords. They were followed by a second pair representing the same firm; these were clad in dark blue coveralls.

Moving more deliberately, the workers were carrying stainless steel cases. The pilot, warm in a wool-lined bomber jacket, emerged to tie down the plane.

The tribal investigator, who had gotten out of his car, recognized one of the suits.

FBI Special Agent Stanley Newman strode forward, stuck out his hand. "Hi, Charlie. Wow, look at your mug! I heard you've been in a fight with a couple of badasses—want to do some bragging?"

"You don't want to hear about it." Moon shook the strong hand, smiled at the familiar face, which was always pinched by some nameless inner anxiety. Newman introduced the Ute to Special Agent Michael Yancey, who insisted that Moon "call me Mike." Stiffly handsome, graying at the temples, the senior member of the FBI team was one of those hardy souls who—having invested all of his considerable confidence in himself—had not a nickel's worth left over to squander on his fellows. Yancey gave the tall Ute a brief sizing-up. *Friendly. Wants to be helpful. Not too bright.* Having gotten Moon "calibrated," he turned his attention to the technicians, who were opening the steel cases to inspect the equipment secured inside. "Cold," Yancey said, rubbing his palms together. Coming from the self-assured man, this needless observation carried the weight of an oracle.

Moon looked toward the clearing sky with a rancher's keen eye for weather. "Another couple of weeks, we'll have considerable snow on the peaks."

Stan Newman was blowing warm breath into his cupped hands. The wiry man—who had been raised in Newark—looked around the vast openness as if he doubted they had landed at the right airstrip. Like maybe this was one of Charlie Moon's pranks. "So where's the senator's home?"

The Ute pointed to the south. "Just over that little rise." *In the man-made oasis.*

The techs, having satisfied themselves that their electronic gear was in good working order, waited several paces away from the Ute and the suits. As if not to contaminate themselves by unnecessary contact with those who paid no heed to Ohm's Law—and had never encountered Maxwell's elegant electromagnetic equations.

Charlie Moon nodded to indicate a Chevrolet Suburban, the designated transportation for airport visitors who arrived when the senator was not present to greet them personally. "You can drive that to the BoxCar headquarters. I'll show you the way." He was heading toward the Expedition when Newman hurried to fall in step beside him. "If you don't mind, I'll hitch a ride with you."

"I'll be glad for the company." He was cranking the engine when the federal agent, cold hands jammed deep into his suit coat pockets, gave the Ute a searching look. "So where's all the cowboys?"

"This isn't a working ranch. Senator doesn't need that many employees."

"Anybody else here besides you?"

"Not a soul. For today, I'm the BoxCar's sole caretaker." The Ute watched the rearview mirror while the techs loaded their gear into the Suburban. "Davidson and his personal assistant boarded his Gulfstream last night, headed for Washington. Before he left, Davidson managed to get everyone off the ranch for several days. Nephew's off to Italy, ranch manager's warming himself on a sandy beach in Costa Rica."

"Lucky devils." Newman stared at the heater button, wished Moon would switch it on. "I hope all the doors are unlocked—even with the senator's signed request to check out his real estate for electronic listening devices, we don't intend to pick any locks."

Moon jangled a large ring of keys.

A sly smile cut the flat space between Stan Newman's beak nose and square chin. "So how come Patch Davidson trusts a slippery guy like you around his silverware?"

"It's one of life's great mysteries, Stan—everybody trusts me."

"Everybody except me, Chucky."

"You were always an exceptional man."

The Suburban, with Special Agent Mike Yancey at the wheel, was belching a stutter of gray puffs from the exhaust pipe. It made a sudden leap forward, stalled, then lurched again.

Moon pulled away from the airstrip.

Newman lost the smile. "What I don't get is why're you going to all this trouble for the senator? You're a happy-go-lucky rancher now. You oughta be out on the range, singin' songs to your cows."

"I have cowboys in my employ who are paid sing to the animals. Besides, me and Patch are neighbors. I'm just being neighborly. And it cuts both ways. If I should come down sick, Patch'd run the combine over my wheat fields. Help raise a barn. Pluck chickens."

"Horse hockey. I bet there's some money in it for you."

"I will draw a modest few dollars for my services."

"Hah—I knew it." The special agent's eyes narrowed. "I hear you're poking around in that assault on the senator."

"More to the point, in the murder of Billy Smoke. Who happens to be an enrolled member of my tribe. If the FBI had arrested his killer, I would not have been asked to look into the matter."

"Don't mess with me, Charlie. I ain't in the mood."

"Haven't had your breakfast?"

"Not even a cuppa coffee."

"When we get to the big house, I'll take care of that."

"Don't change the subject—how'd you get so close to Senator Davidson?"

"Hey, you're the FBI. Given enough time and resources, you'll figure it out."

"Given enough time and a hammer, I'll nail you to the barn door for some petty misdemeanor."

"Like what?"

"Like annoying an agent of the federal government. Now tell me how you got to be the senator's security advisor."

Moon bounced the Expedition over a pothole. "You settle for a hint?"

"Forget hints—you tell me straight out in plain English."

"You won't like it."

"Try me."

"Okay, here goes. For reasons I cannot fathom, the senator doesn't like you federal cops. On the other hand, he is very fond of me. I am almost like a son to him."

The FBI agent snorted. "I don't care if Davidson adopts you—you better not step over the line. If you do, I'll . . ." His words trailed off.

"You getting cold feet?" Moon switched on the heater.

Newman stuck his shoes close to the floor vent. "Only thing worse than a former Indian traffic cop is a smart-ass Indian rancher with a state P.I. license to go snooping."

"You forgot something."

"Oh, yeah—the local chief of police is your best buddy."

"Well, that too. But I also have a very influential next-door neighbor. Who is a senior member of the Senate Judiciary Committee. Which oversees the Justice Department. Which includes the FBI."

"Please—don't remind me." Newman exhaled his martyr's sigh. *Twelve more years to retirement.*

"Now I have a question for you."

"About what?"

"It's about who—Agent Michael Yancey."

"What do you want to know about him?" *Like I'd tell you squat.*

"What brings the chief of the FBI's crack counterespionage team out on a routine security check?"

Stanley Newman's jaw dropped. He stared at the driver. "How the hell did you know Yancey was . . ."

Moon grinned. "You just told me."

"Charlie, that ain't funny." The federal agent clenched his jaw. "You shouldn't a done that. You *know* how that pisses me off."

"Can't help it, Stan—it's sort of a reflex action." Moon pulled to a stop under the spindly branches of a Russian olive. They had arrived at the BoxCar headquarters.

Newman fumbled with the door latch. "Look—don't try

none of your nonsense on Agent Yancey. He ain't a nice guy like me."

The Ute watched the Suburban lurch to a stop behind his Expedition. "I'll try to remember that."

Special Agent Michael Yancey stood with arms folded across his chest. He glared at his silent audience, spitting out words like the head of a commando team about to scale the cliff and take out the long-range German naval guns that would otherwise surely sink half the Allied invasion fleet in the icy channel waters. "Okay, here's the way it works. Me and the technicians go in and get the job done. Agent Newman, you and Mr. Moon wait outside. I should think you fellows will find something to talk about." He shot an accusing look at Newman. "I understand you two are old buddies."

Charlie Moon thought he would give Stan Newman an opportunity to set the man straight on the rules of the game.

Newman started to open his mouth, thought better of it. *I'll let Charlie tell him.*

The Ute told him. "I go in with you."

"Sorry," Yancey said crisply. "It's against established procedure. The techniques we use in a sweep like this are highly sensitive. Even Agent Newman doesn't have the need to know—"

"I don't think you understand," Moon said. "The senator was very clear about this. No one goes into his house without the designated escort—which is me."

The senior agent stared coldly at the Ute. "That is simply unacceptable."

Moon presented a friendly smile to the uptight fed. "If it was up to me, Agent Yancey, you folks could have free run of the place. But it's not my call. I've agreed to represent the senator's position. And his interests."

"Look," Newman said to his superior. "He's right. That was the senator's condition—Charlie has to observe what goes on inside."

"I agreed to no such arrangement," Yancey snapped at

Newman. "Why didn't someone tell me about this?"

Moon concealed his enjoyment of the small drama. *Look out, Mr. Yancey. Stan is getting his bulldog-about-to-bite-a-pork-chop look.*

Newman's response was delivered in a dull, dangerous monotone. "It was in the letter I faxed you last week." *Read your mail, you obnoxious sonofabitch.*

"I recall no such communication." Yancey turned his attention to the amiable Ute. "Our work here must be done in private. Or not at all."

"I'm sorry for the misunderstanding." Moon nodded toward the airstrip. "Might as well head back to your airplane."

Yancey turned toward the techs, as if to issue such an order.

Newman made a face. "I'm tired of flying." *And I'm tired of trying to work with fashion-plate jerks who don't know what the job is before they fly halfway across the country.* "If you don't mind, Charlie, I'll be your guest till I can get someone to come and pick me up."

"No need for that. I'll singe a couple slabs of steak and fry a half dozen eggs. After we've had our breakfast, I'll be glad to run you down to Durango."

Michael Yancey realized that he had made a gamble and lost. But as was his habit, he pushed this knowledge so far into the bottom of his unconscious as to be oblivious to the truth. He assured himself that he was a sane, reasonable man who had the misfortune to be surrounded by bumbling incompetents. This was merely a sorry situation that needed expert managing. The Indian seemed easygoing, but he was stubborn as a mule. Such rustics must be manipulated with skill and cunning. He turned to face the tall Ute. "As you said, Mr. Moon, this is merely a misunderstanding. A bureaucratic mix-up. A problem in communications." *Now a touch of flattery.* "As fellow professionals, it is up to us to find a way to work around it. Here's how I see it. Because you are an official member of the senator's security staff, I propose that you escort us into the house."

Moon responded with a thoughtful nod. "Yeah. That sounds like a workable idea."

Newman rolled his eyes.

Agent Yancey managed not to notice this hint of insubordination. "You must realize, of course, that some of our instrumentation and investigative techniques are quite sensitive."

"No problem," Moon said. "I promise not to look at any of your dials and meters."

Having regained control of a deteriorating situation, Yancey beamed a fatherly smile at the Ute. "Here's how we'll play it. You take us in, but address any remarks only to Special Agent Newman. Do not mention him by name—the bad guys may be listening. Talk about ranching. The weather. Baseball. Anything except what we are here for. Do you understand?"

Moon nodded. *He thinks I'm an idiot.*

Yancey continued: "The techs and I will maintain a strict silence while we're inside. When our work is completed, we will leave by the front entrance. You and Agent Newman will follow immediately." He stared intently at the silent man. "You got that?"

Moon appeared to be expending a great effort to concentrate on the instructions. "Well . . . I think so." He glanced at Newman with a hopeful expression. "If I forget anything, I'll ask Stan what to do. Not out loud, of course—I'll whisper to him."

This arrow barbed with sarcasm sailed past Yancey without pricking his skin. "Right. Agent Newman knows the drill. Just follow his lead."

After a preliminary sweep of the BoxCar headquarters, the techs got down to the serious business of checking the conference room, that inner sanctum where the senator presided over confidential gatherings. Charlie Moon stood just outside with Stanley Newman, watching the coveralled pair—supervised by gestures and handwritten notes from Agent Yancey. Light fixtures and electrical receptacles were disassembled. Panels were unscrewed from a television set, a computer, a microwave oven. Pictures and certificates were removed from frames. And, of course, the telephones were thoroughly examined. Despite his lighthearted promise to take no notice of the gadgetry, the Ute was fascinated by one of the portable instruments. A surreptitious glance at the front panel revealed that the device was a Hallmark 101 Spectrum Analyzer, one-hundred kHz to ten GHz. There was a long, narrow black screen upon which a bright green trace crawled like a skinny worm slithering across a field of invisible pebbles. At a warning look from Agent Yancey, the Ute averted his eyes from the instrument.

Newman followed Moon into the spacious BoxCar headquarters kitchen, where the "designated escort" found a can of Maxwell House and a pot. While the coffee perked, the tribal investigator searched a vast cupboard until he discovered a box of animal cookies.

The men retired to the dining room, seated themselves at an immaculate mahogany table.

"Well," Moon said to the wall, "I hear that beef prices are up seven cents a pound."

Newman, who was pouring cream into his coffee, grunted.

The Ute rancher continued his monologue. "Fine weather we've been having."

The FBI agent scowled at his cup.

Moon passed the cookie box across the table. "I figure this'll be a seriously cold winter. And a long one." He smiled at his comrade. "That's the kind we always have."

This brought no response from the grumpy fed.

"Hey, how about them Cubs?"

Newman frowned at the animal cookie. "He's a real horse's ass."

Moon assumed a quizzical expression. "To whom do you refer?"

"You know damn well." He stuck his paw into the cookie box, scooped out a herd of herbivores.

"Well, Archibald, seeing as there are only two of us

here—all alone in the house—I don't see why you shouldn't say his name out loud."

Newman stuffed a dozen animal pastries into his mouth. "Mawk Hawrses Awss Gbwancy."

"Yes," Moon said. "I hear what you're saying."

Two pots of coffee later, when the animal cookies had been decimated by the pair of voracious carnivores, Agent Yancey showed his aristocratic face at the dining room archway. Stared for a moment at the coffee cups, then at the cookie box—with a yearning, hungry look.

As the man did not officially exist, Charlie Moon pointedly ignored him.

Stanley Newman did likewise.

"Hssst!"

The Ute cocked his ear. "Archibald, did you hear something?"

"Yeah," Newman said with a glance toward the kitchen. "Must've been the teapot."

Yancey was indeed coming to a boil. He jerked his head in a gesture that made it clear the party was over.

Outside, Special Agent Mike Yancey assumed his rightful place. He considered dressing Agent Newman down for unprofessional conduct, thought better of it. The man from New Jersey looked to be highly annoyed—even a bit dangerous. *Best leave the feisty little bastard alone. He might go postal on me.* A confidential written evaluation of his behavior would be the more prudent course of action. The senior agent addressed the Ute. "I appreciate your cooperation with our investigation."

"You're welcome. So what did you find?"

"You'll have to wait for an official report."

"Me, I don't mind waiting till kingdom come." Moon smiled. "But Patch Davidson, he's an impatient sort of fellow."

Michael Yancey weighed his options. "You may inform the senator that we have uncovered no evidence of electronic listening devices in his home." The senior agent turned his back on the tribal investigator, stalked away toward the Suburban.

Moon approached the pair of technicians, neither of whom had uttered a word since their arrival at the airstrip. "You found nothing at all?"

The techs looked toward Yancey's back.

The tribal investigator pressed on. "I appreciate Agent Yancey's helpful statement. It's always nice to know what the boss thinks. But Senator Davidson is the sort of man who'll want to hear from the people actually doing the work. So what do you say—you find a trace of anything?"

The older technician, a skinny man, shrugged. The plump blond woman licked at thin lips, then said, "We found no evidence of surreptitious listening devices."

"That's what Agent Yancey already told me. So how sure are you that the senator's house isn't bugged?"

She looked the tall man straight in the eye. "Absence of evidence is not evidence of absence. Particularly when it comes to detecting hidden electronic devices."

CHAPTER 25

The Entrepreneur

Charlie Moon navigated his recently repaired pickup along Staples Street past a series of business establishments separated by vacant, weed-choked lots. The tribal investigator parked the F-150 in front of a shotgun structure that was squeezed between Fagan's Diesel Engine Repair and Emogene's Florist. The cinder block building, gray and naked under a film of peeling blue paint, was partially concealed by a bowed-over elm whose dead leaves rattled in the dry breeze. He read the words painted on the display window.

PEPPER'S MOBILITY CENTER
Authorized GroundHog Dealer
Bruno Lifts • Carriers
Parts • Sales • Service
In-Home Service Our Specialty
All Major Credit Cards Accepted

On a dusty display stage behind the window, there were fold-up wheelchairs, adjustable aluminum crutches, stainless steel leg braces, fiberglass neck immobilizers, and a host of other products designed to enable the disabled. The centerpiece was a glistening Electric GroundHog. Aside from the color—Sunrise Red—this model appeared to be identical to the senator's scooter.

On the door of the business establishment, there was a small, hand-lettered sign.

Sales Representatives Welcome by Appointment Only
Disobeyers of This Dictum Will Be Dismembered

Moon pushed the door open, heard an electric bell jangle somewhere in the rear of the store. He waited. Presently, the Ute's patience was rewarded.

A person opened a door marked SHOP EMPLOYEES ONLY and emerged from the semidarkness. The figure—clad in khaki shirt and pants and shod in polished black leather boots—leaned on a twisted hickory cane. The brown hair was clipped short, the shoulders broad and muscular, the legs thin and spindly—one grotesquely twisted. A label above a shirt pocket identified the inhabitant of the garment as one BOBBIE PEPPER.

Charlie Moon removed his hat. "Hi. You must be the boss."

The voice was feminine. "I'm the owner. I'm usually here just two days a week, but my manager's out with a kidney stone."

"I'm sorry to hear that, Ms. Pepper—"

"*Professor* Pepper, if you please." She tossed her head back and glared at him. "I teach freshman chemistry at Rocky Mountain Polytechnic."

He took a step backward. "No kidding—you're the famous Dr. Pepper?"

She groaned. "I've only heard that one about a million times."

"Sorry, couldn't help myself." He flashed a smile. "But I want you to know that I have a great respect for our nation's educators."

"Educator—that's a laugh." She snorted. "My function is that of gatekeeper. I'm charged with preventing the bone lazy and mentally challenged from cluttering the hallowed halls of academia. Every single one of those snotty-nosed little sods either makes the grade in my class or it's 'Hit the road Jack.' " The grin turned cheerfully malicious. "But despite my best efforts, somewhat more than half of the mush-heads manage to survive."

"It is always gratifying to meet a whip-cracker who enjoys her work."

She looked the tall man up and down. "You seem sound of limb. What brings such a robust specimen to a business enterprise that caters to the maimed and crippled?"

He was about to respond when she cut him off.

"You must be shopping for somebody else." She approached in a painful hip-wrenching gait.

"I'm not exactly a customer."

The proprietor scowled. "Well, if you're exactly a peddler, I do hope you'll stay for a late lunch. I had me a smart-ass insurance salesman for breakfast this morning, and I have not had time to digest his bones and toenails."

"A free meal is hard to turn down, but time is short and I've got other people to annoy before the sun sets." Moon looked around the store. Boxes of Ace bandages and digital blood-pressure monitors were stacked on an unpainted pine shelf.

The embittered woman followed his gaze with an air of utter despair. "Yes, it's a sure-enough dump. Two years come September—right after the previous owner got his ticket punched—I picked this joint up for two bits. Which was about twenty-four cents too much." She shot him an annoyed look. "Who'n hell *are* you?"

He presented his tribal ID.

The professor squinted at the photograph on the laminated card. "An Indian cop." She made a snorting sound. "Am I supposed to guess why you're here?"

"One of my tribesman has been killed."

"Sad news. But what does it have to do with the price of boiled eggs?"

"Well—"

"If one of your braves got himself snuffed, why aren't

you sniffing around on the reservation for the culprit?"

Moon seemed embarrassed by this question. "We already got way too many Utes in our lockup. So the tribal chairman, he told me to pin *this* murder on a white."

"I have not killed me an Indian for a month of Sundays." A tic of a smile jerked at the edge of her lip. "But right at the moment, I am feeling this strong urge to correct that lapse."

"Thanks for the warning."

Bobbie Pepper eased herself down on a wooden bench, absently tapped the cane against a steel brace under her pant leg. "What's on your mind, beanpole—you really here about some dead Indian?"

"Truth is, I'm interested in that fancy electric scooter in your window."

She looked toward the display. "You thinking about buying a GroundHog?"

"It has crossed my mind."

"Who's the machine for?"

"Elderly friend."

"I could get you a less expensive unit that'll work just as well."

"Nope." The Ute set his jaw. "Got my heart set on a GroundHog."

"Why?"

"It's the best electric scooter on the market."

"What makes you think that?"

"The power of advertising. And the fact that Senator Davidson bought one."

"Well, of course he did," she snapped. "I sold it to him. What I don't understand is why you'd want to squander your money. The G-H is overpriced and it has too damn many useless gadgets. On top of that, it's not made in the good old U.S. of A."

Moon raised his hands protectively. "Whoa, now—ease up! This red-hot sales pitch is too much for a simple country boy. First thing I know, you'll have sold me three or four GroundHogs."

Big smart aleck. She scratched at a wasted leg. "Don't ever say I didn't try to save you some cash money."

"Sign on the window says in-home servicing is your specialty."

"It is highly gratifying to know you can read."

This is a sure-enough mean woman. "Would the senator have his scooter brought here for a tune-up—or would you send someone out to the BoxCar?"

"Most of the repairs are done here. On those occasions when it is not convenient for the customer to return a malfunctioning product to our shop, my manager will go to the client's home and do the repairs. I also make a few service calls myself—for special customers." She smiled, as if at a private joke, then cocked the close-cropped head. "What else do you want to know?"

Moon stared past the rough-hewn woman at the window display. "I'd like to know why the senator purchased that particular make and model. What are the special features. How much it cost him. What does the warranty cover. How many of these things do you sell in a year. And just about anything else you can tell me about the GroundHog."

"What is it, you big totem pole—d'you think I've got nothing better to do than sit around all day and spill my guts to flippant Indian coppers?"

He put the black Stetson on his head. "Just say goodbye and I'll be gone."

She sighed. "Sit down. This'll take me a while, and looking up at you makes my neck ache."

He seated himself beside Professor Pepper.

The lonely woman was pleased to have such interesting company. As the minutes drifted by, she talked and talked and talked.

The tribal investigator listened. And considered. Weighed this unlikely possibility against that undeniable fact. Thought maybe he was onto something.

Charlie Moon closed the door of Pepper's Mobility Center behind him, buttoned his jacket against the stiff breeze that was flinging sand and trash along the narrow street. Holding onto the brim of his hat, he opened the F-150's door, slipped behind the brand-new steering wheel. The cab of his old pickup was not quite as empty as when he'd left it.

This time the uninvited occupant was not a rattlesnake.

But the tough-looking fellow wore a sour scowl under his nose and a shoulder holster under his left armpit. Snuggled in the leather receptacle was a .38-caliber Smith & Wesson revolver that was not an ornament.

The Ute did not start the engine. "I should've locked the doors."

A dry chuckle. "That wouldn't have kept me out."

"How'd you know I was in the neighborhood?"

"It's my business to know."

"If you wanted to see me, you could've come inside the store."

"No way." The chief of police aimed a double-barreled high-caliber glare at the business establishment. "Every time I bump into Professor Pepper, she pisses all over me about how GCPD has never arrested the hit-and-run that crippled her up. Hell, Charlie, it happened way before my time."

"Guess that'd be a hard thing for her to forget."

"The department hasn't forgot about it either—it's still an open case. But enough about ancient history, let's get to the right now. What're you doing here?"

"Checking out the merchandise."

"For what purpose?"

"Well, you know how it goes. You do something that you know is right. But later on, you feel kinda bad about it. Like you should make amends."

"Charlie, what on earth are you talking about?"

"A few days after I rip Eddie Knox's good leg off at the hip, I'll probably start feeling a little bit sorry for him. Next thing you know, I'll want to do something to make amends. Like buy him a wheelchair."

"You got to learn to forgive and forget." Parris turned to study his friend's dark profile. "Knox has cooled off quite a lot since you pitched that big rattler around his neck."

"That why you're squatted in my pickup, to let me know your employee won't be filing charges against me?"

"I told Knox if he gave you any trouble, you'd stake him out to a hill of fire ants and I'd pour an inexpensive brand of honey all over his pitiful, naked, little one-legged carcass. And while the ants nibbled at his tender parts, me'n my savage friend would dance around the campfire and sing sad old cowboy songs."

The Ute nodded. "Works for me."

"I also consulted with the district attorney. Swore on a stack of comic books that when Charlie Moon threw that snake out of his pickup he did not intend any harm to Officer Knox."

"Well there's a bald-faced lie if I ever heard one."

"I know it, and so does the DA. But she gave me her solemn word—no charges that Officer Knox might file against Mr. Charles Moon in connection with the snake incident will be acted upon by her office."

"Thanks, pardner."

"Now tell me the truth, Charlie—why're you here?"

Good question. "Patch Davidson bought his electric scooter from Pepper's Mobility Center."

"And?"

"Well, it's kinda hard to explain."

"You don't think I could understand the intricate workings of your remarkable mind?"

"Them's your words, pardner, not mine."

"Damn. Life just isn't fair. You're blessed with these amazing powers of detection and deduction, and me, I got nothing to trade on but my charming personality, incredible good looks, and natural modesty." Parris bowed his head. "But now that you have dropped me a broad hint, it's all so clear. The criminal's motive is profit—filthy lucre!"

"It is?"

"Sure. Bobbie Pepper crippled the senator so she could sell him a ten-thousand-dollar electric scooter." He looked up with a deeply sad expression. "These sneaky, low-down, two-bit chemistry professors-turned-shopkeepers. All they care about is a greenback dollar—is there nothing they'll stop at?"

Moon frowned at the sandblasted windshield. "Go right ahead, poke fun at your best friend in the whole world."

"I'd sure like to if I had the time, but other duties call." Scott Parris got out of the pickup, raised his hand. A Granite Creek PD black-and-white emerged from a weed-choked alley. The sleek, low-slung Chevrolet whisked the chief of police away.

The Business Consultant

Charlene hurried into the kitchen, jerked her head at the owner-manager-cook of the Mountain Man Bar & Grille. "BoBo, a customer wants to talk to you."

He noted that she had that wild look in her eye. A cigarette hung in his mouth; it bobbled as he spoke, dropping ashes into a cast-iron pot filled with pinto beans. "It one of them crazy bikers?"

The waitress shook her head.

Relieved, BoBo Harper wiped his big hands on a greasy apron. "This customer got a name?"

"It's Mr. Moon."

"That big Indian?" More gray snow fell into the bean pot.

The waitress watched the tobacco ash dissolve in the thick brown broth. "He looks like he's got somethin' on his mind."

BoBo snorted, banged through the swinging door into the restaurant.

Charlie Moon was seated at a table, nursing a cup of heavily sugared coffee. He invited the owner of the establishment to have a seat.

BoBo dropped his butt into the wooden chair with a heavy thump. "So what's your problem?"

The Ute pushed the cup aside. "Last time I was here,

you were complaining about how bad business was."

The greasy man grinned. "Yeah, and you said I should talk to one a them . . ." He fumbled for the words, couldn't find them.

"Business consultant."

"Yeah. One a them." The grin cracked, broke into a sneer. "You found me one that'll work for nothin'?"

Moon nodded. "Me."

"You? What'n hell do *you* know about running a business?"

"I know you've got a big problem, Mr. Harper. But you're too close to the business to see it."

"No, I ain't. It's the bad location, and the new bypass—"

"Ever since I ate here, I been sick to my stomach."

The white man's mouth opened to protest this harsh criticism.

Moon raised a hand to silence him. "I'm going to have my say, then you can have yours." He inhaled a whiff of the stale air. "I don't generally go around bad-mouthing other people's cooking, but the swill you serve here is a disgrace to the great state of Colorado. And your dining room is almost as dirty as your men's room."

"Now you wait just a damn minute—"

"I've got a hound dog that will eat old boots and watermelon rinds. Even chunks of coal. But he'd never set a paw in this place. So it's no wonder you can't draw any local customers except crazies and drunks and dope-pushers."

The big man sucked in a breath, puffed out his chest. "I don't much like your tone."

"I don't much like your chili. Your lemonade tastes like bleach. And from what I've heard, you can't even fry a decent piece of beef."

BoBo's big hands rolled into knotty fists. "I don't have to take this crap. You don't like what I cook, you can eat someplace else."

Charlie Moon shook his head. "Can't let you off that easy."

The big-shouldered man got up, pulled off the stained apron. "So make your move."

The Ute got to his feet, made a nod to the waitress. "Charlene, call nine-one-one. Tell 'em you'll be needing an ambulance."

"Yes sir." She picked up the telephone, punched at the buttons.

"Tell 'em to bring some splints," Moon added. "And a couple pints of blood."

BoBo remembered his waitress's account of the massive bloody-faced biker picking up his teeth off the floor. "Charlene, put that damn phone down." The owner-manager-cook smiled sourly at his disgruntled customer. "Look, fella, I don't need no more trouble here. How about a free meal—on the house."

"Eat *here*?" Moon eyed the man. "You must be joking."

"Okay, then—here's the deal. I'll refund the money you spent on the meal that didn't sit well."

The Ute shook his head. Began to roll up his sleeves.

The owner of the Mountain Man groaned. "Then what the hell do you want from me?"

Charlie Moon told him.

CHAPTER 26

The Invitation

Under the gaze of several onlookers, Henry Buford lifted the frail man from his motorized scooter. He placed the senator gently onto the pickup seat.

"Thank you, Henry." Patch Davidson did a bared-teeth grimace, grunted as he pulled a braced leg into position. The proud man did not complain, but the tight-lipped expression revealed his anguish. It was a never-ending humiliation, depending upon others to accomplish what were formerly life's most trivial tasks.

"This old pickup rides a little rough." Charlie Moon put the folding wheelchair into the pickup bed. "But I hope seeing the Columbine will make it all worthwhile."

"Right," the senator mumbled. *Like I don't have land enough of my own to look at—thirty-six thousand acres of dirt I can't walk on.* But suspecting that he knew what this was about, the politician put on a cheerful smile. "Can't wait to get there."

Moon should have been getting in the truck, but he could not stop looking at Miss James. When she noticed this attention, he fumbled for words. "Dolly Bushman's barbecued beef is the best in the state."

"Indeed," Davidson said. "The culinary skills of your

foreman's wife are legendary." *The grease will probably kill me.*

Henry Buford gave the Ute's F-150 a doubtful once-over. Shaking his head at the ratty-looking vehicle, the BoxCar manager leaned to inspect the senator. "Sir, you need to fasten your belt."

Davidson dismissed this with an impatient wave. "Dammit, Henry, I intend to have a good time today. I will not tolerate you fussing around me."

Unfazed, Buford reached across the distinguished man, fastened the buckle on the shoulder strap. "There, that's better." He patted his boss on the shoulder. "Ol' Charlie Moon slams into some big pothole, we don't want you bumping your noggin on something."

The powerful man uttered a dark curse under his breath. "Henry, you are beginning to grate on my nerves. Depart from me." Davidson slammed the door.

Henry Buford looked over the top of the pickup with a worried expression. "Charlie, you drive carefully."

The Ute rancher assured the BoxCar manager that he would take good care of his precious cargo, and noticed that Allan Pearson was standing on the porch of the BoxCar headquarters. Moon approached the front steps. "It's not too late to change your mind—come along with us. We'll have lots of vegetables on the table. And homemade bread."

"I appreciate the invitation. Really I do." Pearson's eyes darted toward the pickup, then the black Lincoln. "But there are some matters I must attend to."

"Well, we'll miss you."

The young man smiled. *I rather doubt that.*

Henry Buford opened the Lincoln door for Miss James. Once his pretty passenger was securely fastened in, the broad-shouldered man slid into the driver's seat, started the engine.

Davidson was grumbling as Moon drove the pickup away from the BoxCar headquarters. "Dammit. They all treat me like I'm some kind of . . ." *Invalid.*

The Ute shifted down for the steep grade up the long,

barren hogback separating the lush oasis from the arid prairie. "They're just trying to take good care of you."

Senator Davidson fussed with his string tie. "Thankfully, my nephew never makes any fuss over me. But Miss James is constantly expressing concerns for my welfare. And Henry Buford, he's the worst of the lot. Since the assault, he's like an old hen with only one chick. Shadows me wherever I go, lest I should stub my toe on a stone." He turned a crank, lowered the window. The air smelled sweetly of sage and piñon. "Last month, I was back at the Blue Light for the first time since . . ." His face clouded. "Since my injury. It was a small, private party. Just as dessert was being served, this big, hulking man barged into the reserved dining room. He took a look at me, put his hand in his coat pocket. Before you can say 'pickled peppers,' Henry launches himself out of his chair, lands a left hook that almost takes the fellow's head off."

"Good for Henry. Somebody needs to be looking out for you."

"A purple pox on Henry! Turned out the man was seeking an autograph for his mother. I wish he would find someone else to protect—his concern for my physical safety sometimes borders on the absurd."

Moon pulled on this string. "Can't imagine why he likes you so much."

"Obviously, Henry admires my fine personal qualities."

The Ute grinned. "I hadn't thought of that."

The senator was silent for a moment. "It has to do with his brother—Henry's identical twin, Edward."

"The fella in the picture over his fireplace."

"The very same. I don't suppose you want me to tell you about it."

"I don't suppose I could stop you."

"Oh, very well, if you insist." Davidson scowled as he called up the unhappy memory. "Edward Buford was a petroleum engineer, employed by a Houston firm involved in oil exploration. This corporation had a lucrative contract with the Philippine government to perform geological surveys in a vast area of the South Pacific west of Palawan."

"The Spratly Islands?"

"I am impressed with your knowledge of geography. There are supposedly vast quantities of petroleum in the region, so it is not surprising that several other nation-states strongly dispute the Philippine government's assertion to mineral rights in those waters. Other claimants include China. Vietnam. Malaysia."

This was beginning to sound familiar. Moon had read a piece in the *Rocky Mountain News*. "Did Henry's brother die in a plane crash?"

The senator raised a bushy eyebrow. "For a rustic country lawman, you are surprisingly well informed."

"Don't tell anybody, Patch—I enjoy playing the stereotype."

The senator chuckled. "But you sit up late at night, poring over fine print in obscure scholarly journals. Thinking deep thoughts."

Moon's stomach growled. His thoughts drifted to beef and potatoes.

"But you are correct, of course. Edward Buford was last seen boarding a company-owned instrumentation aircraft that was rigged for geomagnetic surveys. Alas, the airplane did not return. A few scraps of wreckage were recovered near a place picturesquely known as Swallow Reef. Sharky waters, so I'm told, which is probably why no bodies were recovered. All onboard were presumed dead."

"Not a pleasant story."

"And it should have ended there. But Henry—who was once employed by the Defense Intelligence Agency—still has contacts within that organization. He heard rumors that his brother had survived. According to this rather melodramatic version of the incident, Edward Buford was allegedly plucked from the rolling waters by a band of fellows who could most charitably be described as cutthroat pirates. These crafty entrepreneurs supposedly sold Edward to a certain party, which, shall we say, had a considerable interest in the petroleum engineer." He smiled at the Ute.

"Tell me now—doesn't that tale sound highly improbable?"

"Holding an American hostage doesn't sound improbable, especially not in the Philippines. I imagine we're talking about an Islamic terrorist group like Abu Sayyaf. They would've taken him to Basilan Island." *And chopped off his head.*

The senator put on his poker face. "I shall neither confirm nor deny your lurid imaginations. The relevant issue is this—Henry was firmly convinced that his brother was being held in captivity. He pleaded with me to use the power of my office to obtain his brother's release. I contacted the director of the CIA, asked him to determine whether there was any possibility that Edward Buford had survived the plane crash. The DCIA approved an off-the-books investigation. Unofficial inquiries were made through the Department of State. Sadly, it all led to nothing."

The Ute was familiar with how the federal bureaucracy worked. And didn't work. "And that was the end of it."

"I wish it were so. Late one afternoon, Henry came to see me. It was a rather poignant meeting—he informed me that it was too late to help Edward. His brother had died while in captivity."

"He hear this from his buddies in the intel community?"

"You would think so. But the source of his information was even more spooky than that." The senator smiled at the small pun. "Henry believed he had some sort of psychic connection with his twin. He told me he knew the precise moment when his brother died—that he had actually experienced Edward's pain as he . . ." A pause. "Forgive me. The account is rather too morbid for repetition."

"I'm sure he appreciated the effort you made on his brother's behalf."

Patch Davidson watched the scenery scroll by the pickup window. "Henry knew that I had done everything possible to help Edward. He was extremely grateful. I've no doubt this is why he has been excessively protective of my person—especially since the assault that left me . . ." As his voice trailed off into a whisper, the paraplegic rubbed at the wasting muscles in his thigh.

Moon was still mulling over the encounter at the Blue Light. "This enthusiastic autograph hunter Henry intercepted—you find out who he was?"

Patch Davidson frowned at the tribal investigator. "Should I have?"

"Would've been a good idea. Maybe he wasn't after an autograph."

The senator shrugged. "Such a sinister thought did not occur to me. After all, we were at the restaurant to celebrate Miss James's birthday."

He muttered, "So, Miss James had a birthday last month."

"Yes she did, Charlie." His distinguished passenger smirked. "I daresay one in twelve of the population shared that same annual experience."

"I was just thinking that—"

"I know very well what you were thinking. Pretty little thing, isn't she?"

The driver nodded. "And smart."

"Indeed, she is. I can see that you are enormously attracted to her mind." Having momentarily forgotten his troubles, Davidson chuckled at his wit.

"I like smart women." *It's smart-aleck old men I can do without.* Moon slowed as they approached the BoxCar gate, which had been opened for the two-vehicle caravan. He waved to the elderly cowboy standing outside the gatehouse, took a left turn onto the paved road. "Maybe you could tell me something."

"Like what?"

"Like what's her first name?"

The canny politician managed to look confused. "Of whom do we speak?"

"You know of whom."

"She hasn't told you?"

Moon held his silence. *If she had, I wouldn't be asking.*

"Then she does not want you to know. It is her way of

keeping you at arm's length, so to speak. In any case, be forewarned—I do not want you wooing my valued personal assistant. Find yourself a willing young lady in Granite Creek. Or Salida. Or Durango."

The Ute did not respond.

The senator hesitated, glanced at the man behind the wheel. "Charlie, there is something you should know. Miss James has recently had some troubles in her life. Serious troubles." Being a deliberate and cautious man, Davidson selected his words with care. "There was a man. Poor fellow died in a dreadful accident."

"I'm sorry to hear that."

"Point is, I am quite certain she is not looking for—oh, what the hell do these modern women call it—a *relationship*. At least not yet."

"I sure do hate to hear bad news."

"Sadly, the world is full of it." Patch Davidson raised a hand to shade his eyes from the bright morning sun.

Moon reached across the cab to lower the visor for his passenger.

Still, the senator squinted.

"There's a hat in the glove compartment."

Davidson found the article of clothing. It was a billed cap sporting an Atlanta Braves patch. He pulled it down to his ears, adjusted the bill to shade his eyes. "So how do I look?"

Moon glanced at the highly respected United States senator. Tufts of gray hair stuck out over his bent-down ears. "Very distinguished."

"No, don't spare my feelings. Be brutally frank."

"Well, I wouldn't want to say . . . ludicrous."

"I am glad to hear it. Or not to hear it, as the case may be. So boil it down to something any half-wit could understand." Patch Davidson's face was split by an idiotic ear-to-ear grin.

This took some careful thought. "Okay. You look like the guy who just won a blue ribbon at the Comstock County cow chip kicking contest."

"Perfect! Come next election, my new look should be good for four percentage points."

"Keep the hat with my compliments." Charlie Moon glanced in the rearview mirror. As if it were tethered to the pickup, the sleek black Lincoln remained precisely twenty yards behind. He wondered what Henry Buford and Miss James were talking about. Whether she was enjoying the ranch manager's company. The Ute forced himself to dismiss these thoughts, concentrate on the road ahead. It was about fifteen miles to the Columbine turnoff. Another seven to the bridge over Too Late Creek, the last landmark before he could see his home. He wondered how many years were ahead before he crossed The River. Ten? Twenty? Or maybe it wouldn't be measured in years. A man could miss a lot by working twelve hours every day. Putting off the good things until lost opportunities were bittersweet memories. The Ute's eyes took on a faraway look.

They drove along in peaceful silence, spending miles and minutes precious beyond measure.

Finally, Moon slowed to turn at the entrance to his vast property. He eased the F-150 under the great wooden arch over the Columbine gate. *Almost home.* A billow of yellow dust puffed up behind them. He slowed to spare those following in the luxury automobile.

Senator Davidson took a deep breath. "Charlie, I have to tell you something. Right at this very moment, I feel better than I have since the night that skulking bastard busted up my legs."

"Glad to hear it."

He puffed out his chest, flexed wiry arms. "This little excursion was a terrific notion."

And so on they went, traveling along the arrow of time.

Davidson found himself mesmerized by a side of the Misery Range he had not seen for ages. The mountain's pale blue skin was wrinkled by meandering crevasses. The alpine heights were swathed in broad skirts of pine, spruce and fir; this lush fabric was streaked by glistening sashes of golden aspen. And all was sweetly illuminated by the soft light of late morning. "Strange thing. I have traveled all my life. Been everywhere. Seen everything. Even after I got crippled up, I didn't slow down as much as you might think. But wherever I go, it's much like the place before."

"There's no place like the Columbine."

"Indeed. I have not been here in years. And I have a feeling today is going to be different—a quite memorable juncture in my busy life."

The Ute slowed for a particularly rutty section of road. *Need to get the big tractor out here, blade this thing off.* "You have a really good time, say nice things about Dolly Bushman's barbecue, maybe I'll invite you over again."

"I will hold you to that." The senator sighed. "Charlie, I may look like a certified idiot in this baseball cap, but I am a seasoned player and I know the score. There is something you want to tell me. I expect it is about what the FBI geeks found in my home."

"That can wait."

"I assure you, I will enjoy my megacalorie meal much more if you tell me now."

"You expecting bad news?"

"Well, of course I am. It is a matter of the most elementary logic. If the FBI technicians had found nothing amiss in the BoxCar headquarters, you could have informed me of that good news inside my home—perhaps in the now-verified security of the conference room where I have conducted so many sensitive meetings. But instead of breaking the news inside my house, you have craftily arranged to get me alone. You could have brought your spacious, comfortable Expedition, but instead you have shoehorned me into this rattletrap pickup."

Moon pretended to be hurt. "I thought you'd appreciate a ride in a real cowboy truck."

"Bah! Save your baloney for white-bread sandwiches. You have made sure there was no room for additional passengers. I have no doubt this was so you could make a confidential report on the results of the Bureau's investigation. Ergo, I may safely conclude that there is precious little security inside the supposed privacy of my walls. I have no doubt that you are about to tell me that my conference room has as many bugs as a Mississippi back porch on a humid night in June. Whatever the FBI has found, I imagine they wish to leave in place for a period of time."

Moon smiled at his reflection in the pitted windshield. "For providing misleading information to the enemy state?"

"Of course. I have read my share of spy thrillers."

The Ute drove on. The lane, now paralleling an irrigation ditch, neatly divided an eighty-acre alfalfa field that had been harvested a week before. Several dozen fat Herefords, switching their tails at buzzing flies, munched contentedly at the green stubble. Not one of the serene bovines gave the passing automobiles a glance.

Finally, the white man could stand the silence no longer. "Well?"

Moon kept his eye on the lane, which twisted around a lumpy clump of piñon-studded knobs. "FBI technicians didn't find anything. Not in the conference room. Or anywhere else inside your house."

Patch Davidson gaped openmouthed at the lovely pastoral scene, magnificently framed by the large windshield. "But . . . that is just absolutely wonderful news." He gave the Ute a doubtful look. "Isn't it?"

"Sure."

"Charlie Moon, you are a hard fellow to gauge. You pass on good news like it was a report of a death in the family."

Moon started to respond, hesitated.

The politician's sensitive antenna went up another notch. "What?"

"Somehow, I know I'm going to regret sticking my nose into your business."

"Undoubtedly. But I cannot stand the suspense. So go ahead, tell me."

"First, I'll ask you a couple of questions."

"You may certainly ask. But I may not choose to respond

to questions that are, let us say . . . of a sensitive nature."

"Fair enough. If you don't want to talk about the matter, I'll let the whole thing drop." *And I'll feel a hundred percent better.*

They passed a small house on the right. "It's been so long since I've been here—isn't that the foreman's quarters?"

"Yeah. But today, Pete and Dolly are up the road at the Columbine headquarters. I expect lunch will be on the table by the time we get there."

There was a full minute of tense silence between them. Then another. "Go ahead, Charlie—ask your damn questions."

"You have any idea when these leaks of sensitive information started?"

"*Alleged* leaks. But to answer your question, no, I do not know. I am reasonably certain that the *suspicions* of a security problem at the BoxCar surfaced fairly recently. I got wind of it . . . well, I would not want to mention a precise date."

"But it was after the murder of Billy Smoke."

The senator thought hard about this enigmatic observation. His brow wrinkled. "Excuse me, but I am unable see any connection between the tragic death of your fellow tribesman and the rumors of a security problem at the BoxCar."

I knew I should have kept my mouth shut. "There probably isn't any connection."

Davidson seemed mildly amused; his tone was almost mocking. "Then, Mr. Detective, where are you going with this mystifying exercise?"

Ten to one, to hell in a hand basket. "Let's make an assumption."

"Name it."

"Let's assume that the people who work at DIA and CIA and those other government spook shops know how to do their jobs."

"Though such a sweeping assumption is highly questionable, I will nevertheless go along with your proposition. But only for the sake of good manners."

"Let's also assume that they have credible evidence that somehow a foreign government is able to eavesdrop on conversations inside the BoxCar headquarters. Even inside your *allegedly* secure conference room."

"You wound me. But very well, let us presume that this is so. But if someone is listening, tell me this—why did the FBI counterespionage geniuses proclaim my home to be free of electronic eavesdropping gadgetry?"

"They did not."

"Pardon me. But I distinctly heard you say that—"

"What I said was that they didn't find anything. Negative results prove nothing."

"I heartily disapprove of such pessimism." The senator looked away toward the beautiful mountains. "I regret that you take an unduly dim perspective on what is unalloyed good news. You would do well to practice a bit of positive thinking." A fat insect splattered on the windshield.

"That sounds like good advice." The creek was coming up. The tribal investigator lifted his foot off the accelerator, allowed the old pickup to slow. "So I'll focus my thoughts on Dolly Bushman's West Texas-style barbecued beef. Heaps of mustard potato salad. Pork and beans baked in brown sugar. Homemade rye bread, still warm from the oven." There was a rumble of loose boards under the pickup wheels. A glimpse of crystalline water spilling over black stones.

"Excellent." The senator's lips were firm. "I quite agree. Let us shun all negative talk. It is unhealthy to search for troubles where there are none—snatch defeat from the jaws of victory, as it were."

But alas, they had already crossed over Too Late Bridge.

The F-150 bumped along the road.

The invisible tether between the pickup and the trailing Lincoln had stretched while Henry Buford eased the big car over the plank bridge.

"This is a hundred-dollar day," the Ute said. "Warm sun-shine. Bluebirds singing. Not a trouble in sight."

"Okay, Charlie, get it over with." Patch Davidson gnawed at a blue-tinged lip. "Go ahead, have your say. Depress me beyond words."

Moon frowned at his passenger. "What're you talking about?"

"Do not be the sharp stone in my shoe—get the thing over with."

"Okay. Think about this. If the bad guys are listening to your private conversations at the BoxCar—and the FBI experts can't turn up anything in your house—maybe the bug ain't in your house."

The senator did not like the undertone of this statement. It was like a glimpse of cloud shadow a few minutes before the boom of thunder shakes a man's castle to the very foundation. "But if there is no electronic eavesdropping gadget in my home, where could it possibly be?"

"I been doing a lot of thinking about that. So I put my-self in the foreign spook's place. If it was my job to record your private conversations, where would I hide the bug? Well, a man can think of all kinds of things. Your private conference room is the obvious spot. Getting it in there would be a problem, but it wouldn't be impossible." He shook his head. "But the FBI couldn't find it, so most likely it ain't there. And then I thought, maybe Senator Davidson should carry the bug around with him."

This time it was the white man who held his tongue.

"But where would I put it—maybe in your shoe heel?"

"I had no idea you had such a fertile imagination."

"Thank you. The bug-in-the-shoe-heel sounds pretty cool, but it don't really suit me. Rich man like you probably owns ten dozen pairs of shoes. Do I have to plant some-thing in all of 'em? And then there's the problem of power for my electronic gadget. Tiny batteries are okay for a little while, but sooner or later they run down. I don't think I want to be sneaking into your shoe closet every few weeks to replace ten dozen batteries. No, I'd much rather put my gadget where there's already some electricity to operate it. And then I have this inspiration. I don't know how it happens. Maybe I see somebody in a supermarket, or on the street. It's a person who always has plenty of electrical energy close at hand, wherever they go. At home, at work, on the street—they've got kilowatt hours to spare."

"Excuse me, Charlie, but I do not share this vision. What is it that you see—the Wichita Lineman attached to a ten-mile lamp cord?"

"Better than that. I see a fella attached to a motorized scooter. Like an electric GroundHog."

As the inner light illuminated his mind, the senator's ruddy face paled. "Oh my God." His hands clenched into fists. "You're suggesting that someone has taken advantage of the fact that I'm an invalid—to commit espionage?"

"In a way."

"But that is absolutely . . ." Davidson searched for the word. Found it. "Absolutely *damnable*." He shot an accusative look at the driver. "So your ploy today was not so much to separate me from my home as from my high-tech electric conveyance."

"Yeah."

Senator Patch Davidson shook his head in a dazed manner. "Forgive me, but this is an absolutely fantastic theory."

"Tell me why."

"The GroundHog is always in my home. Or, on a couple of occasions, in my Georgetown residence."

"Or in your airplane. Or your Senate office. Or the Senate Chamber."

"Well, yes. But the point is, what possible opportunity would a foreign agent have to implant a surreptitious device in it?"

"I've been doing some serious thinking about that."

"And?"

"Haven't come to a conclusion. Still thinking on it."

"I suggest that your expectations are overly optimistic."

"Few minutes ago, you said I was a pessimist."

"A truly first-rate intellect—such as my own—is able to

simultaneously entertain contradictory concepts."

"How about the concept that somebody has wired your GroundHog for sound?"

"Haven't come to a conclusion. Still thinking on it."

"Imitation is the sincerest form of flattery."

"The hell it is." His useless legs were aching. "Charlie, I would like to raise an issue that is of some importance to me."

"Go right ahead."

"Granted, you are gifted with a spectacular—one might even say bizarre—imagination. Even so, I admit that your speculation is not totally without merit. But to put the matter quite bluntly, you have raised an ugly issue that I would just as soon not have heard about. I merely wanted you to act as a watchdog over the FBI snoops while they sniffed about my home. You have gone rather beyond the bounds of your assignment."

"Thank you. I try to give this job all I got."

"The way I see it, a member of my staff who presents me with a problem—"

"A part-time member of your staff."

"Very well, nitpick if you will. A part-time member of my staff who presents me with a problem that I did not previously perceive—that person introduces trouble into my life. The offending person, therefore, has a sacred obligation."

"A part-time member of your staff who has not yet been paid."

"Let us not discuss money—it is crass and vulgar on a social occasion such as this. As I was saying, the person who troubles my mind has an obligation to present a solution to the problem—which will otherwise keep me awake into the wee hours."

"You're a tough guy to work for."

"I suspect that you know what I have in mind."

"Let me make a haphazard guess. Even though I got a king-sized ranch to run—and an investigative assignment from my tribal chairman—you want me to work with the

FBI counterespionage hotshots for a while longer. Talk
them into checking out your Electric GroundHog. So before
the rumors about espionage hit the newspapers, you'll have
it on record that the Bureau experts didn't find a single bug.
Not in your senate office. Not in the BoxCar headquarters.
Not in your electric scooter."

"As you raised the issue of bugs in my faithful little
GroundHog, such a service on your part seems both appropriate and eminently fair. And do not suggest that I find
someone else to perform this small task—you are on my
payroll as security consultant for my western headquarters."

"Seeing as how you bring up the issue of payroll, there's
still the matter of a check and—"

The senator raised a hand to interrupt the protest. "I will
hear no more. You are my official liaison with the Federal
Bureau of Investigation. If they must poke and pry about
the innards of my Electric GroundHog, then so be it. But
it is up to Mr. Moon to make the necessary arrangements.
And see that they do no damage to my wonderful machine."

Moon grinned at his passenger. "I'm glad you see it that
way."

Davidson's face mirrored his astonishment. "Do not tell
me—you have already discussed this wild notion with the
FBI?"

"Okay. I won't tell you."

"And what did they say?"

"The Bureau experts think it's a pretty long shot. And
they're concerned about depriving you of your four-wheel-
drive transportation."

"Well, perhaps I have misjudged Mr. Hoover's opera-
tives—evidently a few of them must have a grain of compassion. But there is no cause for concern. I can do without
the GroundHog overnight. If need be, even for a full day."

"To do the job right, they'll need to have your scooter
for at least a week."

The senator snorted. "That is impossible—I will not
even consider it."

"Yeah. That's what I told 'em. There's no way you

could get along without your wheels for that long. You'd have to rent yourself a backup unit. And rich as you are, you wouldn't be likely to do that."

He turned innocent eyes on the driver. "I wouldn't?"

"Nope. Even though you could afford to buy a brand-new GroundHog and keep the spare in Washington. Which would actually be convenient, because you wouldn't have to fly the original scooter back and forth between Colorado and the capital." Moon added: " 'No,' I said, 'The senator wouldn't ever go to the expense. Not even if the national security of our great Republic was at risk.' "

"Charles, I cannot believe you said such a thing."

"Neither can I."

"True, I do not cast greenbacks to the four winds. But neither am I a penny-pincher."

The tribal investigator shot the senator a sly look. "Then some extra expenses won't be a problem?"

"Well, of course not. Hang the expenses—full speed ahead."

"Now that's the kind of talk I like to hear."

"I hate to admit it, but a duplicate GroundHog is an excellent idea. On this very day, I will instruct Miss James to place an order for another unit."

Moon shook his head. "The counterespionage specialists won't go along with that."

"They won't?"

"Nobody but you and me and the feds can know about the duplicate GroundHog."

"Then how will the purchase be made?"

"Through the FBI's Denver field office. And any kind of check from you is out of the question. We'll hide the expenditure on my credit card."

"I must say, that is very decent of you."

"Not really. I'm talking about my BoxCar card—I'll use your plastic to get a loan from the Stockman's Credit Union. Later on, when I turn in my expense account, the cost of the new GroundHog will be broken up into several cost categories. Travel. Meals. Whatever."

"Of course. Go right ahead—I hereby authorize you to make the expenditure."

"I'm glad you approve." Charlie Moon pulled to a stop under a pair of tired cottonwoods that leaned against each other for support. "I made the application for the loan yesterday."

"I must admit that I am greatly impressed by your audacity. Furthermore, I admire your circuitous—nay, I shall even say *devious*—means of achieving the desired result." Senator Davidson beamed on the younger man. "Charlie, you have all the makings of a crackerjack politician."

Moon frowned at the elder statesman. "Sir, I know I have my shortcomings, but that sort of remark is uncalled for."

CHAPTER 27

The Uninvited

Lunch at the Columbine was a splendid affair. The men ate like wolves; they talked loudly of politics and cattle and the economy and what a great country this was. Miss James attempted to help Dolly Bushman in the kitchen, but the senator's able assistant was gently shooed away from the cookstove. What would it look like—a guest working like a hired hand? Dolly would not rest until all present had had their fill of barbecued beef ribs, baked beans, potato salad, hot baked bread dripping with butter. When Charlie Moon insisted that the woman who had prepared the feast sit and enjoy the fruits of her labor, Dolly finally relented.

Moon was about to take a bite of pie when the telephone on the parlor wall jangled. Pete Bushman made a move to get up from the table, but was stilled by a look from the boss. "We have an answering machine," his employer said.

The caller hung up when the recorded voice asked for a name and number.

Immediately, Pete Bushman's cell phone buzzed. The foreman mumbled something under his bushy beard, got up, and stomped out of the dining room. He stood in the parlor, listened to a torrent of words, barked a few curt orders, pressed a memory button, repeated the previous performance, dialed 911, had another brief conversation.

Moon, who had been watching Pete out of the corner of his eye, got a nod from the grizzled foreman.

By the time the Ute got to the parlor, Pete had opened the glazed gun case.

"What's going on?"

"We got troubles." He pitched the boss a carbine.

Must be the cougar. Moon checked the magazine. It was full. "Two-Toes?"

"Nope. The call was from Alf. He's working on the ir- rigation ditch down at the south alfalfa." Bushman selected an automatic shotgun, loaded it with slug shells. "We got a bunch a yahoos on black motor-sickles comin' up the road hell fer leather. I figger it's that nasty bunch you had a run-in with."

The Ute glanced toward the dining room. "Job One is to protect our guests. Get on the phone and—"

Bushman cut in. "I already told Alf to bring all the men he's got to the headquarters fast as he can. I called the Wyomin' Kyd. He's straw-bossin' some repairs on the east fence line. He'll bring as many hands as he has; any as ain't already armed'll pick up their guns at the bunkhouse. Then I called the state police—told 'em the senator is here on the Columbine and we've got big trouble a-comin' down the road. Cops'll be here fast as they can."

"You did good, Pete."

There was a heavy scratching at the porch door, fol- lowed by a deep-throated bark. Moon opened the door, pointed the large hound toward the dining room. Seeming to understand what was required of him, Sidewinder trotted away to take up a position behind Miss James's chair.

Henry Buford appeared at Moon's elbow, frowned at the grim-faced armed men. "What's up?"

"We may be about to have a problem with some mo- torcycle hooligans." Moon pointed at the gun cabinet. "Take whatever you feel comfortable with."

"I'm already packing." The senator's ranch manager

pulled back his suit jacket to expose a holstered 9mm automatic pistol.

"You'll need more than that," Bushman said.

Buford selected a Remington repeating rifle.

Moon glanced at the grandfather clock in the corner, made a quick calculation. "I think I know where I can stop them."

Pete Bushman set his jaw. "Well, I'm goin' with you."

The Ute rancher shook his head, gave his foreman a look that brooked no argument. "There's no time to discuss this, Pete. You stay here at the headquarters—make sure our guests are safe. Soon as a few of our men show up, send them down the road to find me." He hesitated. "I doubt this situation is as bad as it looks. But if any of those fellas show up here looking for trouble, don't bother with winging 'em—shoot to kill."

Bushman gave the boss a look that expressed his intense desire to do just that.

Moon headed for the door.

Henry Buford hurried along behind the Ute, down the porch steps. "Well, I'm coming with you."

"It would be better if you stayed—"

The BoxCar manager made a barking laugh. "Don't give me any orders—I'm not one of your hired hands."

Moon was sliding into the pickup. "I thought you'd want to stay close to Patch."

Buford's face flushed red. "My responsibility is to keep thugs well away from the senator." He jumped into the passenger side of the pickup, slammed the door. "And the best way to do that is to back you up."

Moon cranked the engine, slammed the gearshift into "low," kicked gravel. "I am happy to have your company."

Buford chuckled. "I heard about how you kicked some ass over at the Mountain Man. Word is, one of those leather-jacketed, drug-pushing terrorists put a big diamondback in your pickup."

"Yeah," the Ute said. *But I'm still here.*

When they approached the bridge over Too Late Creek,

the pickup was doing sixty miles an hour on rough road. The Ute hit the brakes, slid to a sideways stop on the rickety plank structure.

Buford understood. This was the only bridge across the yard-deep stream, and the banks were steep and heavily treed with cottonwood and willow.

The men took up positions behind the pickup. The tall Ute rested his carbine on the cab, the BoxCar manager stood by the tailgate. They heard the understated mumbling of engines. As the seconds ticked away, the throaty rumble grew loader.

Henry Buford blinked into the noonday sun, pulled down the brim of his felt hat. "Here they come."

And there they came. A stampede of savage beasts, enfolded in a billowing cloud of dust.

For a long moment, it appeared that the bikers might collide with the pickup on the plank bridge. But within fifty yards of Too Late Creek, there were yelps from the leaders of the pack, a waving of hands, motorcycles skidding to a stop.

Moon and his backup waited.

Slowly, the dust responded to the pull of gravity, settled on the road.

Dolly Bushman—equally familiar with kitchen appliances and firearms—had left the former to take up the latter. The foreman's wife was stationed at a front window with a double-barreled, twenty-gauge shotgun. The woman was entirely ready to conduct such business as might become necessary. Her husband, who had been tramping from window to window, was muttering incoherently under his beard.

Senator Davidson, having armed himself with a carbine, was waving the weapon around like a club, and demanded, "What in hell is going on—are we under attack?"

The Columbine foreman stuffed a chaw of tobacco into his mouth. "Patch, we got us a situation here. But I wouldn't worry none." *Dammit, where are them no-account cowboys when you need 'em?*

With the hound hovering protectively at her side, Miss James was only mildly alarmed. Whatever was going on, surely Charlie Moon and Henry Buford could manage it. But if things got desperate, she had already decided to use the single rifle left in the gun cabinet.

The senator rolled his manual wheelchair to the front window, beside Dolly Bushman. *If push comes to shove, I'll give a damn good accounting of myself.* He cocked the carbine.

Dolly looked down at the ashen-faced politician. *You live to see another election, you sure enough got my vote.* The plump sentry returned her attention to the window. Though prepared to do battle, she was not overly concerned that it would come to that. *Charlie Moon can handle whatever is out there.*

Half-Ton was in the lead, his great bulk concealing much of the black Harley. The huge man cut his engine, waved to his band of followers. They did the same. The sudden quiet was unnerving.

Pie Eye, stuffed into a sidecar near the middle of the sinister procession, appeared to be in a semivegetative state. His mouth lolled open, the eyes stared blankly.

Moon and his comrade waited.

The motley crew of bikers spewed their hatred at the unexpected obstruction. There were mutters, grunts, shouted obscenities.

The Ute held his silence.

In a voice that could barely be heard, Henry Buford was singing an old hymn. *Shall We Gather At The River . . .*

The oversized leader of the gang blinked at the men behind the pickup, aimed a toothless grin at the Ute, and yelled, "Hey, Injun-cowboy, this any way to make your company welcome?"

The BoxCar manager interrupted his singing. "I make it thirteen. Not counting the veggie."

Moon nodded. A baker's dozen.

Buford was perfectly calm. "Charlie, how do you want to do it?"

"If this goes sour, I'll take the ones to the left. You go for the right side."

"Suits me. And this being your party, you can have seven, I'll take six."

"Sounds fair."

"But I want the fat one."

"You goin' for the easy shot?"

Buford chuckled.

"These crazies make a move, Half-Ton is your meat. But first, let me try talking."

"Talk to this bunch?" Buford snorted. "You might as well recite Kipling to a herd of pigs."

Bushman looked out the kitchen window, saw them coming on the run. *Thank the Lord!* The Columbine foreman threw the back door open to the Wyoming Kyd. Jerome Kyd-mann—the Kyd was from Wyoming, Rhode Island—appeared to be a decade younger than his thirty-four summers. It had not been necessary for the Kyd to arm himself. An incurable romantic, Jerome always wore a brace of blued-steel, ivory-grip Colt .45 six-shooters. This was considered a mild eccentricity on a cattle ranch populated with a congregation of exceedingly strange characters.

A half dozen scruffy-looking Columbine cowboys trooped in behind the well-dressed straw boss. Most of these carried rusty old carbines or revolvers of doubtful reliability.

The small, lean Mexican in a broad-brimmed straw hat was the exception. Griego Santanna had a chrome-plated pistol in his hand, a glistening bowie knife tucked under his belt—a wild, happy glint in his eye. He addressed his inquiry to Pete Bushman: "Ho-kay, where are these *com-ancheros* you want Griego to murder for you?" Fighting was much more fun than mending barbed wire fences.

Miss James, still in the dining room, had not noticed the

arrival of the cowhands. She heard the voices, turned to see the band of cutthroats invading the Columbine headquarters.

The Mexican grinned at her, exposing nine stainless steel teeth. With the intention of amusing the wide-eyed gringo woman, Santanna pulled the bone-handled bowie knife from a beaded leather sheath, rotated the nine-inch blade to display the mirror finish. "*Brillante,*" he said to the attractive lady, and winked. "Very pretty, huh?"

Sidewinder moved in front of the woman, bared a mouthful of impressive teeth at the Mexican.

Moon addressed the chief of the hooligans. "Turn your bikes around—I don't want to see nothing but your backsides getting smaller."

Half-Ton snorted. "What—you gonna send us away just like that?"

"I'm in a charitable mood today. And so far, no harm's been done."

The leader of the pack laughed, his enormous belly shook. "That's 'cause we just got here."

Buford smiled, addressed the bikers in a folksy tone. "Here's some helpful advice for you buncha half-wits—haul your sorry asses outta here while you still can." He took a bead on the fat man.

Half-Ton exchanged a long look with the rough-looking fellow backing up the tall Indian. "Now, that ain't very friendly."

"You're trespassing," the Ute replied. "You fellas want to visit the Columbine, you'll have to call ahead. Get an appointment."

"Hey, don't get your shorts all in a knot, Injun—we just come for a pow-wow."

The Ute wondered where all his cowhands were. "Speak your piece."

"You whooped me and Pie Eye in a fair scrap. We're here for a rematch."

Moon glanced at the blank-faced man in the sidecar. "Your friend don't look ready for a fight."

"You can start with me." Half-Ton grunted as he unloaded his mammoth bulk from the machine.

Moon wondered how long he could keep the man talking. "Looks like you brought along a lot of help."

"They's just spectators. Anyways, you brought one of your buddies. He kin watch, too, if he's got the stomach to see Injun brains and guts splattered all over the ground."

Moon was watching a leather-coated thug who was darting furtive glances down at the sidecar where Pie Eye was deposited. He was muttering to his disabled passenger.

The huge man leaned back and bellowed. "Well, what is it—you gonna fight me?"

Moon kept his gaze focused on the sidecar. "If you got any teeth left in your head, I'd be more than happy to knock 'em out. But this is not the time. Or the place."

Half-Ton turned to grin idiotically at his following of cheerful misfits. "Sounds to me like the big Injun's scairt shitless."

This produced the expected chorus of guffaws and jeers from his entusiastic comrades.

Moon, assuming they had come for the sole purpose of reducing the Columbine to a heap of smoldering ruins, dearly hoped that all they wanted was a fistfight. "You boys head back into town. Tomorrow—let's say noon—I'll meet your Ultimate Leader at the Mountain Man." *And give his fifty-gallon ass a real kicking.*

This suggestion brought a smirk to Half-Ton's battered face. "Sure. And you'll have all your copper friends there to arrest me and my buddies. I don't think so. And don't you think we're scairt a your guns. Me'n alla my boys is packin'." To demonstrate that this was not an empty bluff, the big biker pulled back his leather jacket. Holstered on the belt under his ample belly was an automatic pistol.

Moon watched the biker above the sidecar. "First one to touch his gun is a dead man."

"There's no need fer any shootin'. Come on out from

behind your truck, Injun." Half-Ton raised hamlike fists in an absurd parody of a prizefighter's pose. "We'll duke it out right here, just you'n me. An' after I whoop your sorry ass real good, me'n my boys, we'll go back to town and have us a beer party." The leader of the pack pulled off a tentlike leather jacket. Flexed gigantic biceps.

Moon ground his teeth. *It'd be really stupid. But I am sorely tempted* . . . He noticed that Henry Buford had left the cover of the pickup. The Ute spoke softly. "Henry, don't go out there—"

The heavy rifle cradled in the crook of his arm, the BoxCar ranch manager approached the leader of the pack.

Half-Ton's mouth crinkled into the foolish grin. "Whatta we got here—this hotshot cowboy gonna fight fer his Injun boss?"

Buford smiled at the fat man. "You stupid shit—what do you think you're doing, coming here? Does a slime-slug like you actually think he has a right to associate with human beings?"

The biker's pale eyes widened. The lips curled.

Henry Buford planted the rifle stock on the side of Half-Ton's head. The biker staggered sideways. Another deft swing—the stock landed squarely in the thug's face. The huge man stumbled, fell to his knees, slobbered blood from the almost toothless mouth.

There was an angry murmur among the bikers, hands moved toward concealed weapons. Buford raised the rifle, pointed it at the nearest offender. His tone was deceptively congenial—like a kindly preacher addressing a backward congregation. "Now who among you does not understand the subtle elements of today's message?"

Moon—amazed at this reckless display of courage— managed to find his voice. "Uh . . . Henry, why don't you just come on back here and—"

Pete Bushman appeared at Moon's shoulder. "Okay, boss, I got the big house covered. The Kyd an' a truck fulla armed cowboys'll be here in two minutes flat." He squinted at the scene. "What's goin' on out there?"

"Looks like Henry Buford has taken charge of the situation." The Ute rancher held a bead on the biker with the sidecar, who was muttering something to Pie Eye. "If this goes bad, Pete, take cover till our men get here. Don't get yourself shot."

Half-Ton, still on his knees, shook his bloody head as if attempting to reconnect jumbled circuits in a scrambled-egg brain. He looked up, tried to focus bleary eyes on the man who had poleaxed him.

Henry Buford smiled down at his victim. "Hey, maggot, know what I think?"

Again, Half-Ton shook the massive head.

The BoxCar manager smiled. "I think you're too stupid to live."

The behemoth biker grinned blankly at the standing man. But while he was on his knees, Half-Ton had removed the automatic pistol from his belt holster. This stealthy action had been concealed by his massive belly.

In the sidecar, a blank-faced Pie Eye was fumbling with something wrapped in a red cloth. A charcoal-gray submachine gun.

The Ute squeezed one off from the Winchester carbine. A small hole appeared in Pie Eye's forehead; he slumped. The biker at his side made a grab for the Uzi. Moon put a lump of lead through his chest, another through his neck. The thug tumbled off the machine, sprawling over Pie Eye.

While the BoxCar manager was momentarily distracted by Moon's gunfire, Half-Ton raised his pistol to aim point-blank at Buford's belt buckle.

Buford poked the rifle barrel into Half-Ton's right eye; the top half of the biker's head exploded.

As Pete Bushman would say later, that was when all hell broke loose.

Motorcycle engines roared to life.

Henry Buford dropped to one knee, calmly emptied the rifle into the nearest bikers. A screaming hoodlum fell off his bike; the riderless Harley went head-on into a large cottonwood at the stream's edge. Another motorcycle sailed into Too Late Creek, the ice-cold water turned crimson with the rider's blood. Discarding the 30.06 rifle, Buford drew his pistol, began picking off the remainders, one by one.

Moon wounded another thug, who was attempting to ride his big machine into the BoxCar ranch manager.

Pete Bushman—yowling like an ecstatic savage—fired grape-size shotgun slugs into the leather-clad crowd. The Columbine foreman crippled one fear-crazed biker, sent another lead sphere through a motorcycle gas tank, which exploded in a sphere of searing fire.

As Bushman had promised his boss, a flatbed truck arrived with a dozen Columbine cowboys—all loaded for bear and oozing adrenaline from every pore. There was not much left to shoot at. Of the bikers who had invaded the Columbine, three made it to the front gate. These were picked up by Colorado State Police, converging from two directions in five cruisers at speeds up to one hundred and twenty miles an hour.

Another thug, whose club name was Poppa Weasel, was lying flat on his back, blood oozing from a wound in his abdomen. He thought things just couldn't get worse. He thought wrong. The unfortunate thug looked up to see the small, thin man standing over him.

Griego Santanna had a shiny revolver in one hand, a gigantic knife in the other. The bloodthirsty Mexican grinned to expose a scattering of steel incisors, canines, and bicuspids. "Don't be afraid, señor. It is I, Griego, here to end your terrible suffering. So what do you want—a bullet between your eyes, or the blade across your throat?"

The gut-shot biker gurgled something incoherent. Blood bubbled up between blue lips.

Santanna slipped the bowie knife into its leather holster. "I cannot understand your words, gringo. I think I will shoot you in the heart—so your pretty face will be preserved for the *funerales*." The Mexican cocked the pistol.

Charlie Moon clamped a heavy hand on Santanna's shoulder. "Hey—what do think you're doing?"

"Find yourself another one—this *hombre* is mine." He

closed his left eye, sighted down the barrel. "He will be the twelfth man I have killed." Twelve was a lucky number.

"No he won't," the Ute said.

Annoyed and hurt by this rude intervention, the Mexican hesitated.

Charlie Moon spoke softly. "Here's the deal, Santanna— you pull the trigger, I'll pull your head off. And feed it to the coyotes."

The bewildered man turned to look up at the Indian's face. "You would do that to me, who is about to kill your enemy?"

"Without batting an eye. Now put the *pistola* away."

Santanna grunted, stuck the heavy gun under his belt. "*Si*. You're the *jefe*." To express his disgust, he spat in the dust.

The biker gurgled at his dark, towering savior; tears of gratitude puddled in his bloodshot eyes.

CHAPTER 28

The Lake

Upon receiving word that Colorado's senior United States senator was under siege at the Columbine, the National Guard dispatched a military helicopter carrying six grim-faced members of a Ranger contingent that had been training in hostage rescue procedures at an Air Force base thirty miles north of Granite Creek. These heavily armed men—much like Moon's knife-wielding Mexican cowhand—were extremely disappointed to have no one to kill. "All dressed up and the party's already over," one of the dejected commandos mumbled. Along with the helicopter pilot, they were tasked by the governor of Colorado to provide air cover for a state police convoy that would escort Senator Davidson back to the security of his BoxCar Ranch.

The Columbine was the scene of carefully orchestrated chaos. Ambulances and state police units blocked the narrow ranch lane. Wounded bikers moaned, pleaded pitifully for help from the medics. The deathly silent were zippered into body bags. After the wild shoot-out, it seemed almost miraculous that only four of the intruders were dead.

In deference to the senator, the authorities agreed to take only brief, preliminary statements from the survivors of the shoot-out who had defended the ranch headquarters. Despite howling protests from those few bikers able to speak coherently, it was abundantly clear to the detail commander that Charles Moon, Henry Buford, and Pete Bushman had acted in self-defense while repelling an unprovoked invasion by a gang of armed, vicious thugs. But shootings are shootings, and there were procedures to be followed to the letter. The "incident area" was laced with yellow plastic ribbon, thus blocking all traffic between the Too Late Bridge and the Columbine headquarters. Officers wearing latex gloves gathered evidence from the scene of the shooting, placed said evidence in plastic bags, carefully labeled said bags, laser-scanned said labels to enter the graphics into a ruggedized laptop computer. A uniformed officer snapped almost three hundred shots of bodies, wreckage of expensive motorcycles, bullet holes in Moon's F-150 pickup. As a backup, another trooper made videotapes of the scene. Other officers made precise reference measurements with steel tapes. "I make it seventeen feet, four inches from the right pickup headlight to Motorcycle Number One." All firearms used in the shoot-out were collected, labeled, bagged. The process of sorting out who had shot who—and in what order—would take some time.

Finally, the curtain fell on Act One of the drama. The yellow tape was removed to allow the ill-humored senator to depart. As Henry Buford had not yet been interviewed, a state police officer was assigned to drive the powerful politician back to the BoxCar.

After Senator Davidson was seated in the black Lincoln, Henry Buford jammed the folding wheelchair into the trunk and said good-bye to his employer. He promised to get back to the ranch as soon as the cops turned him loose. The senator shook his loyal friend's hand, thanked him for defending his person.

Responding to a nod from the politician, Moon approached the low-slung vehicle, leaned on the roof. The senator smiled up at the tribal investigator's dark face. "Well, Charlie, this much must be said—you do know how to keep a luncheon guest from getting bored."

The rancher shook his head. "Patch, I'm sorry about all this. It never occurred to me that those knot-heads would trespass on Columbine property, armed to the teeth. Especially in broad daylight."

Davidson reached out to pat his friend's arm. "Don't give it a thought. And proceed with the business we discussed on the way over."

The big car pulled away.

Henry Buford was seated on a cottonwood stump. As if nothing of note had interrupted his day, the BoxCar manager was paring his nails with a short-bladed folding knife.

Charlie Moon wondered whether his guest was as calm as appearances suggested. "How're you doing, Henry?"

"Okay." Buford wiped the glistening black blade on the cuff of his shirt. "But I need to be getting back to the BoxCar." He squinted at a lemon-colored sun that was casting long shadows. "When d'you think these cops will get around to questioning me?"

Moon shrugged. "I don't know. Want me to lean on 'em?"

"Nah." He folded the blade into the handle, dropped the knife into his pocket. "But if they don't get started soon, I may get belligerent."

The rancher grinned. "I sure do appreciate you backing me up today. I had no idea what I was getting into with that wild bunch and—"

Buford raised a hand in protest. "Don't mention it." His leathery face crinkled into a smile. "Most fun I've had in years."

"Well, I'd rather have been fishing." Moon turned to survey the crowd. Miss James was on the headquarters porch, talking to a handsome young state police officer. The pretty woman was repeating her story for the third time while the dashing trooper made copious notes. When he saw the tall rancher approaching—and the look on Moon's face—the young officer dismissed himself with a gallant tip of his hat.

The tall Ute smiled apologetically at his attractive guest. "I'll drive you home."

"Will they let you leave?"

"Sure. I've already been grilled."

The senator's personal assistant pulled a borrowed cotton shawl tightly around her shoulders. "I'm not ready to go back to the BoxCar just yet." She looked south, toward a shallow basin in the valley between the mountain ranges. The pool of water could have been molten blue glass; the surface shimmered in the glow of a promised sunset. "That lake—does it have a name?"

Moon seemed not to have heard the question.

A smile played at the edge of her lips. "Aren't you going to tell me?"

"Sure. Soon as you tell me your name."

She ignored this small impertinence. "Is it a very long walk to the lake?"

"About a mile."

She looked wistfully toward the waters. "Someday, when you have the time, I hope you'll take me out there."

"I'll take you now." Someday might never come.

As they watched the waters glimmer and shimmer in the warm sunlight, a fragrant breeze moved across the surface to the shore, played with the lovely woman's black hair.

Miss James seated herself on the white bark of a fallen aspen trunk, and began to work her long locks into a thick braid.

Charlie Moon sat down beside her. "That looks like an all-day job."

"Not if you help me."

And so he did. Until moonlight danced on the waters.

CHAPTER 29

The Dance

The authorities had departed, taking with them the wounded and the dead. Except for a pair of night riders, the cowboys were in the bunkhouse. Charlie Moon pulled off his socks, stretched out on the oversized bed.

A lonesome wind whispered in dry cottonwood branches, moaned under the eaves.

Down at the riverside barn, a nervous mare whinnied, kicked at her stall.

The Ute waited expectantly for the good-night from his dog.

By some mysterious means, the hound was always aware of the precise moment when his favorite human being was about to fall asleep. Right on schedule, the canine musician bugled a long, melancholy howl.

Taps . . . now eight sweet hours till reveille. Charlie Moon closed his eyes. Yawned. *Good night, old dog. Good night, world.*

The sleepy man had a few more words to say—to The Other. Names were mentioned. Thanks given. Finally, a hopeful petition—a couple of inches of rain would be most welcome. *If you've got some to spare . . .*

For some weary souls, prayer is the perfect soporific.

And sleep cools troubles percolating in the mind. Thus it was for Charlie Moon. The memory of day slipped away, a thick mist of not-knowing settled over him.

Within minutes, the sleeper's eyes began to shift under his lids. Fragments of a much-spliced film slipped over sprockets with missing teeth. Surreal scenes flashed intermittently on the grainy undersurface of his subconscious.

His initial dreams were troubled. The dozen bikers converging on Too Late Creek were multiplied by hundreds, all brandishing bloody swords. The sleek Harleys were transformed into black panthers, slathering mouths hungry for flesh. No matter how many he shot down, the wild savages multiplied. But like the day that had spawned it, this violent panorama also had an end.

He was standing by the placid lake, her warm hand in his. Miss James looked up. "Do you really want to know . . . my secret?"

He did. Very much.

She smiled. "Come closer."

The dreamer leaned.

She whispered her name in his ear.

He could not hear.

Miss James's smile faded. Then her face was gone. The vanishing woman took the lake with her.

He stood alone in a vast, crystalline ballroom. From an invisible ceiling, countless chandeliers were suspended on golden chains over a floor of polished rose quartz. Charlie Moon saw his image on the mirrored surface. From a brand-new black Stetson to the collar of the black tuxedo, and all the way down to the spit-shined cowboy boots, he approved of what he saw. *Yes, sir—fine-looking man.* His image smiled back at him. To achieve perfection, he adjusted the loops on the string tie. *Wish she was here with me.*

From some unknown dimension, a someone entered the vast space.

The dreamer's vision was telescopic. While the woman

was still very far away, he could make out every detail. The long, clinging white gown. Curled, crimson locks. A single snow-white rose over the left ear. The hot eyes burning with a pale blue flame, the face that was paler still.

Moon watched the feminine vision glide toward him.

Within arm's reach, she paused. The pallid coquette raised a miniature silk fan to partially conceal a narrow, freckled face.

He had been expecting someone else. *Miss Brewster?*

She smiled.

So—you ready to talk to me?

Her lips moved. *I would rather dance.*

The well-dressed man felt a surge of panic. *I never learned how.*

I'll show you. She raised graceful, gloved arms, exposed the tip of a red slipper at the hem of her snowy gown.

There must be some way out. *There's no music.*

She folded the fan, pointed with it.

He turned to see a woman who was a perfect reflection of the first. Illuminated by a diffuse pillar of blue light, the look-alike was seated at a massive piano. This second redhead fussily adjusted her sheet music, then began to tease a waltz from ivory keys.

They were gliding along the ballroom floor, then above it.

You are so warm. She laid her head on his chest. *Hold me now. Hold me close.*

Moon felt the fragile form collapse in his arms. The woman's body was not soft. Friable bones rippled under the white gown. Plucked tendons twanged a sad, sonorous hymn. And she was very, very cold.

The sleeper awoke with a start, his muscles tensed. For a long, dark minute—dreading the return of the eerie dream—Charlie Moon kept his eyes open. Stared into darkness. Finally, he got of bed, trudged downstairs, boiled a pot of strong coffee. For almost an hour, he paced around the spacious lower floor of the Columbine headquarters. Despite what Aunt Daisy believed, dreams were not to be taken seriously. They were nothing more than a lot of jumbled thoughts knocking about in a man's mind. Troubling images coalesced into absurd stories, disturbing his sleep. Long before the first hint of a pale yellow glow broke in the east, the Ute rancher decided it was time for breakfast. He scrambled an iron skillet full of scrambled eggs and pork sausage. Charlie Moon was certain that he'd feel better after a solid meal.

He did not.

Scott Parris was sleeping peacefully. Dreaming his own dreams. There were no shoot-outs, no phantom women in formal gowns, no waltzes over infinite ballroom floors. Only the river . . . and Anne, lovely Anne. His fiancée was still with him. They were walking along a shaded forest path that paralleled the rocky banks of a small stream. In the stream were arm-long trout, flashing iridescent hues of neon orange and blue. Anne had gathered a bouquet of wild lupines; he pulled a red wagon filled with small, sweet children in ruffled bonnets. A swarm of bulldog puppies skittered about his feet. It was all so very pleasant.

Suddenly, Anne stopped, turned her face to him, frowned. "Scotty, what's that noise?"

"The telephone," he mumbled. The chief of police groaned, rolled over in his bed. *I will not answer it. No matter how long it rings . . .*

The infernal instrument kept right on making the rude noise.

He made a grab, knocked the telephone onto the floor, snatched the handset on a second grab. "Who the hell is calling me before daylight?"

He heard Ute's familiar bass voice. "Testy this morning, aren't we?"

Parris groaned, fell back on his pillow. "Dammit, Charlie—d'you have any idea what time it is?"

The tribal investigator had anticipated this question. "It's time all good men were up and at it. Early bird gets the bug."

"Worm. Why didn't you call me when the biker-thugs showed up?"

"Pete did all the calling. After that, we were pretty busy."

"Well, I'm kinda hurt not to have got a chance at those hoods."

"Sorry. Next time we have serious trouble, your number'll be the first one that gets dialed. Even if it's the middle of the night."

"So what do you want?"

"I'm going over to Rio Hondo. See if there's any sign of Miss Brewster."

"Knox and Slocum already checked it out." The chief of police rubbed at his forehead. "Didn't I tell you?"

Knox and Slocum together couldn't find a wildcat in a rain barrel. "I'd like to have a look for myself."

"Well, go right ahead—you don't need my permission."

"Thought maybe you'd want to go along with me."

Parris groaned. "What time is it?"

Moon told him.

"Five o'clock in the morning?" The chief of police sat up on the edge of the bed, leaned to squint at the clock. "It's four-fifty-eight."

"So call me liar for two minutes."

Parris stood up, felt a dull pain at the small of his back. *Hope it's not another kidney stone.*

"Hey, pardner—you still there?"

The sleepy man grunted. "When're you heading out to Arroyo Hondo?"

"About forty-five minutes."

Scott Parris closed his eyes, called up today's schedule. "I got a budget meeting with the mayor at nine A.M. sharp. Sorry. I'd lots rather go on a tramp in the woods."

"Budget meeting?" Moon laughed. "You'd rather eat a live porcupine, quills and all."

"Right-o. But the city's business has to get done. Some

of us have to suffer so civilized society can progress."

"Glad it's you and not me, pardner."

"Charlie, you find anything interesting up there, beep me."

"Will do."

CHAPTER 30

Arroyo Hondo

Charlie Moon washed the breakfast dishes, slipped into a fleece-lined denim jacket, popped the battered John B. Stetson on his head, opened the front door onto the redwood-plank porch. The sun behind the house was three discs high. The rancher sniffed at the crisp morning air. *That's better than hot coffee.*

A large something nudged against his leg.

Moon looked down to see the homely hound.

Sidewinder yawned, exposing a mouthful of wicked-looking yellow teeth.

"Mornin', pal. Want to go for a ride?"

The dog responded with something halfway between a snort and a growl.

"I thought so."

The animal, having slept most of the way, suddenly lurched up from the floorboard. Sidewinder got onto the pickup seat, placed large paws on the dashboard. He stared through the sandblasted F-150 windshield, barked once. Then began whining.

Moon smiled at the beast. *How does he know where we're going?* The Forest Road 985 exit was a hundred yards ahead. The narrow lane would wind through several miles of evergreen forest before terminating at what little remained of the long-deserted Arroyo Hondo mining settlement. The Ute slowed, made the turn onto the dirt road.

The hound's long tongue draped over his teeth. Occasionally, Sidewinder would bark—as if to urge the Ute to drive faster.

Moon was lost in his thoughts. This was most likely a fool's errand. But Wilma Brewster—if the redhead who'd spoken to Aunt Daisy *was* Jane Brewster's shy daughter— had hinted that he might find her at the ghost town. He exited the thickest part of the forest, headed down the side of a slope. Moon shifted to low gear, bumped the F-150 along the rutted road. Spruce and ponderosa were gradually replaced by clumps of juniper and piñon. After passing along a sandy streambed, he encountered an uphill grade. The pickup was heading more or less northward, toward the crest of a ridge above the deep arroyo that had provided the remote silver-mining settlement with a name.

When he finally topped the basalt-strewn ridge, the yellow tide of midmorning light was washing over the high plains. The tribal investigator and his dog got out of the Ford pickup. Aside from the clicking sound of the exhaust system cooling, the silence in this remote place was complete. An intense, bone-numbing cold remained from the departed night. He pushed his fists into the fleece-lined pockets of the jacket, swept his gaze over the crumbled ghost town. Remains of rotting shacks dotted the ridge. Not one had a complete roof, but sheets of tin were scattered about like dead leaves in a windy autumn. The depths of the arroyo were honeycombed with crumbling mine shafts. A well-crafted Forest Service sign warned hikers to stay away from these death traps.

The Ute examined the dirt road for any sign of recent visitors. There were a number of tire tracks on the lane. Judging from the street-tread, the most recent were probably left by GCPD police officers Eddie Knox and Piggy Slocum.

Moon took a deep breath and called out. "Helloooo."

An eerie echo called back, like the sound of a wolf howling. He bellowed again. "Heeey . . . anybody here?"

The crisp echo had a mocking tone.

Because it seemed necessary to do *something* after coming all this way, Moon inspected the wreckage of a dozen mining shacks. There was little to be seen except the pathetic artifacts left behind by those who had been dead for many decades. Broken fruit jars. A twisted boot sole. A rusting Model-T truck chassis. The tribal investigator looked into several crumbling mining shafts. He walked around the perimeter of the ghost town for any sign of a camp. Recently discarded trash. A fire pit.

For hours, he searched.

Nothing.

The truth gradually became apparent. *If Wilma Brewster has ever been in this particular Arroyo Hondo, she's long gone.* He made a mental note to ask Scott Parris whether the New Mexico State Police had turned up anything in the Arroyo Hondo down by Taos. Maybe Wilma was holed up there with a boyfriend. He picked up a piece of basalt, sent it sailing into the deep arroyo. Like his investigation, it took a long time hitting bottom.

The tribal investigator took a last look at the long-deserted community. It was hard not to feel the fool. A man was only allotted so much time in Middle World. And time was far too precious a commodity to waste on improbable hunches that bubbled up out of dreams. *And an old woman's tale about a redheaded gal who wants to talk to me but won't.*

The Ute was suddenly aware that he was alone. *Where's that dog?* He called for the animal.

Sidewinder barked an answer—or was it a summons?

Sounds like he's down in the hollow. The saddle in the ridge was filled with scrub oak and lodgepole pine. There were a few towering ponderosas. Moon called again.

The response was a long, baying howl.

He must've treed something. The Ute made his way down the grade.

Sidewinder was stretched out by a large, split ponderosa log. The ancient tree had simply lived out its time, rotted away, taken one too many lightning strikes, fallen to earth.

Moon grinned at the eccentric hound. "What is it—you too lazy to walk?"

The homely canine stared at the human with deep, mournful eyes.

"I hope you don't expect me to carry you back to the truck."

Sidewinder got up, raked a paw over the place where he had made a temporary bed.

The tribal investigator felt a coldness ripple along his spine. He knelt by the animal. Reached out to see what the hound had unearthed. Wisps of hair. Red hair.

As he always had during hard times, Scott Parris stood beside his Ute friend.

Charlie Moon had withdrawn well away from the gaggle of police officers who gawked while Dr. Simpson's assistants used small pointed trowels and stiff paintbrushes to uncover the human remains.

The elderly ME grunted painfully as he pushed himself upright. He paused to brush pine needles off the knees of expensive gray trousers, then walked stiffly toward the pair of lawman.

Parris asked the question. "What have we got?"

"What we have got is a decomposed body." Walter Simpson glanced back at the small excavation. "Female Caucasian. Red hair. Slender build."

The chief of police was annoyed at having to ask. "Any idea how she died?"

"Looks like strangulation. There's a loop of ten-gauge copper wire around her neck."

The Ute didn't want to know. But he heard the words coming out of his mouth. "How long has she been here?"

The ME shrugged. "Later on, I'll be able to tell you

more precisely, but it'll be a matter of several months."

Scott Parris glanced at the Ute's stony face, then spoke to Dr. Simpson. "Wilma Brewster fits the general description. She was reported missing late last December."

The pathologist rubbed at white stubble on his chin. "The condition of the remains is consistent with that time frame." He frowned at the tall Ute. "How'd you find her?"

"I didn't." Moon nodded to indicate the hound.

Sidewinder was watching the evolving excavation with considerable interest.

The curious ME pressed on. "What on earth brought you out here?"

The tribal investigator hesitated. "A tip."

Simpson glared at the taciturn Indian. "Tip from who?"

Moon held his silence.

Scott Parris gave Simpson a look that said, *Back off.*

The inquisitive ME shrugged. "Well, excuse me." He marched off to bark orders at his assistants, who were gingerly removing a red shoe from the shallow grave.

Parris chewed on an oak twig. "So maybe it ain't Wilma Brewster."

Moon shook his head. "It's her."

"If this corpse is Miss Brewster—and she's been dead since December—how could she have talked to your aunt less than a month ago?"

Moon's expression made it clear that he did not care to discuss the subject.

Parris understood. "Oh—yeah." Talking to ghosts was part and parcel of Daisy Perika's trade. His eyes met Moon's. "You don't think . . ."

"No, I don't. And neither do you."

The chief of police shrugged. "It was just a thought."

A new pair of headlights appeared at the edge of the clearing. It was a small, battered Honda. The driver, an elderly heavyset man, went around to the opposite side of the automobile to open the door for his passenger, but the woman was already getting out. She pulled a tattered woolen coat over her shoulders, lifted the yellow tape, and marched past a state police officer who reached out to stop the intruder. Scott Parris made a gesture; the officer gave way.

The chief of the Granite Creek Police Department blocked her view of the excavation, tipped his felt hat. "Hello, Mrs. Brewster."

Jane Brewster tried to look past the broad-shouldered man. "When I heard, I had to come see for myself."

"Look, it's no good—"

The woman was thin-lipped with determination. "Is it my Wilma?"

Parris looked over her head. "We don't have a positive ID yet."

"Tell me what you do have."

The lawman sighed. "Caucasian. Doc Simpson says it's a woman. Probably a young woman."

She said the words in a whisper. "What color's her hair?"

The lawman looked at the sky. The clouds were ugly. Life was ugly. "Red. I'm sorry, Mrs. Brewster."

She nodded to no one in particular. "I knew it'd be my Wilma." She turned away, began to heave with great, gasping sobs. "My God. My daughter's dead—and I'm so dirt-poor I don't even have money to bury her proper."

"Ma'am."

She looked up to see the tall Ute.

He put an arm around her shoulders. "You don't have to worry about burial."

She dabbed at red, swollen eyes. "What do you mean?"

"There's a fine spot on the Columbine, where you can see for miles and miles in every direction. We call it Pine Knob. If you want, we'll put her there."

She stared at this man she had met only once. "That would be very kind of you." Jane Brewster reached out to touch his hand, then hurried back to the small automobile.

The policemen watched the taillights diminish into tiny red points. In less than a minute, the night had swallowed them up.

Parris rubbed at tired eyes. "It's times like this I hate my job."

"I got to take my dog home." Charlie Moon headed back to the pickup. Sidewinder trotted along at his heels.

Darkness followed closely behind.

CHAPTER 31

The Gathering

To the extent that it was humanly possible for a busy parish priest, Father Raes Delfino's life was well organized. And according to his schedule, it was time to visit Daisy Perika. The pastor of St. Ignatius Catholic Church approached this particular duty with an unsettling mixture of apprehension and anticipation. This was partially because the man, who should have been impartial, had a terrible secret hidden in his heart. Among the whole tribe of Utes, Daisy Perika was his favorite. This despite the fact that the elder was often a sharp thorn in his side. The old woman was mischievously irreverent and wholly unpredictable, but this volatile combination provided a welcome seasoning to the cleric's bland diet.

Upon arriving at Daisy's remote trailer home, Father Raes had been gratified to see Charlie Moon's pickup parked under the shade of a juniper. He received a hearty handshake from the amiable Ute, a derisive snort from the tribal elder, who suggested that the priest must have taken a wrong turn off Route 151. There was no bingo game in these parts, nor was there any cash for his long-handled offering plate. In return for these poisonous barbs, Daisy received the gentle man's blessing—which galled her—and a look of stern disapproval from her nephew—which had no effect whatever. These obligatory preliminaries completed, the trio of quite remarkable human beings enjoyed a tasty breakfast of bacon and eggs, which was salted by talk of reservation politics, upcoming events at St. Ignatius, the desperate need for rain.

When Daisy got up to brew fresh coffee, the tribal investigator removed a photograph from his shirt pocket. Knowing that consulting the priest first would arouse his aunt's ire and pique her curiosity, he pushed the likeness across the table to Father Raes. "She look familiar?"

He studied the image. The pale, redheaded woman stared back at him, as if pleading for recognition. He furrowed his brow at the photo, then at Moon. "She does look vaguely familiar, but beyond that I really can't say."

Moon waited for his aunt's reaction.

Having restarted the coffeepot, Daisy untied her apron. Pretending to have taken no notice of the conversation between her nephew and the priest, she made it her business to pass behind Father Raes. And look over his shoulder at the photograph.

Charlie Moon watched the old woman's wooden expression for the least hint of recognition. Hoped there would be none.

Daisy had only intended to make a quick glance. But she could not pull her gaze from the image of the young woman she had seen first at the Wal-Mart, then across the street from Angel's Cafe. This was the very same person that Louise Marie LaForte *could not see in broad daylight.* Unaware that she had been holding her breath, the tribal elder felt her vision blur. She exhaled carbon dioxide, drew in a fresh supply of oxygen.

Moon had seen the truth glinting in the old woman's eyes, but felt compelled to ask. "Somebody you know?"

Hesitant to lie in the priest's presence, Daisy substituted a shrug and an evasion. "Hard to say—these *matukach* all look pretty much alike."

The *matukach* priest smiled.

Moon pressed. "Then you've never seen this woman?"

"Who knows," the elder said. "It's a fuzzy picture."

"Take a closer look." The tribal investigator offered his aunt the photograph.

Daisy backed away, made an urgent dismissive gesture.

Moon withdrew the picture. And his question. The Ute elder would not touch the likeness of a person recently dead. Especially if the death had been violent. *But how does she know?*

Daisy closed her eyes. *God protect us from ghosts and witches and all kinds of evil.*

Immediately, the priest heard a light tapping. He waited for Daisy to open the trailer door, then realized that neither the old woman or her nephew had shown any sign of hearing the sound. *Maybe I imagined it.* But there it was again—a louder knocking. He looked again to the Utes; surely they had heard it this time. Charlie Moon was putting the photograph of the dead woman into his pocket; the old woman had her eyes closed.

A third time: Bang—bang—bang!

Father Raes could see the flimsy door vibrate under the urgent blows.

Though she did not hear the knocking, the shaman sensed the *presence*—and felt a chill. *It must be the pitu-kupf.* Of course, the dwarf knew the priest was in her home—and had come to embarrass her! The little man, once such a shy recluse in his badger hole, had become more bold with the passing years. Not so very long ago, he had shown up in church during Sunday morning Mass, sitting right there in the pew beside her! The old woman fixed her gaze on the trailer door, muttered in the Ute dialect: *"Pága-kwáy!"*

Charlie Moon frowned at his aunt. *Who is she telling to go away?*

Daisy Perika eyeballed her nephew a stern warning. *Don't ask—you don't want to know.*

The knocking ceased. Father Raes felt a rush of relief, but this was mixed with an inexplicable sense of loss. And loneliness. *I should have opened the door myself.*

Moon dismissed the incident from his mind. Aunt Daisy had always been a bit peculiar, and age had only sharpened her eccentricities. The tall man got up from the kitchen table, leaned to peer through the small window. Three Sisters Mesa loomed massively over the mouth of *Cañon del Espiritu*. A cloud-bonnet had lodged itself on the head of the tallest of the legendary Pueblo sisters who, ages ago, had ascended to the heights to escape an Apache raiding party. In response to an urgent prayer for deliverance, the frightened women had been turned to stone by a stroke of lightning. Or so it was said.

Daisy felt the need to say something. "You men want some more coffee?"

Father Raes declined with his usual grace. The old woman's brew was strong enough to etch the enamel off a camel's teeth.

Moon also refused a second cup. "I'd best be heading home." The Columbine was a long, lonesome way north. And driving alone gave a man time to do plenty of thinking. Which was not always a good thing.

She turned off the blue propane flame under the coffee-pot, and assumed a casual tone. "That young woman in the picture—she have a name?"

"Wilma Brewster," her nephew said. "She was a student."

Daisy pretended to be surprised. "Was?"

Charlie Moon pretended to be taken in by his aunt's amateur performance. "Miss Brewster is no longer with us." *Not in this world.*

After a brief prayer for God's protection of Daisy Perika, Charlie Moon, Wilma Brewster—and himself—the Jesuit shepherd took his leave.

Charlie Moon departed in the priest's wake.

Deprived so suddenly of her company, Daisy Perika felt a pang of melancholy.

CHAPTER 32

Nested Visions

The aged woman was feeling every one of her many birthdays. *Except for my toenails, everything in my body aches.* But there was work to be done, and no one else to do it. This being so, she leaned on the stout oak staff with one arm, carried a bucket of well water with the other. Very deliberately—stalk by stalk—she slaked the thirst of three rows of stunted blue corn. When this task was completed, the weary woman paused to straighten her stiff back. *Oh, God . . . I am getting too old to live.*

Shielding her eyes from a bright patch of sky, Daisy squinted to the northwest. A long, leaf-shaped sliver of cloud drifted out from the San Juans to shade Three Sisters Mesa. As she watched, the cloud's shadow slipped over the earth like a wizard's cloak. A sage-tinted breeze was exhaled from the mouth of *Cañon del Espiritu,* whipping the old woman's woolen skirt around skinny legs. The shaman shuddered, pulled her third husband's overcoat tightly around her waist. *Soon it comes—the Moon of Dead Leaves Falling.* But for a while yet, only the highest peaks would be blanketed with white. The threat of a hard frost was of more immediate concern to the gardener than the uncountable mass of six-sided crystals brewing northward over the

Never Summer range. The malicious freeze that would murder her vegetables might be lurking just past tomorrow, planning an icy assault on the tiny garden. Daisy picked the few ripe tomatoes, which would be ruined instantly by a sudden drop in temperature. The green ones—so delicious when sliced, sprinkled with flour and salt, fried in an uncovered iron skillet—would not last into the depths of winter if plucked from the vine. The gardener did not hesitate; she pulled all of the tomato plants up by the roots. These would be stored in a dark space under the trailer.

Another breeze came to ruffle her skirt. This one also carried the spirit of winter—and something else. The shaman raised her nose, sniffed. *It's smoke.* And within the tiny particulates, there was an additional message for her nostrils. The distinct odor of roasting animal flesh. Rabbit, she thought. The Ute elder knew in an instant who would be roasting cottontail up in the Canyon of the Spirits. *The little man. And he might know something about the red-headed woman. Maybe that's why he came knocking on my door.*

Daisy Perika hurriedly stored the modest produce from her arid vegetable garden, stuffed a few selected items into a tattered pillowcase. She had someplace important to go. Something important to do.

The tribal elder started her stiff-legged journey toward the yawning mouth of the canyon. Once between the towering walls of *Cañon del Espiritu*, the grade was slight. A young person would hardly have noticed the climb. But the aged must walk slowly, pause frequently to take deep breaths. This allows time for their weary spirit-shadows to catch up and reattach to their mortal bodies.

Each time Daisy made the trek, it seemed as if her destination had moved farther up the canyon. The sun—which had been low in the east when she departed on her walk—was near its zenith as she approached the badger hole, long since abandoned by the original tenant. She sat down on a small shelf of variegated sandstone. The tribal elder leaned her tired back against the rough bark of a piñon that was even older than herself. Laying the oak staff across her thighs, she closed her eyes. Saw darkness. Then ripples of dim light. Something very much like sleep overcame the bone-tired woman.

The shaman would dream her way into the *pitukupf's* subterranean home.

The bottom of the badger hole had been hollowed out into an oval chamber. A thick cobweb of fine, hairlike roots hung from the ceiling. Sticking on some of these fibers were small, pearled beads of water. Embedded in an arched wall was a long taproot, descending from a middle-aged ponderosa. The flat, earthen floor was randomly cobbled with smooth stones that, eons ago, had tumbled along in an icy glacial stream. On the north wall of the snug chamber, the current occupant had fashioned a small fireplace, where a heap of dry willow twigs crackled with flame. Across the hearth, supported by notched blocks of sandstone, was a blackened oak branch. Mounted on this spit was the headless carcass of an unfortunate rodent. Grease dripped into the fire, popped in the willow embers. Aromatic smoke wafted upward through the thick whiskers of ceiling roots, found its way up through the twisting tunnel, drifted slowly down *Cañon del Espiritu* toward Daisy Perika's home.

Expert in the protocol of such meetings, Daisy held her tongue. The shaman stared at the *pitukupf*. Waited.

The age-old creature was seated on a three-legged stool near the small fire where his meal roasted slowly. He busied himself with some obscure task. For an undetermined time (in this place, ticks and tocks from little clocks cannot measure the mysterious distance between *then* and *now*) Daisy watched the dwarf carve on a hard pine knot with a knife the diminutive craftsman had surely fashioned himself. The instrument's handle was a crescent of knobby elk horn; the blade, resembling a glistening black elm leaf, was cunningly chipped obsidian. The smoky volcanic glass was streaked with ripples of crimson, as if some ancient reptile had been caught in the molten flow and left a bright trail of fossilized blood.

Her patience grew taut and thin. *I can't sit here all day waiting for this little rascal to say something.*

The small craftsman blew fine shavings off the pine knot, into the fire. He held his work up for a critical inspection, then began to whittle again.

She grunted.

The *pitukupf* did not acknowledge the shaman's presence.

Daisy cleared her throat. "You're looking well." *For a sawed-off little runt who must be at least a thousand years old.*

No response.

She tried again, assuming the solicitous tone of a long-lost friend. "Haven't seen you in a long time." After a polite pause, she added, "Somebody knocked on my door yesterday—I thought it might've been you. Thought maybe you wanted to stop by and talk."

The little man seemed determined to prove that his reputation for rudeness was well deserved. Hunched before the small fire on the three-legged stool, he pointedly continued with the work that fully occupied his attention.

The *pitukupf* had his own way of doing things. And his own notion of time. *Well, I'll give him a little longer.* Sitting on the floor of his underground den, she hugged her knees and watched.

Her inconsiderate host continued his concentrated effort to shape the woody object into something that did not look like a pine knot. Occasionally, he would pause to spit into the fire.

Father Raes has warned me a hundred times to stay away from the pitukupf. *Maybe I should have listened to the priest.* The shaman was suddenly struck with the absurd nature of her relationship with this eccentric creature. Like so many times before, here they were again in the abandoned badger hole the little squatter had selected for his home. And as always, they played their assigned roles. She, bringing small gifts to exchange for supposedly priceless information. The *pitukupf*—arrogant to the point of outright nastiness—spurning not only her offerings, but apparently objecting to the shaman's very presence in his domain. But in the end, he always accepted the bits of this and that she brought to loosen his lips. In return, he would break the silence to offer some fragment of information that was so shrouded in dark symbolism as to be practically useless.

Many winters ago, when Daisy had been a young woman, these clandestine meetings had filled her with awe, as if she were touching the edge of the Infinite. Now, with the fullness of age and experience, it was becoming apparent that the little man was little more than a man. A cranky, ugly, old man—the worst sort of that gender. *But nobody drug me here kicking and screaming. I came because I wanted to.* As this understanding grew in her breast, the shaman was beginning to feel a bit of a fool. Daisy Perika was not given to introspection, and this unexpected intrusion of self-knowledge was discomforting. *Well, let's get this over with.* The shaman removed the old pillowcase from her coat pocket, placed it on the earthen floor.

The small creature continued to whittle on the chunk of pine, seemingly uninterested in what the tribal elder had brought to his den.

But as Daisy removed a small sack of tobacco and a half pound of coffee, she was pleased to notice a quick glance from the *pitukupf*—an appreciative flare of hairy nostrils.

Even so, he continued to shape the wood with the stone blade.

Enough is enough. She set her jaw and glared at the side of his craggy little face. "I'm going to tell you something. And you better listen with both of your ugly ears, because I won't say this but once." She waited for a sign that he had taken notice of her. It did seem that the rhythm of his whittling had slowed. "Two times, I've had a talk with a skinny, redheaded *matukach* woman. She told me some strange things, so I wanted to ask you about her. But you probably don't know nothing about the whites and their strange doings."

There was a sudden darkness in his expression. But the elfin craftsman continued with his work.

"And even if you do know something about this woman, it don't matter that much to me. I am tired of your bad manners. Just the same, I'll leave what I brought you." The old woman turned the pillow-case upside down, dumping out a pile of oatmeal cookies.

The *pitukupf* stuck the obsidian blade under his buckskin belt, snatched two cookies, wolfed one down in three frantic bites, got to serious work on the other.

Miserable little glutton. Go ahead—eat yourself sick. "I'm going home now." The Ute elder pushed herself erect. "I don't know if I'll ever come back." She shook a finger at her host. "A mean little fellow like you don't deserve human company."

He stuffed the sack of tobacco under his shirt, looked up at the shaman. An utterly astounding thing happened.

She watched as a single tear formed at the corner of a yellowed eye, made a serpentine course down a leathery cheek. The shaman was slack-jawed with astonishment. It seemed impossible, but . . . *I've hurt his feelings.*

The *pitukupf* had yet another surprise up his sleeve.

He showed his guest a soiled palm. Upon it was what had been a pine knot. Now, the product of his skilled craftsmanship had taken on the shape of a delicate piñon cone. It was a thing of wonder.

The old woman's throat constricted, causing her to croak. "Is this for me?"

He nodded.

Daisy felt a pang of regret for scolding the little man, whose narrow face had taken on the wounded aspect of the martyred saint in the stained glass at St. Ignatius Church. "Well . . . that's very nice of you." She started to drop the carving into her pocket.

The squint-eyed frown on the dwarf's face made it clear that he opposed this action.

The shaman took another look at the gift. It was no longer a mere carving. This was an actual cone. Equally real were the nuts nestled between the segments.

It startled her when the *pitukupf* spoke. As in all previous encounters, he uttered his words in a choppy version of the Ute tongue so ancient that the tribal elder strained to understand.

She stared at the pinecone, then at her frustrated host. "What did you say?"

The dwarf scowled, made an impatient hand-to-mouth gesture.

"You want me to eat them?"

It was quite evident that he did.

Daisy removed several nuts, pried open the split brown hulls with her thumbnail. She placed a tiny kernel into her mouth. Chewed. Delicious. She popped a second tiny delicacy onto her tongue, nodded to communicate her approval.

The dwarf seemed to be quite gratified at this response.

Encouraged, Daisy put a third kernel in her mouth. *Oh my.* This one must be rotten; it was extremely bitter. And getting worse. She made a terrible face.

The *pitukupf*, who appreciated low comedy, slapped his skinny thigh, cackled a horrid laugh.

The shaman tried to spit the stuff out, right in his face. But like a wasp's nest under the eaves, it clung stubbornly to the roof of her mouth.

The dwarf laughed even harder, almost falling off the three-legged stool. Real tears began to drip off his cheeks.

It was clear that she had been the butt of one of the *pitukupf's* crude pranks.

Nasty little imp—I'll get you for this if it takes me the rest of my life!

She swallowed some of the bitter spittle. Coughed. Choked.

And then came the vision.

The shaman saw amazing things—things that made her tremble.

She saw Charlie Moon, clad in traditional beaded buckskins, holding a feathered lance. The tall warrior stood by a spotted mare. Her nephew concentrated all his attention on the beautiful animal, whose thick black mane he was braiding. He seemed unaware of what was behind him—a magnificent tipi whose top reached up to touch the clouds. The conical dwelling, white as the first snow, was decorated with cryptic figures. A helical band of bloodred handprints. Here and there, humpbacked bison snorting fire. Swarming herds of tiny blue horses galloping across an invisible plain. And something that looked like a four-wheeled wooden cart. In the small wagon was a skeletal figure, stripped of all flesh, but with a tuft of white hair radiating from a bulging skull.

The absurd skeleton did not frighten the shaman. That which terrified her came from the mists at the edge of her vision. It was that shadowy, amorphous figure who now routinely visited the world of her dreams—the same evil presence that had beheaded the pale elder.

Daisy tried to call out, warn her nephew. She had no voice.

The nightmare-shadow grew legs. Arms. Took on an almost human form. Placed a large scorpion on the earth behind Charlie Moon. The terrible creature scuttled inside the huge tipi. This done, the evil presence danced a few exaggerated steps—apparently to signify victory—then receded into the mists from whence it had come.

Again, the shaman tried to cry out a warning. She barely managed a mouselike squeak.

Charlie Moon, unaware of the imminent danger, caressed the mare's neck, whispered something into her ear. The spotted pony nodded her handsome head, whinnied.

Oh, God—it's too late. The shaman tensed, waited for the inevitable.

It came.

A blinding flash of white-hot lightning, a horrendous rumble of thunder that shook the earth to its very foundations. Screams, shrieks, groans. Smoke everywhere. And hanging on the smoke, the smell of roasting flesh. But not rabbit flesh.

A great wind came, swept the smoke away.

The earth remained.

The grand tipi was gone.

Charlie Moon was no more.

The spotted pony had likewise vanished.

But not everything had melted away from her horrific vision. The shaman cringed at the pitiful sound of moanings . . . groanings . . . terrible pain. Hungry tongues of flame licked at charred flesh. There were great heaps of blackened corpses—more than she could count.

Some twitched.

CHAPTER 33

An Obscure Illness

Among those who knew him, there were a variety of opinions about Charlie Moon's problem.

Scott Parris thought that it was probably a virus, maybe a touch of the flu. Give ol' Charlie a few more days, he'd be right as rain.

Dolly Bushman offered the opinion that the Ute had too many branding irons in the fire. The rancher was simply overworked. Exhausted. He needed to get away, take a long, restful vacation. For once in a blue moon, her argumentative husband agreed.

Jerome Kydmann thought Moon's problems were related to stress. The boss should slow down, the Kyd said. Delegate more authority. Learn to take things easy.

Alf Marquez had his own take on the matter. The Mexican assured his cowhand companions that the Ute's trouble came from being too rich. If a man owned very much land, had dozens of people working for him, he was bound to worry all the time. And worry sickened the mind. What the Indian needed was to sell off his properties, marry a young woman, raise a flock of children—and at least once a month, get roaring drunk.

An elderly Arapaho cowman conjectured that Charlie

Moon had eaten food that had been cursed by a witch. Or maybe he had gotten the dreaded night sickness, which came from sleeping with the window open. Either way, the cure was well-known. The Ute would benefit from regular sweat baths and smoking kinnikinnik in a red sandstone pipe.

Had she known about the symptoms, Daisy Perika would not have agreed with any of these diagnoses, or the prescribed cures. She would have pronounced her nephew a victim of ghost-sickness, for which there was no reliable treatment. The aged Ute shaman would not have been so far off the mark.

Every night, just moments after he closes his eyes, Charlie Moon drifts off into the same dream. And so it is no wonder that he awakens feeling bone weary. It is very hard on a man—dancing with a redheaded woman who never seems to tire. A woman who will not let go of him until the sun rises.

CHAPTER 34

The Killing

The visitor stood stiff-legged in Henry Buford's kitchen, knees knocking like an old well pump.

The BoxCar manager gave the impression of being quite at ease, and this unnerved his guest all the more. Buford was seated in a straight-backed chair, boots flat on the floor, right elbow resting easily on the dining table. He glanced at the pistol pointed at his chest. All five chambers in the cylinder were loaded. *Serves me right—I brought this on myself. But who wants to live to be a hundred.* "What's the matter?" Buford raised his palms in a mocking gesture of surrender. "There's nothin' to be scared of—you got the drop on ol' Henry. Hell, a blind man couldn't miss at this range."

The response was barely above a whisper. "I really don't want to do this." The short barrel of the shiny revolver wavered ever so slightly.

"Of course you don't," Buford said. "But you don't have any choice—because I know what you've been up to. And you know what I intend to do about it."

The visitor went glassy-eyed.

Buford's grin was a merry one, as if this was a delightful game. "So what're you gonna do—stare me to death?" He shook his head wearily. "Ah, hell—let's get this sorry business done with."

This is like a terrible dream. The unwelcome guest pulled the trigger, heard the explosive discharge, felt the jerking recoil of the pistol grip—saw the fluffy hole blossom in the ranch manager's plaid shirt. It had all happened so very quickly, like a flash of summer lightning. The playful smirk was still on Henry Buford's face.

CHAPTER 35

Strike Three

Charlie Moon was seated across the government-issue desk from Sam Parker, special agent in charge of the FBI's Denver field office. The tribal investigator waited for the *matukach* cop to have his say.

On a dirty sill outside the third-floor window, a fat pigeon made short, jerky steps, occasionally pausing to cock a cherry-red eye at the federal lawman and his Ute visitor. On the street below, an endless chain of automobiles and trucks and buses rumbled by.

Parker—oblivious to feathered creatures and the racket of internal combustion engines—leafed through a report that was neatly bound in a blue plastic cover. He cleared his throat. "Charlie, this is a summary of the findings on Senator Davidson's four-wheel-drive scooter." The SAC glanced at his guest. "Here's the long and short of it. There wasn't anything in the senator's Electric GroundHog that didn't belong there."

The amiable Ute felt his blood pressure rising. "Let's make sure I got this right—I drove all the way to Denver just to hear that your experts didn't find anything?"

"I thought we should have a heart-to-heart conversation." The wide, toothy mouth smiled at him. "Don't take this as a criticism, Charlie. But you seem a wee bit edgy."

"Don't take this as a criticism, Sam—but a fifty-cent phone call would've saved me a long, tiresome drive over the mountains."

The SAC leaned back in his swivel chair. "There were reasons for requesting the pleasure of your company. Any discussion even potentially connecting a United States senator to alleged espionage is far too sensitive to conduct over an open line. And I wanted to see you face-to-face so I could offer you a confidential update." Sam Parker bunched the bushy brows. "I am authorized to inform you that the senator's security leak has been plugged. A member of Davidson's D.C. staff was arrested yesterday, in Falls Church, Virginia. It'll be on the six o'clock news, but I thought you'd want to hear it from me."

The tribal investigator felt his hands go cold. He wanted to say that this was good news. That he was truly sorry he'd wasted the Bureau's valuable time with his hunch that the Electric GroundHog was bugged. But the sting of failure had numbed his lips.

Parker, who had suffered more than a few professional embarrassments, understood. "You're a way better than average country cop, Charlie. But when it comes to crimes like espionage, let the Bureau handle it."

Moon nodded. "Guess I've been playing out of my league."

"Hey, you tried the majors, gave it your best swing—and you struck out. That's a helluva lot better than not ever walking up to the plate. But from now on, leave the fast pitches to the heavy-hitters."

Moon fixed his gaze over the SAC's head, at a framed watercolor of blue and yellow flowers thumbtacked to the wall. *For Daddy*, the youthful artist had scrawled. Proof that somebody loved the fed.

Parker snapped the cover shut on the report.

The tribal investigator pushed himself up from the uncomfortable chair, went to the window. The pigeon turned a blood-tinted eye on the tall man. Made a warbling sound.

Moon muttered a response in the Ute tongue.

The feathered creature departed in a flutter of gray wings.

Denver and the bitter taste of defeat now well behind him, Granite Creek would be visible just over the next ridge. Another hour beyond the town, nestled between the mountains, the Columbine. Home was a powerful, relentless magnet. Always pulling at him.

Charlie Moon thought he might stop just long enough to top off the gas tank, then pass through town to begin the drive across the high, arid prairie toward his ranch. But there was a sharp disagreement from his members. The Ute's long legs informed his brain that they needed stretching. Denied this necessity, they would slowly turn blue, wither up, fall off. His stomach chimed in with an urgent request for sustenance. The requests became demands. The left side of his brain reminded him that there was no pressing need to return immediately to the ranch. Charlie Moon surrendered; he would appease both legs and stomach. He found a parking space between Martin Street and Nelson Avenue, just two blocks from where the three-story brick police station squatted like a lazy toad waiting for a felonious fly. The walk made his legs very happy. His stomach sulked.

Refreshed by this mild exercise, he entered the GCPD building, nodded at the day shift dispatcher, climbed the stairs to the corner office occupied by the chief of police. Scott Parris greeted his best friend, took him into the chief's meeting room where coffee was offered the visitor. Plus a jelly donut. The Ute decided that the best way to dispose of this sweet temptation was with three savage bites.

Parris, though on a steady diet of undercooked broccoli and semi-raw carrots, still suffered the indignity of a slight bulge around the middle. The middle-aged man watched his lean friend with a jealous eye as Moon accepted a second donut, then resisted a third. "I see you're not overly hungry today."

"Saving my appetite for suppertime."

The older man looked down at his belt buckle, sighed.

Moon added sugar to his black coffee. "Thanks for the refreshments."

Parris gave his friend a long, thoughtful appraisal. "You look kinda tired."

"Was up before the sun. Drove over the mountains to Denver. Spent some time with the suits."

"Lucky you."

"So what's happening in your life?"

A melancholy expression spread over the white man's face. "Dismal ain't the word. You know what that woman has done—"

Moon cut him off. "Hold it right there."

"What?"

"When you start moaning about your love life, you get that hang-dog look. It's just too pitiful and I can't bear to see it."

"Well, what'd you like to hear about—my last attack of colitis?"

The Ute considered the offer. "Think I'll pass on that one."

"Then what?"

"Tell me about something you're working on."

Parris waved an arm at the stack of documents on the cluttered table. "I'm working on performance appraisals. Budget estimates. Duty roster for next month."

"This is really sad. You must be doing something worth talking about."

"Not really." The chief of police rubbed at watery eyes. "This job is getting to be a real drag."

"Anything on that big fire and explosion at the airport construction site?"

Parris removed a file from a gray metal cabinet. "We got this report back from the state arson investigator." He opened the folder. "But didn't I already tell you about that?"

The tribal investigator shook his head.

"I guess that's because there was nothing particularly interesting between the covers. Mostly speculation. It's clear enough that something set off the portable propane tank inside the unfinished terminal building. Could've been a trash fire. A lightning strike. Or maybe somebody took a potshot at the fuel tank."

A shot. "Forensics turn up anything on that chunk of lead?"

"Oh, yeah—I'd almost forgot about your big find at the burn site." The chief of police grinned. "The specimen of lead that might possibly be the remains of a high-caliber bullet." Parris searched the arson investigator's report, found the section titled "Miscellaneous Debris," ran his finger down the page until he found a paragraph entitled "Lead Fragment." "You want to read it?"

"Nope. Just give me the executive summary."

"Okay, I'll boil the cabbage down. Based on amounts of trace levels of bismuth and antimony, the lead was mined at a location in southwestern Saskatchewan. Same corporation that mines the ore also uses the refined metal in their product line." Parris recited the list. "High-current electrical terminals for industrial circuit breakers. Electrodes for lead-acid electrolytic cells. Fishing sinkers. And security seals." He bunched his eyebrows at this last entry. "I guess that means those wire seals the electric company puts on their meters—to keep dishonest customers from tampering with the readout."

"But this Canadian company doesn't make bullets."

"Not even a BB for your Daisy rifle." Parris flipped the report aside. "The terminal building was full of all kinds of construction stuff. Welding machines, gasoline and diesel engines, every kind of hand and power tool you can imagine. So after the explosion, I guess we shouldn't be surprised to find almost anything scattered around the ruins."

Moon returned to the coffeepot, refilled his cup. "The construction company—they have insurance coverage?"

"Twelve million and change. But the firm's not in any kind of financial trouble, so if the terminal building was torched, I doubt it was for the insurance. Probably some sicko who loves to see the fire." He wriggled his fingers to imitate flames dancing.

Happy to have this diversion from his troubles, Moon leaned back in his chair. "Could've been kids playing around with matches."

Parris nodded. "Last year we had three juveniles build a campfire inside a barn—where the straw was six inches deep. Fire was out of control before they could get their marshmallows roasted. Loss was over eighty thousand dollars. Poor dairy farmer got wiped out. Dumb-ass kids got a stern lecture from the judge plus a year's probation." Parris shook his head. "I don't know what some of these young people use for brains."

CHAPTER 36

The Chef

Charlie Moon slowed as he passed the Mountain Man Bar & Grille. The graveled parking lot was almost filled. *Quite a crowd for this time of day.* He did a U-turn, pulled into the graveled lot fronting the establishment. *Maybe he took my advice.*

Indeed, the owner of the business had given up his cook's apron. BoBo Harper was at the cash register, smiling as he accepted credit cards, hard cash, and earnest compliments from happy diners. He was still grinning when he saw the Ute. "Hey, fella, glad to see you. This meal's on the house. But while we clear a table, I got somebody I want you to say hello to." He took the Ute by the elbow, guided him through a restaurant crowded with happy customers. BoBo pushed the swinging doors aside, ushered his guest into the kitchen. The formerly filthy den had been transformed. Copper-bottom pans sparkled, the stainless steel sink shined—even the floors were clean.

At the gas range, the new cook was hard at work. Mrs. Brewster looked up to see the new arrival, smiled. BoBo clapped his honored guest on the back. "Jane, I think you've already met Mr. Moon." He winked. "This here fella's my business advisor." With this, the owner departed into the dining room, shouting orders to one of three new waitresses he had hired to help Charlene.

Jane Brewster put aside a ladle. She reached out, captured Charlie Moon in a crushing bear hug.

He winced at the pain in a fractured rib. "What's this all about?"

"You know very well." Her eyes were filling with tears. "Now lean over, you two-legged telephone pole."

He leaned.

She kissed him.

If his dark face could have blushed, it would have.

The cook laughed at the shy man. "I know you recommended me for this job. And don't you deny it—Mr. Harper told me."

Moon grinned. "Looks like business has picked up."

"And I haven't forgot how you made a place on top of that pretty hill for my daughter's grave." Wilma Brewster's mother wiped at her eyes. "Now go out there and find yourself a table—I'm going to fix you something really special."

Charlene seated Moon; the waitress patted him on the shoulder. "Glad to see you back."

"I'm glad to be back."

She put a hand on her hip. "So what'll ya have to drink?"

He thought about it.

"We got real lemonade. Fresh squeezed."

The diner looked doubtful. "Squeezed from what?"

"From cactus apples." She brayed the donkey laugh, slapped him on the arm. "From lemons, of course."

"Then bring me a tall glass."

"You got it, honey."

Twenty minutes later, the cattle rancher was hard at work on a stacked green chili enchilada. The creation was segmented with blue-corn tortillas, laced with onions and tender roast beef, smothered in sharp cheddar cheese. The BoxCar gatekeeper had not exaggerated this woman's culinary skills. Jane Brewster was a rare find.

CHAPTER 37

Trouble

As he had a hundred times before, Charlie Moon drove the Ford pickup westward along his favorite stretch of two-lane highway. It was barely an hour from Granite Creek to the Columbine entrance. He could almost see it. The massive log arch spanning the entrance. The dirt lane crawling like a yellow snake over the high prairie grasslands, skirting the green garments of granite mountains, slipping over rocky ridges. Pete and Dolly Bushman's sturdy log house, set under a cluster of cottonwoods. Finally, the rattling plank bridge over Too Late Creek, and home. *Home.* Now there was a fine word. Like a warm pocket filled with sweet things. Shelter. Food. Sleep. Peace.

Even among the dead bones of autumn, when the prairie grasses were brittle with frost and a stiff breeze swept waves of powdered snow across the highway, he still found a special joy in this short journey. At this moment, the majestic, flint-hard loveliness was more wondrous than on any previous passing. But on this particularly steel-gray day, the tribal investigator was blind to the visual banquet spread out before him. The man's normally buoyant spirit was heavy under the weight of failure. Melancholy thoughts magnified his defeat. *There wasn't anything wrong with the senator's electric scooter. Or anything suspicious about him getting crippled up. I'll never know who killed Wilma Brewster. I'll never see the face of the man who bashed Billy Smoke's head in for a few dollars—or maybe just for the hell of it. And probably would have done the same to Senator Davidson if Oscar Sweetwater hadn't come running with his pistol. Sam Parker was right—I should stick to what I do best. Whatever that is.*

His thoughts were interrupted by a warbling. The tribal investigator found the cell phone in his jacket pocket. "Yeah?"

His aunt's voice crackled in his ear. *"Yeah? That's no way to answer the telephone."*

Moon forced a cheerful tone. "What's up?"

She told him. "I'm not sleeping good."

He grinned into the phone. "Shouldn't be a big problem—brew yourself some of that Red Root tea."

"That wouldn't help, Red Root is for stopping bleeding!"

He assumed a doubtful tone. "You sure about that?"

"Well, of course I'm sure—when a person can't sleep, they need a dose of figwort or bugleweed tea." There was a pause before she began to mutter to herself. "He's got me off the track." A sigh. "Now what was it I wanted to tell him about?"

"Sorry, I don't remember."

"Don't get smart with me, you big jughead." Another pause. "Now I remember. So shut up and listen to what I've got to say."

He shut up, and listened.

The shaman did not mention her visit to the *pitukupf's* underground home, or the fact that her most recent vision had been induced by eating the little man's carved piñon nuts. But she did tell him what she had seen, though she disguised the vision as a dream.

The tribal investigator half-listened to a wild tale about an old man in a wheeled cart, a gigantic tipi that vanished, great heaps of roasted corpses. When the aged storyteller paused for a breath, he felt obliged to offer a sympathetic comment. "That *was* a nightmare on legs."

Nightmare. That reminded her. The Ute elder's voice was heavy with accusation. "It's all your fault, Charlie Moon—you could've stopped it from happening!"

She must still be half asleep. "I could've, huh?"

With uncharacteristic patience, she proceeded to explain. If her nephew had not been so busy with that pretty mare, he would've understood what was going to happen and done something to prevent it. She paused, waiting for his apology.

"I am truly sorry for my many shortcomings." *Next time, I'll try to pay more attention to what you're dreaming.*

Somewhat mollified, Daisy Perika proceeded to tell him about an earlier vision—which she also presented as an unsettling dream.

Moon was moderately entertained by the bizarre account of a shadowy presence that had chopped off a man's head. And not just any man—a distinguished elder. To humor the eccentric old soul, he inquired, "Who was this fella who lost his head?"

Her tone was testy. "I'd rather not say." *You'd just laugh at me.*

He knew how to make her talk. "Yeah. Maybe it's better if you don't tell me—"

She shouted in his ear. "He was a president of the United States of America."

"Which one?"

"Look at a dollar bill," she snapped.

"George Washington?" The grin went ear to ear. "Well, don't worry about him—I'm pretty sure he's already dead. Has been for quite some time." He heard a rude suggestion in the Ute tongue, a sharp click in his ear as she hung up.

Charlie Moon put the cell phone back into his pocket. *Poor old woman; she spends too much time by herself.* Daisy invariably refused his offers to live at the Columbine. *I need to get someone to stay with her.* He wondered where he would find a sensible person who would take on the job of looking after an ill-tempered old woman who lived in a little trailer way out yonder at the mouth of *Cañon del Espiritu*. On top of that, it would have to be someone Daisy would allow in her home. Which, since she couldn't get along with anyone on the face of the earth, made it a daunting challenge indeed.

The pickup topped a rise in the undulating prairie. The western horizon was a deep shade of midnight blue. Hanging over the Misery Range was a single, oddly shaped cloud. It looked like nothing in particular, but the human imagination is compelled to analyze and categorize such amorphous forms. A healthy man's mind might have seen a cauliflower. A huge peanut. Even a fist. The tribal investigator saw a crippled Senator Davidson riding his Electric GroundHog across the endless sky. Moon shook his head, as if to dislodge the sickly illusion. *This is really pitiful. I keep on this way, I'll end up like Aunt Daisy, seeing things where there's nothing to see. Believing my nightmares are real.* He recalled the ancient Ute prescription for good mental health. Six times, he repeated the mantra: *Don't think bad thoughts.* Being a product of his times, he added a positive corollary. *Think good thoughts.* And so he did. *Everything is going to be fine.*

Immediately the pickup engine coughed. Took hold again. Stuttered.

Stopped.

As the power steering hydraulics lost pressure, Moon felt the wheel stiffen in his hands. The truck coasted to a gradual stop on a shoulder where dry grasses leaned flat in the wind. He tried the ignition. Nothing. Dead as last year's hope for a better world. He watched frigid droplets of liquid water ricochet off the F-150's rusty hood, splatter against the windshield. The bomblets were gradually transformed into prickly shards of ice. *Ain't this just swell. Stalled thirty miles from home and it's sleeting parallel to the ground.*

Moon buttoned his jacket to the collar, got out, lifted the hood. *Could be the battery's given up the ghost. Or maybe the alternator's not pumping electricity.* He tried to remember: *When I turned the key, did I hear the starter solenoid click?* He pulled at the high voltage cable sprouting from the autotransformer coil. The thing looked sound enough. Ditto for the spark plug cables. Sleet pelted his neck. Icy water dribbled down his back. *If I'm lucky, it'll be a bad battery connection.*

Charlie Moon spent twenty minutes cleaning both battery terminals, tightening the cable connections. He got into the cab, slammed the door, turned the ignition switch—cranked the engine to life. *All right—things are looking up.* He pulled onto the highway, shifted up to second gear. With no worries to occupy it, his mind shifted to neutral. Seemingly pointless associations were made. White goop. Lead hydroxide carbonate. Lead. Battery terminal. Lead battery terminal. Lead . . .

The needle got stuck.

Lead battery terminal.

Lead battery terminal.

Lead battery terminal.

The tribal investigator jammed the brake pedal to the floor, skidded to a stop on the slippery highway.

My God. Surely not . . .

He sat in the pickup, unable to believe what he was thinking. The sleet departed. The snow came to call, accompanied by its old friend the wind. A minor gale whistled around the sharp edges of the pickup, howled like a pack of starving wolves on a bloody trail. The human being was oblivious to nature's drama.

As one in a dream, Charlie Moon removed a cell phone from the glove compartment, entered a number. There was an almost immediate answer. Miss James's voice was sweet and warm.

He identified himself. "Are you in Washington—with the senator?"

"Why, yes, Charlie. It is so nice to hear from you. Where are—"

"I need to know something."

The smile went out of her voice. "What?"

"Is there a fixed schedule for servicing the senator's electric scooter?"

"I'm not sure—Henry Buford takes care of things like that."

"Things like what?"

"Well, from time to time, Henry charges the batteries. The senator sometimes forgets to plug his machine in when he goes to bed."

"Were the batteries charged before Patch went to Washington?"

"I don't know. But I believe Allan did replace one of the batteries."

"Allan? I thought we were talking about Henry Buford."

There was a brief silence. "Allan said Henry asked him to do it."

Moon chewed on this. It had a bad taste. "Does that seem likely?"

"What do you mean?"

"Has Henry ever asked the senator's nephew to do anything like that before?"

"Well, now that you mention it, no. Henry doesn't trust anyone to mess around with electrical or mechanical things." She laughed. "Henry especially doesn't trust Allan."

"This is very important—which battery did the senator's nephew replace?"

"There's more than one?"

"There are two. The main unit and a backup."

"Oh. Is it important which one was replaced?"

It has to be the backup. "Where is the senator?"

"At the moment, he's with the rest of the Senate in the House Chamber, waiting to hear the president's speech to the joint session."

Moon felt his stomach churn. "What speech?"

"His address on Social Security and Medicare. Wait a minute, I'll check the closed-circuit TV." The line went silent, then: "The president is just entering the chamber. And there's Senator Davidson in the front row." She waited for a response from the Ute. "Charlie?"

Aunt Daisy had dreamed about an old man in a wheeled cart. A great tipi vanishing. Great heaps of burned bodies. And . . . George Washington's head chopped off. Washington *decapitated*. For a brief interval, Moon was deaf—and had the eerie sense that his body had turned to stone.

"Charlie, are you there?"

Moon heard his voice respond in mechanical fashion. "Contact the Secret Service. Tell them there's an explosive device in Senator Davidson's electric scooter. They'll want to call me." He recited his cell phone number to the senator's assistant.

He could feel the mix of fear and disbelief in her voice. "Why on earth do you—"

"Make the call right now. I'm heading for the BoxCar." He pressed the End button on the cell phone, terminating the conversation.

Several miles down the road, the telephone emitted an electronic chirp. The tribal investigator pressed the instrument against his ear. "I'm here."

The voice on the other end was calm as a Sunday morning. "Am I speaking to Mr. Charles Moon?"

"You are."

"I'm Special Agent Adams, United States Secret Service. Our conversation is being recorded."

"No problem."

"You will understand the need to verify your identity, Mr. Moon. Please give me your Social Security number."

The Ute recited nine digits.

Adams passed the information on to Research. "Now tell me what you know about a threat against Senator Davidson."

"I have reason to believe someone has rigged an explosive device on his electric scooter."

The Secret Service agent's response was calm, matter-of-fact, as if they were discussing a weather report predicting sunny days. "What leads you to this conclusion?"

"A while back, a building at local airport construction site was destroyed—fire and explosion. Probable arson. A chunk of lead was found just outside the burned area. Looked like it might've been a large-caliber bullet. But it wasn't a bullet. It was what was left of a battery terminal." *Or a fishing sinker.*

Agent Adams was scribbling notes on a yellow legal pad. "Battery terminal."

"I believe the explosive device is concealed in a twelve-volt storage battery." Moon's mouth was dry as cork. "The airport explosion was probably a test."

"Test?"

Said out loud, this was starting to sound pretty thin. Feeling more and more the imbecile who had leaped into an abyss, the tribal investigator continued his free fall. "Before the bad guy put an explosive battery in the senator's electric scooter, he had to be sure it'd work."

"Electric scooter?"

What is this guy, some kinda damn echo chamber?

"Mr. Moon, are you still there?"

"Yeah."

"Do you have any hard evidence to back up these allegations?"

There was a flinty edge on the Ute's words. "You'll find your hard evidence in Senator Davidson's scooter. It's in the House Chamber, parked right up front—just a few yards from the president of the United States."

"In the absence of supporting evidence, I don't—"

Moon gripped the cell phone so hard the sturdy plastic cracked. "We're wasting time talking. You've got a choice to make—do something useful while there may still be a few minutes left, or just sit on your ass and wait for the explosion."

"I understand your frustration, Mr. Moon, and I assure you that decisions are being made even as we speak." There was a brief interruption as the agent paused to listen to an instruction from a superior, then: "I need more information. Is there any reason to believe that someone has actually installed an explosive device in Senator Davidson's—"

"I talked to the senator's personal assistant a few minutes ago. Miss James confirmed that one of the storage batteries was replaced on his electric scooter. This happened a couple days ago—right before he left for D.C."

"Is a battery replacement unusual?"

"Not if the ranch manager had done it. Henry takes care of stuff like that."

There was a distinct tone of interest in the distant voice. "Who switched the batteries?"

"Allan Pearson. The senator is his uncle."

"You are suggesting that the senator's *nephew* has placed an explosive device in his electric scooter?"

"I'm not suggesting—I'm telling you straight out."

"But what would be the nephew's motive—"

"I don't know. And at the moment, I don't really give a damn."

"Do you have any information about the nature of the explosive device?"

"Like what?"

"Type and quantity of explosive material. How will the detonator be triggered—by remote control or timer?"

"I don't have the least notion. All I can tell you is you'd better do something *right now.*"

"Tell me precisely where you are."

About forty-five minutes from being arrested for filing a nuisance report with the United States Secret Service. "About forty-five miles west of Granite Creek, Colorado. I'm headed toward the BoxCar—that's Patch Davidson's ranch."

"Keep the line open, Mr. Moon."

The tribal investigator turned onto the BoxCar lane, braked the pickup to a skidding halt by the closed gate. The gatehouse was dark inside. Moon banged on the door. Nothing. He turned the knob. Locked. The big man took a step backward, aimed the heel of his boot at a spot just below the doorknob. Drove it home. Wood splintered, fragments of the cast-iron lock mechanism went flying. He unholstered the .357 Magnum revolver, entered the shack, yelled: "Ned Rogers—you in here?"

No response. He switched on the lights. The room that served as the gatekeeper's duty post was not occupied. Moon checked the small bedroom, and a tiny bathroom that smelled strongly of aftershave and urine. Still no Rogers. Which was not surprising. With the BoxCar effectively shut down in the senator's absence, the gatekeeper had probably taken some time off. Moon returned to the room that served as Ned Rogers's lookout station, staring out the north window. *Maybe I'm way off base.* He heard Agent Adam's muffled voice calling his name. The tribal investigator pulled the live cell phone from his jacket pocket, jammed it against his ear. "I'm here."

"Mr. Moon, have you arrived at the senator's ranch?"

"I'm at the BoxCar gatehouse. Ranch headquarters is another six miles up the lane." The log house where Henry Buford lived was closer to four. He really did not want to know but . . . "Have you guys done anything?"

There was a brief hesitation. "On the basis of your call, Mr. Moon, the Senate Chamber has been evacuated."

God help me. If there is no bomb, I am in deep, deep trouble. The tribal investigator inhaled a long breath. "You want me to see if I can find Pearson?"

"We do. Miss James informs us that the senator's nephew has an apartment in the main residence on the ranch property, and also a small house in a more remote location."

"Yeah. The line shack."

"We have not been able to reach Mr. Pearson by telephone in the main residence, and we understand there is no telephone in his other residence."

Moon watched the northern sky—a pale blue sea, here and there whirling swirls of pink and purple. The high country air was charged with electric premonition. Something unseen whispered in his ear, a cold finger prickled the hair on his neck. The Ute was certain that something was about to happen. Something very unpleasant.

In the background of the Ute's consciousness, the federal agent's voice droned on. "We would appreciate it if you would make an attempt to contact Mr. Pearson—inquire about his reason for installing a replacement battery in the senator's electric scooter, then get back to us. And keep in mind that so far as we know, no crime has been committed. We will merely wish to interview Mr. Pearson at length." The special agent added ominously: "And yourself, of course."

Moon felt cold. Like dead meat. "Anything else I can do for you?"

"Not at the moment, but keep your cell phone avail—" There was a sudden, dead silence, as if the line had been disconnected.

For sixteen seconds that lasted half a lifetime, the Ute waited.

Agent Adams voice barked in his ear. "Mr. Moon?"

"I'm still here." *Wish I was somewhere else.*

"I am informed that there has been a tremendous explosion in the Senate Chamber."

"Was anyone—"

"There were no casualties among the senators. But two of our agents and several members of the Capitol Police Bomb Squad are unaccounted for and presumed dead." The Secret Service agent's tone was now hard. "I understand that you are a sworn officer of the law."

"That's right."

"Are you armed?"

"I am."

"The official position of the United States Secret Service is that Mr. Pearson is presumed innocent. If you should have the opportunity, we request that you detain this individual as a material witness." There was a pregnant silence. "But as we realize that Mr. Pearson might turn out to be extremely dangerous, you are expected to use due caution in any attempt to take him into custody. I hope you understand what I'm telling you."

The tribal investigator understood perfectly. This was an unofficial, personal request from a furious federal cop who knew that the wealthy senator's nephew would probably never be indicted, much less go to trial. *If the bastard resists arrest, kill him.*

CHAPTER 38

Firestorm

If the V8 engine had been properly tuned, he would have been flying along at eighty miles an hour. As it was, the F-150 speedometer was bouncing about the sixty-five mark. Charlie Moon was bouncing about the cab. The rational part of his brain reminded him that it was not sensible to drive so fast on the rough road. Another, more elemental part of that mysterious organ urged *hurry hurry hurry*. Praying that he wouldn't blow a bald tire and end up in some deep arroyo with a broken neck, the tribal investigator kept the pedal on the floorboard.

He was less than a minute from Henry Buford's home when a mushroom of coal-black smoke sprouted up, blotting out the northern horizon. An unseen hand painted a fiery smear across the turquoise sky. The Ute investigator topped the ridge over the shallow valley dotted with cottonwoods. The log house was a roaring mass of fire underneath a boiling column of acrid smoke.

If Henry had been inside, he was way past helping.

After finding no sign of life at the edge the roaring inferno, Moon continued on toward the BoxCar headquarters, where recent history was about to be repeated. As he topped the crest of the ridge overlooking the green oasis, the wealthy man's mansion suffered an even more violent fate than Buford's log house. The booming explosion tossed red roof tiles for a thousand yards; a rolling mixture of intensely blue fire and pitch-black smoke grew into a mile-high poisonous mushroom. After a brisk west wind cleared away some of the ground-level smoke, the Ute was surprised to see that none of the outer sandstone walls were standing. After a fruitless attempt to get near the super-heated ruins, he turned east on a dirt lane, aiming the F-150 in the general direction of Dead Mule Notch—and Alan Pearson's line shack. There were several crossroads and forks in the rough lane. He stayed with the electric power line.

Thirty bone-jarring minutes later, the road began to peter out. He followed the utility poles into a shallow canyon between a pair of sandstone mesas that extended out from the sides of the Notch. After passing through a thicket of scrub oak, the tribal investigator pulled the pickup to a jerk-ing halt in front of a ramshackle structure. This had to be it. The sad-faced little building wore a peaked hat of rusty tin; the walls were made of vertical, creosote-soaked pine slabs. At one corner of the structure, a fifty-five-gallon oil drum was placed to catch water from a rusty downspout. A lime-green propane tank was nudged up against the west wall; the metal cylinder seemed to be doing its level best to hold the leaning structure upright. Thirty paces to the rear, there was a wooden privy with a door hanging on a single rusty hinge. He got out of the pickup, made a quick inspection of the ground in front of the cabin. A complex of tire tracks crisscrossed in the brownish-red sand, but there was no sign of Pearson's flashy red motorcycle.

A hand-printed sign was tacked to the door.

> IF YOU WERE NOT INVITED
> YOU ARE NOT WELCOME
> GO AWAY!

Hand resting on the butt of his holstered pistol, Moon called out. The only response was a thin echo off a cliff wall, a raspy call from an unseen raven. He knocked once on the unpainted door, then tried the knob. Locked. The lawman reminded himself that the right and proper thing would be to get a warrant before entering.

Well to hell with that.

For the second time on this singular day, he kicked a door in. Revolver in hand, the tribal investigator entered the musty building. An overpowering stench of stale food and sour beer sucked his breath away.

Moon switched on a penlight, poked bright holes in the soupy near-darkness. The shack enclosed a single rectangular room. A shiny tin fixture sprouting a trio of lightbulbs hung from the ceiling. He pulled at a dangling string to switch on this poor man's chandelier. What he saw complemented the noxious odors. With a little cleaning up, Allan Pearson's hangout could qualify as a pig pen. Bits of cracked brown plaster hung like scabs on the walls, rotting pine rafters were thick with sooty cobwebs. Aside from a sturdy wooden bench under the south window, a rickety pair of straight-backed chairs, and a broken-down old cupboard, there was no furniture worthy of the name. Only a scattering of wooden and cardboard boxes, a bookcase jury-rigged from pine boards set on cinder blocks. An unvented space heater squatted near the wall where the external propane tank gamely played its supporting role. In a corner, there was a small electric refrigerator, its worn compressor chugging away erratically, imitating an outboard motor with fouled spark plugs.

The senator's nephew apparently slept on a mattress on the floor. Littered about at random were bits of dirty clothing, dirtier blankets, biker magazines with sassy-looking pinups on the covers. Stacked in a cobwebbed corner were cardboard boxes of canned goods. Corn, pinto beans, tomato soup, green peas. A large plastic trash container was half filled with empty food cans. A makeshift table—an unpainted sheet of plywood set on a pair of wooden boxes—was littered with unwashed cooking and eating utensils. Plus a scattering of hypodermic syringes and pill bottles.

Only the workbench displayed some semblance of order. On the Formica-covered surface there was a plastic toolbox, a Fluke digital voltmeter, a model 545 Tektronix oscilloscope, a soldering iron, a roll of electrician's tape. But Moon's attention was focused on an AusTex Beef Stew box occupying the precise center of the bench. After a careful inspection that convinced him the box was not boobytrapped, he used the blade of his pocketknife to lift the lid. Inside the cardboard container were a variety of interesting items.

Most prominent to Moon's eye were the disassembled components of a twelve-volt storage battery. The plastic casing had been neatly sawed into upper and lower halves. Lead electrodes were carefully arranged in a glass tray.

A small pressurized tank was propped in a corner of the box. A painted label specified its contents. The liquefied gas was so dangerous that few craftsmen had used it for years, preferring more stable products. But the old-fashioned compound was readily available.

There were also two Kerr canning jars. Each was half filled with a powder, one a rusty brown color, the other silvery in appearance. From his military experience, Moon understood the significance of the contents. By themselves, the powders were harmless enough. But combined in the proper proportions, these were the basic ingredients for a highly potent incendiary. Because the composition was relatively difficult to ignite, a brick of it was safe enough to carry around in your pocket. But once the mix was lit off, it would melt holes through any known metal or alloy. And the fire *could not be extinguished*—the hellish burn continued until the material was entirely consumed. Very, very ugly stuff.

The assassin had left behind a clear account of his malignant method. Surround a pound of the powder composition with a half-gallon of the liquefied gas, conceal the package in a hollowed-out storage battery, ignite the assembly—the result was an extremely impressive explosion and fire. Enough to destroy an unoccupied airport terminal building—or a House Chamber filled with human beings. Allan Pearson was determined to make certain that he received full credit for his nefarious activities.

Moon replaced the lid on the box, went to the open door for a breath of clean air. As his eyes scanned the top of the mesa, the Ute wondered where the senator's nephew had gone to ground. Wherever it was, the quirky young criminal would be a very long way from the BoxCar.

CHAPTER 39

Three Weeks Later

A steaming cup of coffee warming his hand, Charlie Moon waited on the west porch of the Columbine headquarters. The hound stood stiffly beside him, bile-green hatred glinting in his eyes. Man and beast alike watched Stanley Newman emerge from the Ford sedan, march purposefully across the yard. The FBI agent carried a briefcase.

The descendant of wolves moved protectively in front of the human being he had adopted. The animal bared yellowed teeth, rumbled a low growl.

Moon spoke softly. "It's okay, Sidewinder—he works for the government."

The dog, reputed to be a hard-shell Republican, growled louder.

Newman paused at the porch steps, gave the ill-tempered animal a wary look. "He bite?"

"Only when you least expect it." Moon scratched a spot behind the dog's ear.

The beast sniffed at the fed's knees, slobbered on his shoe, lost interest, trotted away to wherever such creatures trot.

The rancher took his guest inside, invited him to sit by the fireplace where an aromatic piñon fire crackled sweetly.

The federal agent seated himself in a leather chair. Closed his eyes. Sighed. *This is the life. Wish I could just stay here with Charlie.*

The Ute jabbed a sooty iron poker at the fire. "How about some coffee."

Newman leaned toward the flames. "Thanks, but I'm all coffeed up."

"Where's your partner, Stan?"

The query echoed from the suit back to the Ute. "Partner?"

"You fellas always travel in pairs." Unless there was a good reason not to—like there shouldn't be a witness to the business conducted.

The visitor danced a nimble sidestep around the question. "You're a curious man, Charlie, you know that?"

"I'm a man who's already talked himself to death about what happened at the BoxCar. Last week, I spent three ten-hour days at the Federal Building in Denver, giving my deposition to a covey of Justice Department lawyers. Which makes me wonder what I could possibly tell you that you don't already know."

"Okay. I guess we might as well get down to brass doorknobs."

"Try tacks."

"What?"

"They're like nails, only shorter. And sharper."

Momentarily disoriented, Newman attempted to blink the glaze off his eyes. "Dammit, I wish you wouldn't derail my chain of thought!"

"Break."

"Huh?"

"Or train."

Newman threw up his hands. "Charlie, what in *hell* are you jabbering about?"

"Sorry—must be my old head injury kicking in. Every now and then, random thoughts come popping into my mind and outta my mouth. Carpet tacks. Links breaking. Old Eighty-Nine derailing." He sighed. "It's embarrassing."

"Well, try to focus your ears on what I'm saying." With no small effort, the special agent gathered a disparate collection of thoughts. "I need to consult with you on some evidence. Bureau forensics has been sifting the ashes in what's left of the log house formerly occupied by Henry Buford. We sure we've found his remains, but it would be helpful to have some confirmation." Having been told of Moon's friendship with the BoxCar ranch manager, he avoided the Ute's pained expression. "According to our clever white-frocked Beakers, the fire reached temperatures well above three thousand degrees Fahrenheit. Except for ceramic and stone, just about everything in Buford's house was either melted or reduced to cinders, so there wasn't much evidence left."

The rancher leaned the poker against the fireplace.

"Where Buford's kitchen used to be, our forensic techs found some powder that had a high calcium content. Almost certainly the remnants of bone, and the distribution of the material was consistent with that of a prone human body." He offered Moon a stack of black-and-white prints. The photo on top showed a barely perceptible grayish outline on a slighter darker field of ash. Other prints showed views of the same material from a variety of angles. "These photos are just the way we found the ruin—nothing has been touched."

Moon began to examine the high-resolution photograph evidence print by print. "No dental evidence?"

The FBI agent shook his head. "Wasn't enough of Buford's teeth left for an ID. If he'd had ceramic dentures, we'd have been in Fat City." Newman extended his palms toward the fireplace, flexed his fingers in the warmth. "We recovered four specimens of melted lead. Average mass was about ten grams—which is consistent with a one hundred and fifty-eight-grain point thirty-eight-caliber slug. One of the presumed bullets was found in close association with the remains, the others were located a few meters away. The body apparently stopped one bullet; the others either missed or passed through the victim. Looks like Buford was shot, then left to burn to a cinder when the house was torched." He lowered his head, studied the tongue-and-groove planking in the hardwood floor. *I hope to God he was dead.*

The blaze in the fireplace sizzled into a sooty plume over a resinous piñon knot. Charlie Moon felt the searing heat on his face. For a fleeting moment, he fancied he could smell burning flesh. With some effort, he dismissed the odorous fantasy.

Newman was giving the Ute a worried look. "Charlie, to the best of your knowledge, did Mr. Buford own a pocketknife?"

Moon searched the dark corners of his memory, found what he was looking for. "I saw him use one at the Columbine—on the day we had that run-in with the motorcycle gang."

"Give me a description."

The tribal investigator reconstructed the image. "Handle was stainless steel. Decorated with some lines—blue, I think. Closed, it was about two, maybe two and a half inches long."

Newman leaned forward, staring holes in his witness. "What about the blade?"

"It was black." The tribal investigator understood. "Must've been ceramic."

The FBI agent's relief at this testimony spread across his face. He unzipped a side pocket on the briefcase, removed a padded manila envelope marked: "EVIDENCE/ BoxCar/Structure 2." Inside the envelope was a sealed plastic bag with an evidence tag that read: "BxCr/Structure 2/Grid 122–430." "About halfway along the bone-powder distribution, which would be near the victim's pelvis—and his hip pocket—our forensics team found this." He offered the packet to the Ute. "Look familiar?"

Moon switched on a floor lamp, stared at the ash-stained contents of the transparent bag. Nothing was left of Buford's pocketknife except the ceramic blade. "That looks like it."

Newman's broad grin split his hatchet face. "Great. We already traced the purchase of a Boker pocketknife of this same model to a cutlery store in Cherry Creek. It was charged to Henry Buford's Visa card, but that was almost four years ago. With your corroboration that he was carrying the knife recently, we got an ID of his remains we can hang our hat on."

The tribal investigator sorted through the remaining photographs, pausing at a print of the charred fireplace. The blackened chimney remained standing. The granite mantelpiece had cracked from the intense heat. Where the pewter candlesticks had stood, there were frozen puddles of dirty gray metal. Aside from this, the mantel was clear and clean; the winds had swept the smaller ash away with Henry Buford's spirit.

The FBI agent drummed his fingers on the arm of his chair. "If you're done with those, I'll put 'em away."

The Ute continued to stare at the image.

Newman reached, took the photos from Moon's hand. "We'll need your signed statement later on the knife blade, but the Denver SAC wanted to get your informal response today." He got up from the chair, held his breath for a moment, gave the comfortable parlor a longing look. "Guess I'm about done here."

Moon raised an eyebrow. This busy man had surely not driven a hundred and seventy miles merely to show him the ceramic blade from Henry Buford's pocketknife. "Stay for lunch, Stan. I'll bake us some potatoes, burn some prime beef."

"That's tempting." Newman stared at his wristwatch without noting the time. "But I need to be going." He headed for the door, paused. "There is one more thing."

Moon suppressed a smile. *Here it comes.*

"Almost forgot," the FBI agent lied. He removed a card from his inside jacket pocket. "I got something I'm supposed to read to you."

"My rights?"

Ignoring the remark, Newman held the card eleven inches from his eyes, cleared his throat. " 'The Director of the Federal Bureau of Investigation, acting upon the instructions of the Attorney General of the United States and in concurrence with the wishes of the director of the United States Secret Service, directs Mr. Charles Moon to make no statement whatever, public or private, regarding any information or opinion he may have that might bear upon the recent explosion in the United States Capitol Building' "— Newman paused for a breath—" 'or any other matter that might be related to said explosion. This direction is made in the interests of national security.' " He put the card back in his pocket.

Directs? Moon stared at his guest. "Why'd they send you?"

Newman made a lopsided grin. " 'Cause me and you are buddies."

The Ute cocked his head. "Since when?"

"Now don't be a *hostile* Indian—your government prefers to keep this arrangement as friendly as possible." He passed the Ute the document and a ballpoint pen. "Sign at the bottom, to verify that you have read the statement."

"Mind if I read it first?"

Newman assumed a wounded expression. "What—you don't trust your federal government?"

Moon took his time examining the fine print, then gave his guest a wry half-smile. "Seeing as how we're such good buddies, I bet you'll be glad to tell me what all this legal mumbo jumbo means."

The FBI agent avoided the Ute's gaze. "It is my official duty to inform you that the agreement is nothing to get uptight about. Just some paperwork to keep the lawyers happy."

"Okay, Stan, you've done your duty. Now tell me what this is all about."

Newman came very near blushing. "Off the record?"

"You're a guest in my home."

"Okay, Chucky, but you never heard me say this. Bottom line—you maintain the discretion for which you are legendary, you are a Friend of Uncle Sam. Which along with about four dollars and fifty cents will get you a tasty cup of vanilla-flavored java at one of those yuppie caffeine saloons. But should you make a slip of the lip, your uncle can and will squash you like a stinkbug."

"If you're joking, it ain't funny."

"I am terminally earnest. There's at least a half dozen ways the Justice Department can nail your hide to the barn."

"Tell me one."

"Okay. You're a material witness. Justice can hold you in protective custody to safeguard your person from vindictive elements of the terrorist conspiracy that attempted to knock off the top dogs in D.C."

"Hold me—how long?"

"Till the snow drifts six feet deep in Tucson on the Fourth of July. And the Cubs win the pennant. And not a stalk of corn grows in Iowa."

Moon helped himself to a long, thoughtful look at the federal agent.

Newman wiped his fingertips across the smooth leather surface of the briefcase. "And that's just for starters—they might even decide to target you as an accomplice."

The Ute could hardly believe his ears. "What did you say?"

"Charlie, traces of your DNA were found inside the cardboard box that the neph—that the unknown person or persons placed over the bomb-making apparatus in Allan Pearson's shack."

"Well of course it was. I probably shed some skin cells when I was opening the lid to—" The Ute's protest was halted by Newman's raised palm.

"Listen to me—there are certain influential elements in Justice who are suggesting that you know altogether too damn much about this case. Proponents of this fascinating line of reasoning are proposing the theory that you are a part of the conspiracy. According to this scenario, Charlie Moon was in cahoots with the terrorist organization— maybe some Native American radicals. But something went sour at the last minute. You got cold feet. Called in the warning to the Secret Service—not to preserve the government, but to eliminate yourself as a probable suspect."

Moon experienced a bizarre sensation; it had the eerie quality of an out-of-body experience. He was not a part of this impossible conversation, but rather an amused witness to it. He heard himself say, "Stan, you know that's crazy."

"Sure I do. I also know that innocent people get sliced and diced every day of the week."

There was a lengthy silence.

In a corner closet, a Mormon cricket chirped.

A clock on the wall struck eleven times. After the last tone had faded, the pendulum continued to click and clack.

Moon came back to earth. He returned the single page to the special agent. "Thanks for the straight talk—I am obliged to you."

"I am obliged to point out that you did not sign the form."

"I cannot see how any good would come from scratching my X on the dotted line."

Newman pocketed the unexecuted agreement. "This will be interpreted by my superiors as an unfriendly gesture. I don't know how I'll explain your lack of cooperation."

Moon felt the heat of righteous anger warming his face. "Explain it this way. I have me a fine lawyer down in Durango town who wears a blue pinstripe suit and a red bow tie. His given name is Walter Price, but he is more commonly known as Crocodile Wally. This man eats live baby ducks for breakfast, big-eyed puppy dogs for lunch, government lawyers for snacks—and picks his teeth with a railroad spike. Your superiors may deal with him."

Newman's lips went thin, his face paled to a sickly yellowish tint. "I am pained to point this out, but in connection with your part-time job as Senator Davidson's security consultant, you applied for and were issued an FBI security clearance, which gives you access to specific categories of classified material. With such access comes certain responsibilities and liabilities. Including fines and imprisonment for unauthorized release of said classified material. I refer you to Section 1,001, Title 18 of the United States Code."

The Ute felt the skin on his face stiffen into a hard mask.

The FBI agent managed to look the Indian straight in the eye. "You are hereby informed that critical information that might be used to apprehend those persons responsible for the attempted decapitation of the United States government is classified. And don't ask me *which* critical information. That information is also classified, and will be continually reviewed and modified by the Security Affairs Committee in the Department of Justice."

Moon mouthed his words in a deceptively mild tone. "So if I say something, it might be the wrong thing. Trouble is, I don't know what the wrong thing is."

"In principle, you will have access to the Bureau's classification manual. We keep a copy at the Denver field office. But precisely *what* is classified is liable to change on a day-by-day basis, according to the whims of the aforesaid Review Committee. And our manual only gets updated about once a month." Newman looked at his shoes. "Make a dumb move, and you could spend the next several years in expensive litigation. Or in the federal can."

"Thanks for pointing this out, Stan."

"Don't mention it. And I really mean that." Newman snapped the latch on his briefcase. "I gotta go now." The FBI agent jerked his head, indicating that Moon should follow him to his car.

Moon followed, wondering whether the FBI agent thought the Columbine headquarters might be wired for sound. And whether Newman might be right. He tried to shrug off this paranoiac notion, but it stuck to him like a bad smell.

A few yards from the porch, the government cop addressed the rancher in a low monotone. "For once, Charlie, listen to what I've got to say. Us Bureau cops appreciate what you've done. The Secret Service grunts would like to pin a medal on your chest. We're on your side."

"That's nice to hear." Moon slowed to match the shorter man's strides. "But I think I hear a 'but' coming."

"But when somebody attempts to decapitate the United States government, and evidence points to the nephew of a powerful U.S. senator—a senator who happens to be one of the president's closest friends and advisors—well, things tend to get more than a bit dicey." The FBI agent stopped at the Ford Taurus, turned to look up at the tall man's face. "Even as we speak, the president of the United States is appointing a blue-ribbon panel to oversee the decap investigation. It'll look pretty much like the Warren Commission. Chief Justice of the Supreme Court, Speaker of the House, director of the CIA, a retired Atlanta police chief, General Motors' CEO, a famous astronaut who is now a U.S. senator—and the list of notables goes on."

"Sounds like a sensible thing to do."

Stanley Newman shook his head. "Do I have to spell it out for you?"

"Maybe you better."

"Okay. I'll talk slow so you can understand. The president and his closest advisors have already reached a decision about what happened. The attempted assassination was carried out by a group of highly organized domestic or international terrorists. It was not an inside job. The senator's nephew was not implicated in any way in the bombing of the House Chamber. There is no scandal associated with Senator Davidson's family or household." The FBI agent looked away from the honest man's face. "And the president's handpicked panel will seek out evidence to support the White House position."

The Ute stared at his visitor. "But the evidence—"

Newman snapped Moon's words off. "The conclusion will be that the bomb-making apparatus you found in the kid's shack was planted by a person or persons unknown."

"Stanley, I already heard through the cop shop grapevine—Allan Pearson's prints were all over that stuff."

Newman ground his teeth. "Charlie, forget what you heard. Even if that fingerprint rumor turned out to be factual, under the current rules it would constitute classified information. And on toppa that, it would be the Justice Department's official position that the actual person or persons responsible for this terrible crime had tricked the senator's nephew into touching those pieces of evidence."

"But—"

"Dammit, there ain't no *but*." He pointed a finger at his mouth. "Charlie, read my lips. Allan Pearson did *not* know that he was planting the explosive battery in the senator's electric scooter. Allan Pearson did *not* bomb Buford's house or the BoxCar headquarters. Allan Pearson did *not* go into hiding."

The Ute stared at the fed. "If he didn't go into hiding, then where is he?"

"In these chaotic times, exactness is a hard commodity to come by." Newman raised his hands. "There was some thought that he might have been kidnapped by the perps. But that theory was rejected. *Officially* Allan Pearson is out there somewhere in the Great Beyond; he dwells in that far place from which no mortal returns. And I do not mean Carter County, Montana."

"You really think he's dead?"

"It is not my job to conjecture about whether or not the nephew's heart still beats. That issue has already been decided in the Oval Office, and in a year or so will be a central finding of the president's handpicked blue-ribbon panel."

"So how'd Patch's nephew die?"

"Allan Pearson perished in the flames of the BoxCar headquarters."

The sense of unreality returned. "Will the blue-ribbon panel have any proof of that?"

"How could they? The fire was sufficiently intense to destroy all evidence of the young man's body."

"Even bone-powder?"

"Charlie, I'm trying to help you, so don't go and piss me off."

"Why wasn't Pearson's motorcycle found at the head-quarters?"

"Whoever is responsible for the deaths of Allan Pearson and Henry Buford either rode or hauled Pearson's red Suzuki two-wheeler to Montrose, left it in a lot behind an establishment known as Buggy Joe's Tavern." He paused. "The FBI has been directed by the U.S. Attorney General to conduct its investigation on the broad assumption that organized terrorists—foreign or domestic—are behind the failed attempt to assassinate the upper echelon of the United States government."

"The same group I might be working with. Unless I keep my mouth shut."

Newman nodded at his distorted reflection on the Taurus fender. "Now you're getting the picture."

The tribal investigator looked off toward the mountains. They seemed impossibly remote and serene. "So it's a whitewash. A cover-up."

Newman shook his head. "Not exactly."

"What does that mean?"

"It means that the current administration does not *want* to know any truth that might turn out to be embarrassing or inconvenient. There's lots of historical precedent. Like when Eisenhower ignored intelligence reports that the Russians held several hundred American soldiers who'd been captured by the Chinese during the Korean so-called police action. Or when Lyndon Johnson didn't want to hear any evidence supporting the theory that Castro was ultimately responsible for the Kennedy assassination." He smirked at the tall man. "And you know damn well I'm right."

The Ute kicked a stone across the yard.

The FBI agent snickered. "You better watch your skinny ass, Charlie Moon."

Sidewinder materialized at the Ute's side. The hound's neck bristled; he snarled at the federal lawman.

Newman backed off a half step, scowled at the animal.

"What is it about me that this ugly dog don't like?"

"You want to hang around for another coupla hours, I'll prepare you a written list."

"That's real accommodating of you."

"Hey, we're old buddies."

"Sayonara, Charlie. And whatever happens, don't say your buddy Stanley didn't warn you." Newman got into the Ford, slammed the door. He started the engine, frowned, lowered the window. "Your ugly dog made me remember something I needed to ask you about. Henry Buford—he have any pets?"

The Ute nodded. "Old bluetick hound. Henry called him Grape-Eye."

"Yeah, that must be the one." The weary FBI agent rubbed his eyes. "About a hundred yards from the ruins of Buford's log house, we found a dog's carcass in an arroyo. It'd been hidden—covered up with stones and brush. Poor mutt'd been shot in the head."

"He loved that old dog." Moon recalled the visit he had made to the ranch manager's home. It seemed like years ago.

Newman stared up at the tall man. "What's on your mind?"

"Officially, I can't say—might turn out to be classified information."

"Don't be cute. Spill it."

"Henry told me the senator's nephew hated dogs—especially Grape-Eye." The tribal investigator looked at the coffee cup in his hand. Like the embers of Henry Buford's house, it had grown cold. "But that can't be important, because officially Allan Pearson didn't have anything to do with killing Henry's dog, shooting Henry, burning down his house, firebombing the BoxCar headquarters to red-hot smithereens—or planting a bomb in the senator's Electric GroundHog."

Newman grinned at this remarkable man, who actually believed the world should make sense. "Charlie, I'm beginning to think you might come out of this with your hide intact."

"Stanley, I intend to do just that."

The federal agent waved, stomped on the accelerator. His departing automobile was cloaked by a billow of yellow dust.

Long after the drone of the small engine was lost in the distance, Charlie Moon did not move. Unaware of Sidewinder's curious gaze, he turned the coffee cup in his hands, watched slanted rays of sunlight reflect off the ebony surface of the tepid liquid. An exceedingly thin film of oil produced a pretty rainbow sheen. He thought about Henry Buford's dead hound, concealed under a pile of rocks and brush. It was easy enough to imagine the senator's warped nephew shooting Henry and killing the victim's dog. But why would he go to the trouble to hide the animal's body? It did not make sense. He supposed that very little Allan Pearson had done in his few years would yield to rational analysis.

Nevertheless, he pondered about the hidden dog carcass until the shadows grew long and diffuse. Finally, the Ute nodded to no one in particular.

Maybe—in a sick, twisted kind of way—it did make sense.

CHAPTER 40

Moon of Dead Leaves Falling

Autumn arrived late at the Columbine, and would be allotted the fleeting period between two crescent moons. Winter, having paused in Montana, made reservations for points farther south, where it would settle in until the return of the sharp-shinned hawk. The high country cares nothing for calendars drafted by the hand of man.

Dolly Bushman fussed about the spacious kitchen, worrying about one thing and another. She pointed a dripping spatula at a cast-iron skillet that was filled to the brim with frying chicken. "Just look at that—the grease all runs to one side."

Her husband eyed the antique appliance. The monstrous thing was solid iron and seriously heavy. "I expect it's the floor that's tilted."

"Don't go making no excuses—I want this stove leveled."

"I'll get around to it tomorrow." *Or maybe the day after tomorrow*. Pete approached the stove, stirred a cedar spoon in a pot of bean and bacon soup, lifted the wooden implement to his mouth. He smacked his lips. "Needs two or three dabs a salt. And just a little pinch a garlic, and then some—"

"You get away from there—don't be messing with my

stuff." His plump wife shot the meddling man a poisonous look.

Pete snorted, but he dropped the spoon into the soup pot. "What's chewin' on your leg, old woman?"

Dolly snatched a matched pair of hemp pot holders off a brass wall hook. "*You* are." The Queen of the Kitchen elbowed the pesky man aside, bent an aching back to remove a steaming peach cobbler from the sooty oven. She thumped the sweet concoction onto the dining table. The foreman's wife stood, staring at the pie—but not seeing it.

Pete Bushman knew the look. *If she don't get it outta her system, she'll start to yapping after we go to bed. And I won't get a wink of sleep.* He seated himself at the table, gave his wife a sideways look. "You might as well tell me now."

Dolly sat down beside her husband, kept her eye on the pie. "It's Charlie Moon."

Pete waited for the rest to come out.

She wiped her hands on an apron. "Something is wrong with that man."

Her husband reached for an enameled coffeepot sitting on a square of Mexican tile, poured himself half a cup.

Dolly looked accusingly at her bushy-faced mate. "And don't tell me you haven't noticed."

Okay, I won't. Pete took a sip of the weak brew. Made a face. *I'd rather drink warmed-over goat piss.*

"Charlie hardly ever stops by anymore. And when he does, he won't have a thing to eat."

Pete raised an eyebrow. That sure didn't sound like the boss. The big Ute generally put away enough food to keep three lumberjacks well nourished.

"He won't even have a cup of coffee," she added.

Her husband stared cross-eyed at his cup. *Well, I don't blame him, for that.*

"And he hardly ever goes into town anymore. Doesn't answer any of his phone calls. Since those troubles over at the BoxCar, I get thirty or forty calls a day for him here. I had to unplug the phone so's I could get some work done."

"Who is it wants to talk to the boss?"

"For one, his aunt what's-her-name—you know, that funny little lady."

"That crazy old Injun woman is about funny as a boil on my ass."

"Shut up, Pete." Dolly was trying to remember the other names. "And Charlie's friend Mr. Parris calls every day. And Senator Davidson. And that young woman who works for the senator—what's her name?"

"Miss James." *Pretty little thing.* Pete leered under the brushy beard.

"And there's been a half dozen calls from some uppity lawyer who claims she works for the Justice Department. I told her Charlie don't want to talk to a living soul. Not even the president of the United States of America. And that's the truth. He just stays up there in that big house. All by himself."

Sounds like weak blood. Charlie probably needs a good dose of cod-liver oil. "I expect he must be feeling a little peaked."

"Well, of course he is," Dolly snapped.

Pete reached for a graham cracker.

She slapped his hand. "Not till after supper."

The foreman scowled at his wife. *Damn crabby old woman.* "So when is supper goin' to be ready?"

She sniffed. "We are not talking about you stuffin' your face—we are talking about Charlie Moon." Dolly rapped a knuckle on the table. "I'd wager he's lost ten, maybe fifteen pounds. And the man was skinny as a fence rail to start with."

"Well, I don't know what we can do about it."

"You could go up there and talk to him."

"What could I say?"

Dolly shook a finger at her husband. "You better think of something."

"I think better on a full stomach," Pete grumped.

Pete Bushman knocked on the heavy oak door.

The inside of the Columbine headquarters was silent as a tomb.

He knocked again.

Still nothing.

The foreman cupped a hand by his mouth and yelled. "Hey, boss—you in there?"

The silence was thick as cheap molasses.

Bushman tried the porcelain doorknob. It turned. He poked his bushy face inside. It was dark. "Helllooo—anybody home?"

Moon's deep voice rumbled across the parlor. "C'mon in, Pete. And shut the door behind you."

The foreman did as instructed, waited for his eyes to adjust to the inner twilight.

"Have a seat," the disembodied voice said.

Pete Bushman flopped down on a carved Spanish bench. The boss was seated in a maple rocking chair, but he wasn't rocking. "It's a nice day outside."

The Ute made a grunting sound.

The foreman leaned back, crossed his legs. "So how're you gettin' along?"

There was a long, empty silence before Moon spoke. "What do you want, Pete?"

"Well, I been feelin' a little low lately. Thought I'd drop by and see the boss. Figured maybe he'd crack a joke or somethin'—cheer an old man up."

The Ute stared at a split pine log crackling in the massive fireplace. If a man watched a blaze like this for a million-million years, the flames would never be exactly the same. But then nothing was ever the same. From one second to the next, everything changed. Even the stones.

Pete Bushman grinned. "An' I do feel a world better. Yes sir—your company is a real tonic. We could bottle it an' sell it for six dollars a half-pint."

"Speak your piece."

Dolly's right. Something is wrong with him. For the first time since he'd met the amiable Ute, the Columbine foreman felt uneasy in Charlie Moon's presence. "Well, we got us a big ranchin' operation to look after. I thought we might talk some business."

"We?"

Bushman picked at an inch of loose thread sprouting from the knee of his patched khakis. "I know I always let on that I don't want no interference from the owner. But that's just my way. From time to time, a foreman has to have a talk with the boss."

"Okay," the boss said. "Let's talk."

"We got some decisions to make. About what to do with the winter pasture over by Crystal Springs. Like how many cows to put on it."

"You can make that decision."

Bushman grimaced, yanked at the string on his trouser leg. Now it was six inches long. "And there's that big he-cat up in the Notch."

The Ute leaned forward in the rocker until he felt the warmth of the fire on his dark face. "That mountain lion been causing us more trouble?"

The foreman nodded. "Old Two-Toes pulled down two heifers just in the past week."

The owner of the ranch got up. Began to pace back and forth in front of the fireplace. "You sure it's Two-Toes?"

"Sure I'm sure. Last kill was yesterday, down by the river. Alf Marquez found his tracks in the wet sand."

Charlie Moon stooped, put a powder-dry cottonwood log on the fire. "I'll look into it." He turned to the foreman. "Anything else?"

"Well, Dolly wants you to come by and have some peach cobbler."

His back to the popping flames, the Ute stood like a post. "That's kind of her. Tell your wife I appreciate the invitation."

Bushman knew he was being dismissed. He got up, turned to go—then stopped. "Charlie, you won't want to hear this, but I don't give a squeaky fart. So here's what I got to say—it ain't healthy to sit around in the dark."

There was a smile in the Ute's voice. "Thanks for stopping by."

CHAPTER 41

Dead Mule Notch

The hound's mournful night song had been sung; Sidewinder had slunk off to the barn to find his rest in a bed of straw. Charlie Moon lay on his bed. The weary man stared at the ceiling. He wanted to be finished with this business for good. But more immediately, he wanted sleep. Sleep without dreams.

As is so often the case in this world, he did not get that which he so desired.

The Ute rancher spent a week on horseback. Before dawn, he would saddle Paducah. Swaybacked, heavy-footed, the color of dirty dishwater, the big animal was nothing to look at. He was, in fact, a sight to make a stockman's eyes ache— a sorry piece of horseflesh. On top of that, the brute was not the most intelligent animal in the Columbine corrals. But Paducah had this outstanding characteristic—he was totally unafraid of anything God had put upon the earth. The horse did not rear at the sight of a rattlesnake coiled at his feet. The discharge of a rifle within an inch of his ear was but a slight annoyance. Most importantly for the Ute's purposes, Paducah did not even flinch at the scent or sight of a mountain lion. In the opinion of those Columbine cowhands most familiar with the equine mind, this latter trait was proof of the horse's complete lack of common sense.

Charlie Moon spent long, tiresome hours riding along the foot of the great slot in the Misery Range. On the evening of the second day, just inside the fence line, the rancher discovered the remains of a white-faced heifer. Near the carcass, he found the two-toed paw print.

On the third day, the hunter began a systematic search of the Notch that would eventually take him up to the crest of that rocky pass through the mountains. It was hard work and no paycheck, but there were excellent fringe benefits. The autumn air carried a life-renewing crispness. The pale green, gold, and orange of aspens was intermixed with the dark cones of perfectly formed spruce. At the crest of the wide gap in the mountain range, the Misery cliffs were honeycombed with natural caves and horizontal hard-rock mines where tempting veins of silver had played out well before Mr. Wright flew his flimsy contraption over the sands of Kitty Hawk. The caverns were suitable homes for black bear. Hibernating rattlesnakes. And far more dangerous predators. The Ute did find the odd cougar track here and there, though the pad marks were rarely less than a week old.

At midday, he would find a spot that was protected from the brisk west winds. When they were not near one of the tiny streams that trickled from clefts in the blue granite, Paducah would get a fair share from the rider's canteens of well water. While the Ute ate a piece of dark bread, the gentle beast would enjoy a portion of corn or barley from the saddlebags. Having finished the grain, the horse would pull on those few sprigs of grass that could be found between fractured stones and weathered boulders that littered the saddle of the Notch. What may have occupied the horse's brain during these pleasant hours must remain a matter of conjecture. But all day long, the man's mind was filled with many things. Charlie Moon thought about reliable horses. Fat Herefords. Faithful hounds. Hard winters.

Old friends. Unpaid bills. And of course—the woman. From time to time, he also thought about the mountain lion, a big cat whose foot had been mutilated by the jaws of a steel trap. The aging, gimpy predator was unable to run down elk or deer. Two-Toes had nothing left to hunt but domestic animals. Or, just possibly, human beings. The Ute had developed a sympathy for the beast. But the cougar was a potential danger to the Columbine cowboys. And the rancher was responsible for the safety of his employees.

On the sixth day, Charlie Moon knew what he had to do.

The Marksman

Pete Bushman was sitting by the fire, warming his feet. Having heard no one approach his door, the Columbine foreman was startled by the heavy knock.

Dolly hurried to the window. "It's *him*."

He pulled on his boots. "Him *who?*"

"Charlie Moon."

Bushman found the Ute standing by the front porch. The rider had looped the horse's reins around a post. Paducah looked fitter than normal, dopey as usual, and highly pleased with himself. "It's good to see you, boss." But it was not. Charlie Moon was hollow-eyed and pitifully thin. "Why doncha come inside?"

Moon seemed not to have heard the invitation. He looked off toward the Notch. "Pete, who's our best shot?"

The foreman rubbed at bushy whiskers. Studied about it. "With a pistol or a long gun?"

"Long gun."

"From a horse, or on foot?"

Moon considered the question. "On foot."

"Well, that'd be the Wyomin' Kyd."

The Ute was mildly surprised. "Jerome Kydmann's that good?"

The foreman grinned under the unkempt beard. "Imagine a grasshopper at fifty paces. Now that 'hopper, he's got a

flea sittin' on his left eyebrow. And that flea has got a
eensy-teensy red chigger bug squattin' on his kneecap."

With some effort, Moon managed to capture this image.

"That young dandy can shoot the chigger off'n the flea's
knee without doin' the least harm to the flea. And it's such
a clean shot, why the grasshopper, he won't bat an eyelash."

Moon shook his head. "The Kyd's too green. I need a
man with more experience."

Bushman's eyes twinkled. "You want somebody to
shoot that big cat for you, I'm your man."

The rancher gave his employee a long, appreciative look.
"You could get the job done, all right. But I don't think
Dolly would ever let me hear the last of it if something bad
happened to her husband."

"Hmmph," Bushman snorted. "She'd find herself another man ten minutes after the funeral."

Moon smiled. "How about Santanna?"

"That mean-assed Mexican?" The foreman shrugged. "I
guess he can shoot well enough. And he's probably killed
about as many mountain lions and bears as he has men—
at least to hear him tell it. But he don't have a rifle; you'd
have to loan him one."

Moon loosed the reins from the post, mounted the
homely horse. "Send Santanna around to the house first
thing tomorrow." The Ute wheeled the animal, calling back,
"And don't give him any work to do—I'll be keeping him
busy for a while." He reigned the horse to a stop, looked
back at his foreman. "Tell all the hands—and this goes for
you, too—I don't want anyone going near the Notch. And
that includes Pine Knob."

Pete Bushman nodded. Dead Mule Notch was the big
cat's territory. And ever since the redheaded woman's body
had been buried on the Knob, that lonesome place had been
off-limits. Nobody but the boss ever went up there. Or
wanted to. Some of the cowhands believed the hilltop was
haunted by the young woman. Alf Marquez swore he had
seen her spirit floating around the crest of the Knob. The

Arapaho claimed that at twilight and dawn the ghost showed itself as a curling wisp of yellowish smoke. In dark of night, the disembodied spirit took on the appearance of a forked flame, split like the tongue of a viper.

The foreman watched the big Indian ride off on the ugly horse, turned to see Dolly's round, rosy face in the doorway.

Her dark eyes were fairly popping out of the sockets. "What was that all about?"

Dolly's husband puffed up his chest. "I told you I'd get the boss outta the house. After I told him about how ol' Two-Toes had brought down them heifers, he's been out checkin' for signs every day. He wouldn't say, but I betcha six bits to a nickel, that Injun's found the hole where that big cat sleeps—and he's plannin' to put 'im outta business."

"Well, he mustn't try to do it by himself."

"He's borrowed Santanna. That Mexican's a professional hunter—he's killed himself a dozen cougars." *Leastways, that's what he claims.*

Dolly shook her head. "I'm glad Charlie's getting outside again. But I sure hope that mountain lion don't sink his teeth into him." *Or even that awful Mexican.*

The Assignment

Griego Santanna showed up at the Columbine headquarters fifteen minutes after the sun popped over the eastern range. Having guessed what the *jefe* had in mind, the Mexican set about telling him how to go about getting the job done. "First, we'll borrow some redbones or bloodhounds that—"

"No dogs," the Ute said.

Santanna stared at the boss. "But dogs is the best way to—"

Charlie Moon pointed at a chair. "Have a seat. We'll talk while we have some breakfast." The Ute fried pork chops and eggs for the feisty man from Zacatecas. The Ute ate half a pone of cold cornbread with a cup of black, unsweetened coffee. In addition to sharing his table, the rancher shared his idea about how Santanna might bag a dangerous predator.

The Mexican listened in rapt silence, occasionally nodding.

Finally, Moon bowed his head, stared at clenched fists. "This thing has to be done, and by rights it's my job. But I can't bring myself to pull the trigger. That's why I was hoping you might be willing to. . . ." He hesitated. It was far too much to ask of a hired hand. Even a hard man like this one.

Griego Santanna smiled, exposing the glistening stainless steel teeth. "When do I get started?"

Moon looked toward a west-facing window. Dead Mule Notch was glowing in golden sunlight. "Early tomorrow morning, a good hour before first light. And you'll have to stay out there alone, till well after dark. I don't know how many days this'll take, but you'll have to stay at it till you get a bead on him." After a long, heavy silence, the Ute spoke. "I don't want him wounded. If you pull the trigger, he has to be shot dead."

"*Si, Jefe.* I understand." And he did. Perfectly.

A Hole in the Ground

Pete Bushman stomped into his house, plopped into the comfortable embrace of a creaky reclining chair. He mumbled to himself, knowing this would attract his wife's attention.

Dolly, who had been listening to the local news, switched off the fifty-eight-year-old General Electric vacuum tube radio. "What is it?"

Her husband shook his head. "I just can't figger it out."

Busy cleaning a mixing bowl, she waited for the next installment.

"Every morning, soon's the sun comes up, the boss rides that ugly ol' hoss up to the top of Pine Knob."

She frowned. "What is he doing up there?"

He pulled at his whiskers. "He's diggin'."

Dolly turned to stare at her husband. "Digging *what?*"

"Woman, you wouldn't believe it if I told you."

Her eyes became large. "Charlie's digging up that Brewster woman's grave?"

Annoyed, Bushman shook his head. "Hell no, he's diggin' *another* hole—right next to where she's buried. After he lays his shovel down, he stands by that redheaded gal's grave with his hat off. Like he was goin' to her funeral, over and over."

This made the woman shudder. "What on earth would he do that for?"

Her husband stared at the beamed ceiling, sighed. "Who knows why these Injuns does the peculiar things they do?" In a knowing tone, the foreman added: "They ain't like us."

Dolly sat down near her man, gave him a suspicious look. "How do you know what Charlie's doing up there?" The boss had ordered everyone to stay away from Pine Knob.

Pete Bushman reached into his jacket pocket, produced a dusty pair of binoculars. With a smug expression, he waved the optical instrument under his wife's nose.

"Shame on you, spying on Charlie Moon."

"I'm the foreman of this here outfit—it's my job to know what's goin' on."

Dolly grudgingly admitted that he had a point. But the report gnawed at her. "There must be a reason he's up there digging a hole in the ground."

Her husband shook his head. "There ain't but one reason—he has finally gone crazy as a spotted coot." He reached across the table, removed the lid from a century-old crockery milk pot. He found a long plug of chewing tobacco inside, began unwrapping the foil cover.

Very slowly, the woman twisted her white apron into a knot. "I thought Charlie and Santanna were hunting that mountain lion."

"That Mexican goes out before daylight, comes back after dark. And he keeps to himself—don't say a word to nobody about what he's up to. I figger Santanna's scrounging around up yonder in the Notch, lookin' for a sign. Once he finds the big cat's den, I expect the boss will help him kill it."

"I thought Charlie Moon had already found the den."

Bushman shrugged.

Dolly looked blankly at the faded wallpaper. "They should bring in some trained dogs."

Her husband shook his head. "The boss, he don't believe in usin' dogs to run down what he's huntin'."

"Well, that's just plain silly, and dangerous. He's still not thinking right."

The foreman shrugged. "I think it's some kind of Injun thing. Mixin' dogs and cougars is bad medicine."

"After you talked to him about Two-Toes, I thought Charlie would get better." Dolly shook her head. "But I shouldn't be surprised. That's what happens when you give a woman's job to a man."

Old fusspot. "Then why don't you do somethin' yourself."

"I think I will."

He did not like the sound of this. "Like what?"

"I'll call in some serious help." Dolly was staring at the telephone.

CHAPTER 42

The Woman

As he rode Paducah back to the Columbine headquarters, the rancher was lost in his solitary thoughts. Drawing near, he saw the white Dodge van parked between the F-150 and the Expedition. It looked like one of the BoxCar fleet. *What's going on? I told Pete Bushman No Visitors.* And then he saw her.

Miss James's trim form was concealed under a fashionable trench coat.

This must be Dolly's doing. As the Ute dismounted, he tried hard to maintain a solemn expression. Did not quite manage it.

The pretty woman returned the smile. "Hello."

"Hello yourself. Is Patch back in Colorado?"

She shook her head. "The senator will be staying at his home in Georgetown until the new headquarters is completed on the BoxCar. He instructed me to convey his warmest regards—he is extremely grateful for what you've done."

"I don't expect you came all the way to Colorado to tell me that."

"I hope you don't mind my showing up unannounced. I realize that you need your solitude right now, but . . ." The carefully rehearsed words faded away. *He is so terribly thin.* "I do hope you're well—I mean . . ."

"Some of my hired help hold the opinion that I am not altogether healthy." He tapped his temple. "Up here."

Miss James found herself at a loss for words.

He approached so close she could smell him. "What do you think?"

Her already enormous eyes grew larger. "Well, I really don't—"

The seven-foot man enfolded the little woman in a bear hug, lifted her off the ground. A slipper dropped from her foot.

"Charlie—what *are* you doing?"

"Being my natural self."

The other shoe fell to earth. She relaxed in the unexpected embrace. "And I had thought you were such a shy man."

"You thought wrong, Abigail."

"That is not my name."

"Then tell me."

Her nose was almost touching his. She smiled. "Why should I?"

" 'Cause I'm not putting you down till I know."

"Oh, all right then. It's Jane."

"Missy, bald-face lies won't get you nowhere."

"Well I'm not telling you—so there."

"Then we'll stay right here till the sun goes down and the moon comes up. And the sun comes up again."

Miss James put her arms around his neck. "Perhaps some sort of compromise is in order."

"I'm listening."

"Tell me the name of your lovely lake."

"And you'll do likewise?"

She nodded.

"I don't completely trust you. You go first."

She looked at his jacket collar. "It's . . . Jesse."

He rolled this revelation over in his mind. *Jesse James. That's not so bad. It coulda been Frank.*

"Oh, I just *knew* you'd do that."

"Do what?"

"Grin like an ape."

He managed a melancholy expression. "How's this?"

"Much better." She giggled. "Now keep your side of the bargain."

"Well, I might as well tell you the truth. The lake's never had an actual name—"

"Charlie, that's not fair!"

"—but from now on and forever and then some, it's Lake Jesse."

Her eyes were luminous in the twilight. "You should not tease me."

"Before the dark of the moon, I will plant a big sign by the water's edge." *If I'm still alive.*

"Very well, I believe you. Now I think . . . perhaps you should put me down."

She doesn't sound like she really means it. "I'll have to think on it."

"My goodness, what else do you want?"

"I'm altogether too shy to say." He looked away. "So I'm hoping you already know."

She did. And kissed him. And kissed him again.

Miss Jesse James's feet did not touch the ground. Not until the sun blushed crimson, dipped its face in darkness . . . and an apricot moon peeked over the mountains.

CHAPTER 43

On Pine Knob

From dawn to dusk, Charlie Moon went about his solitary business. When darkness came, he slept. And dreamed. Day and night, the women were always on his mind.

Mostly, he thought about the pretty lady who had kissed him, the black-haired beauty whose blood ran warm. This one invited him to live—to share her life.

And then there was . . . the *other*. That pale, redheaded phantom who trespassed the boundaries of his dreams. And danced with the dreamer. This one lay in her grave, waiting for that companion who was destined to join her. She was not to be denied.

The man with the troubled mind had made his choice. And having made it, there were preparations to be made. Moon lifted a scoop of rocky soil from the deep slot, set the long-handled shovel aside. The hole looked deep enough.

Satisfied with his work, the rancher went to check on his mount. On each visit, he tied the horse to a different aspen sapling. By this means, the animal was assured of a fresh patch of grass to graze upon. On this day, the horse had had time enough to nip away every sprig. Paducah lifted his head, snorted at the man who had been working without pause since shortly after sunrise.

With all the patience and cunning of his kind, the predator approached. Slowly. Silently.

The rancher surveyed his domain. Two ranges of granite mountains rose up on the boundaries of the Columbine, the Buckhorns to frame the sun's rising, the Miserys to conceal its setting. Toward that place where the snows are made, rolling gray-green hills were dotted with spruce and pine. He gazed to the south, admiring the ribbon of river. Even at this distance, he could hear the hushed whisper of icy waters rushing over moss-sheened basalt boulders. It was a fine, muscular stream, rolling on to a distant appointment with the briny deep.

On the far bank, there was a scattering of buildings around the Columbine headquarters. His home was perched on a bulge above the flood plain. A mile past the massive log dwelling, shining in the sun, Lake Jesse. Before long, a thin glazing of ice would begin forming along its willowed banks.

Autumn was a sweet time.

Winter was not.

Some fine day, spring would come again. The Ute had always been grateful to see tender new leaves, the blossoming of prairie flowers. But the Moon of New Grass was far over the horizon, and a man never knew when he might wake up to his last day in Middle World. This being so, time must not be frittered away as if it was merely an empty space between then and now, birth and the grave. Again, the pretty woman came to mind. The Columbine was an awesomely silent and empty space, where even summer nights were touched by coldness. Under normal circumstances, he would be ready to take on a full-time partner.

But these were the worst of days. The shadow of death walked along behind him.

His digging done, the gaunt man turned toward the red-headed woman's lonesome grave, removed the dusty black

Stetson. He bowed his head, closed his eyes. Prayed for the
repose of the dancing woman's soul. He could not have
estimated how long he stood before the pair of silent
graves, one occupied, another waiting for a tenant. Shadows
leaned to the east, grew long and diffuse. He did not move
from his desolate post.

From a clump of scrub oak, a pair of alert eyes was focused
on the Ute.

A crisp northwesterly breeze swept across the crest of Pine
Knob, hummed a brittle hymn in the dry juniper spines,
rattled brassy leaves in a clone of aspens. Having played
its piece, the wind slipped away to ripple the surface of the
glacial lake beyond the river. Moon's tiny corner of the
vast universe fell silent.

The man standing at the edge of the pit was in another
place. He dreamed the dreams of his ancestors. Somewhere
far beyond yesterday, he saw great oceans of buffalo flow-
ing over the high plains in a black flood. He heard the
excited shouts of mounted hunters, the snorting of horses.
Something drifted past the Ute's nostrils—the sweet aroma
of animal flesh roasting over small campfires. He heard the
jubilant songs of chanting women, the laughter of children.

Slowly, slowly, all these yesterdays melted away.

The painted warriors were gone with the spirit of the
buffalo. The deer remained, and the elk. And the big cougar
who had been taking fat young cattle from the Columbine
pastures. Moon had returned to the eternal present—the
Now.

The Ute sensed the pitiless predator, stepping over a
fallen log. Pausing to sniff the scent-tinged air. Strong tendons stretched, taut muscles rippled.

He's coming. The haunted man wondered whether he
would live or die. It seemed to matter little. Father Raes
Delfino had once told him that a man does not truly live
until he is willing to cast his life away.

Somewhere behind him, Charlie Moon heard sharp

wings cut the air as a startled raven took to the sky with a croaking call of warning.

He's here. The Ute did not raise his head or open his eyes. He was completely at peace. That which had not yet begun was already finished. What was preordained would come to pass.

There was the barest hint of rustling dry grass underfoot.

Hat in hand, Charlie Moon kept his vigil between the open pit and the young woman's grave.

The predator paused. Gazed at the back of the tall, bare-headed man.

Paducah snorted, stamped a heavy hoof.

The Ute uttered his first words in three days. "Hello, Henry."

CHAPTER 44

Cave Man

"Well, you do amaze me." This declaration was followed by a raspy chuckle that trailed off into a cough.

Charlie Moon opened his eyes, turned to see his visitor. Camouflage deer hunter's coveralls hung like a tattered tent on Henry Buford's gaunt frame. The man's face was concealed under a bristly growth of new whiskers, a woolen sock hat was pulled down to ears and eyebrows. By the smell of him, he had not bathed for quite some time. The sight of the uninvited guest might have been comical—except for the Winchester carbine resting in the crook of his left arm.

Buford's finger was tucked inside the trigger guard. He bared a few teeth in a foxy, yellow-tinted grin. "You don't seem overly surprised to see me."

The Ute stared without blinking. "I'm surprised to see you looking so poorly."

"Charlie, I am bone-tired from all my labors. After I'm done with this business, I aim to sit myself down in an old rockin' chair." *And rock myself far away from here.*

"I wouldn't think hard work would bother a tough old boot like you."

"I haven't been getting enough sleep." *The bad dreams*

won't go away. Buford gave the open grave a sideways glance. "You been acting awfully peculiar, cowboy. Days on end, out here all by yourself." *And unarmed.*

"You concerned about my health?"

Buford nodded. "Concerned—and curious. Thought I should come check on you." He raised an eyebrow. "You must've known all along I was up yonder in the Notch."

And I knew you'd be coming down to the Knob. The Ute looked toward the rift in the Misery Range. It was not nearly so deep as the dark divide that cleaved his soul.

The assassin rubbed a callused thumb across the carbine hammer. "What beats me is—how'd you know?"

The man who was cut asunder did not respond.

"You still got a minute or two, Charlie. So don't be so damn modest—satisfy my curiosity."

"In a scrap with a hardcase like Henry Buford, it was hard to believe the senator's nephew came out on top."

"I appreciate your confidence in me, cowboy. Really I do. But you must've had more'n that to go on."

"The young man was a vegetarian."

The puzzled man cocked his head at the Ute. "And you don't think carrot-chompers ever commit violent acts?"

"The bomb-making evidence in Pearson's cabin was in a box. A box that come from the grocery store packed with twenty-four cans of stew. *Beef* stew."

Buford rolled this over, looked at all sides of it. "That don't prove nothin'. Allan coulda picked up that empty box in an alley."

Moon nodded. "Yeah, that's what I thought. Until an FBI agent showed me some pictures of your burned-out house. I looked for something that should've been on your mantelpiece. It wasn't there."

Henry Buford stared past the tribal investigator. "The old Indian axe head Daddy gave me. I tried, but I just couldn't leave it behind."

"But you left your dog." *Left him dead.*

The assassin wiped the back of a hand across his eyes. "I couldn't take Grape-Eye with me. Soon as somebody come within a hundred yards of my hideout, that floppy-eared idiot would've barked and gave me away. And I couldn't leave him behind. Damn old mutt would've sniffed out my trail, followed me into the Notch. Probably brought a dozen cops with him."

"All the same, it takes a pretty cold hand to shoot his own dog."

"Had to be done." He added hoarsely, "Grape-Eye understood. Right before I . . . put him to sleep, he licked my hand."

The Ute wondered what it would be like to drift off into that final sleep. He lifted his gaze to the mountains. "When I was up there looking for the cougar, I found a couple of boot prints. Figured you were holed up in one of the caves. But it didn't seem sensible to go looking too close. Didn't want to tempt you to take a potshot at me."

"I appreciate that. But why didn't you send the feds up there after me?"

"Way I see it, Henry, finishing this sorry business is between you and me."

"Then we see things eye to eye." Buford pointed his chin at the headstone over the young woman's grave. "Why'd you plant her here?" *To torment me?*

Moon watched the two-legged predator. "Why did you kill her?"

"Wasn't like you think, Charlie." *You couldn't even imagine. . . .*

"Tell me what it was like."

Henry Buford's eyes glazed over. "She happened along one night when I didn't want any company. So I did what was necessary."

"What'd she see that made her so dangerous?"

"It wasn't what she saw." *Turn the word around.* "It's what she *was*. . . ."

"A campus police officer."

"Nah, that didn't bother me." Buford's voice dropped to a low mutter. "She was something . . . something I can't tell you about." *The dancing woman. From my nightmares.*

He's not making any sense. "What were you doing when she happened along?"

The murderer's lips cracked a mischievous grin. "That's for me to know—and you to find out."

"I already found out."

"The hell you did."

"She saw you stuffing sand in a sock."

Buford stared wide-eyed at the tribal investigator. "Now who told you about that?"

Charlie Moon almost smiled. "My aunt Daisy."

He's bullshitting me. "Your aunt?"

"That old woman tells me all kinds of things." *Crazy, impossible things.*

"How'n hell would your aunt know what happened that night—was she there, too?"

The Ute shook his head.

"Then how—"

"A young, redheaded woman told her." Moon turned his face toward Wilma Brewster's grave.

Buford glanced at the mound of earth, quickly averted his eyes. "When was this?"

"Few weeks ago."

"I'm surprised at you, Charlie. Never thought you'd lie to me."

"I don't lie."

"That gal's been stone cold dead since last December." Buford's face had gone a shade more pale. "So it's not possible she talked to your aunt anytime recently."

"I know." The Ute squinted at the pale blue infinity floating above the Columbine.

"So what're you sayin' to me?"

"Henry, there was a time when I thought I had things pretty much figured out. But as the years pass by . . ." It was hard to put into words.

Buford attempted a smirk. "You telling me you believe in ghosts?"

Moon shook his head. "But they don't seem to care

whether I believe in 'em or not." *When the shadows fall, they come calling.*

Clearly unnerved by such talk, the visitor pointed the carbine at the open pit beside Wilma Brewster's resting place. "Who's that for—you?"

"Beginning to look that way."

This response produced an odd expression on Buford's grimy face. "You got class, Charlie. From the first minute I laid eyes on you, I says to myself, 'There is a man worthy of respect.' "

The Ute fell silent.

The winds returned to moan over the Knob. Tree limbs rattled like dry bones.

Buford shivered from an inner coldness. *Why doesn't he say something?* "What're you thinking about, Charlie?"

"About how you went into town that night. Waited behind the Blue Light for Billy Smoke to show up with Patch Davidson's Lincoln. After you beat him to death with the rebar, you waited for the senator to come out of the restaurant. You tapped Patch on the head with the sock just hard enough to addle him—then used the iron bar on his knees. Fixed him so he'd never walk again."

"I'm sorry about your Indian friend."

"Billy Smoke wasn't a friend of mine. But I'm glad to know you're sorry about something." Moon's brow furrowed. "You help the senator select his motorized wheelchair?"

"Nah. Ol' Patch, he picked out the Electric GroundHog all by himself." Buford scratched at his belly. "He's always been a lazy old bastard, so I knew he'd want something that did all the work for him. But it didn't matter all that much whether the chair had a battery or not. I could've hid the explosive in a seat cushion. Even inside a wheel."

"How'd you get Allan Pearson to install the battery in the senator's GroundHog?"

"Easy as eating a hot buttered biscuit. Dumb-ass kid followed me around like a puppy, did anything I told him to. Day the senator was leaving for D.C., I told Allan my back was acting up, asked him to replace the backup storage battery with a freshly charged unit." Buford snickered. "And charged it was, my man." He was looking past Charlie Moon, as if the Ute was an insignificant bystander in this small drama. "You should thank me for removing the senator's nephew from this vale of toil and tears."

"Why should I do that?"

"That crack-sniffing misfit was worried you were going to expose his illegal business activities. Allan paid his drug-running motorcycle freaks to put you outta business. After you whipped a couple of 'em, and that big rattlesnake didn't bite you, Allan sent the whole bunch of 'em over to the Columbine, knowingly putting the senator's life at risk. That really pissed me off, Charlie. I had to keep the old man alive and healthy till he'd served my purpose. Patch was the centerpiece of my plan." Lovingly, the assassin stroked the cold carbine barrel. "Day before the main event, I set an explosive charge in the ranch headquarters. And a little firebomb in my house. Then I invited Allan over to my place for a drink. Told the little pissant I knew how he'd sent his motorcycle-freak buddies to the Columbine. He pleaded with me not to tell his uncle. I slapped his face so hard he slobbered."

"And then you shot him—like you shot your dog."

Buford squinted at the Ute. "Charlie, please don't take this as a mean-spirited criticism, but you do have an annoying tendency to think the very worst of me."

"Sorry if I hurt your feelings. I suppose Pearson must've shot himself. Three or four times."

Buford spat tobacco juice into the dust. "The scrap between me'n the punk was a fair deal. Hell, it was more'n fair. I gave him a loaded revolver, told him we was gonna have us a reg'lar Old West shoot-out."

"Why would you want to do a reckless thing like that?"

The storyteller ignored the question. "It was quite a moment, Charlie. There we are, eyeball to eyeball. The kid's piece is in his hand, my old Colt's on the kitchen table."

"Sounds like you had a death wish."

He glowered at the Ute. "It's bad manners to interrupt a man's story with pointless commentary."

"I'll keep that in mind. So what happened next?"

"The pathetic little coward started whining, begged me to call it off. 'Nuts,' I says, 'Don't shame yourself, kid.' Allan, he commences to beg some more. Tells me he 'really don't want to do this.' It was enough to make a grown man throw up his breakfast. But when I reached for my *pistola*, he sure took a pop at me." Buford threw his head back, a laugh rattled deep in the broad chest. "Damn near got me, too—slug popped through the armpit of my best wool shirt. But one shot was all he got off—I nailed the little pissant right good." He sighted down a crooked finger. "Bam-bam-bam. It was a nice, tight pattern—three times through the pump. I slipped my fireproof folding knife into his pocket, left him right there on the floor."

"Then you planted the bomb-making evidence in his shack."

Buford nodded. "I'd been collecting that stuff for months. Allan had bought most of it for me, so his prints were all over it. And after that job was done, I hauled his shiny little motorbike over to Montrose, stashed it behind a run-down bar. A few minutes before the GroundHog was *supposed* to blow sky-high under Patch Davidson's ass— he shot his adversary an annoyed look—"Allan's mortal remains got cremated in my house." The killer's eyes took on a faraway look. "And in case you're wondering, I'm not even a little bit sorry. No-sirree, not the least fraction of a smidgen."

The Ute took a deep breath, exhaled. "The senator trusted you—treated you like a son."

"I only had one daddy." He added in a whisper: "And one brother."

"So this whole business was about your twin."

The barrel of Buford's carbine was pointing at a spot between the Ute's boots. "What do you know about that?"

"Patch Davidson told me you believed your brother had survived that plane crash—"

"Believe, hell!" Pain spread over Buford's face like a rash. "You ever hear of China's Detention Center Number Twelve?" He shook his head. "No, I guess you didn't. Well, it's about ten clicks south of a dirty little burg called Bin-yang. Which is in Guangxi Province. Which I imagine is also not familiar to you. But you can take my word for it—I got some A-Number-One contacts in the intel community. DIA's China Section knew exactly where Ed was, what kind of pig slop the Chinks gave him to eat, how he slept in his own filth." His voice thick with emotion, Buford paused in an attempt to calm himself. "I went to the senator, told him about it—asked for his help. Patch promised me he'd check with the CIA. If they could confirm my brother's location, he'd lean on the State Department, get them to confront the Chinese government—and demand Ed's release. Few weeks later, Patch told me he'd done his level best, but the intel about my brother had turned out to be bogus." Buford shook his head.

Moon watched the carbine barrel. "And you didn't believe him."

"That damned old politician was doing what he does best—lying through his teeth. My DIA contact told me what really happened. A deep-pocket special interest group was worried about upsetting trade negotiations with the Chinese. These businessmen were tight with a block of very influential congressmen. 'Stop annoying our trading partners with these unsubstantiated charges about holding an American prisoner,' these good ol' boys tell Patch, 'and you can have whatever you want for Colorado.' Well, Patch feels which way the wind is blowing. So he trades my brother for some construction projects. Something sweet for his *constituents*." He spat out the word.

"Like the preschool, where you filled your sock with sand."

"I thought that was a nice twist—take a piece of what Patch had accepted in exchange for my brother's life, and knock that lying politician in the head with it. But that was just for starters. Don't forget what I did to his fancy new airport."

Moon had not forgotten.

"It was sweet to behold, Charlie my man. I took the first of my supercharged storage batteries out there in the middle of the night. Blew the Patch Davidson Terminal Building all to hell and gone." Buford smiled at his audience. "I hope you appreciate the delicate irony of my choice for a test site."

The Ute held his silence. *Let him talk.*

The unhappy man was eager to talk. "But I'm getting ahead of my story. A few weeks after Patch accepted these bribes on behalf of the fine citizens of the great state of Colorado, my brother was executed. Shot in the head." His eyes were oddly blank, as if he had been blind from birth. "It's a queer thing—being a twin. The night Ed's end came, it was daytime on this side of the world. I was over at the senator's trout pond, working on the windmill pump. I felt the side of my head explode. For a moment, I thought, 'My God, somebody has bushwhacked me.' But there wasn't any wound—and not a drop of blood. I realized it wasn't *me* that'd been shot in the head. It was Ed. But that Chinese bullet didn't quite finish my brother off." He waved the carbine like a baton. "It was an awful experience, Charlie— worse than you could ever imagine." Buford shuddered. "And then . . . then I felt the little knives."

Though bathed in sunshine, Moon felt a dreadful chill. "Knives?"

Henry Buford looked toward the clouded horizon, as if he could see far beyond it. "In the People's Democratic Republic, nothing much goes to waste. Oftentimes, right after a prisoner is executed, useful body parts are removed from the corpse. Whatever the government can sell on the transplant market. Eyes. Kidneys. Heart. Even skin. Problem was—Ed wasn't quite dead yet when those Chinese butchers went to work on him." He blinked at the Ute. "Charlie, d'you have any idea what it feels like to have your eyes gouged out . . . strips of skin peeled off your back and legs . . . being gutted like a carp?"

Moon tried to speak. Words, if there were any, stubbornly refused his summons.

Buford licked at chapped lips. "Poor Ed. He struggled and twitched some, but he wasn't able to yell . . . I had to do the screamin' for him. And I yelled bloody murder till my throat went dry as chalk." Milky tears formed in the hard man's eyes, trickled down leathery, sunburned cheeks. "After a long, long time, the torment was finally over. Ed's spirit slipped away from the pain." The man's eyes went cold and flat. "And my soul drifted away at the same time—I don't know where to. Funny thing is, my body still don't know it. These old legs just keep on walking, this big mouth keeps on talking. But way down deep inside, I've been dead ever since that awful day." He turned his head to stare at the silent, dark-skinned man. "You have a brother?"

The Ute shook his head.

"Even if you did, you still wouldn't understand. Multiply a brother by ten times ten, you've almost got a twin. If the senator had done the right thing, Ed would've been released—sent back to the good ol' U.S. of A."

"I wish it'd worked out that way."

"Wishes are free, chum, so let's help ourselves. Me, I wish I'd never known about what happened to Ed. *Knowing* is what got me rolling downhill." Henry Buford wiped at reddened eyes. "I spent hours on end just sitting in the dark, knowing I was slipping into the quicksand, but I couldn't pull myself out. Late one night, I came within a gnat's eyelash of putting a bullet through my brain." He shifted his gaze to the young woman's resting place. "That's when I realized I had to get a firm grip on myself. What I needed was some serious work to occupy my mind. So I started thinking—how could I make a payback? It was kind of a daydream, where I'd even the score with Patch and the whole corrupt U.S. government." Buford seemed mesmerized by the tombstone at the head of Wilma Brewster's

grave. He thought he saw something move near the granite
slab. Something like smoke. "Long as I kept busy, it was
almost like being alive. I just had to keep plugging along
till the job was done."

Charlie Moon found his voice. "You set yourself an am-
bitious goal—cutting off the head of the United States government."

"Yes, I did." *Ed would be proud of me.* "You know, it
is just amazing what one determined sonofabitch can accomplish if he sets his mind to it."

"Aside from murdering three people and crippling an old
man, what did you accomplish?"

"Charlie, you have got a way of cutting right to the bone.
Except for your interference, everything I planned
would've worked slick as snail spit." He pointed the carbine
barrel at the tribal investigator's left knee. "So I hereby
hold you personally responsible for messing things up."

"Thanks, Henry. But if I hadn't figured out what you
were up to, something else would've gone wrong. You'd
never have pulled it off."

Buford's blood pressure spiked; his eyes popped dan-
gerously. "Why would you say a mean thing like that?"

Keep him talking. "Your scheme was way too complicated."

"It was not!" He stamped his foot. "It was a nice,
straightforward plan. If you'd left things alone, I'd have got
it done right well."

"Think so, do you?"

"I *know* so. That's why I had to come down from the
mountain—to square things between us."

"There's been enough killing."

Buford lips curled into a mirthless grin. "How much is
enough?"

"Henry—lay the carbine down."

The killer squinted at the sky, where a red-tailed hawk
etched an elegant ellipse over Pine Knob. "If I give myself
up, what's in it for me?"

"I expect you've got an even shot at living out your full threescore and ten."

"Sure. With room and board provided by Uncle Sammy."

"Wouldn't be all that bad. Three squares a day. Clean sheets on the bed. Hot shower. A library. Better than living in a cave with lice and fleas."

"And I'd have lots of time to pray about my multitude of sins."

"There's that, too."

Buford spoke barely above a whisper. "Would you come and visit me?"

"Yes. I would."

"I don't doubt it for a second." The sinner pulled off the sock hat, shook his shaggy head. "But I could not live behind the walls." He began to raise the carbine barrel. "I'd rather be hunted down and shot."

Moon banged each word home with a hammer. "Henry, listen to what I'm telling you—being alive is better than being dead."

He smiled at the tall, thin man. "Now tell me the honest truth—do you really care all that much about staying in this sad old world?"

The Ute had nothing left to say.

Henry Buford felt an electrifying thrill. Like on his eighth birthday, when he had climbed aboard the mammoth Greyhound bus to go see Indianapolis for the very first time. "Feels strange, don't it, cowboy—standing here, straddling that Great Divide?" The wind had fallen utterly silent. The assassin thumbed the Winchester hammer, the metallic snap was audible for a hundred yards.

Charlie Moon closed his eyes. *Oh, God . . . I do not want this.*

Buford aimed at the Ute's chest, his finger tightened on the trigger. *Life in this world is nothing but pain and sorrow, Charlie. Just let it go . . . let it go . . .*

Moon let it go. The black hat dropped from his hand.

It was over in the flicker of sunlight off rippling waters.

• • •

Before the John B. Stetson touched the earth, a seven-millimeter hollow-point bee hummed past Moon's shoulder. A fractional second before the rifle's throaty bark boomed in from sixty-one yards away, the lead cylinder punctured the sternum dead center over Henry Buford's heart. Before the man's head hit the ground, the spirit had left him.

Charlie Moon knew this was so—he saw it go.

And he *thought* he saw something else.

Growing rapidly from a mere pinprick of intense blue light, it took on form. The luminescent mist assumed the appearance of a skinny, floppy-eared dog. The phantom canine licked at an unseen hand, the long tail wagged.

The Ute assured himself that the apparition was a product of his troubled mind.

Sixty-one yards away, Griego Santanna stood up in a cluster of scrub oak. It had all gone according to plan. The *jefe* had staked himself out until the gringo came down from the mountains. Curiosity was very strong bait, but he wondered—had the tall man somehow *called* the bad man to the knob? The Mexican had known of stranger things happening. He yelled. "Hey, *Indio*, you cut that very close." *But another tick-tock an' I was gonna pop him anyhow.*

Charlie Moon closed his eyes, prayed to be blind to that which should remain unseen. This done, he peered through slit lids. The vaporous canine had departed. To some far place.

But the ghostly illusion had been replaced with something far worse—images of Henry Buford, sitting alone in the darkness, unable to put a bullet through his head. Henry Buford, wading into a dozen armed bikers, hot lead pellets flying like popcorn. Henry Buford, giving Allan Pearson the first shot. The final image was the most unsettling of all. Henry Buford, aiming a carbine at a man he did not intend to shoot? Moon tried to fight off the terrible, bone-gnawing

suspicion. *Henry tried to remove himself from this world,
but couldn't. So he was looking for somebody to do it for
him. The murderous bikers. Allan Pearson. And maybe . . .
me.* The Ute investigator considered his options. *I don't
have to know. I'll throw his Winchester in the hole with
him, forget about the whole thing.* But he knew better. *I
wouldn't be able to get it out of my mind . . . always wondering. Sooner or later, I'd have to come back up here, dig
it up again.* He reached for the fallen man's carbine. It was
as he had suspected. No cartridge in the chamber. The magazine was empty. *Henry's been scouting me. He knew Santanna was in the brush with a rifle.* The troubled man had
come to Pine Knob to die. And he'd got it done right well.

The shooter was approaching in hurried, eager strides.
Griego Santanna paused three paces from the body. "He
dead?"

Moon nodded, tried hard to sound pleased. "Good shot."

Santanna rested a hand on the hilt of the bowie knife
tucked under his belt. "Uh—I don't guess you'd let me cut
off his ears."

"No. Don't guess I would." He frowned at the short,
wiry man. "Where're you from, Santanna?"

The Mexican pointed the rifle barrel southward. "I have
me a little goat ranch near Camacho."

The Ute looked toward Mexico. "Camacho, huh?"

Santanna nodded. "It is a village in Zacatecas State."

"You have a family?"

Santanna rolled expressive brown eyes. "A wife who is
a *brujo*. And six daughters."

"I bet you'd like to pay them a visit."

The Mexican grunted. "Last time I saw my woman, she
put a spell on me that made my gums bleed."

"No wife is perfect," the Ute observed.

"She also stuck me with a butcher knife—and the children laughed when I bled." He pulled up his cotton shirt
to display a shiny, four-inch-long scar on his belly. "I am
afraid of that woman—she is *demente*."

"I'm sorry to hear that. But you'd better to go back to

Mexico anyway. And stay south of the border till things cool down."

"How long will that take?"

Moon thought about it. "Ten, maybe fifteen years."

Santanna nodded sadly at the injustice of it all. Kill just one gringo and the American Federales never, never stopped looking for you. The sharpshooter squinted at the fresh corpse. "What about him?"

"Henry's gone," Moon muttered. *And I helped him go.*

Santanna gave the *jefe* a hopeful look. "Go on home; I will put the dirt on him for you." *After I cut off his ears.*

"I'll take care of things here." Moon pulled the rifle from the Mexican's hands, wiped Santanna's prints off with a bandanna. "This should be the end of it. But if it ever comes up, you were not here. You don't know a thing about it." The Ute left a dozen of his own prints on the long gun—including one on the trigger.

"*Jefe*—even though you will not let me take his ears, I appreciate what you have done for me."

The Ute blinked at the unpredictable man. "What?"

"When you did not let me shoot that motorcycle gringo, I was very angry. But now I understand that you are a fair man, and a wise one. You were saving this better one for me." Sunlight glinted on the steel teeth. "It was a great honor to murder this *hombre* for you."

Moon knew that he would never be able to explain the significance of what Santanna had done on the crest of this windswept hill. "When you get to the river, give your hands a good washing."

The Mexican wondered whether this was some peculiar *Indio* cleansing ritual. "Okay, *jefe*—if it pleases you, I will clean my hands."

The Ute stared at his own hands. Fancied he saw Buford's blood dripping off the tips of his fingers. "And wash your face, too."

Santanna touched fingertips to his cheek. "My face?"

"When you fire a rifle, you get more powder residue on your nose than on your trigger finger. If you get stopped by the police between here and the border, I don't want them to find any nitrates on your hands *or* your face."

Griego Santanna stared at the strange Indian, then raised a hand in solemn salute. *"Adios, Señor Luna."* The man from Zacatecas State turned his face toward the river. This had been a very good day, and so he whistled as he walked. When he tired of whistling, the Mexican sang a happy song about a man who had slit the throat of his nagging mother-in-law, stole her sow pig, spotted billy goat, and seven dominiker chickens.

Once Santanna's slight form was reduced to a speck on the horizon, Charlie Moon untied a fringed Circle of Life blanket from behind his saddle. He wrapped the corpse, tied the bundle with a length of yellow nylon rope, lowered Buford's body into the deep slit. Digging the hole six feet into the rocky ground had been work enough. Filling the inhabited grave was hard labor indeed. Each scoop of sandy soil was heavier than the one before. When the hole was filled level, the laborer tamped down loose earth with the long-handled shovel, spread the excess soil around. By the middle of next summer there would be no evidence of a second burial.

Moon stood between the graves. It seemed both eerie and fitting that Henry now slept beside Wilma. He said an earnest prayer for those two souls whose paths had met at a violent intersection. But an "amen" was not the proper way to end this. His voice was just above a whisper. "Henry, I don't know if you can hear me. But I got something I need to say." He took a deep breath. "You needed killing."

A raven landed on the crest of a dead piñon. Cocked its head at the tall, dark man.

After a pause, Moon continued his melancholy speech. "I will say this—when it's too late for talking and there's nothing left to do but break some bones, there's no man I'd rather have by my side. I'm glad you were with me on Too Late bridge." His final words were the hardest to say.

"Truth is, Henry—I liked you." *And I'll miss you.*

His sad duty done, Moon got into the saddle. On the way home, he told himself that there was at least one thing to be grateful for—this sad business was finally finished.

The winds returned to the barren hilltop. They came to groan and sigh in the stunted trees, to hum mournful hymns in the sage, to conjure up twisting little swirls of sand. The elfin dust devils danced over the fresh grave.

CHAPTER 45

The Invitation

Pete Bushman leaned against a post on the headquarters porch, watched the approach of the Indian. The foreman noted the Remington rifle balanced on the saddle. *So the boss decided to do the shooting after all.* He waited for Charlie Moon to tell him about it.

The Ute nodded at his employee.

"I heard a shot. You nail that big cat?"

The rancher got off the horse, patted the amiable beast on the neck. "Not this time."

Bushman grinned under his beard. "Ol' Two-Toes give you the slip, eh?"

"Well, you know what they say."

The foreman chewed contentedly on a wad of Beechwood Tobacco. "No, I don't. What do they say?"

"Tomorrow's another day."

"Oh, yeah. That one." *I'll ask him, but he'll say no. Just like he has ever since he got silly in the head.* "Dolly, she wants you to come over to our place tonight. For some supper."

Moon looked to the north. Wisps of gray mist drifted across Pine Knob. It was time to turn a new corner. "Don't mind if I do."

The Meal

Unable to conceal her satisfaction, Dolly Bushman beamed as Charlie Moon enjoyed a man-sized meal. Roast beef. Boiled potatoes. Pinto beans. Sourdough bread. Strawberry jam cake.

His supper finished, the rancher thanked the cook, returned to the Columbine headquarters.

The Cut-In

A minute before midnight, Charlie Moon climbed the stairs, got into bed, pulled the covers to his chin. He turned off the light, waited for Sidewinder's good night.

The old hound bayed once, twice. Three times.

Eager to trade all of the day's troubles for a taste of sweet oblivion, the weary man descended into the deepest of bottomless sleeps.

It was not possible to turn back, or even to slow his movement. Propelled along a winding path through a vast gray expanse of thirsty mesquite and wilted rabbit grass, the dreamer was pulled toward the distant timbre of discordant music. Presently, the trail ended at a destination. He found himself standing before a run-down clapboard building that had never felt the refreshing touch of paint. A thin, sallow-faced man in faded overalls was seated on the sagging front porch. He kept an eye on the visitor. An old dog lay with his muzzle touching the door. Moon approached; the gaunt man raised a hand, shook his head. Denied entry, the dreamer moved to the side of the structure. He wiped away the grime on a window patterned with spiderweb cracks. Peered through. The dance hall was illuminated by the wan flicker of a single back taper.

He knew the redhaired woman would be there.

She was, and was again. One of her was seated at a rickety piano, daintily fingering random keys. Her second self was on the dirty dance floor—swinging, swaying, laughing with a wild delight known only to the demented.

Charlie Moon knew for certain that he would never feel the terrible embrace of the dancer again. This knowledge should have brought blessed relief. But what he saw inside the twilight interior made him shudder so hard that his bones rattled.

The man from the porch appeared by his side, offered a strong hand to steady the pilgrim.

For a silent interlude, they watched together. When it pleased him to do so, the guardian of the decrepit dance hall spoke. The voice rumbled up from that deep pit where the dropped stone never hits bottom. "Ask me your questions."

The dreamer heard himself respond. "Which of them is Wilma?"

"Neither. She has never been here—and never shall she be."

"Then who are these women?"

"There are no women here."

"When will this end?"

"At first light."

The dreamer was not comforted by these words. "When will that be?"

There was no answer to this final question.

Finding himself alone at the window, Moon returned to the porch. The man was seated in a straight-backed chair, hands folded in his lap. The guardian ignored the dreamer. The scrawny dog had not moved from its position near the door.

There was something disturbingly familiar about the animal. Moon approached for a closer look. The hound turned its head. Under the left ear, a small, round hole. Worming a crooked path down the animal's neck from the bullet wound, a long black track of congealed blood.

The creature took a long, hopeful look at Charlie Moon.

Inside the clapboard shack, the piano clinks madly.
Rotting boards creak.

Insane laughter shrieks.
The dancing woman clutches the new arrival ever so
tightly.
She will hold onto him for tomorrow and tomorrow and
tomorrow. Until . . .

The Call

Charlie Moon sat straight up in his bed. After a moment's reflection he got to his feet, pulled a blanket around his shoulders. The Ute paced back and forth in the near darkness, thought long and hard about it. Finally, at the striking of the clock, he stopped in midstride. There was but one thing to do—and it must be done right now. He switched on a table lamp, picked up the telephone, dialed a number he knew by heart from his years of service with the SUPD. The distant machine warbled six times before he heard the sleepy voice in his ear.

"St. Ignatius." *If this is a crank call, may God smite you.*

"Father Raes?"

"No, this is my butler." A pause. "Charlie—is that you?"

"Yeah."

"Oh dear God—is it your aunt Daisy? Has she—"

"No, she's okay." *Far as I know.* "Sorry to wake you up."

"I accept your perfunctory apology with remarkable grace." The Jesuit priest yawned into the telephone. "Now what's this about?"

"Official business."

"Yours or mine?"

"Uh . . . yours. Mostly."

"I am listening."

The Ute hesitated. "I need you to . . . ahh . . . hear my confession." *There. I said it.*

Dead silence.

"Father Raes, you there?"

"Charlie Moon, you have not come to confession since

you were fourteen years old. If this middle-of-the-night call is your idea of a joke—"

"It's no joke. I need your help."

"Help with what?"

"Can't discuss it over the phone."

"Will you at least reveal the nature of the problem? If you're in some kind of trouble, tell me where you are and I'll leave immediately—"

"No, I'll come to you." Moon selected his words with care. "It's someone else who needs your help—I'm kinda standing in for him."

"Is this other party in danger of imminent death?"

"No." *He's well past that.*

"So. No one is dying." There was a brief silence while the priest weighed the possibilities. "May I safely presume that this is a bona fide spiritual emergency?"

"Oh, yeah—that's what it is, all right."

"Charlie, may I inquire as to why this enigmatic telephone call could not have been put off until tomorrow morning?"

Moon consulted his bedside clock. "Well, technically, it's tomorrow morning right now."

God give me strength. There was a creaking of bed springs. "I'll put on a pot of coffee." Another yawn. "When shall I expect you?"

"I'll be there when the sun comes up."

"Very well then," the Jesuit priest said. "I'll expect you at first light."

"Right." *That should do just fine.*

Charlie Moon sat on the edge of his bed, stared through the bedroom window at the vast sprinkling of white-hot lights. He had read somewhere that there were countless swirling galaxies, and more stars than there are grains of sand upon the earth. Moreover, Father Raes had once shared a sweet mystery with an inquisitive youth—these sparkling gems were strewn across the cold, black void of Middle World by a Creator whose love and extravagance knows no bounds. And despite all the pain and darkness that had haunted his life, and all of the deep mysteries that were beyond understanding, Charlie Moon had always wanted to believe the priest's comforting words.

CHAPTER 46

The Door

Troubled by the Ute's peculiar telephone call, Father Raes Delfino pulled on his wool overcoat, left the rectory, walked across a parking lot to the church. He unlocked the front entrance to St. Ignatius, pulled the heavy door shut behind him, thumbed the latch. Inside was much like outside. Still. Cold. Dark. He flicked a light switch. Nothing. *Oh, balderdash! That freaky furnace motor must've tripped the main breaker again. I'll have to light a candle.* He fumbled in his pockets, could not find the small box of matches. *Wonderful.*

He waited until his eyes had adjusted to the rosy glow of moonlight filtering in through stained-glass windows, then approached the altar. The lonely man kneeled, crossed himself. He prayed for Charlie Moon. For Charlie's anonymous friend. But even as he spoke to God, the priest's mind was engaged by the nagging problem with the furnace. Who could he call to make the necessary repairs, and with what would he pay them? Remembering why he had come to the altar, the priest refocused his attention on his proper business. *Charlie will be here with the sun. And I must be ready to offer what aid and comfort I can.* But the Jesuit priest—trained as an anthropologist—knew well that he was no pastor. He was a scholar, a former professor who found it tedious to minister to these few marginal Christians who slipped in for Mass on Sunday mornings, then went about their worldly ways until the Sabbath came round again. There were notable exceptions, of course. But most came to the Lord's table not for strength and renewal, but for comfort and pardon. And not a few behaved as if God had given Moses the Ten Suggestions. While he tasted these sour thoughts, a familiar voice whispered in his left ear: *These simple people are hardly worth the bother. You should do something more important with your life.*

The priest responded promptly. *Begone, Satan—depart from me!*

Having dismissed the Father of Lies, the man of God struggled to put away his dismal thoughts. And he did. Except for one. The crusty academic had long harbored a suspicion that the bishop had sent him to this Godforsaken outpost as punishment for some unrepented transgression. Most probably, he mused, the sin of pride. Father Raes was not a great admirer of the bishop who ruled from Pueblo, and at the moment he was not altogether happy with his Creator. He spoke aloud: "Father of our Lord Jesus Christ, I speak to you every day, every night—even in my sleep I call out to you. When will you answer me?"

Having more than a mustard seed of faith, the supplicant waited, half expecting the explicit response his earnest prayer deserved. He heard only the whisper of wind in the eaves.

But a sweet stillness came over him.

All thought ceased.

Time passed, unnoticed and unmeasured.

The blissful experience was abruptly interrupted by the sound of a light tapping. Barely noticing the intrusion, Father Raes thought it must be the product of his imagination. He did not bother to open his eyes.

But there it was again—knuckles rapping on the door.

Annoyed, the priest pushed himself erect, marched down

the aisle toward the front entrance, reached to open the
door—hesitated. Something was wrong about this. It was
far too early for Charlie Moon's arrival; the sun was still
well below the twin crests of the Piedra Peaks. And there
was no light inside the sanctuary, not even a candle flame.
How could anyone know I'm here? The answer was all too
obvious. *This person has been watching the church since I
came inside.* Which certainly qualified as suspicious behavior.

Father Raes was not a timid man, but neither was he
reckless. Only last month, the aged pastor of the First Methodist Church had been brutally assaulted by a crazed drug
addict who broke into his study—and that despicable crime
was committed in the middle of the day! *It's a lucky thing
I locked the door behind me.* He thought of summoning
help, but there was no telephone in the church. He held his
breath, then: "You out there—what do you want?"

There was a mumbled reply. Something about being
cold . . . hungry.

It's a ruse—to get me to open the door. "I'm sorry—
this is not a convenient time. Later on today, come to the
rectory."

Thump—thump—thump. Louder this time—*urgent.*

Father Raes retreated to the altar, selected a massive
bronze candlestick. Heartened by the heft of this formidable
weapon, he called out in a tone meant to intimidate, "Who
are you?"

Now the response was crisp and clear, the words perfectly distinct.

Moreover, he recognized the voice.

The priest's vision blurred, the cord was cut. At once,
he was both here and *there. Here,* his knees buckled. *There,*
an irresistible twist of vertigo pulled him in into a whirlpool
of spiraling emptiness. *Here,* he fell sprawling before the
altar, arms outstretched. *There,* he floated in absolute noth-
ingness. *Here,* the heavy candlestick slipped from his grasp,
rolled across the oak floor. *There,* the loosed soul said to
itself, *I have died.*

But he was not dead. Quite the opposite.

Indeed, shortly after the sun rose, Father Raes had recovered sufficiently to hear Charlie Moon's tale, and his confession. On his knees, the priest prayed for the souls of Billy Smoke, Wilma Brewster, Allan Pearson. He also interceded with God on behalf of Henry Buford's tortured soul. When his earnest prayer was completed, the priest knew with absolute certainty that his supplication had been heard and acted upon. The gates of Hell had not prevailed. The dance hall had been shut down for all eternity.

This was a most remarkable event in the life of the parish priest. But as men grow old, the light of the mind dims. As the autumn years slipped by, his memory of the intercession would gradually fade.

But long after the Jesuit's dark hair had paled to snowy white, he would perfectly recall that singular encounter with the unexpected visitor who had stood at the door—and knocked. At the moment he gave up his final breath, the priest would whisper, repeating his fearful challenge . . . *Who are you?*

I am the light of the world.

Keep reading for an excerpt from
James D. Doss's next mystery

THE WITCH'S TONGUE

NOW AVAILABLE FROM ST. MARTIN'S/
MINOTAUR PAPERBACKS!

Nearly thirteen thousand summers have passed since that splendid morning when the first human footprints appeared between these towering canyon walls. But in all the years since that singular event, not one good thing has happened here. This being the case, hardly anyone visits this remote and dreadful place—though the rare exception is worthy of mention.

Consider Jacob Gourd Rattle.

Cloaked in twilight shadows, the solitary man holds a pointed stick in his hand. With the terrible intensity of a fanatic, the meticulous draftsman draws a coffin-sized rectangle in the sand. Satisfied with the length and breadth of his plan, he considers its depth.

The customary six feet is what he had in mind, but the soil is packed with stones and there will be tangles of roots to cut. The laborer balances rocks and roots against the weight of tradition. The scales hesitate, then tilt to accommodate his predisposition.

THE TRIBAL ELDER

Daisy Perika is a crusty old recluse; much preferring her
lonely wilderness home to a more comfortable house in
Ignacio. Because the dirt road to her small dwelling is
treacherous even in dry weather, the Ute elder's flesh-and-
blood visitors are few and far between. For the determined
hiker, her dwelling is a three-hour walk from the paved
road. For the motorized pilgrim blessed with fortitude and
four-wheel drive, the journey can be completed in twenty-
nine spine-jarring minutes. By the light of the waning
moon, the amber-eyed owl wings her way from here to
there in scarcely any time at all.

Whether locomoting by foot or wheel or wing, the traveler eventually encounters a collection of sandstone mesas
rising above the arid prairie grasslands. Each of these isolated plateaus is separated from its neighbor by a deep,
sinuous canyon. Three Sisters Mesa is bordered on the west
by the narrow, meandering *Cañon del Serpiente*, and on its
sunrise side by *Cañon del Espiritu*. This latter chasm is,
according to Daisy Perika, a place where the spirits con-
gregate.

Perilously near the yawning mouth of Spirit Canyon,
almost concealed among a cluster of juniper and piñon—
is her modest house-trailer. Resembling an over-sized metal
mailbox, the Ute woman's home stands confidently on
stubby legs of cinder blocks. Scorched by decades of blis-
tering sun, pelted by wind-driven sleet and sand, its once-
glistening surface is now spotted and blotched by a sooty
oxide pox. Now and then, a rivet pops. Beneath the thin
aluminum skin, brittle steel bones fracture and crack. At
sunrise and sunset, corroded joints expand and contract,
making awful creaks and squeaks. When they work at all,
electrical things sizzle and sputter. On her cook stove, blue
circles of propane flame flicker and flutter. In the deep
trough of night, the ghost in the thing utters painful groans
and quaking shudders. The shaman's home should have

collapsed long ago, and died a quiet death. But like its stubborn occupant, the structure remains. Moreover, it is a place where things tend to happen. Special things. And from time to time, distinguished visitors come to call. On this very day, for example.

In the small kitchen, seated at the table, see the kindly man of God—the tight-lipped woman.

THE PRIEST

Having completed his prayer, Father Raes Delfino opened his eyes, saw the Ute elder's prune-skin face staring at him. *Daisy seems upset. Perhaps she has already guessed what I am about to tell her.* He had known the peculiar woman far too long to underestimate her powers. He hesitated, then got on with it. "I came to see you today—because I wanted you to be the first to know."

Daisy Perika held her breath, waited to hear the bad news. *He don't look healthy.*

The Catholic priest smiled at this meddling gossip, this wicked prankster, this see-sawing backslider, this troublesome woman who persisted in her conversations with the dwarf-spirit—this most beloved member of his flock. "Just this morning, I posted a letter to the bishop. I am asking his permission to retire."

Oh, God—I knew it. He's dying! She laid one trembling hand over the other. "When?"

"It is not for me to say." The cleric stirred his coffee. "But I expect it will take at least six months—perhaps a year, for the ecclesiastical wheels to grind their grist."

He must have a cancer. "You're sick."

"Oh no, I am quite well." He chuckled. *Far better than I have ever been.*

"Then why . . ." The old woman's words trailed off down the path to nowhere.

He reached across the table, took her hand in his. "Because, dear lady—it is time."

Daisy brushed away the single tear coursing its way

down her face. "Where'll you go—to one of them old priest's homes?" She snorted. "Sit in a wheel-chair with a bib over your shirt while somebody feeds you oatmeal from a table spoon?"

This produced a belly-laugh. "Gracious me, I hope not."

Her tone was accusing. "But you'll move away from the reservation." *A long way away. And I'll never see you again in Middle World.*

He gave her a thoughtful look. "If God is willing, I will find a quiet place to rest." *And pray.*

I know what it is! The elder screwed up her courage. "Some people in Ignacio say you've been acting funny lately." She added darkly: "They claim you haven't been paying attention to church business—that you go around all day mumbling prayers and psalms. And singing to yourself."

"God forgive me, it is true." The holy man put on a repentant expression. "Now you see why I must be replaced by someone younger. A practical no-nonsense priest, who will get things done."

Daisy was not fooled by this evasive response. "There's even some that say you've had some kind of a *religious* experience." Her tone was distinctly accusing.

Father Raes arched an eyebrow. "Do they now?"

She nodded, pierced him with a flinty look. "Some say you saw an angel in the church one night. Others say you saw—" But *that* could not be repeated. "Is that why you're bailing out?"

He frowned. "Now Daisy—do you really believe I'd let a bit of gossip drive me away?"

"You know what I mean. Are you retiring because you had a vision?" Daisy Perika encountered astounding apparitions once or twice every month, and the old shaman was not thinking about retiring.

The priest assumed his severe persona. "We will not discuss such rumors." Having done his duty, he softened his tone. "But I assure you—I am not retiring from the active priesthood because of anything I have *seen*." This was literally true. It was, in fact, what he had *heard*. But this would never be revealed to another mortal. Especially not to this Ute Catholic, who was a shaman on the side. Or was it the other way around? *God have mercy on our souls.*

The subject was thus dismissed. They talked for a while of other matters.

About Daisy's nephew, tribal investigator Charlie Moon.

About God and his Son. And the Holy Spirit.

Stern admonitions were given. And sweet blessings.

Promises were made.

And finally, good-byes.

ADRIFT

Daisy Perika stood on the wooden porch attached to her trailer home, wrinkled hands gripping the pine rail. The sounds of the priest's automobile were lost in the winds. Thick mists billowed and rolled out of the wide mouth of *Cañon del Espiritu*. The old woman felt as if her feet were slipping on the deck of a small ship tossed by a heaving, unseen sea. As the porch began to creak and sway beneath her feet, she craned her neck forward—straining to get a glimpse of that familiar landscape that must be out there still. It was not. For a terrifying moment, she was almost convinced that the pale blue sky, the piñon-crested mesas, the sinuous brown canyons—had never been. But in the pocket her mind, she had kept them, and could perceive them there. As she held on to the rail of the rolling craft, the elderly Catholic meditated on the Captain of her soul.

Presently, the sea-mists thinned.

The little porch became steady again.

The Ute shaman squinted at the massive stone figures waiting patiently on the crest of Three Sisters Mesa. Could those petrified women see through the mists of time and space? And the *pitukupf* who lived far up *Cañon del Espiritu* in the abandoned badger-hole—could the dwarf reveal when the priest would leave her, and where Father Raes would go? This thought gave the old woman some slight sense of confidence. Everything would work out. One way or another, it always did. Maybe no replacement would be found for the priest. Then the bishop in Pueblo would tell Father Raes he had to stay for a few years more.

At least until I am gone from Middle World . . .

Daisy rubbed a sore hip and sighed. *I'll go inside, heat up the chili stew.*

But not so very far away, where a man had drawn four lines in the sand—a blacker pot had already begin to brew.

To the typical observer, the trio of Mute Ones do not resemble human beings. Not in the least.

This being the case, it could hardly be expected that they would look anything at all like three Pueblo women who had been petrified (depending upon the version of the legend) by either a feat of malicious sorcery or an act of supernatural mercy. To the uninformed eye, the massive monoliths appear to be merely three huge humps of weathered sandstone that were squatting atop the mesa eons before saber-toothed tigers and majestic mammoths roamed the foothills of those mountains that would eventually be Christened *San Juan* by the Spanish invaders. According to the tale the Ute shaman told—and Daisy Perika would not tolerate the least hint of skepticism—after fleeing to the top of the mesa to escape an Apache raiding party, the trio of Pueblo women had prayed for deliverance from their ruthless pursuers. Their bodies had been turned to stone, their spirits set free to enter Upper World. Daisy also asserted that the sandstone women were not quite nine hundred years old and that before the remarkable event, the top of the canyon had been flat as a billiard table. Local geologists dared not contend the point with the hard-eyed woman.

Whatever the ages of the sandstone towers, the deep canyons that snaked and twisted and turned and twined along the edges of Three Sisters Mesa were ancient beyond imagining. And being so very old, there were some rather odd *things* that lingered between their walls. According to Daisy, some were wispy remnants of material bodies. There

were others (so she said) that had never occupied a house
of flesh. The shaman knew this to be true; she had encountered a score or more of them and often chatted with
those who were lonely. The shaman's knowledge was not
limited to the spirits. Because she prepared medicines, the
tribal elder knew every plant that grew in this wilderness.
She begged their pardon for harvesting flowers, berries,
leaves, stems, and roots. She was acquainted with all the
animals, too, and greeted each of them by name. Some
returned the compliment. But there were a few odd features
in these shadowy depths that even Daisy Perika knew little
about.

For example, consider that canyon that is stretched out
closest to the sunset.

The shaman did not know that ages and ages ago, halfway up the cliffs, a thick basaltic layer had bridged the
chasm. Though having little utility except for the occasional
lizard or mouse or fuzzy caterpillar who wished to cross
over the shady depths, it was nevertheless a wondrous thing
to behold. Or would have been, had human beings arrived
in time to see it. Alas, the marvelous formation had collapsed a hundred millennia before the most recent ice age.
In the bottom of the canyon, portions of the fallen bridge
have cracked and weathered and washed away in seasonal
floods. Even so, some evidence remains. A few black basalt
slabs are still half-buried in the sandy floor, and there are
lofty remnants of the ancient span. Opposed on the sheer
cliffs are a pair of dark projections. Well above the Three
Sisters side of the canyon, a black basaltic shelf juts out
prominently from crumbling sandstone. On the wall across
the way, a smaller sibling mimics its mate.

In the early autumn of 1883, a Scottish prospector on
the way to Fort Garland happened by, riding a fat black
ginny mule, leading a gray donkey. This European was
cursed with a touch of superstition, blessed with a wry
sense of humor. While sipping black tea by his campfire,
the traveler named the larger protrusion the Witch's
Tongue, and made note of this small bit of vanity in his

diary. Across the canyon, the smaller shelf cried out for similar recognition. And so the pliant pilgrim from Portnacroish dubbed it the Witch's Thumb, and penned this also on the yellowed page.

The seeker after gold was murdered six months later in *Los Ojos* by a swarthy prostitute who appropriated the Scotsman's poke, his Winchester carbine with the silver-inlaid maple stock—even his little writing-book. Because she could not read, the sporting woman traded the dead man's diary to a U.S. Army cartographer for three Havana Provincial cigars. Sadly, the unfortunate prospector's name has been forgotten.

The Witch's Tongue and Thumb have not.

It may have been due to a few unfortunate references to *brujos*, or recurring tales of hunters and trappers who had fallen into that twilight crack in the earth never to surface again—or it may have been a more subtle hint of evil sensed by tribal elders. But the canyon was always known to the Utes as a *bad* place. So bad that in the mid-twentieth century the Tribal Council had (in its collective wisdom) officially pronounced the six-mile crevasse off-limits except to members of the tribe. But there were, as there must always be, exceptions to the rule.

From time to time, a privileged few were granted special passes. These hardy souls were typically archaeologists, anthropologists, biologists, or geologists—and always *matukach*. The reckless white-skins did not believe in the People's legends, and so had some measure of protection from those unspeakable things that haunted the canyon.

The more sensible folk among the Southern Utes would not have thought of visiting this forbidden place; even the braggarts and scoffers and show-offs generally came up with an acceptable reason to avoid its dark recesses. And so it was that human beings—particularly tribal members— were not to be found in this particular canyon.

Except for the exceptions.

THE EXCAVATION

Between the canyon walls, beneath the cloud-shrouded slit of sky, the lonely soul attended to his solemn business. He was confident that in this forbidden place, his enterprise would be safe from prying eyes.

Vain are the thoughts of men.

Jacob Gourd Rattle was already being watched.

> *Opposite the Witch's black Tongue, perched on the Witch's black Thumb—reclines the cougar. Her unblinking yellow eyes are focused on the man on the canyon floor. She does not wonder about what the peculiar biped is doing down there—such complex thoughts are not in her nature. The hungry feline licks her lips. Imagines how his warm flesh will taste.*

The busy man was unaware of the mountain lion's pitiless stare—or even the fact that she was there. As Jacob Gourd Rattle removed earth and stones from the hole in the ground, he concentrated on the happy thought that the troublesome woman was not with him.

Kicks Dogs would return, of course. She always did.

But, Jacob hoped—not until the appointed time.

Not until his work here was done.

Charlie Moon would have been quite interested in Jacob Gourd Rattle's clandestine activities, but the tribal investigator was a long drive to the north of the Southern Ute reservation. And like the man digging the grave in the canyon, Daisy Perika's nephew was also engaged in important business.

The three serious men were in the antiquarian's storage room, seated around an unusual table.

Charlie Moon—intent on the delightful task of fleecing

his friends of their currency—hardly noticed the furniture.

Scott Parris had already described the card table as "kinda sissy for a man's game of gut-bucket poker."

The mildly miffed owner—who made his quite comfortable living buying and selling fine antiques—informed his gaming companions that they had the distinct honor to rest their elbows on a genuine George II demi-lune mahogany card and tea table with a two-fold top, baize-lined surface with wells. Not to mention club legs and pad feet— thank you very much.

Ralph Briggs' semi-brutish guests had not been impressed.

On the mantel piece, a Victorian brass lantern clock twirled its delicate hands in the slowest of motions to measure the flow of that indefinable river called Time. When it chimed once to announce the eleventh hour, it so happened that Scott Parris was the dealer. The broad-shouldered, sandy-haired, blue-eyed chief of Granite Creek PD was also the heavy loser.

Charlie Moon was down by eight blue chips, but not defeated. The Indian was laying low, waiting for his chance to ambush this mismatched pair of *matukach*.

Ralph Briggs, banker of the game, was nearly twelve hundred dollars up. Hoping to get away while the getting was good, he faked a yawn. "Last hand?"

Scott Parris took a sip of black coffee from a china cup that was almost as translucent as the antiquarian's ploy. "Okay," he said. "But how about we switch to Leadville stakes and White Mule rules."

The Ute nodded his assent.

Ralph Briggs considered protesting, saw the flinty look on the white policeman's face, thought better of it. "Very well, Scott."

Parris rubbed his hands together. "Then let's play poker, gents."

Each of the gamblers anted in a white chip.

The chief of police shuffled, offered the cards to the player on his right.

Charlie Moon cut the deck, passed it back to the dealer.

Scott Parris dealt five rectangles to each of the players, pulled his own hand close to his chin. *Garbage*. He looked to the antiquarian. "Okay, Ralph—how many do you need?"

The smallish man pursed his lips. "Two will do."

The dealer dealt the pair.

Ralph Briggs looked at his new hand. *Well, now. Look at that.*

Parris eyed his best friend. "Charlie?"

Moon wore a mask that grinned. "I am happy with what I'm holding."

Parris snorted at the Ute. "Dealer takes three," he said and did. *More garbage!* He squinted over his pitiful cards at the antique dealer.

Ralph Briggs raised a thin eyebrow at the crafty Indian, eyed his Hearty flush. *I shall demolish Mr. Moon.* On a pretense of miserly caution, he started to push four white chips to the center of the table, hesitated—withdrew half of the pale quartet.

The Ute sniffed the air and smelled the musky odor of deceit. "I'll see that pitiful wager." He offered up two whites. "And raise—this much." The tribal investigator baited the pot with four red chips.

Parris folded. "I hate this game. I hate it more than dentist drills and cod liver oil and income taxes."

As if some dark magic might have transformed the cards since his last furtive glance, Briggs examined what he was holding with exaggerated care. *Moon is bluffing.* "I shall see you," he offered a quartet of matching reds, "and raise you—thusly." The antiquarian sent two blue chips to join their lesser friends.

The Ute called and raised again. Six blue chips.

The dapper little man in the tweed suit did the same. Six and Six more.

"You are a bulldog, Ralph." Charlie Moon pondered his next move. "But I am feeling reckless. So I'll see that and raise you . . . hmm . . . how much? Oh what the hey, a greenback dollar means nothin' to a fella like me. I will risk all I've got." He pushed a multicolor pile of chips to gorge the pot.

The folded chief of police stared goggle-eyed at the players.

As a matter of civilized principle, Ralph Briggs firmly refused to sweat. In lieu of this means by which common men cool their skin, his high forehead beaded with tasteful pearls of unscented perspiration. *The Indian is bluffing. I know it!* He opened his mouth to call, but his churning stomach had the last five words. *But if he is not . . .* His fingers refused to touch the last of his chips. The antiquarian choked. And folded.

The Ute placed his cards face-down, raked in the red-white-and-blue pot, offered his surly adversaries the consolation of a melancholy sigh. "You fellas are the lucky ones. After you've hit the hay tonight, you'll only think about how bad you played for maybe an hour or two or three. But before the sun comes up, you'll finally get worn out from all your moaning and groaning, and drift off to a troubled sleep. But me—I'll be up all night long." He flashed a toothy smile. "Counting my winnings."

Scott Parris shook his head, glanced at the other beaten man. "Ralph, don't you just *hate* it when he does that?"

Ralph Briggs glared at Charlie Moon. *Yes. Indeed I do.*

While the winner was donning on his fleece-lined denim jacket and black John B. Stetson hat, Briggs counted and recounted the meager remnant of his chips. He mumbled: "I just *know* Charlie was holding trash—I should have called."

Parris leaned close to Briggs and whispered. "That Ute never bluffs."

Ralph Briggs desperately wanted a reason to feel better. "Never?"

The town cop shook his head. "Never. If you'd have called, he would've cleaned you out."

After the chief of police had departed for hearth and home, the antique dealer followed the Indian into the display room of his expensive, exclusive shop. *I should not ask, but*—"Charles, just between friends, and just this once—I wonder if I could impose upon you to tell me what—"

The seven-foot Ute stopped in mid-stride, looked down at the smaller man. Charlie Moon shook his head in a gesture that suggested a mix of sadness and disappointment. "Ralph, it is one of Nature's fundamental laws—if a player wants to see the hand a man is holding, he has to lay his money down. But you did not call my bet."

"You are absolutely right, of course." Briggs looked away and had the grace to blush. "I do not know what came over me. It must be the lateness of the hour."

"Don't worry about it." Moon clapped him on the back. "Because you and me are buddies—I have already forgot you asked."

"I am eternally grateful—and you are very gracious."

Moon took a look around. "I might want to make a purchase from your store."

The vulgar reference to a *store* made the pale man wince. "Do you have something particular in mind?"

"I will know it when I see it. Or maybe the other way around."

The businessman made a half-hearted gesture. "Feel free to browse." With a greedy glint in his eye, Ralph Briggs watched Charlie Moon examine this and that. He wondered about a number of things. For instance—on top of his winnings, how much more hard cash did the full-time rancher, part-time tribal cop have in his hip pocket? And how much would he be willing to part with?

As it came to pass, the Ute was separated from the white man by a rift of cultures and a finely crafted walnut display case. The latter barrier was glazed with brittle Venetian glass that cast the contents in a pale bluish hue. On the top shelf, a remarkable assortment of collectibles was laid out on a plush carpet of purple felt.

An 1857 French Army dental kit, neatly packaged in a

small wooden box that presented a silvered mirror on the open lid.

An ivory crescent of walrus tusk, delicately engraved with the ghostly form of a four-masted Boston whaling vessel, sails still billowed by phantom winds.

Representing the Yankee invasion of the Confederate States of America, a corroded assortment of powdery-white lead bullets, silver medals, brass buttons, bronze belt buckles.

A diamond-studded bracelet and magnificent emerald ring worn by the lovely young heiress of the Flint Hill and Nacogdoches Oil Company on the very night she drove her black 1949 Packard convertible into Attoyac Bayou.

The centerpiece of the display was a .45 caliber Colt Peacemaker with ivory grips. According to the information card, the single-action revolver had been presented to Chief Ouray by his first wife, Black Mare.

The proprietor of The Compleate Antiquarian observed his potential customer with intense professional curiosity. Though the Ute had a glance for each of the fascinating objects, Moon's gaze would invariably be pulled back to that *special item*. Of course. Now Ralph Briggs thought he understood what the Indian was doing here. The proprietor allowed himself a knowing smile. "See anything you fancy?"

Charlie Moon pointed at the item that had caught his eye. "How much do you want for that?"

The owner of the establishment unlocked the case. "The Colt Peacemaker?"

The Ute shook his head, tapped his finger on the glass.

"Oh, *that*." He arched an eyebrow at Moon. "What on earth would a hard-case cow-pie-kicking cowboy like you want with—"

"How much?"

After a perfectly timed dramatic pause, Briggs told him how much.

Charlie Moon swallowed hard.